PRAISE FOR LUCINDA BRANT

'Brant has carved a niche for herself in this particular patch of history and she is gifted in weaving both story and history into a compelling read.'
Fiona Ingram, *Readers Favorite*

'Witty prose and well-researched context, skillfully drawn characters you'll be captivated by, are the main features in her style.'
Maria Grazia Spila, *Fly High*

'True talent is when an author creates an in-depth backstory of intricately woven together complicated characters and events and yet the reader starts on page one, right in the middle of the action and is none the wiser to the author's machinations, only having eyes for what is happening on each and every page, eagerly turning to the next.'
Eliza Knight, *History Undressed*

'Brant has a deft palette for historical detail which contributes to a strong backbone for the narrative. The characters are larger than life and its not hard to read with a visual image in mind. Brant's writing is filled with freshness and wit... highly recommended.'
Prudence J. Batten, *Mesmered's Blog*

'Once again I am in awe of Lucinda's originality to go outside of the norm and use historical moments to create an elaborate story.'
Crystal, *For Your Amusement: My Life*

'Grab a glass of wine, a quiet corner and plan to read the night away. The intricate web that Lucinda Brant constructs with a most amazing cast of characters is sure to keep you mesmerized.'
SWurman, *Night Owl Reviews*

Midnight Marriage

A GEORGIAN HISTORICAL ROMANCE

Roxton Series Book 2

LUCINDA BRANT

Published by Sprigleaf
sprigleaf.com

ISBN 978-0-9872430-2-7

FOR
GEORGETTE, TAYLOR & JEAN

$\mathscr{P}$rologue

Gloucestershire, England *1760*

$\mathscr{D}$eborah woke from a deep sleep to the sounds of a hasty late night arrival in the cobbled courtyard below her bedchamber window. Commands were barked out at drowsy-eyed stable boys and carriage wheels spun and slid to an abrupt halt. At first the girl thought it all part of her dream but the clip clop of horses hooves on uneven stone did not seem possible in the cool of a forest clearing. Otto was making beautiful music with his viola while she swung higher and higher on the rope swing, her silk petticoats billowing out between her long stockinged legs. She was sure if she swung higher her toes would touch the clouds. They both laughed and sang and it was such a lovely sunny day. Then the sun went behind a cloud and Otto disappeared and she fell off the swing at its highest point. Someone was shaking her awake. Fervent whispering opened her eyes and she blinked into the light of one taper held up by her nurse.

Before she had time to fully wake, Nurse pulled back the warm coverlet and threw a dressing gown over Deborah's thin shoulders. Then with shaking hands the woman pushed a tumbler into her hand and guided the cup to her lips, telling her to drink up. Deb did as she was told. She grimaced. The medicine was the same foul-tasting brew she had been given just before bedtime. It had put her into a deep, deep sleep. So why was she being got out of bed if she was meant to fall asleep again?

Nurse evaded the question. She straightened the girl's lace edged night cap, brought forward over one shoulder the single long thick plait of dark red hair, needlessly straightening the white bow; all the while muttering for Miss Deb to be a good girl and do as she was told and her prayers would be answered.

Drowsy and barefoot, Deborah was abandoned by her nurse at the door to Sir Gerald's book room. The passageway was dark and cold and the book room was no better. At the furthest end of this masculine sanctuary blazed a fire in the grate but it did not beckon her with the prospect of warmth and comfort. She went forward when ordered by her brother Sir Gerald, a glance at the two strangers taking refreshment after a hard ride. They had divested themselves of their great coats but the tall gentleman with the white hair and strong aquiline nose still wore his sword, the ornate hilt visible under the skirts of his rich black velvet frockcoat with silver lacings.

Deborah could not help staring at this imperious ancient stranger, whose close-shaven cheeks were etched with the lines of time; his hair and eyebrows as white as the soft lace ruffles which fell over his thin white hands. She had never seen an emerald as large as the one in the gold ring he wore on his left hand. She imagined he must be a hundred years old.

When he turned bright dark eyes upon her and beckoned her closer with the crook of one long finger she hesitated, swaying slightly. A sharp word from her brother moved her feet and through a mental fog that threatened to overwhelm her she remembered her manners at last and lowered her gaze to the floor. When she came to stand before this imperious ancient stranger she shivered, not from fear because she did not know what or whom to fear, but from the cold night breeze coming in through the open window. She made a wobbly curtsy and placidly waited to be spoken to first, gaze obediently remaining on the Turkey rug.

The stranger's voice was surprisingly deep and strong for one so old.

"What is your age, child?"

"I had my twelfth birthday six days ago, sir."

He frowned and over his shoulder said something in French to the little gray-haired man who stood at his elbow. He was answered in kind and the ancient stranger nodded and addressed Sir Gerald in his own tongue.

"She is far too young."

"But—your Grace, she is of age!" Sir Gerald assured him with an eager nervous smile. "The bishop raised no objection. Twelve is the age of consent for a female."

"That is true, Monseigneur," agreed the little man. "But it is for your Grace to decide... I do not know of an alternative."

"Surely your Grace has not changed his mind?" whined Sir Gerald. "Bishop Ramsay was not pleased to be summonsed here, your Grace, and if the ceremony is not to go ahead..."

"Your sister is not fifteen as you led me to believe, Cavendish," enunciated the ancient stranger in an arctic voice.

Sir Gerald gave a snort that ended in a nervous laugh. "Your Grace! Twelve or fifteen: three years hardly matters."

Deborah glanced up in time to witness the look of disgust that crossed the lined face of the ancient gentleman and she wondered what he found to fault in her. She knew she was only passably pretty. Sir Gerald despaired of her plain, brown looks, but she was not disfigured and her features were unremarkable. She was considered tall for her age but she was not so awkwardly big boned that this stranger had the right to pull a face at her in her own home. And why did her brother wear such a silly smile on his round fleshy face and stare expectantly at the arrogant ancient man as if his whole dependence rested on his will? He was acting as one of his own lackeys did before him. She had never seen her brother bow and scrape to anyone. It was strange indeed.

Deborah felt the black eyes regarding her from under heavy lids and she forced herself to look the ancient gentleman in the face without blinking. But she could not stop herself blushing when his gaze dropped to her bare feet and travelled slowly up the length of her nightgown to the brush tip of her single thick plait of dark red hair which touched her thigh, then on up over the swell of her budding breasts to rest on the lopsided bow tied under her chin that kept her nightcap in place. He then looked into her brown eyes again and she met his gaze openly through eyes that felt filled with oil and thus did not see clearly because the medicine she had drunk was beginning to take effect. A small crooked smile played on the ancient gentleman's thin lips and Deborah wished she had the courage to tell him his manners were lacking in one so old. His question to her brother bleached her cheeks.

"Has she commenced menstruating?"

Sir Gerald was dumbstruck. "Your—your Grace?"

"You heard the question well enough, Cavendish," prompted the gray-haired companion of the ancient one.

But even though Sir Gerald's mouth worked he could not speak.

Deborah, feeling as if her head was full of cotton wool, sluggishly answered for him. "Two—two months ago."

All three men turned and looked down at her then, as if finally acknowledging her mental as well as physical existence. Sir Gerald frowned but the ancient stranger and his friend smiled, the ancient one politely inclining his white head to her in thanks for her response. He seemed about to address her directly when a commotion in the passageway distracted them all. The gray-haired companion disappeared into the shadows and out of the room. He was gone for several minutes and in the interval no one spoke. Sir Gerald brooded; once or twice looking at his sister with mute disapproval while the ancient stranger calmly waited by the open window and fastidiously took snuff from a gold and enamel snuffbox.

Into the book room came a gentleman dressed in a cleric's robes, but these were no ordinary robes; they were edged in ermine and were of velvet and gold thread. He carried an ornately decorated Bible and wore a magnificent, old-fashioned, powdered wig with three curls above each fleshy ear. Deborah knew this to be Bishop Ramsay. He had arrived at the house earlier that day and set the servants on their ears with his imperious demands. Nurse said Cook was at her wits' end. The bishop took one look at Deborah in her nightclothes and put up his bushy brows. He ignored his host in favor of the ancient stranger over whose outstretched hand he bowed deeply. Deborah thought it odd that a bishop should bend to this old gentleman; he must be someone very illustrious indeed. Just then the little gray-haired man came out of the shadows looking worried.

"They've dragged him out of the carriage, your Grace," he announced then hesitated.

"And… Martin?" asked the ancient gentleman with uncanny perceptibility.

"He's downed another bottle, your Grace," Martin apologized.

"Then he will endure the ceremony better than the rest of us," came the flat reply.

"The marriage is to go ahead as planned?" Sir Gerald asked eagerly.

The ancient stranger did not look at him. "I have no choice."

He said this in such a weary tone that even Deborah, for all her youth and inexperience, heard the deep note of sadness in the mellow voice. She wondered what troubled him. The fact that these men were talking about a marriage ceremony barely registered with her. After all, no one had spoken to her of marriage. And everyone knew that when a girl was of marriageable age she had to leave the schoolroom and be launched in society during the Season and attend plenty of balls and routs and meet many eligible gentlemen, one of whom she would fall in love with and hopefully he would be the one who asked her brother for her hand in the usual manner. Marriages did not happen in the dead of night, between strangers. And they certainly did not happen in nightgowns after taking a measured dose of laudanum. There were formalities and mysterious things called settlements and a proper order to such a momentous step in a girl's life.

But Deborah was wrong and knew she was terribly wrong when her brother led her to the bishop, who called her a little sparrow of a bride and pinched her chin in a fatherly way, saying what a great honor had been bestowed upon her and her family for she had been chosen to be the wife of the Duke of Roxton's heir.

Her first thought was that she was asleep. It was the medicine Nurse had woken her to take had changed her beautiful dream with Otto in the forest to this nightmare in which she appeared to be the central character of a Shakespearean tragedy. Perhaps if she tried hard enough to think about waking it would happen and Nurse would be there with a glass of milk and soothing words. She closed her eyes, swaying and dry in the mouth. But she did not wake up from the nightmare. She was so bewildered she could not speak nor could she move. Panic welled up within her. She wished with all her heart that Otto would come home and save her. She wanted to cry. There were hot tears behind her eyelids but for some reason she was incapable of crying. So why was she sobbing? She soon realized it was not her. The quiet sobbing came from the doorway and distracted her enough that she momentarily forgot that she was in a nightmare.

A tall, well-built youth with a mop of tight black curls was being supported at each elbow by two burly servants in livery. He was not so drunk that he could not walk and so he told his captors in a growl of angry words. But the more he struggled to be free of them, kicking out his stockinged legs and balling his fists, the harder the grip on his elbows and he soon gave up the fight and returned to weeping into his velvet frockcoat.

An awkward silence followed as the boy was brought to stand beside Deborah. A languid movement of dismissal from the ancient gentleman and the burly servants retreated into the shadows.

Deborah stole a blinking glance at the weeping boy but he had turned away from her to face the ancient gentleman and addressed him in French, his voice breaking into sobs between sentences. He spoke faster than she could ever hope to understand but he used the words *mon père*: Father, over and over. Deb could not believe that this white haired old man could possibly be this boy's father. Surely he meant *grand-père*? And as she continued to stare at father and son, the boy suddenly broke into English. His words were so full of hatred that Deborah's face was not the only one to brighten with intense embarrassment.

"It's *all* your fault! *Your* fault," the boy screamed at the ancient gentleman, his fists clenching and unclenching with rage. "Why should *I* be banished for *your* sins? Does my presence make you uncomfortable, *Monseigneur*, now that I know the sordid truth? You can't bear the truth about yourself, there's the irony!" he added bitterly. "Poor Maman. To think she's had to live with your-your *disgusting* secrets all these years—"

"Alston, that will do," cut in the gray-haired companion. "You're drunk. In the morning you will regret—"

The boy tore his tearful gaze from his father to stare at the man at his side. "*Regret?* Regret knowing the truth about *him?* Never!" he spat out, lip trembling uncontrollably. "You've known all along, haven't you, Martin? Why didn't you tell *me?*

6

I'm his *heir*. I have a right to know. A-a *right*." He began to sob again and dashed a silken sleeve across his wet face. "*Mon Dieu*, I'm cursed. *Cursed*."

"It's all in your head, my son," the ancient gentleman said quietly.

This made the youth give a bark of hysterical laughter that broke in the middle. "In my head? Then it's a lie? A lie that His Grace the most noble Duke of Roxton, *my father*, has littered the land with ill-gotten *bastards*—"

The slap across his face knocked the boy off his feet and left the Duke nursing a smarting hand. Deborah watched him turn his back and walk into the shadows while at her feet the boy picked himself up to his silken knees, a hand to his stinging cheek. The gray-haired gentleman known as Martin put an arm about the boy's shaking shoulders and with a glance at Deborah said in a soothing voice,

"If you ever want to see your mother again, marry this girl. Then you and I can be on our way to France."

The youth gripped Martin's arm convulsively, his tear-stained face close to his. "If I do as he wants, may I see Maman before we sail? May I, Martin? *Please*. I must see her before we go. I *must*."

Martin shook his head sadly. "The early birth of your baby brother has left her very weak, my boy. She needs time to recover; the rest is up to God."

The youth broke into fresh sobs. "He'll never let me see her again! I know it, Martin. *Never*."

Deborah's brown eyes widened and she held her breath, awaiting the gray-haired gentleman's response. When he looked over the youth's bowed head of black curls and smiled at her kindly she felt a great relief. Though why she should feel anything but panic and dread at the prospect that lay before her she could not explain. Perhaps it was because she did not believe any of this was real. It was a laudanum-induced dream and soon she would wake up. If only she could shake her head free of cotton wool.

"After the ceremony, I am taking my godson to France and then on to Rome and Greece," Martin told her in a confiding tone, adding for good measure, as if living up to the promise in his smile, "We will be away for many years. Do you understand, *ma cherie*?"

Deborah nodded. There was something oddly reassuring in

Martin's smile, as if he would protect her from this strange sad boy and the consequences of this hasty midnight marriage. France was over the water. And Greece and Rome were so far away that it took months and months of travelling to reach such exotic countries; Otto had told her so. Suddenly she felt safe. Soon she knew she would wake up. All she had to do was lie still and wait for Nurse to wake her with the breakfast tray. This boy was going away for many years. She would never see him again after tonight. The sooner the bishop performed the ceremony the sooner she would wake up and forget this bad dream ever happened.

Martin's words of reassurance had an effect on the boy too for he pulled out of the man's embrace and dashed the curls from his eyes. The bishop quickly came to stand before these two children with his bible open and proceedings began in a rush; as if there was no assurance the boy's capitulation would last long enough for the exchange of vows, or that the girl who swayed on her feet and had a gaze that seemed incapable of blinking would be able to stand upright for very much longer. The bishop's fears seemed justified when all of a sudden the boy began to chuckle under his breath, disconcerting the bishop enough for him to pause on two occasions, and Deborah to blink uncomprehendingly up at the boy to see what he found so amusing. Finally the boy had to share his amusement with his ancient parent who stood behind him like a sentry made of marble.

"*Monseigneur.* Is this plain, awkward *bird witted* creature the best you could find to marry your heir?" he threw over his shoulder in arrogant bitterness. "Surely my lineage begs better?"

"Her pedigree is as good as yours, my son."

The youth sniggered. "What an illustrious union to be sure! Something of which you all must be very proud. *Pshaw*," and snatched up Deborah's hand when requested by the bishop. Obediently he repeated the words that would make them husband and wife. Deborah too had repeated the words after the bishop but she had said them without comprehending and had no idea what this boy's Christian names were, despite there being a string of them, because she could not take her eyes off his face. Her nightmare had unexpectedly turned into a wondrous dream. Her youthful husband was the handsomest boy she had ever seen in paints or real life; but it was his eyes that held her mesmerized. They were green, but not just any green, a deep emerald green. The same color as the large square cut emerald on the thin white hand of the ancient stranger Deborah was convinced had to be a hundred years old.

One

Bath, England *1769*

*J*ulian Hesham thought he had died and gone to Heaven. But angels did not punctuate their harp playing with *damns* and *blasts*. He supposed the music in Heaven to be a gentle plucking of the strings, the melody more *largo* than *allegro*. He was not musically inclined but the cacophony that assaulted his ears was a frenzied piece of playing, irritating to the nerves. If he was to slowly bleed to death, much better to do so in the peace and quiet of a spring morning, with only the attendant sounds of an awakening forest. He wished the musician a hundred miles away. That the fiddler might prove his salvation did not cross his mind. It did not occur to him to call out for help. But for the jarring musical cords of the apostrophizing fiddler he may very well have slipped into an unbroken sleep.

He was slumped under a birch tree. To the casual observer he had the appearance of a gentleman sleeping-off an evening of heavy drinking. Long, muscular legs were sprawled out before him, neckcloth and silk embroidered waistcoat were disorderly, boots muddy, strong, square chin rested on his chest, and a lock of thick black hair, having escaped its ribbon, fell forward into his eyes. His right arm was limp in the leaf-litter beside which was his discarded rapier. His left hand he had shoved inside his flowered waistcoat to hold a folded handkerchief to a place just under his ribs where a thrust from his opponent's foil had entered deep into the muscle.

Suddenly the music stopped. The wood was again at peace. Julian sighed his relief. In the silence there was the unmistakable click of a pistol being cocked, and this brought his chin up. Standing only a few feet away at the edge of the clearing was a youth in a blue velvet riding frock, not holding a pistol but a viola. Julian guessed he was about nine years of age; the same age as his much younger brother.

When the boy-musician jammed the viola under his chin and set bow to strings again, Julian shook his head and brought the recital to a halt before it began. He was not about to be a willing audience to more screeching, however curious to know the musician's next move.

"I'm certain you're very good on the night, but couldn't you rehearse elsewhere?" he asked conversationally. When the boy-musician spun about on a heel, almost dropping his bow, he added, "At your feet." And smiled weakly when the boy took an involuntary step backward. "Do me the favor of fetching my frockcoat. It's behind you... There's a flask... In the right hand pocket..."

The boy-musician took the viola away from under his chin. "What do you want with a flask? You look as if you've drunk enough."

"What deplorable manners you have," Julian complained, adding when the boy-musician continued to hesitate, "I mean you no harm. And even if I was a footpad I'm too knocked about to attempt to do you a mischief."

This speech was an effort and Julian's breathing became labored. The boy-musician watched a spasm of pain cross the handsome features and wondered what he should do. The man's face was too pale, the strong mouth too blue and the breathing now short and quick. It was then that the boy-musician saw the dark spreading stain seeping out from under the soiled waistcoat.

"Good God! He's injured!" came the cry and in such an altered voice to that of the boy-musician that Julian, through supreme effort of will, looked up. A pair of damp brown eyes regarded him with concern and a cool feminine hand touched his forehead.

Julian grinned and promptly fainted.

"Damned fool!" muttered the young woman, laying aside her pistol and hurriedly unscrewing the lid of a monogrammed silver flask handed to her by the boy-musician. She glanced up at her nephew. "Jack. Take Bannock and fetch Dr. Medlow. Tell him a man's been injured. Don't mention it's a sword wound."

The boy-musician hesitated. "Will you be all right left alone with him, Aunt Deb?"

She smiled reassuringly. "Yes, I'll be fine, Jack. I have my pistol, remember?" And watched her nephew scurry off before turning her attention once more to the injured duelist. Gently, she tilted back his head and slowly dribbled the contents of the silver flask between his cold and parched lips. "It won't be my fault if you die," she admonished him as one does a naughty child. "But it would serve you to rights for being foolish enough to fight a duel!"

"No. It won't be your fault," Julian murmured at last. "Thank you. Another sip, if you please." He let his head fall back into the circle of her embrace and looked up into a flushed face framed by an over-abundance of dark red hair. "Does he always play his fiddle punctuated with oaths? It adds color but it would offend Herr Bach."

"It's not a fiddle, it's a viola. And not Bach but Herr Telemann. And the oaths were mine, not Jack's. I'm out of practice. He's not."

"And the—er—pistol?"

"Mine," Deb admitted truthfully and promptly changed the subject. "What did you think of the composition we were rehearsing?"

"I didn't like it at all."

She laughed good-naturedly, showing lovely pearly-white teeth.

"Perhaps in another setting, after a few more days of practice, and…" Julian paused, distracted by the faint feminine scent at her white throat. "That's very pleasant," he announced with surprise. "As a rule females wear far too much scent. Is it lavender or something else? Rosewater, perhaps?"

"You're a lunatic. How can you talk pleasantries while you're bleeding all over me?" She gently sat him upright against the tree trunk and brushed down her petticoats as she got to her feet. "Don't laugh; it will only make your suffering worse. If I don't do something to staunch the bleeding you'll die, and I've enough to worry me without a corpse adding to my difficulties."

"My dear girl, don't put yourself to any trouble. I'm sure I'll last until the saw-bones arrives."

Deb wasn't listening. She was thinking. The last thing she wanted was for this gentleman to die on her. Besides, she would be in enough trouble explaining away to her stiff-necked brother what she and Jack were doing in the Avon forest, alone, and with their violas. Sir Gerald loathed their music making nearly as much as he loathed Jack's very existence. What could she use to make bandages? She groaned. She supposed she'd have to sacrifice her shirt (it was one of Otto's anyway). To cover her nakedness she'd borrow the gentleman's frockcoat. "I'll have to use his cravat, too," she said aloud as she unbuttoned the mannish shirt at her throat and promptly pulled it up over her head. She scooped up the gentleman's discarded frockcoat and disappeared behind a tree.

"H-how old did you say you were?" Julian asked conversationally, an appreciative audience to her undressing and disappointed that he was only permitted a view of her lovely narrow back and straight shoulders in the thin cotton chemise.

"I didn't. You may detest my viola playing," she called out, "but I am considered good in a crisis."

"What are you doing back there? Please don't go to any trouble…"

"I assure you, I won't do more than is necessary to keep you alive until Dr. Medlow arrives."

Deb stepped out from behind the tree, the frockcoat hanging loose about her shoulders and arms and buttoned to her chin, the narrow lapels pulled up about her slender throat and tickling her small ears. She knelt beside Julian and went to work ripping up her shirt to make bandages.

"I'm going to have to remove your waistcoat and shirt," she said, addressing the torn strips of fabric. "I'll be as gentle as I'm able."

"I'm sure you shall," came the murmured reply.

He submitted with good grace to having his silk cravat pulled this way and that; the diamond pin extracted with care and put aside, but it took great presence of mind for him to sit up, straighten his leg and remove the hand that was pressed to the wound. At the latter he fainted with the pain but made a swift recovery, gaze riveted to the girl's face: On the expressive brown eyes, the straight indifferent nose and the full bottom lip that quivered ever so slightly. Several curls had escaped from their pins and fell across her flushed cheek. Julian could not decide on their color; were they a dark strawberry blonde or were they more an autumnal red? He was certain he had never seen such rich red hair before, or such shine. He would have remembered such a particular color. The question consumed all his thoughts as he was stripped out of a richly embroidered waistcoat to reveal a shirt wet and heavy with his own blood.

Removing the shirt presented a problem for Deb. She knew her patient did not have the strength to raise his arms above his shoulders to slip the shirt over his head, so it would have to be torn from his back. Yet that was no easy thing. The cloth about the wound was wet with blood and had adhered to the slit in the man's muscular chest like glued paper to a wall. But Deb did not dwell on the pain she was about to inflict. It only had to be endured for the briefest of moments.

Decided, she took hold of the opened shirt front and ripped it left and right off the broad shoulders. It took three tugs to rent the fine fabric; the third tore the cloth from neck to waist, exposing a wide expanse of chest matted with hair the same raven-black color as that which covered the gentleman's head. For an instant her eyes registered surprise. The silk cravat, the richness of the exquisite fabric of waistcoat and frockcoat, the patrician features, all had concealed the measure of the man's muscle. It gave her hope for a full recovery. Such a well-exercised physique would stand him in good stead; but only if the wound could be staunched, and at once.

Julian suffered these ministrations with great fortitude; surprised the girl possessed such strong constitutional powers. It seemed that the sight of blood did not bother her in the slightest. She merely wrinkled her nose, not in response to any feelings of squeamishness, but in an enquiring, interested sort of way. He was about to make a quip about the dual sensibilities of being female and a musician but the quip died on his pale lips and was replaced with a guttural oath from deep within his throat, for suddenly his whole being convulsed with an unbearable pain.

Deb had carefully peeled away the sodden shirt from the wound, exposing a deep gash under the rib cage in the gentleman's right side. Examining it, she said in a detached voice,

"I don't think he meant to kill you, or your opponent has no notion of anatomy. The slice is deep but if he'd wanted to kill you he'd have pinked you on the left..."

Then, without warning, she pressed a wad of folded cloth over the wound, and so firmly that to Julian it was as if her whole fist had been thrust through the slit to mingle with his entrails and meet up with his spine. Disorientated with pain, he fought to remain conscious. His limp hand was placed over the dressing and he was told in a strident voice to keep it there with a firm pressure until the makeshift bandage was securely about his chest to hold the padding in place.

It was no easy task to bind up the wound. Deb managed to slip the bandage once around her patient's taut stomach, but having achieved this much the gentleman's eyelids fluttered and he promptly fainted. Quickly, she scrambled up, roughly pulled aside the layers of her petticoats to free her long stockinged legs and straddled the man's inert thighs in time to catch the full weight of his upper body against her shoulder as he pitched forward. She was almost knocked off her knees but managed to put her shoulder into his upper chest and at such an angle that it permitted her arms to remain free. This enabled her to pass the bandage freely across the width of his wide bare back. She did this several times, each time pulling the binding tighter so that the wound was sealed and the padding secure under the wrappings.

Certain that her shoulder was bruised and her back about to buckle under the man's weight, she quickly groped about the tangled tree roots for the diamond-headed stickpin she had set aside. With the pin secured through the top layers of her makeshift bandage, she used her remaining strength to set her patient upright and gently leaned him back against the birch tree. But he did not look at all comfortable and so without a thought to modesty she stripped off his frockcoat, folded the embroidered silk garment up into a bundle and successfully placed this soft pillow behind his strong neck, thus avoiding his raven head banging back against the tree trunk with a great thud.

Exhausted and feeling the need to catch her breath, Deb just sat there in her thin cotton chemise: straddled atop her patient's muscular thighs, petticoats bunched up over her knees and exposing her long stockinged legs to the world. She felt bruised, battered and on the verge of tears.

"How dare you do this to me!" she demanded of the unconscious gentleman and picked up the flask, uncertain whether to force the rest of its contents down his throat or dash the liquid in his face. "You're probably a notorious criminal and well served to be left to bleed to death! My misfortune to stumble across you." She leaned forward and poured a drop of brandy between the parted lips. "I'm a fool," she murmured, scanning his angular face. "I don't think you can be a criminal. Your eyes are too honest... and you are far too swooningly handsome to be—Oh! You ungrateful brute! Unhand me!" she yelped, for Julian had her hard by the wrist and the flask fell into the grass. "That hurts!"

Julian looked into the flushed face close up to his and blinked. "Promise me you won't run off."

Deb gave a twisted smile. "Afraid I mean to leave you to the footpads?" she goaded, plying at the strong fingers about her wrist.

"No. I want... I want to talk to you."

"Save your strength for the physician. Oh, do let me go! You'll bruise my flesh."

He released her and she sat up.

"I haven't the strength to make you stay. But I'm apt to decline into a blue melancholy without you." He swallowed and closed his eyes and spent a few moments regaining his breath. "That would wound my pride far greater than any wound to my body."

Deb was suddenly curious. "Who did this to you?"

"Men of little consequence." He sighed his annoyance. "They weren't particularly good swordsmen. Uncle Lucian will be disgusted with me."

"Uncle Lucian?"

"Premier swordsman in France and England in his day. He thinks I lack grace in my movements. He's right."

"You should have shot 'em!" Deb said savagely.

Julian smiled. "Uncle Lucian? I know he thinks me a sad trial on my parents and never has a good word to say on my behalf but—"

"Silly! Not Uncle Lucian, the cowardly curs who did this to you. Why didn't you use pistols? Much quicker result and you need not break a sweat."

"Precisely. Uncle Lucian deplores the methods of chivalry employed by the modern youth."

"But you're not exactly—Sorry!"

"I'm hardly in my dotage, dear girl," Julian drawled. "And to a man in his sixties, five and twenty is barely of an age to be out of leading strings."

"Oh! Well, that's not old at all," Deb agreed. "Actually, I thought you older—Oh dear! I have the most wretched tongue and am forever saying the first thing that comes to mind."

"Don't let it bother you," he said dryly, gaze flickering across her bare shoulders and slim arms. "I expect you thought me older because I'm graying at the temples?"

Deb met his gaze. "How—how many swordsmen were there?"

"Three."

"*Three?* That's unfair and dishonorable."

"Yes. Tell me your name."

"Name?" she repeated with downcast eyes, suddenly feeling self-conscious. "My name is unimportant."

"I'm sorry you had to ruin your shirt," he apologized after a short silence. When she looked away, out to the forest, unable to meet the steady gaze of his clear green eyes, he said gently, "Won't you tell me why you and—Jack? Yes, Jack, are fiddling in the forest at this hour? Wouldn't the schoolroom be a more appropriate place?"

"I-I—must go…"

"My name is Julian," he continued. "I can't thank you if I don't know your name."

"I told you. It's not important. I'd have done the same for-for—Oh! *Anyone.*"

"I see. Is it necessary for you to carry a pistol?"

Deb threw him a sullen look. "You're very busy."

"Are you in trouble?"

"That's none of your concern."

"If you are, I'd like to offer my assistance."

"Is that so?" she said with a twisted smile. "When do you think you will be in a position to offer your services? A month; two months from now?"

"I'm not about to beg," he replied mildly.

"I didn't mean to sound ungrateful," she apologized; face a

mask of hard indifference. "It's just that you can't help. So, please, forget you ever saw us or that I have a pistol. If Gerry ever found out... I'll go and meet up with Dr. Medlow; show him the way through the forest."

"Must you carry a pistol?" he persisted in the same gentle tone.

Deb regarded him steadily then made up her mind that there could be little harm in confiding just a little bit about herself, especially to such a willing ear. Besides, it might just take his mind off the pain in his side. "My brother Gerry—*Gerald*—doesn't know about the pistol. It belonged to Otto who gave it to me just before he died and said that I must keep it on me always when I am out alone. Otto was my other brother and my best friend and Jack's father. He was a splendid musician and Jack has his talent. If Jack is to go to Paris to be tutored under Evelyn Ffolkes, then he must practice. But as Gerry has forbidden us to play our violas, Jack and I come out here to be alone, and so the servants won't report back to him. So you see, that's why I carry a pistol."

"Gerry has no ear for music?"

Deb's brown eyes lit up. "Gerry is tone deaf."

"Hence he has no appreciation of Jack's talent."

"Precisely!"

Julian's breathing became labored again and he half-closed his eyes. Deb thought he was about to faint again until he smiled and said in a contrived tone of disinterest, "I dare say Gerry has the same lack of appreciation for beauty. If you were my sister I'd take better care of you. I certainly wouldn't allow you out of the schoolroom, dressed in a man's shirt and without a corset."

"You obviously have no idea what it's like to be spied upon!" she said indignantly. "I can't be expected to sneak out of the house with Jack if I must first wake my maid to lace me into a corset. Brigitte would have the whole house up within five minutes of my departure."

"Well then, that certainly excuses you."

"And you are a bad judge of age. I will be one and twenty *very* soon."

"Accept my apologies. You look much younger. Perhaps because you aren't wearing your corset...?"

Deb gaped at him. "Because I'm not wearing my corset?" she

repeated incredulously. "Your manners are appalling. If you weren't wounded I'd—I'd—"

"Yes?" he asked expectantly, shoulders shaking with silent laughter. "You would...?"

A crimson flush washed over her breasts and up her throat but Deb bravely looked him in the eyes to tell him what she thought of his insolence when she noticed a spot of fresh blood on the bandage and that he was trembling.

"You're shivering!" she announced, all embarrassment forgotten.

"Yes. I'm cold and can't move my legs. No matter, the physician will be here shortly."

Only then did she realize that as well as being practically naked from the waist up she was still straddled atop the injured duelist's thighs and had been comfortably seated on his lap for quite some time. Hiding her embarrassment behind anger, she admonished him as she scrambled off his long legs and brushed down the layers of her crushed petticoats.

"You should've said something instead of letting me sit there rattling on at you!"

"And cut short our _tête-à-tête_? Now _that_ would've been bad mannered."

"You must be a lunatic!"

"Yes, I must be," Julian answered with a private smile and closed his eyes.

Two

When next Julian Hesham, Marquis of Alston, looked out on
the world there were three pairs of eyes peering down at him in
anxious silence. He thought himself still in the forest and looked
about for a pair of brown eyes belonging to the boy-musician's
aunt. But his head nestled amongst soft down pillows and he was
lying in a big bed. He closed his eyes again. Looking. Thinking.
Both were too much for him. His head seemed too large for his
weak body and when he tried to raise an arm he found he was
too feeble to perform even this simple task.

"He opened his eyes. That's a good sign," said an unfamiliar,
well-satisfied voice. "The fever's broken, thanks be to God. I will
come again on the morrow. If he has a restless night, give him
the tincture of opium—"

"No—opium," Julian interrupted in a sluggish voice. "Frew?
Tell M'sieur Physician I won't—"

"Yes, my lord. No opium, my lord," agreed the hovering valet.
"Just a teaspoon if absolutely—"

"No!" growled his master and fixed a stare on the one face
he did not recognize. "When can I get up?"

"In a sennight, my lord."

"Sennight? How many nights have I been here?"

"Three, my lord."

"Three? Good God!"

"Yes," answered the physician with a smile. "And you're
making excellent progress, thanks to Mr. Ellicott's—"

"Martin?" Julian interrupted and turned his head on the pillow to look down the foot of the bed at an elderly gentleman with grizzled hair. "Have I been a sad trial, *mon parrain?*"

Martin Ellicott smiled and shook his head. He showed the physician to the door and then returned to pull up a chair beside the bed, motioning away his lordship's hovering valet with a slight wave. "How do you feel?"

They spoke in French.

"Passable," Julian replied. "I have a thumping headache. Have I really been tossing about in bed for three nights?"

"Yes. You contracted a chill that turned into a fever. That is not important now. You must rest and regain your strength."

"Always in and out of some scrape, aye, Martin?" Julian grinned self-consciously. "But this time it was not of my making. If you can believe me."

"I never doubt you, M'sieur."

"*M'sieur?* When has my godfather ever called me anything but Julian when we are private?" He frowned. "Ah. Your expression, or should I say, lack of one, gives you away. You look remarkably like *mon père* when you put on that face. Did you learn from Father or vice a versa? Never mind. You are about to lecture me on my folly."

"No. Not now. Could you eat something?"

"I don't know. Mayhap something other than that pap I seem to recall having pushed down my throat." He watched the old man stand slowly. "Martin," he said abruptly, "was I ever lucid during those days?"

"Occasionally." He gave a rare smile. "Always in French."

Julian sighed. "Thank God for that." He looked past his godfather. "Did I make mention of any particular circumstance?"

Martin Ellicott was silent a moment and it brought the younger man's eyes back to his face. "You asked that your parents not be told. I did not tell them. You know I would not distress their Graces for the world. I need not add that *Monseigneur*—"

"I am well aware of the Duke of Roxton's uncanny ability to know my every move. He'll be as mad as hell-fire but I'll deal with that when the time comes. Anything else?"

"No."

"Oh… Then I must have dreamed… I seem to recall asking you—"

"—about a young lady with brown eyes?"

"Yes. She patched me up."

"Is that so?" mused Martin Ellicott, a twinkle in his eye.

"I didn't conjure up this female in some opium induced dream. She is flesh and blood."

"If she is the one who bandaged you up, then you do indeed owe her a debt of gratitude." Martin Ellicott executed a neat bow. "Now you must rest and I will send Frew in with a tray of something palatable. Tomorrow we will discuss what is to be done to find your savior."

The Marquis gave a grunt of laughter that made him grimace. "Well, I'd hate for you to think me as weak-brained as Uncle Lucian—"

The old man gave an involuntary shudder. "No one could be as weak-brained as that."

"—but you shouldn't have difficulty finding her. She sneaks out to the Avon forest to play her viola because Gerry don't like it one bit. Then again he's tone deaf, so he wouldn't, would he?"

Martin Ellicott refrained from commenting and went out of the room. Opium, he thought. It had to be the opium.

The young woman with the brown eyes who occupied the Marquis of Alston's thoughts in his sickbed waking hours was Miss Deborah Cavendish who lived in a tall, narrow fronted house on the east side of Milsom Street, two doors up from the Octagon Proprietary Chapel. It was a respectable address, close to all the amenities of town and only a short walk to the newly opened Upper Assembly Rooms. Yet, it was not considered a fashionable place to reside by the first families. The street housed chapels and trade, and the great rumble of traffic during the Season was considered unpleasant. The buildings lacked the style and elegance and aspect to be found in Queens Square, the Circus or Gay Street. Such an address might do for the seasonal lodger but could not be considered a comfortable or respectable address for a Cavendish.

Yet the house and its situation suited Deb. So much the better to be crammed in amongst seasonal lodgers, faceless chapel-goers and industrious merchants, who had more to do with their time and energy than to squander it in idle conversation, as did the Quality. The Quality spent their time at the Pump room sweating out their ills in the hot water of the King's Bath; ingested scandal with their morning glasses of mineral water, and later in the day, sipped tea laced with the latest gossip in the Assembly Rooms.

Not that Deb was out to shun Bath society or its jostle of habitués. She was often to be seen at the offered entertainments; promenading in the Pump Room; dancing at the Assembly Room Balls; and taking breakfast with a party across the river Avon at Sydney Gardens. She had become a well-known favorite of the year-round inhabitants; indeed was sought after to play at cards with the old infirm gentlemen whose membership boasted three retired Colonels, a General and a sprinkling of be-knighted self-made men. And there were the widows, titled, genteel and mercantile, all hypochondriacs of one form or another who confided their ills to dear Miss Cavendish.

Yet, she was politely over-looked by the most intimate of circles, made up exclusively of the sons and daughters and cousins of the first families in the land. These illustrious personages readily rubbed shoulders with all degrees of society at the public entertainments but were highly selective as to who could enter their drawing rooms or put their feet under the dining room table. It was not that Deb's lineage was to be sneered at, after all she was a Cavendish and cousin to the fifth Duke of Devonshire and a considerable heiress.

Deb's social consequence and respectability was severely tarnished by her volatility of character. When she was just sixteen years old she had left the sanctuary of her brother's house against his wishes and travelled to the Continent to look after her ill brother, a musician who was the black sheep of the family. Her two years on the Continent may have been overlooked, after all her disobedience to her brother Sir Gerald was due to her devotion to her brother Otto who sadly, but thankfully for the family's good name, died in Paris before he could disgrace the family further.

Deb had re-surfaced in Bath, fresh-faced and looking for all the world as if scandal had never touched her lovely form but with her orphaned nephew in tow. The nephew was the product of Otto's coupling with a wandering gypsy. That Miss Cavendish chose to give the boy a roof over his swarthy head when her elder brother Sir Gerald had at first refused to acknowledge such base offspring scandalized society to such a degree that speculation was rife about the sort of life Miss Cavendish had led on the Continent and provided the tea table gossips with a plethora of conjecture.

Deb had heard the whisperings, saw the lascivious glances of disreputable men, and the hostile looks of upright matrons. It would have been too simple to say she did not care in the least what was thought of her, she did. But she also knew there was nothing she could do to change society's opinion of her. That was carved in stone. As long as society kept its distance and did not interfere in her life, she was quite content to co-exist with her peers.

And so it was with head held high that she stepped out of a sedan chair and paid off the chairmen, green velvet riding skirts over one arm, and entered Bath's noisy and crowded Pump room in search of her sister-in-law, Lady Mary Cavendish. She had been about to ride out for a breakfast engagement with her French tutor; an elderly gentleman who had settled in a quaint Queen Anne House on the outskirts of town after a lifetime's service in the employ of some illustrious but nameless French aristocrat. Lady Mary's hastily scrawled note arrived as she was dressing and requested her immediate presence in the Pump room.

It surprised Deb that Mary had come to town so early in the Season. Not to have forewarned her of such plans made Deb suspicious. It would be too much of a coincidence for Mary to be in Bath the precise week Deb was making plans to quit the declining waterhole for Paris. She suspected her odious brother had once again sent his wife in his place. Deb had no proof but she believed he kept abreast of her every move by paying a member of her household to spy.

Deb found Lady Mary seated at a window overlooking the King's Bath and caught in conversation with a stiff-necked society matron who rose immediately Deb came through the crowd towards them.

"Don't get up, Lady Reigate," Deb said cheerfully. "I came only to say good morning to Lady Mary."

"Deb! How good of you to come," said Lady Mary, fluttering her fan in agitation, a sidelong glance at her conversationalist. "Will you take a glass of water with us?"

Deb leaned over to kiss Lady Mary's cheek. "No, thank you. I hate the taste and it's quite fouled you know."

"Good day, Lady Mary," Lady Reigate said with an outstretched hand and a curt nod in Deb's direction. "It's reassuring to see a familiar face so early in the season. You will come to my soiree? I want to hear all about how your cousin the Duchess is holding up, what with her son embroiled in another seduction scandal. Not that I blame Alston. So handsome and so virile, is it any wonder silly French girls swoon at the sight of him? But such a trial on his poor Mamma. Do come on Tuesday, won't you?"

"Thank you for the invitation," said Lady Mary, pulling Deb down beside her. "Thank goodness you came when you did," she said with a sigh, Lady Reigate barely out of earshot. "I've heard enough about Alston's degrading behavior not to want to be subjected to a moral monologue of his ills by that creature!" She noticed Deb's riding skirts. "I haven't upset your morning plans, have I?"

Deb was staring down at the waders in the King's Bath, smiling at the bobbing figures in their ridiculous brown gowns and small bars of soap on floating plates. "Not at all, dearest. I intend to ride out to keep my engagement. But your note expressed some urgency. I hope little Theodora isn't ill?"

"Theodora? Oh, no. Your little niece is very well indeed and I hated to leave her with Nurse at such a time. She is teething y'know. But Sir Gerald is tied up with tenant matters and cannot get away to see you himself for at least a sennight so he thought it best I come to Bath in his stead."

Deb couldn't help a crooked smile. "If Gerry is tied up with estate matters for a sennight then I do see the urgency for your visit." When Lady Mary appeared suitably blank faced Deb shook her head. "I'm sorry you came all this way for little return, Mary. I won't alter my travel plans."

"So it is true." Lady Mary moaned. She grasped Deb's gloved

hand. "I wanted to call on you in Milsom Street but I feared finding a hallway stacked with trunks and so thought it best to talk with you here, in a public place where we could be private."

"Dearest Mary, how like you to think it more private here in a crowded Pump Room than within my four walls; and yet how true. Yes, my hallway is piled high with luggage because I intend taking Jack to Paris as soon as I receive word from Mr. Ffolkes. Colonel Thistlewaite! How do you do?" Deb acknowledged, hand out-stretched to a middle-aged gentleman who had broken away from his own party to bow before Deb with a flourish. "Permit me to present my sister Lady Mary Cavendish." To which the portly gentleman in purple silken knee breeches and saffron yellow frockcoat with black lacings bowed over Lady Mary's little plump hand, a twinkle in his jaundiced watery eye. "You mustn't mind the Colonel," Deb continued with a bright smile. "He admires all the pretty females with the eye of a connoisseur."

"Have you been out riding, my dear Miss Cavendish?" he asked, his whole attention returning to Deb; the sister thought pretty but not animated enough for this military man. "For shame that you did not spare a thought for Colonel Thistlewaite."

"You cannot join me upon this occasion, Colonel, for I go to my French lesson as usual. Lady Mary, Colonel Thistlewaite and I are Hazard partners, are we not, Colonel?"

"And fleece all comers!" laughed the Colonel. "You haven't forgotten our engagement this afternoon?"

"With the Brownlowes? Not I."

When the Colonel politely took his leave to join his cronies at the far end of the room, Lady Mary said in a thin voice of disapproval, "You don't sit down with him to cards, Deb?"

"I do, Mary."

"Can't you guess what he is?"

"Why of course."

"I wish you wouldn't," complained Lady Mary. "The way he looked at you, and those others over there with him. I don't know who they are, of course because—"

"Then you must not judge them. They're old and quite harmless, I assure you."

"But what would Sir Gerald think if he knew you—"

27

"—played cards with a retired regiment? What do I care for Gerry's censure?" She said this with a careless shrug but there was an edge to her voice that should have warned Lady Mary to beware. The latter was not very quick on the uptake and rushed headlong into a defence of her husband and thus disaster.

"I'm sure you think them harmless enough, and mayhap they are," she lectured. "But you were never one to worry your head over gossip, but it really does matter what people think of you if you are to marry well; particularly after your fool-hardy behavior in running off to Paris to care for Otto. As I am older than you, and married, I feel I can speak with some authority—"

Deb stood up and shook out her petticoats. "Mary, you're wasting your time to try and persuade me not to go to Paris. I must: For Jack. He has progressed far beyond what I can teach him. He needs an experienced tutor such as Mr. Ffolkes. I only await his letter of reply to leave this watering hole. You should return to Theodora who needs you. It was quite selfish of Gerry to make you come."

"I hate to continually remind you of what happened in Paris when Sir Gerald had to drag you home before you eloped with Mr. Ffolkes—"

"Then don't!" Deb said through gritted teeth.

"How do we—you—know you won't fall in love with him all over again when you see him?" Lady Mary said in a small voice. "It's been years but I know Evelyn still holds a candle for you. He never married and says he never shall. Sir Gerald thinks—"

"Oh, for God's sake, Mary! You are being ridiculous," Deb said dismissively. "Would it be such a bad thing if Mr. Ffolkes offered for me again? After all, he is nephew of a duke and will one day be a Viscount. Gerry should be pleased not worried. I could do worse."

Much worse, thought Lady Mary, if the rumors about a certain Mr. Robert Thesiger pursuing her sister-in-law proved true. She wrung her gloved hands. The interview was not going as planned; how she and her husband had discussed it should progress if she was to convince Deb to remain in Bath. And the Pump Room was not the place to continue such a conversation.

"You'll be late for your ride, Deborah," she said quietly.

"And you're quite right. And I do not understand Sir Gerald's opposition to Evelyn's proposal."

Deb put up her brows. She couldn't remember the last time Lady Mary had openly admitted to disagreeing with her husband. And something must truly be bothering Mary for her to call her Deborah in such a formal manner. "Come for morning tea tomorrow. Jack is home for the holidays and would welcome a visit from his aunt. Now I must leave you for I can't keep Joseph walking the horses forever. Oh, dear. Here comes Mrs. Overton with her toothy son. The Overtons are exceedingly well connected and Sir Henry left a plum, so I am told. *Au revoir.*"

With a sinking feeling Lady Mary watched Deb escape across the hall only to be waylaid by the one person whom she had come to Bath to warn Deb against.

Mr. Robert Thesiger was a broad-shouldered gentleman of average height and good looks who made the most of what God had given him with an exquisite sense of dress and exceptionally polished manners. He was resplendent in an Italian silk frock adorned with sprays of silk-threaded flowers on the close, upturned cuffs and hem of the short skirts, his midnight blue cashmere breeches fit him like a glove and a short waistcoat from which dangled many gold fob chains and seals was sure to start a trend. His highly polished black leather shoes with their enormous tongues carried a higher than average heel that was said to be all the rage in Paris. To romantically minded young ladies the mysterious dueling scar which cut the length of his left cheek elevated his masculinity to that of the swooningly handsome.

Yet, despite his charming good looks and prospects of inheriting an ancient title, Mr. Thesiger's marriageability was severely compromised by his shoddy parentage. He was the acknowledged heir to his father's baronetcy, a man of papist inclinations and Jacobite tendencies who had danced attendance on the Young Pretender in Rome and retired a semi-invalid to Bath; yet it was his mother's scandalous reputation which had brought Robert's pedigree into question.

A French Comtesse, at the time of her separation from Baron Thesiger Therese Duras-Valfons had publicly declared her only child not to be the son of her husband but the bastard offspring of an

English duke, whose mistress she had been at that time. She had gone so as far as to proclaim that her son had been fathered by this notorious duke while on a Hunt with the King of France. Not many moons after impregnating his mistress, the English duke up and married a girl young enough to be his daughter.

Robert Thesiger did himself no favors by his devotion to his mother, a woman whose sordid reputation sank even further when she became the mistress of a French tax-collector for mere pecuniary gain. Yet Mr. Thesiger's frequent visits to his father's bedside went a long way to redeeming him in the eyes of Society's matrons, who looked upon him as a potential son-in-law for their daughters. That he was courting an Englishwoman, and none other than Deborah Cavendish who was worth fifty thousand pounds, was proof positive to all but Society's sticklers that Baron Thesiger must indeed be the gentleman's sire.

He had been watching Deb out of the corner of an eye while she spoke with Lady Mary Cavendish and merely awaited the opportunity to waylay her. He strolled about the Great Pump room with the two Miss Reigates; the pretty but freckled twins of an impoverished Viscount. Their mother, Lady Reigate, was just being complimented on their deportment when Robert Thesiger suddenly took his leave of the girls and presented himself to Deb Cavendish. Envious friends sympathized with Lady Reigate. After all, Deb Cavendish was always in her best looks in a riding habit; perhaps a little too masculine in cut, but how well it suited the young woman with the Amazonian stature and unusually dark red hair. What was Lady Reigate's opinion?

"Miss Cavendish! One moment, if you please," purred Mr. Thesiger, touching her arm. Startled into dropping her hat, he promptly restored it to her, pleased to have momentarily put her off guard.

"Oh! It's only you," she said bluntly. "I thought for a moment... No. How foolish of me. How are you, Mr. Thesiger?"

He smiled and bowed over her gloved hand. "My feelings are sadly bruised. Who did you wish me to be?"

"I can't stay. Joseph is walking the horses."

"A pity I'm not dressed to accompany you. Did you come looking for me?"

"I came to see my sister. She's just arrived."

"Ah. The lovely Lady Mary. She didn't drag the very correct Sir Gerald with her, I hope?"

Deb laughed and, slowing her stride to a walk, allowed him to slip her arm through his. "Gerry leave his pigs and cows?"

"Then I shall pay Lady Mary a morning call," said Mr. Thesiger with a quick smile. "I still maintain you came to find me. I can tell by the look in your eyes you are annoyed with me for not being at the recital."

"How extraordinary you should say so," she said conversationally. "It is a talent you need to perfect. I am not so foolish or so shallow."

"You are piqued because business kept me in Paris longer than I anticipated."

"Business with blue or green eyes?"

This made him laugh softly. "Blue," he confessed. "The adorable Dominique is more beautiful than you, my dear, but she has none of your wit or fire. Jealous?"

"No. That requires an effort I do not feel inclined to exert on your behalf."

He was not fooled by her light tone. That she kept her eyes straight ahead, never once looking at him told him what he wanted to know. "Touché." He smiled and bowed to a passing couple seeking his attention, saying to Deb, "These verbal sparring matches you and I indulge in are amusing, but it is time we progressed, Miss Cavendish."

"What a fantasy you have weaved," Deb answered lightly and withdrew her hand from his silk sleeve as they had come full circle and stood to one side of the front doors. "I am sorry to disappoint you, Mr. Thesiger, but I cannot give you the answer you seek."

"You won't disappoint me," he said in an under-voice.

"Paris must have been dull indeed," she commented, allowing her gaze to wander out the front doors onto the street.

"I am a patient man, but I am no saint, my dear."

"You had my answer before you left for Paris. I own to being a fickle creature, but I have not changed my mind."

Mr. Thesiger followed her into the morning sunshine, side-stepping an elderly couple being wheeled about by their attendants, and grabbed her arm before she could go to her groom, a short, stocky man of Italian extraction who now took a step forward at this cavalier treatment of his mistress. "It is not an answer I am willing to accept."

"Do you imagine this is the way to go about getting what you want? What fine manners you have, sir!"

Mr. Thesiger recovered himself almost at once and dropped his hand to his side but not before raising it in a gesture of annoyance. "Forgive me," he stated woodenly and retreated with a curt bow, saying as he straightened himself, "I am determined to win you, Miss Cavendish."

"I admire such single-minded purpose, Mr. Thesiger. It does you credit. I only wish I knew my own heart half as well," she apologized as she put on her hat, running a gloved hand down the length of the plume. "You may think it a female whim, Mr. Thesiger, but I cannot entertain any marriage proposal that does not—not engage my—my feelings."

"And if I was to tell you that you and only you have engaged my feelings, Miss Cavendish?"

Deb regarded him with a lop-sided smile. He was quite dashing and she should have been flattered but his words embarrassed her because she could not return his regard. She expected more, indeed knew there had to be more than mere fondness for the man with whom she would spend the rest of her life. She wanted a certain sort of unexplainable something to happen to her when a gentleman proposed marriage. Perhaps she was being stupidly romantic...? Still, it was the way she felt and she could not change. "No doubt you have these same feelings for blue or green eyes, Mr. Thesiger," she quipped and left him standing on the footpath.

Deb and her groom were some distance from the town center when she slowed her pace to enjoy the open fields and morning air, free of the bustle and noise of town. She was thinking about what Lady Mary had said regarding Evelyn Ffolkes still holding a candle for her, and how she might feel when she saw him again. Four years had almost passed since those heady months spent in Paris with Otto and his musician friends and although she and Evelyn corresponded erratically she had not once thought more of him than as a dear friend; Otto's closest friend. Then Joseph cantered up and rudely disturbed her peace.

"Been pressin' you again, has he?"

"Who?"

"That prosy dandy."

"Mr. Thesiger? He doesn't press," she answered mildly. "He merely persists."

"What charmin' manners he's got," Joseph said with a snort. That he spoke to his mistress with all the familiarity of a gruff uncle was due to the fact that he had known her from the cradle. He had been her brother Otto's valet, and after his master's untimely death had taken it upon himself to act as Deb's major domo.

"Why do you dislike Mr. Thesiger?"

Joseph looked between his horse's ears. "Beggin' your pardon, ma'am, but he pretends to be more French than he is English, despite his papa being English to the core, and that's enough for me!"

"That's not reason enough to dislike him. He may make Paris his principal place of residence, after all his mamma is French, yet he goes to considerable effort to regularly visit his ailing father—"

"Eager to get his hands on that ancient Baronetcy, is my guess," Joseph muttered.

"You judge him too harshly," Deb answered stridently, "as does the rest of society."

Joseph decided to keep his opinions about Mr. Thesiger to himself and they rode on in silence until turning into a laneway with a set of high gates proclaiming the entrance to a small estate set well back off the main road and surrounded on three sides by forest. Joseph jumped down to swing the gates wide. Mature oak trees lined either side of a drive that led up to a Queen Anne red brick house set in twenty acres of parkland. At the bottom of the well-cared-for gardens flowed the river Avon.

The house was in sight when Deb next spoke, a determined look on her face as she struggled to overcome a desire to ask after the injured duelist. To her annoyance, she often found her thoughts wandering in his direction and speaking about him never failed to heighten her color.

"Joseph... you did...you did enquire after my injured duelist with Dr. Medlow?"

Back astride his mount, Joseph cast her a sly glance and kept his features perfectly composed. "No sooner had Medlow tended him than along comes a carriage to take your duelist away, to who knows where. The saw-bones didn't recognize the arms on the door and none of the servants either. Vanished that's what he's done."

"The carriage must have stopped at one of the respectable inns. He couldn't have travelled far in that condition."

"I enquired at the less respectable inns too. I know you said he's a gentleman, but just cause he's dressed in a duke's garments don't make him one." He glanced at Deb again and said to goad her, "He could've won the fineries from some poor sot of an impoverished lord. Seen that done before. You'd be surprised how many coves go about dressed as if they've got two or three titles to their name! I remember in Turin—"

"Nonsense! He is a gentleman. He—His features are such…"

"Plenty of 'em come out on the wrong side of the blanket these days. If rumor is to be believed, so did Mr. Robert Thesiger. Shocking it is how the nobility have littered the countryside with their by-blows."

Unconsciously Deb stiffened in the saddle. "The rumors about Mr. Thesiger's shoddy parentage are hardly his fault. It can't be easy for him, having a mother who is a notorious whore. But as the Baron owns him, I think we can safely ignore the rumors." She glanced slyly at Joseph. "As for my injured duelist, you did give my description of him to the landlords?"

"To the word. And none have seen him. Though, if they had, I've no doubt about 'em rememberin' your man. Now let me see… Tall with raven hair and the greenest of green eyes. And he's got muscle and a very charming smile. Not to mention a great gaping hole in his side. No. I don't think a landlord or his servants would miss a man like that, d'you?"

Deb felt she had to say something in her defence. "You needn't think I've lost my heart to some nameless duelist! The notion is absurd. I'm merely curious to know how he got on. There is nothing unusual in that, given my exertions on his behalf. What a wasted effort if later he was to die of his wounds."

Joseph helped her dismount and bowed, saying in a low voice, for their host had come out onto the gravel drive to greet them,

"A damn shame, ma'am, as you say."

Deb cast him a dark look and then turned to her host with gloved hand outstretched. "Ah, M'sieur, forgive my lateness. I trust I've not kept you waiting your breakfast? *Ma belle souer* has newly arrived in town and I spent a little time with her in the Pump Room. It is not an easy place to escape."

They spoke in French.

"*J'ai regret*, it is as you say, Mlle," the old gentleman answered, patting her gloved hand.

Soberly dressed and in his sixties, he nonetheless had alert, bright eyes and upright gait. Deb did not know much about his background, only that he had been in the service of some magnificent personage whom from time to time he had mentioned as *Monseigneur*. Deb concluded his employer had been a French Duc. She had met him in the Pump Room when she had first come to Bath and found they had a similar taste in music and painting. He spoke impeccable French and once, when she had lamented her inability to find a suitable native speaker of that tongue, he had offered his services. She had been coming to his house once a week ever since. She had not seen him in three weeks, he sending a note to say he would be out of town. Now, as they stood on the gravel drive she asked him about his stay away, and after looking at her blankly for a moment recovered enough to smile but change the subject.

"Today we will sit outside," he said escorting her through the hall to the back of the house where there was a broad terrace overlooking the lawn and river beyond. "My godson is staying with me and I have asked that he join us. I hope you don't object? He too is a native French speaker. And I should like for the two of you to meet."

"Your godson? How delightful!" Deb dropped her gloves into the crown of her hat and set it aside on the low terrace wall. "I only hope he can bear with my conversation. It is a fortnight since I saw you last. As you know, my cook is a poor substitute and hardly a fit person to converse with. She teaches me many idiomatic sentences that would turn your ears very red, M'sieur."

"That," he said, handing her a glass of wine, "I can readily believe."

He excused himself and disappeared into the house, leaving Deb to contemplate the summer garden and the inviting coolness of the river. She wondered if anybody swam down by the little pier, or went out in the skiff moored to one of the pylons: possibly the old man's godson. She wondered at the godson's age. He might be just a schoolboy. Someone Jack might like to have as a friend now that he was home from school. The thought had barely time to register when she was startled into dropping her wine glass. It smashed on the stones of the terrace, the last drops of wine splashing the hem of her petticoats. She spun about, flustered, eyes wide in astonished disbelief.

A voice, masculine and pleasantly drawling, had spoken to her back. "*Excusez-moi, mlle.* My godfather—No, that won't do," he continued in English. "You may speak excellent French, but I prefer introductions to be conducted in English."

The words were hardly out of his mouth when Deb had her little disaster with the wine glass and spun about to find herself confronted with her injured duelist of the wood; seemingly fully-recovered, more handsome then her remembrance of him, and at least three inches taller than her previous estimation.

"Good God!" she blurted out. "What are *you* doing here?"

Three

Two hours before Deb was due to arrive at Martin Ellicott's Queen Anne house, the Marquis of Alston and his godfather were seated on the terrace, immersed in reading the London newssheets, drinking strong black coffee and keeping their own counsel.

The old man had been up and dressed since dawn. A lifetime of habit could not be easily broken, as hard as he tried to enjoy a leisurely morning in bed. He walked about the gardens, sat on the pier awhile and came back to the house to speak to his housekeeper about the arrangements for a late breakfast. He had then ordered a pot of coffee and settled himself on the terrace to re-read a letter received the day before. There was a similar billet awaiting the Marquis; the messenger arriving after his lordship had retired for the evening.

The Marquis was still in the dressing stage when he joined his godfather on the terrace. He had suffered Frew's ministrations: to be shaved and his natural hair combed off his face and secured in a silk bag with a large velvet ribbon tied at the nape of his neck, and to be put in a white linen shirt and velvet breeches. He had even permitted the fastidious valet to adjust the silk cravat about his throat, but he refused to be shrugged into an embroidered waistcoat until he had consumed his morning coffee. In horror did Frew watch his master negligently throw a brocade banyan over his meticulous dressing and go downstairs with this bedchamber article left hanging loose.

Martin Ellicott looked up from the printed page and eyed his godson with the critical eye of a man who had valeted a duke for more than thirty years. The son would never match the father for sartorial elegance, but the boy was more handsome, except when he frowned. He was frowning now, hands thrust deep in the pockets of his dressing gown, shoulders slightly hunched. The frown caused Martin to put up the newssheet to hide a smile. When the Marquis pulled such a face he was his ancient parent. Such an observation would hardly have pleased either nobleman.

"How did you sleep?" he asked conversationally.

"I had the most appalling thought this morning," said Julian, looking out across the manicured lawn. "It was while Frew was fussing at me to put on a waistcoat. Did you ever fuss at my father? I dare say not." He sighed. "Martin. What if she has left Bath? I've assumed all along she resides in town. But she might very well live in London, or Wales or-or—Northumberland, for all we know about her. And we don't know the first thing, do we? Playing a viola isn't much to go on. And you can't make polite enquiries after a girl who carries a pistol and escapes to the forest to play her viola in peace. I distinctly remember her brown eyes because they are lovely. As for the rest of her face, I'm rather vague." He looked at the newssheet concealing his godfather's face. "Are you certain you've exhausted all possible avenues of enquiry? I thought Bath the sort of place crawling with poets and would-be artists and musicians."

"Sit down and have a dish of coffee," said the old man and set the sugar bowl in front of the Marquis. "The London papers arrived last night, as did letters from his Grace. One is addressed to you."

"Ah," said the Marquis absently and sipped at his coffee. He seemed not to have heard, so intent was he to pursue his thoughts, with little regard for the feelings of his listener who was tiring of the monologue on the mysterious lady fiddler. "There must be a hundred musicians in Bath. And not all of them play a viola. She might give lessons or take lessons. She has to get her music from someone. Then again, she might just have been passing through. There are always the inns. What do you think?" He addressed the raised newssheet and as it did not answer him he said with a laugh, as if reading Martin Ellicott's thoughts, "My convalescence has turned me into a great bore! If you hadn't found me bound up with makeshift bandages I dare say you'd think I'd seen an apparition to be forever boring on about my fiddler."

"Whether this young lady exists or not, my lord, I am grateful to her for aiding your quick recovery," Martin answered diplomatically. "Your determination to solve the mystery has got you out of bed quicker than any medicinal." He put the newssheet aside. "However, a week of sitting about the house with only my humble self for company, and the lack of physical exercise, has magnified your little mystery into—forgive me—an obsession."

"Thank you for being frank," Julian muttered.

"As for pursuing all avenues of enquiry," continued the old man, "I am confident all the usual channels have been exhausted. That is, only persons relied upon to remain discreet were approached. You told me once, you believe this female to be in some sort of trouble. Carrying a loaded pistol would indicate she may be in more trouble than is worth your while. Playing a viola in the forest at dawn with only her young nephew for chaperone and a loaded pistol for protection is hardly ladylike behavior."

Julian's eyes danced. "Martin, just because you spent a lifetime steeped in my father's vice doesn't mean that every female who crosses the path of the son is fit only to grace his bed. I am hardly worthy of the Duke's reputation. After all, he did not meet Maman until well into his third decade. And it must have been a most shocking reputation at that, because, even after all these years, it's stuck."

"The Duke has been devoted to your mother since the day they met!"

"All right. All right," the Marquis grumbled good-naturedly. "Don't get nettled. Why shouldn't he be devoted? Her loveliness is matched by her sweet temperament. Sometimes I wish—No, don't build up steam under your cravat; just because I was going to wish her a little bit of age and ugliness. I know you're as besotted as my father."

Martin Ellicott's face changed color. Julian had never seen the old man blush and it embarrassed him as much as it did the blusher. He picked up the letter and fiddled with the seal, giving his god-father an excuse to retreat behind the pages of his newssheet. Although the letter's direction was written in his father's elegant fist, the contents belonged to his mother. As always with her it was written in French, with only a sprinkling of English. He read the two pages of closely written script, saying without looking up, "They are staying in London until the end of the month and then taking Harry down to Treat for the holidays. It seems *Tante* Estée is unwell yet again. When isn't she coming down with something? Poor old *Oncle* Lucian! Maman has persuaded them to spend a few weeks at Treat; says the country air will do *Tante* good. She tells me she wrote to you in *mon père's* letter. She ends by hoping I am well and to see me at Treat on the –th." He folded the parchment and slipped it into his banyan pocket. "No hint she knows of my latest folly. And your missive from my esteemed pater? Well! You needn't pretend he doesn't know because I am persuaded he must, just by the look on your face."

Martin refilled their dishes. He looked pensive as he liberally sugared his coffee, and he did no more than glance at the Marquis. "When your fever broke, the first question you asked was if your parents knew if you were injured and the circumstance of your injury."

"And you assured me you did not tell them."

"I did not. Yet, your father knew—"

"Damn!"

"—and was here—"

"*Parbleu.* No."

"—for one night," continued the old man. "He would have stayed another but I persuaded him, with the physician's help, that you were out of danger. If not for the fact Mme la Duchesse knew you were coming to Bath M'sieur le Duc's presence here would have made Her Grace decidedly suspicious."

"Now do I ever feel the jack-pudding," Julian remarked, wiping a hand over his mouth. "I'm sorry, Martin. I hope he wasn't too difficult. His arctic tempers can freeze over a room. This means I will have to tell him everything, of course," he said more to himself and took out his snuffbox. "He may already know…"

"A word of advice, Julian. You will never keep anything from Monseigneur. Not where his family, his name, Her Grace— especially your mother—are concerned. I don't pretend to know all his methods, but if he desires to involve himself, he will, and count no cost. You are best to tell him everything."

"His letter to you, did it confide anything?"

"M'sieur le Duc confides in no one. He merely enquired after your health. He did say I may tell you your unworthy adversaries are now returned to Paris. He did not mention them by name, and I do not care to know."

Julian took snuff and shut the gold box with a snap, a hard light in the green eyes. "Interesting. Exceedingly interesting."

A lackey came out to clear away the tray and dishes and to enquire if the table should be set for breakfast. The nod was given, an eye on the Marquis who was looking particularly grim about the mouth. Before Martin could suggest he change into a waistcoat in anticipation of the imminent arrival of their morning guest, the Marquis was half-way across the terrace and saying,

"I must be mended enough to ride into town. Have one of the horses saddled, would you? I won't be home for dinner."

"May I suggest the carriage, rather than a saddle, my lord? The physician did say—"

"He can go to the devil! I've wasted enough time poking about here."

"As you say, my lord," the old man answered calmly, following the Marquis through to the back parlor and into the expanse of hallway. "If I may remind your lordship that the wearing of swords is not permitted in town."

"Eh? Not permitted? By whose order? But thank you for the advice. I won't need my sword. I'll carry a pistol." He stopped at the bottom of the staircase to put a hand on the old man's shoulder. "I'm not about to be foolish. I merely want to make a few enquiries of my own about my lady fiddler. Ah, did you think I had other plans? No. Not yet. That matter can wait. The charming scar below my ribs will serve as a reminder of that unfinished business." He caught the butler hovering in the doorway and called out to him. "What is it, Fibber?"

"Miss Cavendish has arrived, my lord."

"Miss Cavendish? Here?" Julian scowled. "*Now?*"

"Very well, Fibber," said Martin, dismissing the butler. "We spoke yesterday of the best method of approaching this delicate situation, my lord," he said to the still scowling Marquis.

"Did we?"

"Yes. It was decided, given your mishap and the fact you do not immediately want your identity made known to your wife, it would be for the best if you were to meet her here under unexceptional circumstances. This is Miss Cavendish's usual visiting day, so her suspicions are unlikely to be aroused by the presence of my godson."

"A chance to look-over the filly before purchase, aye, Martin?" Julian teased, an edge to his voice.

"I need not remind your lordship that the—um—purchase was made a long time ago," he gently apologized.

Julian took snuff. "Are you certain she has no recollection of that night?"

Martin Ellicott bravely looked his godson in the eye. "On direction of your father I made it my business to befriend the Marchioness—or Miss Cavendish as she is still known to the world—and it is my considered opinion that the young woman has no recollection whatsoever of that unfortunate evening. Her family and yours permitted her to remain ignorant of her marriage and thus her elevated station, until such time as you came to claim her. Thus we have arrived at a highly delicate situation that requires, I am sorry to say, extreme care on your part."

Julian heard the note of censure in the old man's voice and his smile was bitter. "Every man has his Achilles heel, Martin; even His Grace of Roxton. Surely you can't blame the Duke for marrying his heir in haste? Nine years banished to roam the Continent gave me ample time and opportunity to make an imprudent match just to spite him." When his godfather looked unconvinced he leaned his wide shoulders against the polished mahogany balustrade and said flatly, "So my wife has no recollection of our midnight marriage. So she's turned out to be a social misfit who made a bolt for Paris; that doesn't greatly concern me either. Her prig of a brother has repeatedly assured the Duke that my wife's virtue remains intact, and that's the main thing, isn't it? But if I don't rein her in *now* and for long enough to get her with child, you tell me there's every likelihood she'll repeat the Paris fiasco, and this time elope with Cousin Evelyn if that piece of vermin, Robert Thesiger, doesn't get to her first? Now *that* I won't allow." He grinned. "Once she's met me and not my title she'll soon forget the existence of my rivals."

Martin Ellicott regarded his godson impassively. It was easy to understand why the young man was so arrogantly self-assured; he had looks, breeding and was destined to inherit an ancient and exceedingly wealthy title. He came from a long line of arrogant noblemen who knew their own worth and counted no cost in achieving their wants and desires. Arranged marriages were commonplace and considered the only way of ensuring lineage, land and wealth remained within the confines of the aristocracy. Still, Martin was left with a nagging doubt as to the infallibility of such arrangements and he voiced his concern saying calmly, "Your parents have a very different marriage from the one your father arranged for you, Julian."

The Marquis was dismissive. "Ha! An aberration. Anyone will tell you so." He went up the stairs two at a time and on the second landing looked down at his godfather with a sly grin. "I always suspected you of harboring romantical notions; now it is confirmed."

"When you speak in that manner you so remind me of Lord Vallentine!" Martin Ellicott said stiffly.

"Good God! Do I? How distressing for you. I hope she is half-way to being pretty."

"I leave that decision entirely in your hands, my lord," the old man threw over his shoulder as he hurried out of doors.

When Julian descended the stairs some ten minutes later he was shrugged into a close-bodied embroidered waistcoat of Venetian silk; diamond buckles on his shoes, and feeling absurdly nervous at the prospect of meeting the female his father had forcibly married him to when he was barely sixteen years old. He hardly remembered the events of that fateful night. He'd been blind drunk and what details he did remember were so painful that he'd conveniently blocked them from his memory. Thus he had not the slightest idea what his wife looked like, only the impression of a small brown haired girl with a frown. Nor had he given her a single thought since.

That he was wedded for better or worse, the choice of bride taken wholly away from him, did not bother him. Marriages for people of his station in life were arranged and for the sole purpose of ensuring continuance of the line. But then Julian had the most appalling thought: What if his wife was cross-eyed and pudding-shaped, or pock-fretten with bad teeth or worse still, resembled her brother, that mealy-mouthed, egg-headed bore Sir Gerald Cavendish? God forbid! How was he to beget an heir under such appallingly difficult conditions? Drunk? Drugged? Would he be able to perform at all?

He hurried out onto the terrace with the frightening image of having to bed a female version of Sir Gerald Cavendish lurking in the back of his mind and found his wife alone on the terrace. She was admiring the gardens and sipping wine from a crystal glass. She had her back to him, and had he stopped to really look at her he would have noticed the deep autumn tones to her upswept hair. But he was not in the habit of summing up females on the straightness of their backs and height alone. He did not mean to startle her but he did, and in the confusion that followed he stared not at her but at the smashed glass and the damage done to the hem of her petticoats. It was her exclamation that instantly brought his green eyed gaze up to her face.

If Deb was startled into uttering an impudent sentence, Julian was momentarily struck speechless. He could not believe his luck. Standing before him was his beautiful fiddler of the forest. Her majestic figure was perfection itself in a deep green velvet riding habit with wide lapels and square low cut neckline that complimented her cream complexion and deep red hair. Horrid images of a female Sir Gerald burst like a soap bubble as he stepped forward and, without a second thought, firmly took hold of her hands.

"Forgive me," she was saying, her brown eyes searching his handsome smiling face. "I did not mean to be so horridly ill-mannered. You gave me quite a shock. Oh, but it is *such* a relief to see you looking so well. You can't know." She gave a nervous laugh at his widening smile. "I had visions—horrible ones—that my clumsy attempt—"

"Never clumsy."

"If not clumsy, then unskilled. Allow me that," she said, returning the pressure of his hands, oblivious to her surroundings

44

and the fact the butler, agog with curiosity, had twice stepped out onto the terrace. "Oh, but you do look well," she sighed with satisfaction.

A lackey came out from behind the butler with pan and brush and quickly set to sweeping up the shards of broken glass from Deb's smashed wine glass. This broke the spell for Deb and she quickly pulled her hands free and crossed to the table, feeling the heat in her cheeks. The Marquis followed, one sharp soft word directed at the crouching servant. The moment of intimacy between them was over. Julian saw it in the tilt of her chin and the determined set to her full mouth.

"If you think I've given away your forest forays," he said softly at her ear as he pulled her out a chair, "you are sadly mistaken in my character."

"Thank you. I never thought you would."

"Miss Cavendish," he began and smiled crookedly at her quick frowning glance. He took his place at the table directly opposite her. "Now you are being foolish. It is only reasonable I should know your name if you came to visit Martin."

Deb looked down at her lap where her hands were pressed firmly together. "Yes, of course. Damn. What a muddle."

He smiled and privately wondered if their meeting had not been fated all along. "Does Martin know you play your viola in the wood—?"

"*No.*"

"No, I don't suppose he can," he agreed, thinking that if his godfather had known about his wife's penchant for playing a fiddle in the forest he would have set it all down in one of his regular missives to the Duke. "Poor Martin. I put him to the unnecessary trouble of trying to find you."

This did bring her gaze up to his face. She gasped. "You made enquiries about me?"

"Discreet enquiries, Miss Cavendish."

"Thank you very much! No doubt whomever you asked thought you fit for Bedlam. I just hope it doesn't reach the ears of—"

"—tone deaf Gerry perhaps?"

This made her laugh. "So you remember that, do you?" She put out her dish. "May I please have some coffee?"

"Certainly. Where are my manners? I don't know where Martin has disappeared. Problems in the kitchen, I suspect. He has a temperamental French housekeeper."

"I sympathize. I have a temperamental French cook who regularly sullies my ears with the most unladylike of idiomatic sentences."

"Most lamentable," he mocked. "Martin tells me your French is very good indeed... and that you spent some time on the Continent...?"

"This coffee is very good."

"Yes, it is. But I'm not interested in the coffee. I'm interested in you, Miss Cavendish. *Comment vous appelez-vous?*"

Deb stared into her dish. "My name? Claudia Deborah Georgiana Cavendish. Dreadful mouthful, isn't it? I prefer my second name."

"I knew I would have it from you eventually!" he said with a smile. "Deborah or Deb? I like both. And the—er—Cavendish?" he asked, although he knew well enough her family's long illustrious history.

"Deb. And if you must know, my great-grandfather was the younger brother of the first Duke of Devonshire. I am cousin to the present Duke through both sides of my family. Quite a lineage, isn't it?" she said nonchalantly. "If you count such social intangibles as important."

"I see that you don't."

"Why should I? Oh, it is all very awe inspiring on paper. The name Cavendish gets one in the door at important social occasions. It doesn't matter to the toadeaters and trencherflies that, like my father, I too am a Black Cavendish. He had three wives, y'know."

"Your father had *three* wives?" Julian commented encouragingly.

"The second was positively unsuitable: An Opera singer. He did redeem himself by marrying my mother, a Boscawen. Her family is on the roll of Norman nobles."

"The Norman rolls? Now *that* is impressive."

Deb peeped up at him, wondering if he was laughing at her. But as he sat with his chin cupped in his hand and his green-eyed gaze riveted to her face, all interested enquiry, she rattled on for want of something to mask the sensation that he made her feel as if she was sitting too close to an open fire.

"I suppose if one wanted to one could throw one's relatives about, especially now as the name of Cavendish is connected to practically everyone who is politically and socially important," she commented with a shrug. "My brother, Sir Gerald, lives for all that sort of nonsense. He's very good at lacing his conversation with his titled relatives. It adds to his self-consequence, and that he has in abundance."

The Marquis pulled a face. "Sir Gerald is a positive bore."

Deb laughed. "Yes, he is, isn't he? But he married a sweet creature who'd been left on the shelf: unrequited love for a rakish cousin, so my brother Otto said. That must redeem Gerry somewhat." She leaned forward, as if fearing to be overheard and said confidentially, "I secretly suspect my brother was aware of Mary's lineage well before he ever realized she was pretty."

"The cad!"

"Mary's cousin is a duchess. I won't bother you with the name. Suffice that the Duke's family is on the roll of Norman nobles and, Mary tells me, is the largest land owner in the kingdom."

"Dear me! An ancient name, a title and half of England: You see me all agog."

"Well you needn't feel humbled. Gerry toad eats them enough for all of us."

"Does your brother have anything to recommend him?"

"I'm sure, given time, I shall think of something," she said simply, her brown eyes alight with mischief. She dimpled delightfully when he put up his brows in expectation of her suggesting at least one redeeming feature that Sir Gerald might possess. "He is forever plagued with having me for a sister. Although he does enjoy the sympathy this elicits. You needn't appear so interested. I'm not about to tell you why I'm a Black Cavendish. But you really should feel for Gerry's position."

"I certainly will not!" he said and sat up. "The fellow is not only a bore but devoid of sentiment. I hope you won't expect me to receive him once our marriage is publicly known, regardless of his sweet wife and her connections."

"I avoid him at all costs, so I don't see why you should—" She blinked and the breath caught in her throat. "You're absurd! You don't know the first thing about me. My name and face aren't sufficient reason to want to marry me—oh! You're as impertinent as ever!"

Julian grinned. He was enjoying himself hugely. "You're adorable."

"Mad," she said with conviction, showing him her profile, chin tilted in affront. "I-I wish I'd never set eyes on you!"

"That's a shame because I'm very glad I set eyes on you." As he said this he was playing with the sugar in the ornate silver sugar bowl, eyes seemingly on the spilling grains as he tipped over the spoon, yet his whole concentration was on her. "Naturally you have my word that your—um—lack of corset will not be disclosed to anyone, particularly odious Gerry." When her jaw swung open and the color reignited in her cheeks he couldn't help a lop-sided grin, adding matter-of-factly, "Of course, as your husband, I would counsel the wearing of corsets in public."

Now Deb was angry. "You may think it a great piece of funning to-to *flirt* with me but—"

"And I thought you'd taken a fancy to me...?"

"Did you indeed?" she answered with arched brows. "I'd say you were feverish at the time."

Julian gave a bark of laughter. "Please! Don't make me laugh or Dr. Medlow will have to put his needle and thread into me again." When she said nothing, lips pressed firmly together, he put out his hand across the table and said in quite a different voice, "I am in earnest."

She ignored the hand, saying in a small voice, "If you knew the first thing about me, about my family, you wouldn't use me in this way. Besides, what do I know of you or your connections? My groom thinks you're an adventurer."

"An adventurer? He could think worse. Are you in the habit of discussing gentlemen with your groom?"

"Joseph was my brother Otto's major domo. After Otto's death, he took it upon himself to look after me. But that has nothing to do with anything!"

"It does. That I'm considered a worthy topic of discussion with the estimable Joseph gives me hope. More coffee, Miss Cavendish?"

"No! Yes! Oh, where is M'sieur Ellicott?"

"Gone to Paris to fetch our breakfast, the time he's taking about it. Fibber!?" Julian called out over his shoulder. "Find out what's happened to our breakfast. Miss Cavendish and I are ravenously hungry. A roll, an egg, whatever you can scavenge. And while you're about it, find out what's happened to your master." He called out to the retreating butler's stiff back, "And more coffee!" then turned a smile on Deb to catch her staring at him in a penetrating manner. "My name isn't branded on the back of my scalp, y'know. That's better. I do so like your smile. And you have the loveliest eyes, and your hair... I've been trying to decide if it is red or brown. It is unusual. Sort of an autumn-leaf red, isn't it?"

"This is all very gallant, but it's getting you nowhere," she said crushingly. "No doubt I ought to be flattered. I'm sure your charm is irresistible to the vast majority of females."

"That's hard to say," he said with a thoughtful frown. "It depends on what sort of female you mean. If you mean the sort you are unlikely ever to meet, I don't waste a lot of words on them. And if you mean females of your quality, I am inclined to believe they hear none of it because they don't know the real me. They are only interested in what they will get by marrying me."

For one moment Deb thought him in jest, and when she realized he was being perfectly serious she giggled. "You are the most extraordinary man I've ever met. I should think you only have to enter a room to set all female hearts aflutter. And five minutes in your company would put the seal on your worth as a gentleman."

The Marquis nodded absently, looked unconvinced and sighed in feigned resignation. Her frown of embarrassment at speaking so candidly made him smile to himself but he said perfectly seriously,

"If you feel I must acknowledge your boring brother then I suppose we will have to invite him to dinner upon occasion. But I put my foot down at having him to stay over a weekend. I loathe trencherflies as much as you do."

"Will you be serious?" she demanded.

"I've never been more so. Drink your coffee, or do you want a fresh dish? That one you've let go cold."

Deb decided it was impossible to talk to a lunatic. She put his silly mood down to the effects of the medicinal drugs he'd been given to dull the pain of his injury. He was obviously an outrageous flirt who was not to be taken seriously. She suspected that he was being familiar with her because she had come to his rescue and thus was deserving of his attentions for the moment. Yet there was no denying that for the briefest of moments the prospect of accepting his outlandish offer of marriage exhilarated her. Of course she banished the thought as soon as she had conjured it up. And mentally upbraided herself for allowing this handsome stranger to so easily put her off balance.

Why couldn't she control the heat in her face?

Martin Ellicott saw her heightened color as he stepped out on to the terrace from the French windows. He had been hovering in the back parlor, awaiting his opportunity to join the Marquis and his guest, and as he sat down at the table he wondered what his godson had said to make the young woman blush and look coy. But he kept his thoughts to himself and his face suitably blank and signaled to Fibber and two lackeys to bring the breakfast things.

"Back from Paris so soon, *mon parrain?*"

"A minor disaster in the kitchen," the old man lied. "*Excusez-moi, mlle.* I hope my godson has kept you suitably entertained in my absence? Try one of these excellent rolls."

"Thank you, M'sieur. *Entertained*, yes," Deb answered, an eye on the Marquis who was plying his plate with roast beef, eggs, slices of bread and a sliver of pie. "A roll and perhaps a little butter. *Merci.*"

Julian glanced up from inspecting the contents of a covered dish. "Fussy appetite, eh?"

"Not at all! I usually eat a good breakfast. It's just that I—I seem to be drowning in coffee." His sad shake of the head goaded her into retorting, "I see you possess a bottomless pit for a stomach!"

"Yes," he answered with a laugh and devoured a slice of roast beef.

Martin Ellicott listened to these exchanges, saw the looks that passed between his godson and Miss Cavendish, and felt a stranger at his own table. The two young people spoke with a familiarity of long standing, which pleased him more than he cared to admit. Miss Cavendish might maintain a semblance of decorum in her demeanor but her replies to his lordship's playful banter stripped away her façade of indifference. As for his godson, he was enjoying himself hugely, no doubt because he had the upper hand in this meeting. The old man was of the opinion that Miss Cavendish's exceptional beauty was the reason his godson had the appearance of a well-satisfied cat who has discovered that the bowl of water put before it is in fact a dish of fresh rich cream.

"Martin will vouch that *mon père* refuses to sit down with me at the breakfast table. He positively shudders to watch me tuck into a hearty meal such as this at so early an hour. Is that not so, *mon parrain?*"

"Your father must be a gentleman of infinite sensibility," Deb teased.

"M'sieur le du—" Martin began, stumbled on the name and immediately corrected himself. A sharp, open look from the Marquis warned him to be on his guard. "M-My godson has an appetite beyond his father's comprehension."

Julian finished off the pie with the last of the coffee, an appreciative wink at his godfather that did not go unnoticed by Deborah. "Maman blames herself. She has a sparrow's appetite, yet when she was pregnant with me she craved all this. Rather an omen. Poor *mon père*," he laughed, "how he must have suffered."

Martin Ellicott thought such intimate conversation unfit for the ears of a young lady and his whole being stiffened. Yet he needn't have concerned himself Miss Cavendish would take offence. She barely heard a word Julian had said for she had fixed on her host's quickly corrected slip of the tongue and the wink of secret understanding that had passed between the two men. Her gaze flew across the table to the Marquis, who was looking at her intently, before she lowered it to the contents of her coffee dish.

"Ah. Apologies," he said as he pushed back his chair to stand. "Martin will be appalled at my lack of manners." He made her a short bow. "Allow me to introduce myself: Julian Hesham Esq." He glanced at the old man. "Miss Cavendish and I have been discussing our marriage—"

Deb's eyes immediately lifted from her coffee dish as a ready blush of embarrassment seized her throat and cheeks. It was one thing to jest of marriage with her in private conversation, quite another to continue the jest in front of her host who, one swift glance in his direction told Deb the old man was in utter disbelief at his godson's pronouncement.

"You must stop this nonsense at once," she demanded in a low voice, up on her feet.

"—and how I put my foot down at inviting her brother Sir Gerald to stay overnight," the Marquis finished off, both men instantly on their feet the moment she scraped back her chair.

"It wouldn't have mattered to me one jot had you been an adventurer," Deb continued, napkin cast aside. "But to tease a girl you have only met once and in-in trying circumstances, a girl you know not the first particular about and who knows nothing about you, with an offer of marriage, an obligation you have no intention of fulfilling, is beyond *forgiveness*."

Julian appealed to Martin Ellicott. "Tell her I am in earnest, *mon parrain*."

"I do not know what circles you mix in, Mr. Hesham, if that is in truth your name, but in the society to which I belong, your actions would not only be considered heartless but unconscionable! And—and those of a-a *lunatic*."

"Please, Miss Cavendish, if you would—"

"Why do you smile? Do you think it amusing? Do you see me as an object of fun, sir? To a gentleman of your address, adventurer or no, I suppose a spinster nearing her twenty-first birthday must amuse someone used to the attentions of—oh! a dozen females at every ball and rout. Well, I assure you, yours is not the only marriage proposal I've ever received! In fact, the ones I have received were in earnest, not made as a cruel jest! Indeed I had one this morning. And from a gentleman who would never make me such an offer unless he truly meant it!"

"I repeat: *I* am in earnest."

"To think I went to the trouble of bandaging you up!"

"And a very good job of bandaging you did too. May I know the fellow's name who proposed to you?"

"No. You may not!" she breathed indignantly and then opened wide her brown eyes at his look of amusement. "Oh, I see. You don't believe me, is that it?"

"Of course I believe you, Miss Cavendish," he assured her, following Deb to the low wall, a handkerchief at the ready. "It's just that I wonder why you have not accepted one of these proposals before now…?"

Deb rounded on him then and he found it hard to keep a straight face because she was scowling at him and it brought back a flash of vivid memory, of a thin shouldered bare-foot girl in an over large nightgown. It amazed him to think he had not recalled her before now.

"I will not take offence at that remark because you do not know my history," she said in a low voice, the scowl deepening spying the handkerchief in his hand. "If you must know Black Cavendishs do not receive many marriage proposals. Certainly not from respectable gentlemen! I dare say you are not respectable or I wouldn't have found you bleeding to death from a sword wound and you certainly would not have offered me marriage."

He quickly put away the handkerchief. "I assure you, it was not my object to offend you, Miss Cavendish. I am merely curious to know of any potential rivals for your hand."

"Is that so?" she said, tongue in cheek. "As my hand is not engaged there is little point in divulging the names of my suitors to you. Now you must excuse me, M'sieur," she said politely, addressing the old man who stood woodenly by the table trans-fixed by the conversation between the couple, "I have packing to do. Thank you for the breakfast. I hope to see you in the Pump Room before I leave for Paris. *Au revoir.*"

"Leaving for Paris soon, Miss Cavendish?" Julian persisted, following Deb down the terrace steps to the pebbled path that led to the stables.

Deb stopped and turned on him, the scowl returning. "If you must know, I am taking my nephew to Paris within the next few days, where, undoubtedly, I will receive more marriage proposals from dashing adventurers. Good day, sir!"

"Not if I can help it," Julian muttered, returning to the terrace. He propped one leg on the low wall and took snuff, maintaining a face of polite indifference under his godfather's steady gaze. "Cousin Mary is in town," he said conversationally. "I hope dull Gerry isn't. I must pay her my respects. I'll drive the chariot. Do you have any errands for Frew?"

"Julian…" the old man said and faltered, trying to collect his thoughts. "Miss Cavendish isn't the… She couldn't possibly be…

Mon Dieu. What a coincidence! It is quite a shock. I had no idea she ventured into the woods to play her viola. As for a loaded pistol... I cannot believe I did not discover these things before now."

The Marquis snapped shut his snuffbox, a hard brilliance to his emerald green eyes. "Don't let it worry you, Martin." He dared to smile to himself as the image of the thin shouldered girl in the overlarge nightgown faded, bringing into sharp relief a young woman straddled across his thighs in a transparent cotton chemise that failed to adequately cover her exquisite breasts. "You may leave the discovering to me..."

Four

"Come to keep an old lady company, Deb?" asked Harriet, Dowager Marchioness of Cleveland, shifting her heavy satin petticoats and her bulk to the end of the settee to allow Deb to sit beside her. "You won't see much from back here. That Reigate creature, with her turban and plumes enough for a whole bird, is blocking everyone's view of the floor. I've a mind to have Waverley shoot the thing to put it out of its misery!"

General Waverley leaned across from the next settee and enquired calmly, "Bird or beast, my dear?"

"Ha! Ha! I believe you'd do it too if you had your pistol," laughed Lady Cleveland and gave his lace covered knuckles a playful rap with her fan. "Say hello to Deb, you rogue."

"How are you Miss Cavendish?" asked the General, kissing the gloved hand extended to him.

"Better for escaping to the back of the room. I left Lady Mary talking to Lord Orminster. He pounced on us as soon as we entered the vestibule and insisted on finding us seats in the front row." Deb peered over her fan, out across the sea of powdered heads. "Poor lamb; he's still with her."

"Fred is a bore," said Lady Cleveland. "I don't suppose little Mary Cavendish will think so."

"Because she is married to one, my lady?" Deb enquired.

Lady Cleveland looked about in alarm. "She didn't bring him with her, did she?"

"No."

"Knows a thing or two about horses," opinioned the General with firm nod.

Lady Cleveland and Deb exchanged a significant look, the ancient Marchioness rolling her eyes heavenward, causing Deb to laugh. "We missed you at cards this afternoon, my dear. I hope it wasn't on account of Thistlewaite's win on Wednesday last?"

Deb shook her head and leaned toward the Marchioness so as not to be overheard, their bare shoulders touching and Deb's fan up to hide her words. "If Gerry comes to hear of it, poor Mary will carry the burden of my lost guineas. He actually sent her to keep an eye on me. As if he doesn't get a surfeit of gossip from Saunders already."

Lady Cleveland's eyes bulged. "Your butler spies for your brother?"

Deb nodded.

"Good God! That's monstrous. Get rid of him at once!"

"For Gerry to set another in his place? No, I thank you. The thing is, Saunders doesn't know that I know what he's up to. And he is good at his job."

"How did you learn of his treachery?" asked the Marchioness, her fan waving in agitated movements across her bejeweled ample bosom; all interest in her surroundings momentarily forgotten. "You didn't catch him spying through a keyhole or-or scribbling notes on his cuff? Horrid man."

"Nothing quite so exciting. Joseph always suspected Saunders was less than loyal. I hate to think what methods he employed but he found a sheet of paper, part of a letter addressed to my brother. Joseph says it was a discarded copy. Somehow I don't believe him."

"Who cares where or how he got it. He did. But why must you be spied upon?"

Deb lowered her fan and shrugged. "All that comes to mind is that Gerry's life is so dull that reading Saunders' accounts of my paltry existence in Bath is an improvement on his own. Poor Mary."

"P-poor M-Mary indeed!" blustered Lady Cleveland, her double chins bouncing with laughter. "Don't the gal amuse him?"

"Can one amuse the dead, my lady?"

This sent the old lady into such whoops of laughter that several heads turned in her direction. That Deb Cavendish sat between Lady Cleveland and General Waverley surprised no one. That she was the cause of the old Marchioness's coughing fit was taken for granted. Wherever Deb Cavendish was there was sure to be some scene or other. She never disappointed the disapprovers.

"I said it would be Deb Cavendish," breathed Mrs. Dawkins-Smythe. "I said, if there is a disturbance trust her to be at the center of it. Sitting up there with the likes of Harriet Cleveland, who should be at home in bed at her age. Flaunting those diamonds. Do you think they are real, Sarah?"

"Harriet Cleveland wear paste?" exclaimed Lady Reigate, craning her squat neck to better view Deb Cavendish. "The woman is merchant born and bred. She knows the value of a good investment. And she made certain her third and last husband had a title into the bargain. Vulgar creature." She turned away, annoyed at herself for staring too long at Deb Cavendish's flawless complexion.

Mrs. Dawkins-Smythe saw the envy and smiled smugly. "She is lovely, isn't she?" And to twist the knife further, "Is it a wonder Mr. Thesiger seeks her out? She always dresses splendidly, to the envy of us all. That sapphire blue gown is divine and shows off her statuesque figure to perfection."

"Vulgar!"

Mrs. Dawkins-Smythe smiled sweetly. "Not a match for your two beauties, to be sure, Sarah. But no one can deny Deb is a diamond of the first—"

"Flawed! Remember her flight to France, to her brother's sick-bed so it was put about. But it is generally acknowledged that she attempted to elope with a musician. A *musician*. No wonder she remains unmarried. No parent wants a bolter for a daughter-in-law," retorted Lady Reigate and presented her friend with a view of her profile, her daughter Sophia having completed the minuet with Mr. Thesiger. She expected him to ask Rachel for the final minuet and was all smiles as he deposited Sophia into her care once again. But he did not ask Rachel. Nor did he hover to make light conversation. He took his leave and mother and daughters watched him saunter off and disappear to the back of the room. His choice for the second minuet froze their smiles.

Deb, who had been fanning Lady Cleveland, while General Waverley fed her sips of iced lemon water to take away the cough, glanced over her shoulder, wondering why there was a sudden hush to the crowd. She had not intended to dance, that was why she had chosen to sit at the back of the room. But she knew she could not refuse to dance the minuet with Robert Thesiger. So it was with a fixed smile that she took his hand and went out onto the dance floor; one couple in the middle of the vast ballroom, scrutinized by an audience of upwards of five hundred people.

It was not a dislike of dancing which gave her a dread of being Mr. Thesiger's dance partner. She enjoyed the country-dances very much. But the minuet was the most public of all dances at the Assemblies and she knew that those mammas with eligible daughters must be willing her to trip, to make a wrong step, to appear awkward and stilted if just to show their own daughters to better advantage. She might smile and look as if she was enjoying herself in the company of her partner, but underneath she was trembling and praying she would not make a fool of herself in front of all Bath society.

As they turned and touched hands Robert Thesiger came near enough to say, "You suppose that by turning me away at your door this afternoon I would magically disappear?"

"Can you? I did not know you for a conjurer, Mr. Thesiger," she quipped and gave him her hand again as they moved across the floorboards toward the orchestra.

"You could do worse than I, my dear Miss Cavendish."

Deb's thoughts went immediately to her injured duelist. Yes, she could do worse indeed! She mentally castigated herself for even thinking about him at all. She had promised herself that she would not spend one thought on him the entire Assembly. She felt a fool. She had been consumed for weeks by fears for her injured duelist's well-being but after his cavalier treatment of her that very morning she was now furious with him for teasingly pretending to want to marry her. The gall of the man!

"Miss Cavendish…?"

Deb blinked at her dancing partner. "Mr. Thesiger?" She came to a sense of her surroundings and said kindly, "You seem to have forgotten that when I marry I must have Sir Gerald's approval."

"Ah. Yes. And yet, it is my belief you use Sir Gerald like one does a shield. You bring him out to hide behind, hoping he will protect you from all manner of declarations from prospective suitors, only to throw dull Gerry in a corner, forgotten, when your suitors are in retreat."

Deb could not deny this because it was true. Whenever she felt the need to put a stop to the verbose compliments of over-eager gentlemen callers she routinely trotted out her brother's name which produced an immediate effect; not unlike dousing the hopeful gentlemen with the contents of a pail of cold water. Yet, Mr. Thesiger remained persistent and she really had no wish to hurt his feelings. After all, unlike a certain other gentleman, Robert Thesiger was nothing if not sincere in his wish to marry her. She made no comment and they continued along the dance floor, Mr. Thesiger squeezing her hand before releasing her and saying with a sad smile,

"I have been mistaken in you, Miss Cavendish. I had taken you for an independent thinker." The quick angry knot between Deb's brows was evidence enough that he had made a direct hit and he added in a voice full of resignation, "I had no idea you held to medieval principles."

It was impossible for her to answer him, such was the sequence of their dance movements, but as they came together again, he circling her sweeping petticoats, she was angered enough by his comment to retort, "I am not at liberty until my twenty-first birthday. Then I may do and say and marry whom I please."

He smiled, the scar on his left cheek puckering up, and made her a bow, the white lace at his wrists sweeping the polished floorboards. "It warms my heart to hear you say so. And to know that in less than a month you will be freed from your brother's shackles."

"Is that so, Mr. Thesiger?" Deb said with some surprise, intrigued he should be so blunt in his opinions about matters that were none of his business. "You and I are the only ones who hold to the belief that I am shackled."

He gave her a sidelong glance. "I have heard a rumor, of course it is absurd but I will mention it anyway, that Sir Gerald has plans to marry you off to the Marquis of Alston."

"I beg your pardon? Gerry betrothe me to the Duke of Roxton's rakehell heir?" Deb stopped dead in the middle of the floor, forgetting where she was and that a hundred pair of envious eyes watched her every move. Robert Thesiger's idea was so absurd she wanted to giggle. "No one has seen Lord Alston on English soil since he was a youth. Sir Gerald certainly hasn't had the pleasure of his company or he would be lacing his correspondence with his lordship this and his lordship that." She was skeptically amused. "What an absurd and quite fanciful notion, Mr. Thesiger."

Robert Thesiger smiled weakly and made her his final bow, the lace ruffles at his wrists again sweeping the floor. "That you are to marry Lord Alston or that he is debauched beyond redemption?"

Deb frowned and remembered to curtsy. "I can assure you that my brother has never put to me such a ridiculous proposal nor have I any desire, despite my brother's slavish devotion to the Roxtons, to ally myself with that family. As for the latter?" She shrugged her lovely bare shoulders. "Everyone has heard the whispers about the Marquis's many mistresses, his Parisian orgies and his total disregard for his good name. That does not mean there is any truth in the rumors, of course." Without expecting an answer she teased him, "Perhaps you have attended one his lordship's Bacchanalian affairs and can make comment?"

Robert Thesiger's smile did not waver, yet there was no laughter in his blue eyes. The music had ceased and the crowd began to shift in their seats, restless for the country-dances to commence. He did not take her flippant remark as intended. "You will excuse me if I do not give an account of our history here and now, Miss Cavendish. Suffice for me to say that Lord Alston and I were once intimately acquainted. Indeed, when we were boys we were enough alike to be taken for brothers. But now, sadly, I have no wish to be associated with a nobleman who lives such a depraved existence, so depraved in fact that unlike other noblemen's sons, Alston chooses to live outside the unwritten rules of his kind. He does not confine his whoring to females of his own class, or to women who make a living from their favors. He preys on the innocent daughters of the Parisian middle-class; girls who are ignorant of the ways of the aristocracy and thus are easily taken in by the debonair Marquis. Alston offers them marriage like one offers a pretty girl compliments, and when he has gained their confidence with this lie he deflowers them and moves on to pick the next budding rose."

Deb put up her gloved hand, nauseous at the prospect of ever coming into contact with such a predatory creature. "Please, Mr. Thesiger, I have heard quite enough. If what you say is true, and I have no reason to doubt you, then he is certainly beyond redemption." She rested her fingers in the crook of the silken sleeve he offered her and allowed him to escort her from the dance floor. "You may rest easy, sir," she said, looking into his blue eyes, blue eyes that remained troubled. "When I marry it will be to a gentleman of my choosing. Sir Gerald has as much reason to hope of his sister agreeing to an arranged marriage with the Marquis as a leper has of being cured."

Robert Thesiger smiled with relief, the tension easing in the dueling scar that indented his left cheek. "Thank you, Miss Cavendish. I always knew you for a female of independent mind. Thus I will continue to hope."

"I have already told you..." Deb began and faulted, angry for becoming flustered in a public place and before this gentleman who had never been anything but open and patient about his intentions. "Please, you must excuse me. I need refreshment."

"Allow me to accompany you—"

"No! No, there really is no need, thank you," said Deb and picking up her satin petticoats made a hasty exit for the refreshments, shouldering her way through the laughing groups forming for the country-dances, neither looking left or right. She was about to follow two couples through to the Octagon room when the lace flounce at her elbow was ruthlessly tugged and a voice from behind a column whispered near her ear,

"Come outside."

She stood quite still, a shiver passing across her bare neck and the oddest sensation knotting inside her chest. She wondered if the voice had been conjured up in her mind, but she did not hesitate to hurry out of doors.

With an indulgent eye, Lady Cleveland watched Deb Cavendish and Robert Thesiger part and go their separate ways at the end of the minuet, her gaze following Deb as she crossed the room. She stopped briefly near a column and then disappeared, not into the refreshment rooms, but out the entrance doors and into the night. A gentleman who had been lingering on the fringes of the dance floor, seemingly content to hover by a pillar and scan the room with his gold quizzing-glass, lifted his shoulder off the marble support and sauntered out into the night air not two steps behind Miss Cavendish.

He was tall, broad shouldered and it was his patrician profile that alerted Lady Cleveland as to his identity.

"Waverley! Look!" she breathed, sitting forward on the settee, a hand hard gripping the General's large silken knee. "I'd know that nose anywhere. There's no mistaking it. He's more handsome than his father, though Roxton has more presence. Ah, but the son, he has so much charm. I wonder…"

General Waverley put up his quizzing-glass but missed his chance at a view of Lord Alston. "Who's that you say, Harriet?" he asked, a magnified eye turned on her ladyship. "Not the satyr's son? Here? No doubt you've heard 'bout the latest mischief he's caught up in?"

"Mischief?"

"Rumor has it he was run out of Paris by a M'sieur Farmer-General for seducing his unmarried daughter."

Lady Cleveland gaped at him.

The General nodded. "M'sieur Farmer-General followed him across the Channel with two of his cronies and demanded satisfaction." He shook his head at the thought. "Imagine! A common little Frenchy demanding satisfaction of an English duke's son. It don't bear thinking about. Trumped-up little peasant." He lowered his voice. "Just between you and me, Harriet: Do you think there's any truth to the rumor the boy's touched in the belfry?"

Lady Cleveland's bosom swelled. "Touched? Roxton's son, *touched*? For shame, Henry! And the Duke one of your Newmarket cronies."

General Waverley shrugged, embarrassed at having voiced the doubt that he knew many privately held about the Marquis of Alston. "You can't deny, Harriet, that Alston's had a dark cloud hanging over him since that disgraceful episode in his Eton days.

Why, it stands to reason we are left to wonder at the strength of his brain when one considers his unforgiveable behavior toward his dear mamma. Such a divine beauty…"

"He was a mere boy, Henry."

"A boy mayhap, but that don't excuse such insane behavior, does it?" continued the General, made confident by Lady Cleveland's slump of the shoulders. "He and that cousin of his, Ffolkes, were hell-raisers at school. Expelled on two occasions and only taken back because old Roxton is a Duke."

"My dear Henry, have you never considered that Alston was led astray by his cousin and not the other way round, as is common report?"

"Aye. That's a possibility," conceded the General. "But that don't excuse Alston's insane—some would dare suggest *Oedipal*—behavior toward his mother, now does it?"

The Dowager Marchioness shifted uncomfortably on her seat, painted mouth puckered up with annoyance. "No, it doesn't, Henry, but… The Roxton marriage is not in the common way, and to a sensitive youth that circumstance is rather difficult to explain." She unfurled her fan with a snap and rallied. "Besides, we will never know the absolute truth of that night and as the boy's brain seems perfectly recovered it is better we not dwell on it."

General Waverley could offer no argument, but added, "But what do you make of the persistent rumor that the Roxtons' other son is also weak-brained? Complications at birth, it's said. He's only nine years old but a physician's been his shadow since he could walk because he has those fits. What's it called… the *Falling Sickness*, that's it! Now if that don't point to a weak brain in that family—"

Lady Cleveland gave a dismissive snort. "Idiotic rot!"

Despite a full moon bathing the cobbles in an eerie light, linkboys lounged about under the portico, there to light tapers for a small fee and accompany those who chose to walk home. Chairmen waited by their sedan chairs, exchanging gossip and ribald anecdotes. A carriage stood in the road with its steps folded down and the door wide, a footman in livery patiently waiting the arrival of its owner. Deb took all this in as she stepped out into the cool night air and looked about her, feeling rather foolish when approached by a link boy. She did not have her cloak and was rightly at a loss, standing in the street unaccompanied.

"May I compliment you on your dancing, Miss Cavendish. Or was it the skill of your partner which showed you to best advantage?" drawled a pleasing masculine voice, its owner hidden deep in the long shadows of the building.

Deb waved away the linkboy.

"Why am I not surprised to find you lurking in darkness, Mr. Hesham?" she asked conversationally, although she was annoyed at feeling oddly elated her injured duelist had sought her out despite her angry rebuff earlier that day. "Is it that adventurers prefer the exciting company to be found in alleyways to that to be had under the bright lights of a dance floor?"

Julian grinned. "You find me living up to a reputation I neither want or deserve. Come closer. I don't bite, my dear."

"Why did I not spy you on the dance floor?" she asked in a voice she hoped sounded disinterested. "Do you dislike dances, sir?"

"I dislike being the center of attention."

"Indeed! I hope you are worthy of your own high opinion."

"It is your opinion of me that matters," he said calmly as he guided her further into the shadows. When she tried to withdraw her gloved hand he would not let her go.

"Forgive me," Deb apologized and dared to look up at him. It was a mistake. The light in his green eyes was all gentleness and she quickly looked away. "That remark was exceedingly stupid and uncalled for."

"I've come to take my leave of you, Miss Cavendish."

Deb gave a start. "You—you are going away?"

He smiled at her quick look of dismay. "For a few days. To reassure my parents I am alive and well."

"I see," she said, keeping the disappointment from her voice. She drew a little away, her bare shoulders suddenly cold, and shivered. "Of course you must go to them. They will be anxious after your health." She caught his smile and added defiantly,

"Not that you need justify your absence to me—"

"May I call on you when I return?"

"—as we are the merest of acquaintances."

"Mere acquaintances, Miss Cavendish?" he enquired lightly. "You, who have seen me stripped of this decorative façade?" He drew her up against him. "I meant every word I said to you this morning. No. Don't bite my head off. I am *not* an adventurer and I am *not* in jest. I am in earnest."

"If you care anything for me you will have done with this taunting!"

"I assure you my intentions are wholly honorable," he whispered near her ear.

Deb's throat constricted. Why did she feel emotionally vulnerable with this man when others had tried and failed? She wanted to be angry with him. At the very least, to be able to coolly rebuff him as she had Robert Thesiger. She had never permitted emotion to rule good sense and yet here she was going weak at the knees with a complete stranger! What lunacy had come over her? Not since she had run away to be with Otto in Paris had she felt like scattering caution to the four winds. She had let her heart rule her head upon that occasion and never regretted her decision. Otto had needed her and she had loved him dearly. But Otto was her brother and there was never any doubt that her sisterly devotion would be returned with brotherly love. But this was different. This gentleman was not her brother.

Indeed he was so unlike a brother that the sensible course of action was to demand that he unhand her at once and flee back inside to the light and crowds within the Assembly rooms. And yet she stayed within the circle of his embrace. His sheer physicality, the warmth of him, the faint smell of his masculine cologne, stirred in her feelings and sensations that threatened to overwhelm her. She tried to rally herself before she said or did something that could not be undone.

"If you are an honorable gentleman you would do well to keep your distance. I… I have a checkered past! I ran away from home when I was sixteen," she blurted out, speaking to the complicated knot in his cravat. "I'm considered by good society as an *eccentric*." When he remained silent she peeped up at him, adding, "An eccentric like my cousin Henry, the scientist, and my brother Otto, who was a great musician. You cannot seriously want—"

"—you?" he said, smiling into her eyes. "Most certainly I do."

"—a female who plays a viola with her nephew in the forest—"

He laughed in his throat. "—without her corset!"

"—against the wishes of her brother Gerry."

"Ah, the one snag in my eagerness for us to be man and wife without delay."

Deb blinked. "Not wearing my corset?"

Julian smiled to himself catching the apprehension in her voice, yet he made himself look very grave. "No, not your corset," he said levelly and pinched her chin. "Although, as your husband, I will demand you wear one in public. Yet, in private…" He stooped to kiss her mouth and momentarily unable to master his self-restraint pulled her hard up against his chest, wanting again to feel the pressure of her long stockinged legs wrapped around his thighs. "Damn these layered petticoats…"

"Please! No!" she demanded and pushed back, though she had instinctively returned his kiss. "I've never—You mustn't think that just because I want you to-to—*kiss* me that I am—I'm the sort of female who wants to be taken advantage of!"

Despite the acute ache in his loins he let her go saying patiently, "I've no intention of taking advantage of you, my dear girl. I am here to make certain that that circumstance doesn't befall you." When she continued to regard him with uncertainty he sighed and said flippantly, "The snag isn't your corset, or put more correctly, lack of one, my doubting beauty, but *Gerald*. He may be your brother and a Cavendish but he is a bore and a toady and his French tongue grates on the ear. I will not have him to stay with us over a weekend. Dinner, yes, but not to sleep under my roof. Never."

Deb relaxed and tried not to giggle. "Gerry? A snag? Are you ever serious?"

He tilted her chin with one finger. "I have never been more so."

Deb colored painfully. "And what of the loaded pistol?"

"Ah. Two snags. No loaded pistols. If you've a taste for shooting, by all means take to my pheasants, but no pistols."

She swallowed and made one last half-hearted attempt to turn him away by admitting, "I am under my brother's guardianship until my twenty-first birthday. He would never agree to-to…"

"Have I been mistaken in you, Miss Cavendish?" he murmured as he brought her back into the circle of his embrace and this time kissed her very gently. His mouth barely brushed against her slightly parted lips. "I thought you and I were like-minded souls. That you too believed in love at first sight…"

His words registered somewhere at the back of her mind as she craved another kiss, a proper kiss: the promise in the light, feathery touch of his salty mouth on hers so deliciously wicked that she felt strangely exhilarated, as if he had heightened all her senses at once. But it was the warm, tingling feeling from somewhere deep within her that was the real surprise. That and the knotted feeling in her chest that threatened to choke the life out of her.

"Damn your conceit, sir," she murmured as her arms went up about his neck and her mouth hungrily met his.

The shadows cast in the moonlight were no protection against the inquisitive patrons taking their leave of the Assembly Rooms. Half a dozen pairs of eyes had riveted themselves to the stooped broad back of the Marquis of Alston. To enable a better view of the embracing couple, a gentleman dressed in puce velvet waved his Malacca cane about at two link boys and ordered them to shine light upon that side of the building. Movement and sound ceased under the portico. Shocked and outraged to find an embracing couple kissing in the shadows, several matrons put up their fans at the sight; such licentious behavior was not to be tolerated at an Assembly ball. One titled lady, a Methodist with two eligible daughters in tow, went so far as to loudly voice her opinion so that even those standing in the street could hear her venomous tongue.

"Yes, you may blush, Rachel, as every female in Bath must blush at such wantonness! I thought we were at the Upper Assembly Rooms, but it is obvious we have strayed into a bordello!"

There was a snort of laughter from a nondescript gentleman closest the doors and a nervous giggle from one of the ladies. Then all at once farewells were picked up where they had left off because the Marquis had turned a broad shoulder, careful to keep Deb shielded from curious glances, and glared at the onlookers in speechless fury. He fixed a disdainful gaze on the titled Methodist lady.

Lady Reigate noticed that the group on the portico had fallen silent and that all veiled eyes were turned in her direction. She wondered why and glanced back at the couple half in shadow. She received a momentous shock. She was sure it had to be a trick of the light, for the gentleman's angular features and tall wide frame so reminded her of the Marquis of Alston that this gentleman could very well be his twin. But everyone knew the Marquis lived in Paris... Or did he?

Lady Reigate had another look at the immobile gentleman. He was regarding her with such an expression of haughty contempt that instinctively she dropped into a respectful curtsy, not willing to chance that he wasn't the Duke of Roxton's heir. When she straightened his broad back was to her. Outrageous expectations of her eldest daughter one day becoming a duchess came to a crashing end.

Deb was fussing with her mussed hair and pinning up a few stray curls, and although she had heard Lady Reigate's spiteful remarks she missed the woman's curtsy to rank because the Marquis's tall frame had shielded her from the curious onlookers spilling out onto the portico. With her hair pinned up again, she stepped out from behind him, grateful the crowd was dispersing, and in time to see Lady Reigate's carriage set to.

"You mustn't mind our resident Methodist," she said conversationally. "She barely acknowledges my existence, yet her pride won't allow her to ignore me because I am a Cavendish. And Cavendishs do not lurk in shadows with men of unknown social consequence." She frowned. "I hope she won't mention this to Mary..."

"I think you will find that Lady Reigate has a pressing London engagement and must quit Bath immediately."

Deb put up her brows. "How do you know her ladyship by name? I did not tell you."

All the coldness went out of Julian's voice. He grinned and chided Deb under the chin. "You may have found me in the forest but I am not a mushroom."

"Oh! Yes, how silly of me!" Deb said, flustered. She looked at him from under her long dark lashes, saying hesitantly, "I expect you know Lady Reigate from London and she—"

"—has two daughters of marriageable age," he interrupted and smiled to himself when she nodded and looked anywhere but up at him. He drew her closer. "But I have no desire to kiss them."

This pleased Deb more than she cared to acknowledge. Still, doubt lingered. "Tomorrow you will regret—"

"Never. When I return I am going to take you for a carriage ride."

"And after that?"

"Ah, that depends on how you conduct yourself."

She plucked a stray hair from the lapel of his embroidered waistcoat. "And if I fail to conduct myself...?"

He chuckled and lightly kissed her forehead. "Then we shall dispense with the formalities and ride straight into our future." He made her a bow, slightly stiff in its execution. "Now, Miss Cavendish, if you would permit me to propose—No, that sounds stuffy. Deb, will you—will you do me the honor of being my wife?"

"Ah! There you are, Miss Cavendish," hailed a voice from the portico.

Mr. Thesiger came lightly down the steps carrying Deb's cloak over one arm.

Immediately, Deb stepped into the light without giving her injured duelist a response and met Robert Thesiger half way, eager that he should not find her conversing with a stranger in the shadows. She had no wish to answer questions, nor did she want to deal with Robert Thesiger's disappointment and censure at what would be seen by all, even the most free thinking residents of Bath, as most unladylike behavior. She was so flustered at such an awkward circumstance that she sighed her relief when Lady Mary followed Robert Thesiger out under the portico and hailed her with a wave of her fan. "There's Lady Mary. I must go to her."

Robert Thesiger placed the cloak about her shoulders, while he continued to peer into the darkness of the narrow lane. He was certain he had detected a large shape move off and knew his eyes had not deceived him when there was the sound of footfall on the uneven cobbles disappearing down the laneway.

"My dear Miss Cavendish, you're shivering," he purred, making a mental note to question the linkboys for a description of the stranger in Miss Cavendish's company. "I'd never forgive myself if you were to catch cold. Allow me to escort you to Lady Mary's carriage."

Before she had gathered her wits she found herself beside Lady Mary, with Robert Thesiger ushering up the rear. A fleeting glance over her shoulder confirmed that her injured duelist had indeed vanished into the night, just as magically as he had appeared at her side in the Octagon room. With a sinking feeling, she wondered what tomorrow would bring, if indeed her injured duelist would ever return to Bath to take her for the promised carriage ride.

Five

The Duke of Roxton signed his name to the document and handed it to his secretary to fix the ink with a wash of sand. That being the last order of business, his Grace put the quill in the silver Standish and waved away the hovering secretary, who stood by his chair holding a Malacca headed cane and with a supportive arm ready to assist him to his feet.

The Duke had never needed assistance before and he wasn't about to start needing it now, despite his physician's insistence that the use of a cane would make walking less of an effort and thus help regulate his breathing, and this in turn would ease the congestion in his lungs. It made perfect sense, but to a nobleman who had all his adult life, up until a month ago, woken with the sun, was astride a horse every morning and kept late hours, the trappings of the sick and dying were to be resisted until the last breath left his body. His secretary knew this, but fresh from graduating from Oxford, he was eager to please. He was also in awe of his noble employer and, the Duke had to smile to himself, a little in love with the Duchess: but who wasn't in love with his beautiful wife? If he was truthful with himself, it was her vitality, youth and eternal optimism that gave him the iron will to live for many more years to come.

The secretary dismissed, the Duke lingered a little longer by his wide mahogany desk, a glance down the length of the library to where his son and heir was patiently waiting to speak with him. The boy had been waiting for nearly an hour, and the Duke had kept him waiting until he had decided how best to approach the subject uppermost in his mind. Yet, Julian did not seem to mind the wait. In fact, he had taken a bundle of day-old newssheets to the far end of the library and was casually reading through them, stretched out on a sofa, a hand behind the tapestry cushions under his head.

The Duke walked slowly to the far end of the long room and warmed his white hands at the second fireplace. When he turned about it was to find Julian on his feet, hands thrust deep in the pockets of his silk embroidered frockcoat and awaiting his pleasure.

A tug of the tapestry bell-pull and the butler came soft-footed to his master's side. A word spoken and the servant retreated to return with a footman carrying a tray laden with breakfast items, and with a silver coffee urn that the butler placed on its pedestal on the low table between the two sofas. Neither nobleman had said a word to the other and kept their own counsel while the butler was in the room. When they were finally alone, the Duke returned to the fireplace, and his son poured out the coffee into two porcelain mugs, which he then set on the table. A wave from his father and he helped himself to the hot rolls, slices of ham and wedge of pie.

"Your mother said you would not stop to eat your breakfast at the Bull and Feather," the Duke remarked, taking up his mug and setting it on the mantle. "That establishment's fare must be lamentably lacking or you—er—have a higher regard for my opinion than I at first supposed?"

Julian cocked an eye at his father but said nothing, finishing off a second roll before pushing aside the plate. He drank down his coffee and poured a second dish. "The fare at the Bull and Feather is rather good, sir; the venison pie, excellent."

The Duke smiled thinly and took out his snuffbox. "I am glad to hear it. I must increase my head of deer so that you can continue to enjoy such excellent venison pie. I trust I did not tear you away from—er—unfinished business?"

"Your letter stated that I present myself at my earliest convenience and so I have; convenient or otherwise. I'm glad I find you well, sir."

"You can dispense with the niceties, Alston," the Duke replied bluntly. "I am no better and no worse than when I last saw you in Paris. I see that your appetite has returned, therefore I take it that you are fully recovered from your—er—mishap?"

"Yes, sir. I only wish that you had not been inconvenienced—"

"You should have thought of that before you crossed swords!" the Duke enunciated coldly and turned to the fire, angry for letting emotion get the better of him, and the interview just begun. He took a moment to collect himself before continuing. "Those fools were beneath your touch. You had no right to engage them in a bloody struggle."

Julian regarded his father's rigid back and snow-white mane with a private smile; he knew him better than he knew himself: anger masked parental concern. "The fight was thrust upon me, sir," he explained calmly. "Lefebvre and his sons followed me from Dover. I had no idea I was being pursued until ambushed in the Avon forest. The old fool was determined to have satisfaction, whatever my arguments to the contrary. A determined man, a man who believes himself grossly abused, does not listen to reason. How was I to tell him he was beneath my consideration?"

The Duke pushed an errant log back into the grate with the toe of his black leather shoe, the large diamond-encrusted shoe buckle glinting in the firelight. "I realize that the pistol is fast becoming the preferred dueling weapon of the modern youth. In my opinion, it is a rather—er—crude and inaccurate method of dealing with one's opponent. A rapier thrust to a precise point on the body is the much neater, cleaner and gentlemanly way of ridding oneself of an annoyance. Did M'sieur's determination make you forget all your years of training?"

"No, sir. Those years of training allowed me to fend off Lefebvre's two sons, who quickly gave up the attempt on orders of their father, but it was no easy matter getting myself into a position where I could be pinked without killing the old man. I could have disposed of Lefebvre on more than four occasions during our encounter. My object was to give him the satisfaction of spilling my blood without slicing up my entrails."

The Duke regarded his son with considerable surprise. "If that was your objective then I am all admiration for your skill. But you find me momentarily stunned as to why you thought it necessary to carry out such an elaborate deception. Why didn't you—er—finish them off?"

"As you say, those thugs were beneath my touch. As for M'sieur Farmer-General…" The Marquis held his father's steady gaze. "He is an old man. Old men should die in their beds."

There was a moment's pause before the Duke inclined his white head. He took snuff and turned back to the fire. And although he continued to stand with his back ramrod straight, Julian could tell it was an effort for his father because his breathing was audible. He decided there was no point in delaying the inevitable.

"Sir. Killing M'sieur Lefebvre would only have strengthened the case against me. Think what his lawyers would have made of that? Isn't it enough that I stand accused of a crime I did not commit, without being branded a coward? How convenient for a nobleman to use his prerogative to settle a dispute with a duel. My opponent would be silenced, the threatened lawsuit dropped, but it would not wipe away the doubt of my guilt."

"Enlighten me, if you will," the Duke drawled, "how you come to be threatened with a French lawsuit for breach of promise?"

"If you know about the threat, then I need hardly elaborate further."

"Indeed?" said the Duke with a sneer. "Then am I to presume there is substance to M'sieur's claims?"

"Yeast alone does not make bread, sir."

"Undoubtedly. Yet, it is the yeast which defines the substance."

Julian pushed a hand through his thick black curls and walked away from the fireplace before turning on a heel to come back and stand before his father. "It was never my intention to involve you."

"You are my son, thus I am involved. Why does Lefebvre hold to the stubborn belief you offered his daughter marriage?"

"I have no idea, sir. The notion is absurd."

"Quite absurd," Roxton agreed, regarding his son with the dispassionate eye of a nobleman with half a century's experience of the fairer sex. "You did not perhaps offer Mademoiselle the inducement of your name in the—er—heat of the moment?"

The son's lip curled as he looked his father in the eyes. "That question is rather academic, is it not, given that I am already married?"

"You have relieved me of an anxiety I never thought warranted; you are, after all, my son."

"Then it must please you that I went to Bath for the express purpose of meeting my wife. It is time my marriage is more than a marriage in name only."

The Duke was pleased. Pleased that his son's hastily arranged marriage almost a decade earlier would finally be consummated and thus legalized beyond doubt. It was about time his son took on the responsibility of husband and, hopefully, in the not too distant future, that of father. The physician's depressing prognosis had made the Duke eager to see his line secured beyond his immediate family.

"Am I to congratulate Martin on his descriptive powers?" the Duke asked with a rare twinkle in his black eyes.

"If you are asking if Martin's prose leans to flowery exaggeration," Julian responded with a shrug, "then the answer is no. Deborah is beautiful but no more beautiful than the beauties trotted out on the marriage market season after season. She's a bit of an Amazon, with the temperament to match. She speaks her mind and knows what she wants. But that's not such a bad thing and preferable to a doe-eyed creature with cotton between the ears."

A muscle quivered at the corner of the Duke's thin mouth. "Indeed. But does she want you, Julian?"

The Marquis shrugged again. "When I left her she was half way to falling in love with Julian Hesham. After an absence of a fortnight, I believe she'll marry me out of hand when I return to Bath."

"You feel it is necessary to go through with this deception rather than tell her the truth?"

"Sir, she has no recollection of the night we were married. The shock of the truth could turn her against me, whatever her feelings, and then where would that leave me? I won't bed a reluctant female, even if she is my wife." He smiled crookedly. "Thus I thought it prudent to allow her to believe me a common man."

The Duke was intrigued. "Such consideration humbles me. Your morals are indeed far better than mine."

"You misplace my consideration, sir," the Marquis stated flatly. "You, like I, do not desire to see my wife seduced into bigamous wedlock, be it with Cousin Evelyn, some unnamed suitor or the son of Mme Duras-Valfons."

"Yet, we are not rid of the problem of M'sieur Farmer-General and the alleged ruin of his daughter," the Duke said smoothly to turn the conversation from a topic he found distasteful and beneath his notice. Unlike a handful of his noble contemporaries, who willingly and unashamedly acknowledged bastard offspring, his arrogance and pride would never allow him to do so, nor would he discuss Mme Duras-Valfons's lurid claims with his son and heir. Still, the boy's remarks smarted and more than he cared to admit. "Mlle Lefebvre's statement to the Lieutenant of Police names the Marquis of Alston as her seducer."

Julian gave a huff of embarrassed laughter. "That document of high drama? It's fit only for the stage."

The Duke regarded him with a cold, unblinking stare. "I think I've lived enough of life not to be at all shocked by anything you may care to tell me."

"As I said, sir, I don't bed reluctant females."

"Lefebvre's lawyers say they have evidence that supports the girl's claim she was seduced with the promise of marriage."

"They may say what they please; it is a lie."

The Duke inclined his head. "I believe you. You should know that this matter has come to the attention of the French Ambassador here at the Court of St James's. The Duc de Guisnes is sympathetic to your cause." The Duke sighed his annoyance. "Unfortunately, he and his contacts in Paris can do little to shut-up the girl's father. As a tax-collector Lefebvre has more power in Paris than any noble, and as a man who believes he has been grossly wronged, he will stop at nothing to see his honor avenged." The Duke sneered. "He is so eaten up with his own self-consequence that he had the audacity and self-conceit to force a duel on you!"

The Marquis made his father a low bow. "I am determined to clear our name, sir. If it comes to a trial, so be it."

"I applaud your sentiments, Julian, but you are under no obliga-tion to give satisfaction. Although, had your adversary been one of us, your impromptu duel would have seen an end to the matter, honor satisfied. You are of the English aristocracy. You cannot be brought before a French court of law unless application is made to our sovereign by His French Majesty's representative at the Court of St. James's. The French Ambassador has given me his word he will not make such an application. M'sieur Farmer-General may puff out his consequence until he—er—pops, but he will soon come to his senses and realize it is pointless to pursue such untouchable prey. I am reasonably confident that when this fact is made clear to him he will—er—crawl back under the floorboards where he belongs."

Julian grinned. "I envy you your supreme indifference to your fellows, sir. And I wish I had but a thimbleful of your sangfroid; your arrogance is rightly justified. But I cannot sit about waiting for the dust to settle on this matter." He added seriously, "It is my belief that the accusation brought against me is a deliberate attempt to bring discredit upon our family. The girl is merely the excuse. Nor am I ignorant of Lefebvre's connections and his motivations. I am sorry if my decision to push the matter to a just conclusion disappoints you, Father."

The Duke was not surprised by his son's declaration. After all, he is his mother's son, he told himself, and with those same clear emerald-green eyes. "You do not disappoint me, Julian," he answered quietly. He too harbored a nagging suspicion there was an undercurrent to this imbroglio that had little to do with a girl's ruin, and was surprised his son was of the same opinion, but he did not care to discuss these thoughts for the present. "I am still regarded as somebody at Versailles, but Paris is of an altogether different political complexion. Even His French Majesty has difficulty controlling the *parlements*. Whatever action your lawyers deem necessary I will have delayed until after your honeymoon. I will do what I can. Or perhaps I—er—interfere?"

"No, sir. Thank you," Julian answered sincerely and kissed the long white hand extended to him.

Lady Mary entered Deb's Milsom Street townhouse and discovered a state of domestic chaos. The front hallway was stacked with traveling trunks, narrowing the passageway, causing Lady Mary to pick up her voluminous hooped petticoats and walk crab-like behind the long-suffering butler, who ushered her into the front parlor. Saunders apologized for the state of the hallway and for keeping her ladyship waiting on the doorstep. He had been indisposed and Philip the footman was nowhere to be found. There was the melodic sounds of strings playing somewhere above Lady Mary's head. A scream and a string of abusive French came from the back of the house. Saunders had not closed the parlor door. Lady Mary watched in wide-eyed astonishment as an animal, possibly a dog, she hoped it wasn't a large rat, slipped along the polished wood floor of the passageway and collided with a portmanteau before bounding up the staircase out of sight. It was pursued by a stout woman in an apron whose floured fist was raised above her head.

Saunders gave an audible sigh of long-suffering as he bowed himself out of the room.

Not many moments later the parlor door was flung wide and a boy with long legs and a head of dark copper curls falling into his eyes bounded into the room with a large rat on a lead, which on closer inspection turned out to be a puppy. Mary knew nothing of dogs so had little idea as to its breed or disposition. But she did know something of their habits and she shrunk back into the sofa cushions, a hand to her voluminous petticoats.

"Down, Nero! *Down!*" Jack commanded and gave a tug on the puppy's lead. He went on a knee and received a lick across his face. "Good boy! Good boy! Hello, Aunt Mary! Saunders told me you'd come to call." He made her a bow. "Aunt Deb's upstairs. We've been busy on a composition I wrote. This is Nero. My best friend Harry made a present of him. He won't bite but he does jump. Aunt Deb says I must keep him on a lead when there are visitors, and because Alice doesn't like dogs. But Aunt Deb likes him and Joseph promised to keep him while I'm away. Do you like dogs, my lady? Would you care to give Nero a pat?"

"Oh, no! That's very kind of you, but no. I won't, Jack. Thank you," Lady Mary said with a smile that made Jack smile despite her refusal to touch Nero.

"He won't bite or drool on your petticoats like Sir Gerald's beagles. He's a whippet and very well behaved."

"There you are!" declared a voice from the doorway. It was Joseph. He took a step into the room, saw Lady Mary, and remembered his bow when Nero trotted up and nuzzled his hand. "Beggin' your pardon, m'lady. Out with you and that brute, Master Jack."

"Nero isn't a brute. He isn't even a dog yet."

"He'll be mincemeat for pies if Alice gets her hands on him. Cook is blaming your friend for the disappearance of a good chop. And by the looks of the wag on that tail he swallowed it all right! Sorry to be of bother to your ladyship."

"We weren't bothering you, were we, Aunt Mary?"

"No. Not at all, Jack," Lady Mary responded with a smile, yet she was relieved to have the dog on the other side of the room.

"If you want to come along with me, we'd best be on our way," Joseph told Jack. "And before Miss Deb changes her mind." He bowed to Lady Mary. "Beggin' your ladyship's pardon for the state of things around here but it's on account of our impending journey."

"I've been invited to stay with Harry. Joe's taking me there. He lives in a palace in Hampshire," Jack explained excitedly, adding, "You mustn't mind Aunt Deb. She hasn't been very friendly to anybody in days. We're hoping a letter from Paris will arrive to improve her mood, aren't we, Joe?"

"Now that ain't for anyone's ears but ours, Master Jack," Joseph was heard to say as he closed over the door.

Saunders appeared with the tea tray and informed her ladyship that his mistress would join her directly. Hardly had he shut the door when there was another commotion in the passageway; it seemed to travel out onto the street, then there was silence once again. Lady Mary sighed her relief only to sit bolt upright when the door was flung back and Deb sailed into the room.

"Well! Who'd have thought one little puppy would cause such a fuss!" she said with annoyance. She shut the door on the butler and rolled down the sleeves of a mannish white shirt that looked as if it belonged to a footman and which was buttoned over her bodice. "Did Jack show you his puppy? Friendly little thing. A gift from his school friend Harry, who has invited him to stay for a couple of weeks," she rattled on as she poured out the tea into two porcelain dishes. She put the teapot back on its stand and set the milk jug and sugar bowl in front of Mary but did not sit down, preferring to stand by the window with its view of the busy street. "I couldn't say no, could I? So our journey to Paris is put back yet again. Oh well, it can't be helped. That should please you, Mary; that I remain in Bath...?"

"I came to tell you that Sir Gerald arrived in town last night," Lady Mary said quietly, a keen eye on her sister-in-law who looked preoccupied. The fact she did not react to the news of her brother's arrival was evidence enough that she was more than usually distracted. "Is anything the matter, dearest?"

Deb did not answer because there was a curious lump in her throat. She merely shrugged and looked out of the window, braiding and unbraiding a handful of the long deep red curls that fell forward over one shoulder. Her thoughts were a complete muddle and she hadn't slept well in days. It was all the fault of her injured duelist and that kiss in the shadows of the Assembly Rooms. She was apprehensive and knew she had no good reason to be. He said he would return to Bath to take her for a drive in the park and it had only been a little over a sennight since their kiss in the shadows, so why should she worry he didn't mean to keep his word? Eight days wasn't very long at all. His parents might live the other side of England, for all she knew...

But with every day that passed her conviction grew that he had merely amused himself with her. Perhaps he was an adventurer out for her fortune? Her brother Gerry had spent years drumming it into her that men were interested in her for one reason and one reason only: she was an heiress. She was too tall; her walk too mannish; her eyes were the wrong color to be considered pretty, he said. She certainly wasn't blonde, blue-eyed and petite like Mary. She should have known better than to lose her heart to a handsome stranger found in the Avon forest bleeding from a sword wound! Where had her wits been wandering? And Lady Mary was looking at her in such a forlorn way that suggested she felt sorry for her and that made Deb madder than anything.

"I really must see to the rest of Jack's packing," said Deb, tugging at the bell-pull. "If there is going to be any food to put on the table for dinner after this morning's tantrums by Cook. So I'm sorry to cut short your visit. I expect you need to get home to Gerry—Good God! What has happened *now*?"

As she spoke there was a series of thuds overhead accompanied by a scuffle of boots and the familiar bark of Nero, and lastly a shout of laughter. Lady Mary was on her feet the moment the butler stepped into the room with his usual look of long-suffering on his marble countenance.

"Well, Saunders?" Deb asked, trying to glimpse into the passageway, but the commotion had moved on to another part of the house. "If you're going to tell me Cook has taken a cleaver to Nero, or is chasing Jack about the pantry mouthing Gallic obscenities, I don't want to know. Or are you about to give notice?"

"Not at all, ma'am."

"It is a brave man indeed who can weather one grubby schoolboy and his faithful hound."

Saunders ignored the sarcasm, saying, "There is a gentleman come to call, ma'am. He put his boot in the door and followed Master Jack and Mr. Joseph—"

Before Deb could answer Lady Mary interrupted her.

"You can't possibly admit a gentleman to your parlor dressed-dress—"

"Mary, I don't see why Bath should be denied a look at my olive-green petticoats. Don't pretend to be shocked for Saunders's sake," Deb said with a sly glance at her butler. "If the visitor came into the house with Jack and Joseph it is probably Fotheringay or General Waverley. And as neither of those two elderly campaigners can walk without the aid of a Bath chair they are hardly likely to ravish me in these fetching garments."

"Deb! Please—"

"Call Lady Mary's chair, Saunders."

Lady Mary sat down again. "I am staying. It's what Sir Gerald would want me to do."

"Well, Saunders? Don't gape at me."

The butler hovered in indecision and looked from one stubborn face to the other. He was prepared to wait out the argument until he was startled into moving away from the doorway by a soft word from the visitor, who had slipped into the room unannounced.

"It is most inappropriate of you to receive a gentleman dressed like a-a *bohemian*," Lady Mary lectured with a sniff of disapproval, "You've not even put a comb through your curls. And *that* is a man's shirt!"

"Can you guess to whom it belongs?" Deb teased.

"When you say such provoking things is it any wonder people are willing to believe the worst about you? Yesterday I had a visit from Mrs. Dawkins-Smythe—"

"My dear Mary, you really must learn to be politely rude. Toad-eating you again, was she?"

"Toad-eating?" gasped Lady Mary. "No. She was not toad-eating me! She came, she said, on a mission of mercy. She had the information from Lady Reigate and thus thought it best that I know that there is indeed truth in the rumor doing the rounds of Bath's drawing rooms, so that I could prepare Sir Gerald for the worst."

"Mary? I have no idea what you are talking about. Why do you have your handkerchief at the ready?"

Lady Mary sat up straight, the white handkerchief crushed in a gloved hand. "Deb, is there any truth to the rumor you were seen in the shadows of the Assembly Rooms last week with—with a—"

"—apparition?"

"You know perfectly well what Lady Reigate witnessed!"

"No, I do not." Deb smiled wickedly. "I was rather preoccupied at the time to take notice, be it vision or no."

"So it is true," Lady Mary announced in tragic accents. "You allowed a-a—*lothario* to kiss you! How-how—*common.*"

Deb laughed, but her eyes were very hard. "Common? No. There is nothing common about him."

"You think it amusing to have people ogle you, talk about you, think you *fast?*"

"Damn and blast what people think of me!" Deb growled, though this masked a genuine hurt that her sister-in-law was prepared to think the worst of her.

"Oh, Deb, when you talk like that I lose all hope of you making a good match. Is it any wonder Sir Gerald despairs of you—Oh! What—*You?*" Lady Mary stuttered and stared straight ahead as one who had seen a ghost, completely losing her train of thought.

Deb slowly turned from the window and came face to face with her injured duelist, dressed for riding in thigh tight buff breeches, dark blue riding frockcoat with embroidered cuffs and highly polished jockey boots. His wide shoulders were up against the closed door and his arms were folded across his chest. There was an appreciable twinkle in his eye and although he bowed to both ladies, his eyes were all for Deb.

At the same time as the Marquis of Alston was being admitted to Deb's townhouse, her brother, Sir Gerald Cavendish, was sitting down to a late breakfast of coddled eggs, bread and butter and strong cup of tea. Sir Gerald drank only green tea and from a cup, not a dish. He had especially ordered a porcelain tea service in mint green with gold trim, and the cups had handles: The latest thing; none of those old-fashioned oriental dishes. He was certain he would set a trend. He intended to send an identical tea service to his cousin by marriage, the Duchess of Roxton. If it found favor with Her Grace it would find favor with the Duke, and he so wanted to be looked on with favor by his exalted relatives by marriage. He smiled to himself at being so clever. Yes, the Duchess could not but be charmed by his gift.

He glanced at the clock on the mantle and frowned. Where was his wife? She should have returned from his sister's house by now. How much time was needed to tell Deborah her brother had arrived in town and expected her to present herself in his drawing room at noon? He had wanted to send a lackey with the summons, but Mary had insisted on doing the errand herself. Some nonsense about Deborah taking the news of his arrival in a better frame of mind if Mary told her in person. Females. He would never understand them.

Two hours. What could be keeping her? He hated wasting time. At least his time last night had been well spent. He smiled smugly to himself. This year Mary must give him a son. If she did not...? That eventuality did not bear thinking about. But he did think about it. Constantly.

Without a son, his nephew, John George (Jack) Cavendish, the product of sickly Otto's coupling with a filthy gypsy, remained his heir. That his half-breed nephew might one day inherit his baronetcy made him ill with worry. So did his sister Claudia Deborah Georgiana, who had grown into an obstinate and free thinking Amazon. Had his sister been obedient and docile and been guided by him he would have relished the task of one day informing her that it was all due to his efforts that she was destined to be a duchess. But Deborah had preferred rebellious Otto's company and had run away to live with the family's black sheep who lived with a pack of gypsy musicians in Paris.

Sir Gerald shuddered every time he remembered the Duke's wrath for allowing his sister to bolt, and the humiliation he had endured finding her living amongst gypsies, with his brother dead and she on the verge of eloping with a musician! In a moment of distasteful weakness he had even permitted her to bring Otto's orphaned brat back with them. Permitting her to set up house with Jack in Bath had been the carrot, not only to get her aboard ship, but also to settle down and remain on English soil until her husband returned from exile to claim her.

Sir Gerald thanked God the Marquis of Alston had finally come to his senses and decided to collect his bride, and before she became embroiled in any further scandalous episodes. After all, with a dowry in excess of fifty thousand pounds Deb attracted suitors. One suitor remained doggedly persistent and had impudently written to Sir Gerald on more than three occasions requesting permission to court his sister. The man had wealth and address, but his base parentage was enough that, had Deborah been unmarried, his suit would have been rejected as a matter of course. It was because of Mr. Robert Thesiger's persistence that Sir Gerald found himself in Bath when he should have been seeing to important estate matters.

He put up a thick finger for a footman to refill his teacup and was sprinkling in a precise measure of a half-teaspoon of sugar when the butler slid into the room and announced a caller. Before Sir Gerald could order his butler to inform the unwanted visitor that he was not at home, the guest walked into the breakfast parlor as if he belonged there.

It was Robert Thesiger and the sip of tea on Sir Gerald's tongue turned to tar.

The wide-eyed butler looked from his master to Robert Thesiger and back again. Sir Gerald put down his cup with deliberate slowness and tugged at the lace at his wrists with a long sniff of displeasure. It was an elaborate display of pompous superiority that masked a social uneasiness at coming face to face with this social pariah. His first thought was that Thesiger's presence in his house must not come to the attention of the Marquis of Alston. The second was to find an excuse to get rid of him quick, before his wife returned and was forced to receive him.

"So good of you to interrupt your breakfast to see me, Sir Gerald," Robert Thesiger drawled and took out his snuffbox, a significant stare at the butler who still hovered in the doorway. He waited for the servant to close the door on his back before taking up a position by the window, forcing Sir Gerald to move his whole body or suffer a crick in the neck. Before Sir Gerald could form words to protest his intrusion, Robert Thesiger added bluntly, "Has Lord Alston arrived in Bath, my lord?"

"Lord Alston's whereabouts are hardly anyone's concern but his own, sir."

Robert Thesiger smiled broadly. "I beg your lordship not to waste my time with a petty show of offended sensibilities. He is either in town or he is not."

Sir Gerald shot to his feet and tossed his napkin on the table. "I will not stand here in my own home and be subjected to such rude enquiry! You, sir, will leave my house at once!"

Robert Thesiger stood between Sir Gerald and the bell pull. "I will certainly leave, as soon as you assure me you have no intention of marrying your sister to Lord Alston."

"I beg your pardon?" Sir Gerald spluttered, so affronted that he groped for a suitable response to such an outrageous suggestion. "You dare to give me advice on a matter—a matter which is none of your concern and which is of the most private and most delicate—"

"If you care for your sister you will reject Alston's offer out-right," Robert Thesiger interrupted. "After all, you can't be ignorant of the fact his lordship is embroiled in a French lawsuit. I shouldn't wonder if the scandal isn't in the French dallies by the end of the month."

Sir Gerald was still finding it hard to control his features least of all put a coherent sentence together. He had never before been addressed so bluntly by a complete stranger and in his own home, but at the mention of a French lawsuit he found his voice, saying with contempt, "If you're referring to that common little tax-collector and his designing daughter, I heard about that at the club at least three weeks ago. The odds are ten to one in favor of Alston winning if it goes to trial, which we very much doubt." He pulled at the points of his silk striped waistcoat and stretched his neck; mention of his club restoring his feeling of superiority over this ill-bred creature. "That Parisian upstart can be nothing more than a petty nuisance to a nobleman of Alston's breeding. I wouldn't be at all surprised if he refuses to acknowledge such an absurd lawsuit."

"Time to get your nose out from between his buttocks," Robert Thesiger sneered softly in French, adding in English, "Alston's uneven temperament is but a whisper in polite circles; his sexually twisted conduct toward his mother, all but forgotten. Yet, when this civil action makes it to court, the true nature of his depravity will become sordid public property. You wish to ally yourself with one such as he, allow your sister to become that degenerate's wife?"

"Eh? You know about that Hanover Square business?" Sir Gerald asked incredulously, curiosity getting the better of him. "I'd heard a rumor—but I never believed—"

"—that in a drunken rage he denounced the Duchess his mother to the world as a whore and a witch?" Robert Thesiger put up his black brows. "Is that the actions of a sane man, Sir Gerald?"

"Sounds a lot of theatrical clap-trap!"

But Sir Gerald's quick brick-red blush belied his dismissive bluster.

Robert Thesiger's smile was smug. "It does, doesn't it? I, like you, would've reacted as you have now had I not been with Alston that night. We'd come down from Eton together, the three of us, Alston, Evelyn Ffolkes and myself." He flicked open his snuffbox. "Brothers in arms, you could say. Evelyn and I there to support our kin in his hour of need. All of us drunk. But not too drunk that we weren't repulsed by Alston's unreasonable demands on his own mother."

Sir Gerald needed a glass of claret to steady his disordered nerves. But having none at hand he gripped the table edge for support.

"Alston is about to become embroiled in a public scandal," Thesiger continued with a sad smile and a frown between his black brows. "This time the Duke can't banish him, even if he wanted to. Nor can the circumstances be hushed up and conveniently forgotten. What a shame your wife must forever share kin with a man who has overstepped the bounds of common decency by seducing and then abandoning the daughter of a Farmer-General." He took snuff, an eye on Sir Gerald to make certain he was digesting every word. "The pretty little thing—and she is pretty, very pretty— had returned from her convent school only a matter of weeks before Alston seduced her with the promise of marriage—"

"Marriage? An English nobleman marry a middle-class Frenchy?" Sir Gerald scoffed pompously. "Unthinkable!"

"Why not, when he did not mean it? It was merely a ploy to get her petticoats up over her luscious thighs. Unfortunately he made the mistake of hunting down a female from a class that does not play by the rules of the aristocracy. The pretty little thing had no idea he did not mean it, nor knew how to rebuff him in her own house. Imagine then the Farmer-General's horror when he learnt his daughter's carefully nurtured virginity had been ransacked by an Englishman of rank and fortune. He was determined Alston should do the honorable thing and marry his daughter."

"The man's an insufferable trencherfly!" Sir Gerald pulled a face full of revulsion. "The son of duke ally himself with a family of tax-collectors? Preposterous!"

"*Mon Dieu*," Robert Thesiger muttered in French, "you're so far up his arse, you're breathing *merde*. Yes, think of the disgrace for the House of Roxton," he drawled in English, the sarcasm lost on his listener. "Alston has been named in a lawsuit for breach of promise. A preliminary investigation has begun; witnesses for both sides have been called. A judge will question them. Legal representatives for M'sieur Farmer-General are in London. The Duke of Roxton was called before the French Ambassador."

Sir Gerald felt suddenly hot and sweaty. He did not like drama in his life. And he certainly did not want scandal attached to his good name. It had taken him years to recover from Otto and Deborah's deplorably wayward conduct. He blinked at Robert Thesiger and asked in a voice of doom, "The Duke called before the French Ambassador? Why?"

"To ensure Roxton's precious son and heir returns to Paris for the trial."

"Surely the Duke will be able to—"

"—do what, Sir Gerald?" Thesiger scoffed. "M'sieur Farmer-General is not prepared to settle out of court. He wants his lordship up before judge and jury. The Parisian authorities are determined to make Alston an example of the unbridled aristocratic lasciviousness that infects the good citizens of Paris." He put up his brows. "You want your sister married to such a man?"

Sir Gerald was ashen faced and sullen. "It's nothing to do with me now."

Robert Thesiger looked haughty. "As your sister's guardian, it has everything to do with you, sir!"

Sir Gerald's ashen hue turned to puce and he puffed out his cheeks. "How dare you tell me my business, you...you..." Then he realized how he could immediately end this uncomfortable interview and rid his house of this product of degeneracy. He smiled smugly at his unwanted guest, saying conceitedly, "Much you know of the matter. Lord Alston is with my sister as we speak—"

"*What?*"

Robert Thesiger shouldered past Sir Gerald to get to the door, wrenched it open and turned and sneered at Sir Gerald, who was mopping his glistening brow with his discarded napkin, relieved that the man had taken the bait.

"I hope for your sake, sir, that your sister has more brain and wit than you! Or you may yet see her and your precious family name ruined beyond social salvation."

Six

"You did keep your promise!" Deb declared with a smile and took a step toward her injured duelist. Then she checked herself, blushing to the roots of her auburn hair, for her spontaneity surely gave away her feelings.

"Yes. I'm here to take you for a ride about the park as promised," Julian said conversationally, as if it was only yesterday he had kissed her in the shadows of the Assembly Rooms. "There is a chill in the breeze so you will need to fetch a wrap and your bonnet."

Lady Mary gaped at both of them and rallied herself enough to say, "Deb can't go riding dressed—"

"Yes, I would like that," Deb interrupted, not looking at her injured duelist for he was smiling at her in that way that made her feel ridiculously happy. "Don't wait for me, Mary."

Julian opened the door for her to pass into the corridor then closed it and turned to Lady Mary, who was on her feet, blushing furiously and looking out of sorts.

"You can't allow Deb to—" she began and was cut off.

"Has it never occurred to you that every time you say no to Deb she will instantly defy you?" he interrupted calmly. "Got a devil of a temper, too, I'll warrant. Born with it, by the color of her hair. And she is very young, for all her worldly façade."

"I suppose you gleaned all of this from one kiss at the Assembly Ball?" Lady Mary asked frigidly.

"No, dearest cousin," Julian said simply. "It comes from having many years' experience of your sex."

"Well!" breathed Lady Mary. "You needn't brag about your conquests to me!"

He shrugged. "Think what a dull dog I'd be if at five and twenty I hadn't notched up a few conquests."

"I don't care to know how many females you've ruined!"

He smiled and said softly, "Only those wanting to be ruined, Mary."

"You may think it vastly amusing, my lord, to seduce Deb in the shadows of the Assembly Room—"

Julian sighed. "Mary. Don't get yourself in a passion over matters which you can neither influence or alter."

Lady Mary lifted her chin defiantly. "You may have ruined the daughter of a French tax collector but I won't allow you to ruin Deborah's chances of marrying well. It has taken Sir Gerald and me years and considerable effort to bring Deb back from the brink of social disaster after she bolted to Paris." When her cousin put up his brows in interest she became flustered. "Not that *that* is any of your concern." Adding in an about face that would have surprised her husband, "When Robert Thesiger asks her I know she will accept him, despite his-his unfortunate parentage."

"Robert has asked her," Julian said flatly. "She has refused him on no less than three occasions."

"How-how do you know this?"

"I have made it my business to know," he drawled. "One must protect one's investment."

"Investment?"

The Marquis came to stand beside her. "Listen to me, Mary. Why do you think Thesiger is pursuing Deb? Why is he so keen for her to accept his offer of marriage when he is at liberty to pursue any female of his choosing?" When his cousin continued to blink uncomprehendingly up at him he sighed. "By enticing Deb into wedlock and bedding her he will have his revenge on a family name he can never call his own."

Lady Mary's eyes widened. So the sordid rumors were true. She had heard the whispers about Robert Thesiger's parentage but she had never had confirmation that the man was indeed her cousin's half-brother and thus the Duke of Roxton's bastard son.

Still, that did not adequately explain why the Marquis was also pursuing Deborah, unless he and Robert Thesiger were locked in some bizarre battle with Deb's virtue as the prize. Knowing a little of their history at Eton, she could well believe it.

"You are at the same liberty as Mr. Thesiger to choose any female," she said as she maneuvered her wide hooped petticoats between the furniture to stand by the window because her cousin was too close for comfort. "Why Deborah?"

Julian frowned down at his intricately engraved initials on the polished lid of his gold snuffbox. "Because Deborah Cavendish is my wife."

"Your *wife*?"

"Yes."

"How? When? It can't be true!"

"We were married off as children, just before I was sent to the Continent. Deb has no recollection of that night and it was thought in our best interests that she and the rest of society remain ignorant of the match until my return. I ask that you not say anything to her." He smiled crookedly. "She knows me only as Julian Hesham and I would prefer her to go on thinking me a gentleman of no particular family for the time being. If she was to discover the circumstances behind our union before I've had a chance to make her my wife in more than name only—"

"You intend to bed her without telling her who you really are?" Lady Mary was outraged. "You think it preferable that she be deceived into your bed than be married honestly and willingly to Robert Thesiger?" She gave a hysterical laugh that broke in the middle. "You think she will accept with equanimity a husband capable of turning on his own mother—"

Quick as lightening he lashed out and grabbed Lady Mary about the wrist and pulled her hard up against his chest, his red face stuck in hers. "You know nothing—*nothing!*" he snarled, green eyes ablaze with fury. He pushed her away and turned to regain his composure, angry with himself for letting his cousin's words get the better of him. "Don't interfere in this, Madam," he added coldly, squaring his shoulders and adjusting his shirt-sleeves just as the door was flung wide. "Well, Jack, where is your Aunt Deborah?" he asked, forcing a smile.

Lady Mary threw her cousin a look of resentment and rushed out into the hall. Her head thudded and her heart pounded. She had the beginnings of a terrible megrim. She needed to return home as quickly as possible to tell her husband. She really couldn't believe Sir Gerald would be party to such a horrid scheme of deceit against his own sister. He must do something to save Deborah from her unconscionable cousin.

"Mary? I thought you'd gone," said Deb, descending the stairs in a many-petticoated gown of pale-blue silk, embroidered in the Chinese manner on tight bodice and hem with flowers and singing birds. The low, square-cut bodice was made respectable by the expert arrangement of a thin silk tasseled shawl draped across her bare shoulders. She peered in the large gilt looking glass in the hall and patted into place her upswept hair, several sprung curls allowed to fall over one shoulder. She frowned, catching her sister-in-law's reflection. "Are you perfectly well, Mary?"

"I have the headache!" Lady Mary announced shrilly, feeling wretched, more so because Deborah looked positively radiant in her ignorance, and scrambled into her waiting sedan chair.

Deb followed her.

"I hope it wasn't Nero's antics that brought on your headache, dearest," Deb said cheerfully at the window of the sedan chair, a suspicious glance at Jack, the wayward puppy and lastly at her injured duelist, all of whom stood in the hallway. The latter shrugged his wide shoulders, denying all implication in Lady Mary's failing health. "If we see Mrs. Dawkin-Smythe in the park, shall I tell her to visit you with one of her restorative jellies?"

"No! I couldn't bear it! Not now!" Lady Mary exclaimed in a shattered voice, and with a sob banged on the side of the door with the closed sticks of her fan, eager for the two burly chair-men to lift her chair up on its long poles. She then threw herself against the damask upholstery and was unceremoniously bounced away out into the street.

"Poor Mary," Deb said with a concerned frown, twirling her straw bonnet by its ribands. "Gerry has come to town and now she won't have a moment's peace."

"Aunt Mary is always complaining of a headache," Jack commented.

"I don't recall asking for your opinion, you rude boy," Deborah said sternly but with such laughter in her eyes that Jack grinned. She turned to Julian, saying, "I didn't mean to keep you waiting above a minute, but Brigitte threatened to throw herself from the second landing if I stepped outside without first changing into this fetching gown and allowing her to put up my hair." She glanced at her nephew. "Well, Jack, I thought you'd promised to help Joseph?"

Her nephew looked expectantly at the Marquis.

"I have consented to allow Master Cavendish to ride with us about the park," Julian said, taking Deb's arm and leading her a little way up the street to where his open carriage and four awaited. "His reward for getting your butler off my back." He looked over his shoulder to make sure the boy was behind them. "Yes, you may bring that black brute with you. But you and he must sit up front with Thomas and behave. Which means leaving your aunt and I in peace. Agreed?"

"Famous! Thank you, sir! I won't be a nuisance. Promise!"

Deb sat back against the plush red velvet upholstery and tied on her bonnet, a sideways glance at Julian as he settled himself beside her.

"I don't pretend to understand how you came to take Jack into your confidence, but it is clear he is firmly in your camp already."

"Why, Miss Cavendish, I do believe you think me capable of underhandedness. And for the sole purpose of gaining your un-dying devotion. That bow will never do! Come here," he said, and proceeded to retie the ribands of her bonnet. "Head up! Good girl." With a nod to his driver, they set off up Milsom Street at a leisurely trot.

They had not gone very far when a gentleman on horseback reigned in alongside and proceeded to accompany the carriage on its journey.

It was Robert Thesiger.

"Miss Cavendish! What a delight to see you out of doors!" Robert Thesiger called out from astride a magnificent black stallion. He carried a pearl handled riding crop and he used this to reign-in his mount beside the open carriage. He inclined his head to both occupants, but whereas Deb returned the salutation, Julian stared straight ahead, as if the man was not there at all.

The carriage stopped at a congested intersection where a wagon and a travelling coach were vying for space.

"It required only the right inducement, Mr. Thesiger," Deb called out teasingly.

Robert Thesiger's smile was tight. "I must speak with you, Miss Cavendish," he demanded, a glance at the Marquis. "It is a matter of the upmost urgency."

Deb stared at him keenly and noted the sheen of perspiration on his forehead. "Has something happened? Is Lady Mary truly ill? Did you see her just now in her chair?"

"No, Miss Cavendish, I have not seen Lady Mary!" Robert Thesiger snapped, a note of desperation creeping into the normally cool voice. "This matter concerns you and I!"

Deb breathed easier knowing Mary was all right and settled herself against the velvet upholstery. "I am most happy for you to call on me this afternoon, Mr. Thesiger," she called out to him with a smile. "But I have quite made up my mind to take a turn about the park before nuncheon."

When Julian put an arm over the back of the seat and let his fingers toy with one of Deb's curls, she glanced up at Robert Thesiger, who still rode beside the carriage, and was surprised by his thunderous expression. She was unsure what angered him more: being ignored by her travelling companion who continued to stare out at the opposite side of the road, thus affording them a view of the back of his head, or the fact her travelling companion signaled his possession by playing with her hair.

"Miss Cavendish! I must insist!" Robert Thesiger demanded, kicking his mount into action, an eye on the road and eager to keep up with the Marquis's horses as the carriage moved off to merge with the flow of traffic. Receiving no response from her, he appealed to the driver, shouting to be heard over the carriage wheels on the cobbles. "Master Cavendish! I say, Master Cavendish, order the driver to pull over!" he called out to Jack up on the box beside Thomas. "Your aunt must return home this instant! Master Cavendish? Do you hear?"

Jack turned to take direction, not from Robert Thesiger but from the Marquis. Julian shook his head slightly, and Jack nodded.

He put up his shoulders at Robert Thesiger, as if there was nothing he could do, and faced forward again.

Robert Thesiger was so incensed that he swung his mount violently to the left and galloped around the back of the carriage to reign in beside where sat the Marquis. "Enjoy your hour of triumph," he snarled in French, a gloved hand hard gripped on the carriage door. "It'll be your last! Lawyers from Paris carry a warrant for your arrest." When Julian continued to stare straight ahead as if not spoken to, crossing his legs in a leisurely fashion, Robert Thesiger leaned so far forward in the saddle that the brim of his hat almost tickled his lordship's ear. "M'sieur Lefebvre is intent that French justice expose you to the world for the despicable cad you really are. *Our father* can't protect you this time."

This did make Julian turn. He stared Robert Thesiger full in the face, as if he'd spoken a language he did not understand, but then he winked and broke into a wide grin saying in French, "Better a despicable cad than an ill-gotten bastard. *Foutre le camp.*"

A thump of the boards with his boot and Julian's driver gave the horses their heads and the carriage took off, swerved around two gentlemen officers on horseback, narrowly passed between a wagon laden with kegs and an open barouche carrying three elderly ladies, and was half way up the street before Robert Thesiger had completely righted himself in the saddle; Julian acknowledging him without turning around by a wave of one gloved hand held high above his head.

Deb sat in thoughtful silence a long time after Robert Thesiger was left by the kerb but it was not until the town was behind them, and the carriage rattling along the Wells road, that Deb came to a sense of her surroundings.

"Where are you taking me?" she demanded, sitting bolt upright.

"I've kidnapped you, Miss Cavendish." When this quip fell flat, Julian smiled ruefully. "That is, only if you wish to be kidnapped."

"Well! It was very unromantic of you to invite Jack along, not to mention that black fiend with four legs." She looked sideways at him. "Or are you about to off-load them at the nearest inn with the ransom note?"

He laughed and the tension eased in his shoulders. "How is it you know me so well? And of course you never wavered in your conviction that I would return to Bath for you, did you, Miss Cavendish?"

"May I know why you gave Mr. Thesiger the brush off just now?" she asked, ignoring his question. "You seemed determined to ignore his existence."

Julian gave a ghost of a laugh. "I've been trying to do that since Eton, Miss Cavendish, but the fellow refuses to go away."

Deb tried to sound disinterested. "You were at Eton together? How intriguing."

"No. It was a dead bore," he answered flatly and abruptly changed the subject and the language with a question of his own in French. "How long have you had the care of your nephew?"

"Since Jack was five years old," she answered in kind, following his lead. "Gerry did not want the care of him; poor little chap. You see, Jack's mamma, Rosa, was a gypsy…Well, that's all ancient history now. I brought Jack back from Paris and we set up house in Bath."

"You must have been very young to take charge of a small boy."

"I was not quite eighteen," she answered, and in a more rallying tone, "And that was three years ago and I would rather—"

"May I know why you were living with Jack's family in Paris," he interrupted, "and not under Sir Gerald's protection here in England?"

Deb bit her lip. The conversation had taken a dangerous turn and she was unsure how best to steer it clear of a topic she would rather not discuss. Yet, it was far better to have the story from her than hear a distorted version from a stranger. She took a moment to consider her words, all the while conscious of her injured duelist's gaze upon her. A mile down the road she glanced up at him and said in a measured tone, "When I was sixteen I ran away to Paris to care for my brother Otto who was very ill. Otto went off on the Grand Tour just after my tenth birthday and never came home. He preferred a bohemian existence as a musician, and as he had married totally inappropriately he couldn't return home even if he wanted to, not that he did want to because he and Rosa had a wonderful life together amongst the musical community in Paris. Rosa was heavy with child and could not care for a sick husband, a small boy and herself all on her own. She-she and the babe died in childbed just after I reached Paris."

"And after Otto's death you and Jack returned home without incident?" Julian asked gently, knowing full well that this was not the case but hoping she would refute the statement without his prompting.

Deb took a deep breath and stared out at the blur of fields. "I wish it had been uneventful…" She met his gaze openly and smiled ruefully. "Otto's best friend Evelyn, who is also a splendid musician, wanted to marry me but he needed the permission of his father and of his uncle the Duke of Roxton, as that old roué is head of his family. They refused him."

"Understandable. You were both too young to be contemplating marriage,"

"Too young?" Deb looked thoughtful. "No, I don't believe that was the reason at all. Plenty of children are married off by their parents at a far earlier age."

"Perhaps the Duke and Evelyn's father felt your feelings weren't entirely fixed?"

"Not *fixed*? It is obvious you have no idea how this business is conducted. Character and disposition are irrelevant, as are the opinions of the prospective bride and groom. What matters to noblemen such as the Duke of Roxton is the legal union: the transfer of money and property; the connection of one family to another; the consolidation of power and prestige. Feelings have no role to play in such contractual arrangements."

Julian stared at the toe of his polished boot, a private smile hovering about his curved mouth. "But as you and Evelyn were not *cold-bloodedly* contracted to one another, perhaps Evelyn's family were not persuaded you would make him a suitable wife?"

Deb turned her head and gaped at him. "Not suitable? A Cavendish heiress not suitable to marry the son of a Viscount?"

Julian shook his head sadly. "Ah, my dear Miss Cavendish, despite your protests to the contrary, I see that wealth and title do matter to you."

Deb turned away, mortified at being so conceited as to throw her name and fortune in his face. Taking a peek at him she soon realized that despite his grave look he was laughing at her. She

97

stared at the box where Jack sat holding the reins, Nero licking his face. Yet she saw none of it. Evelyn had offered to marry her and she had refused him. He had protested that he loved her and had not merely offered her his name out of loyalty to Otto. But Deb had rejected him because she had not loved him enough to elope with him.

As it turned out, the Duke of Roxton had discovered Evelyn's plans and had forbidden his nephew to marry her. She had been relieved, but ashamed to think the Duke and Evelyn's father had rejected her despite her being a considerable heiress. She had had to conclude her unsuitability was because she was thought volatile of character; running away to Paris and her involvement with Otto, the black sheep of her family, and his gypsy wife, was surely proof of that. Yet she believed she had done nothing wrong, indeed, had responded to her heart and in the only way she knew how. So why did she still feel ashamed every time she thought of the consequences of her flight to Paris?

"There is no need for you to involve yourself with me," she said sullenly. "Nothing came of Evelyn's offer of marriage. So there is an end to it."

He shifted to sit opposite her and possessed himself of her gloved hands, but she could not look at him. He frowned. "You allow me to kiss you and yet you say I am not to involve myself with you?"

"I wanted you to kiss me," Deb answered truthfully, gaze on her hands in his. "But I don't want you to involve yourself with me. There is a difference in the two."

"Are you in the habit of allowing gentlemen of the merest acquaintance to kiss you?"

Deb gaped at him and felt the heat burning in her cheeks.

"Just because I won't unburden myself on you, and yet permitted you to kiss me, that I am—that I have—Why! Yes!" she said, changing her tune at his spreading smile. "Dozens! Not dozens, but too many to count. And in public. So you can banish that smug smile!"

"More and more do I sympathize with dull Gerry," he said with a sad shake of his handsome head. "And Evelyn doesn't know how fortunate he is. Better he concentrate on his music than have to wife a female who is in the habit of kissing dozens of gentlemen in public. You saved him from a marriage that could only have ended in disaster."

Deb tried to pull her hands free but he would not let go.

"You know not the first thing about me or him, for that matter, to pass judgment on either of us! That you have the audacity to tell me to my face... Stop this carriage at once!" When he grinned and ignored her plea to have the carriage pull over she said, "You are a fiend and a brute! After such an appalling roasting I've no intention of telling you anything!"

"No? I can wait it out. Thomas has his orders. He will keep on driving until the horses give out if need be, or I give the order to pull up. And I wouldn't be concerned with Jack's welfare. There's a basket of foodstuffs under the box. He, at least, won't go hungry."

"You won't coerce me in this way," she stated, but did not sound particularly convincing because she was trying very hard not to laugh. "There is nothing to tell. I say and do the most shocking things to relieve a natural boredom—nothing more."

Julian folded his arms, black curls back against the velvet upholstery, and closed his eyes. "You may wake me when you feel ready for confidences."

Five minutes passed. Deb pretended to enjoy the countryside and Julian kept his word, only once opening an eye to take a peek at his hostage, quick to close it when she glanced his way. The road was beginning to climb and the horses slowed, but there was no sign of an inn or a farmhouse and Jack was happily biting into an apple.

"Why should I unburden myself on you when I am certain you must have as many secrets to tell?" Deb demanded. "I don't know the first thing about you." When this was greeted with continued silence, she let out a great breath of exasperation, shifted on the seat, and turned to view the deep woods that now lined both sides of the winding road. She could see that he was going to be stubborn so she had to offer him something if only to get him to be pleasant enough to take her home again. She was surprised when it was he who broke the long silence between them.

"Have you fallen in love, Miss Cavendish?"

At this Deb's throat constricted and her cheeks burned. Her gaze flew up to his face and then she looked away just as swiftly, wanting to refute the question, yet unable to do so because it was true. She had fallen in love, inexplicably and without good reason, with him, but she could not bring herself to say so. She felt foolish, not knowing how he felt, whether he returned her regard, and if he cared enough for her to flout convention and disregard Sir Gerald's opposition and society's censure to elope with her.

"Miss Cavendish," he said firmly, "are you in love with Robert Thesiger?"

"Robert Thesiger?" Deb was so taken aback that her color deepened at such a blunt suggestion. "Why would you think me in love with Mr. Thesiger?"

"I saw you together at the Assembly Ball."

Deb put up her chin. "I hardly think that dancing the minuet with a gentleman constitutes a love match, do you, sir?"

"Yet, his display just now on horseback... He was most insistent that you speak with him...?"

At this, Deb looked down at her gloved hands, embarrassed. "I cannot return Mr. Thesiger's regard. And he is a most persistent gentleman." She peered up at Julian through her lashes. "But you asked if I am in love with him, and the answer is no, I am not."

"I am relieved to hear you say so. I have no wish to come between a love match."

"Mr. Thesiger and I are friends. Just because I am not in love with him does not mean I do not champion his friendship. I refuse to be prejudiced by his questionable parentage."

"My dear girl, let me assure you that his motives are far more questionable than his parentage," Julian drawled and sprung down from the carriage, for it had come to stand in a narrow wooded lane.

He assisted Deb to firm ground and turned away before she could respond, to watch Jack run off up the path that led into the wood, Nero at his boot heels. A word to his driver, and he escorted Deb along the same path, a basket in one hand, and in the other, of all things to bring on a drive, a cricket bat! She soon knew why. Up ahead, through a break in the forest, was a clearing. Beyond the clearing, the river, and across the water, undulating farming land. Over the first rise, a curl of smoke drifted up into the darkening clouds.

Jack was busy collecting sticks for the stumps of a wicket he had marked out, while Nero devoted himself to ferreting out possible rabbit holes on the edge of the clearing. A blanket spread out, the basket deposited, the cricket ball found in amongst the food-stuffs, and Julian turned to Deb with a small bow.

"If you will be so kind as to do the honors with the contents of the basket I shall endeavor to entertain your nephew; part of the bargain I'm afraid."

Deb frowned as she took off her bonnet. "You're not going to play at cricket in your condition, surely? It cannot be many weeks since you were stitched up."

"It has been three weeks, five days and several hours since we first met," he said and was pleased when she blushed and looked anywhere but at him. "I am better mended than you realize and am quite capable of bowling a ball. But I won't. I shall leave that treat for Jack. I shall merely bat and let Jack bowl me out. Excuse me. You will find a bottle of excellent burgundy and two goblets in the basket."

Jack proved a tireless competitor and would not give up the game until he had bowled Julian out for a third time. Once he caught and bowled him, which sent Jack into such spasms of delight that it had Nero barking loud and long, thinking his young master in danger of losing his life. It took Deb much coaxing with a succulent slice of lamb before Nero forgot the danger and thought of his stomach. He trotted over to Deb, ears down and obeyed her command to be a good dog and eat his dinner without a fuss. For his obedience he received a pat on the flank. Julian and Jack soon followed, bat and ball let fall into the leaf litter beside the feast laid out on the blanket.

"Well done, Jack. That was a splendid catch," said Deb with a smile. "Your father would've been proud. Otto played at school," she explained to Julian, handing him a goblet of burgundy, the intervening interval of cricket serving to make her feel very much at ease again. "And before he went to the Continent, I spent Saturday afternoons at the village green watching him play at cricket with the local farmers' sons."

"Your aunt is beyond price, Jack. Plays a viola, tells me she is a crack shot with a pistol and, not only does she like the game of cricket, she understands it." Julian bit into a slice of pie, a wink at his young friend. "Will you mind sharing her?"

Jack grinned. "I've seen Aunt Deb take the corner off a playing card at ten paces. Joseph made her as mad as hellfire once and she had him hold up the King of Diamonds in the back parlor and—"

"Jack! That will do!"

"And what, Jack?" Julian asked, passing the boy a wedge of venison and mushroom pie.

Jack ate hungrily of the pie but hesitated to give Julian an answer, but he received such an encouraging look from him that he couldn't help a little family disloyalty. "The shot hit its mark all right, but it shattered the big looking glass over the fireplace. Alice was still picking up the shards two weeks later."

"Thank you very much, John George Cavendish," Deb said without heat. "You failed to add that the said looking glass had the most hideous frame imaginable. No one was sorry to see it go, except Sir Gerald."

"Only because Uncle was forever sneaking into the back parlor to peer into that glass," Jack confessed, adding for Julian's benefit, "Uncle Gerald is always fixing his wig. But no amount of fixing is going to make a difference. He still looks like an egg fitted with a cozy!"

Deb opened her mouth to upbraid her nephew for such lack of respect but instead she giggled behind her hand. "He does look like an egg, doesn't he? Oh dear! I shall never be able to view him the same way again! P-poor M-Mary."

"Well, I don't want to look like an egg," Jack confided, falling back onto the blanket and staring up into a sky gathering clouds. "I'm going to wear my own hair—always. My friend Harry says his brother *and* his papa both wear their own hair." He looked across at Deb. "Harry, well his name isn't really Harry, it's Lord Henri-Antoine, but he likes to be called Harry and he don't like it to be known he speaks French better than he does Shakespeare's English. Well, Harry says that his papa has always worn his own hair and he's ancient. Harry says his papa wore his coronet in the processional at the coronation of King George the Second. I wouldn't have believed it had any other fellow told me, but Harry never lies."

"Perhaps Harry meant to say his grandpapa?" Deb suggested.

Jack sat up on an elbow. He selected a chunk of cheese from the platter put before him. "No, Aunt Deb. But he does look like a *Grand* papa. He was dressed all in black velvet with silver lacings and his hair is white like fresh snow and he wears the largest emerald ring I've ever seen—"

"Snow-white hair and a large emerald ring," Deb repeated, a sudden vivid remembrance in her mind's eye of a dream she'd had as a child, of an ancient gentleman with bright black eyes, white hair, and on a long white finger a large square cut emerald that glinted in the firelight. He was someone very important but he was very sad. "He looked a hundred years old..." she murmured to herself.

"He came to school in the most magnificent coach and six," Jack was saying, hardly drawing breath, such was his excitement to tell his aunt about Harry's papa. "The horses were all black high-steppers and the coach was of black lacquer with gold-leaf everywhere, and there were six outriders in scarlet and silver livery! It had us fellows at the windows when we should've been at our Latin, but who could think of grammar at such a time?"

"Who indeed," Julian commented, and in a tone that did not encourage Jack to continue. He rummaged in the basket for a fruit knife to cut up an apple, slices of which he offered to Deb. "It will rain in the next hour..."

"Are you certain it was an emerald, Jack?" Deb asked quietly, unconsciously taking the apple slices Julian offered her from the knife's edge.

The boy nodded. "It was a green stone. As green as your eyes, sir. Pardon, sir. That's an emerald, isn't it, Aunt Deb?"

Deb nodded, distracted, as she turned to look into Julian's eyes. She knew they were green but she had not realized just how emerald green they truly were. They were beautiful eyes; eyes that reminded her of a sad boy in one of her dreams. She was on a swing and Otto was there with her. And then the boy was there, sobbing uncontrollably, and Otto was not. Nurse had told her it was just a bad dream brought on by the medicine she had been given, for some minor ailment she now could not remember, and to forget all about it...

"Are you sure this ancient gentleman came to collect Harry? That he wasn't just visiting the school for some other purpose?" Deb persisted.

"Why this sudden fascination with white haired old men, Miss Cavendish?" Julian asked lightly. "Some men do wear their own hair, be it white, brown or black. Or perhaps we are confusing white hair with powdered hair or a wig?"

Jack shook his head and answered before his aunt could speak. "No, sir. It was his own hair. Harry told me his papa wears his own hair. And Harry's papa came to the school because Harry had taken one of his turns."

"Turns?" Deb prodded gently, an eye on Julian who was frowning, paused in mid-slice with knife and apple.

Jack was uncomfortable talking about his friend's malady, only because he knew Harry hated to have it discussed. But he wanted to explain himself to his aunt and this gentleman who had been so kind to them. "Harry suffers with the falling sickness. He never knows when it's going to happen. Sometimes he'll get a terrible headache and then he just faints dead away. Just like that! He says he was born with it. And that's why his papa came to school: to take him home after one of his attacks. He has his own physician and his mamma—"

"Dear me, Master Jack! Are you Lord Henri's self-appointed confessor?" Julian interrupted coldly, getting up off the blanket and roughly brushing down his breeches. "What gives you the right to share such intimate details with us when they were obviously told you in the strictest confidence?"

"No, sir," Jack answered quietly, coloring up as he scrambled to his feet. "I mean, yes, sir, he did tell me in confidence. It's just that Harry is my best friend in the whole world." When Julian turned to pick up the empty burgundy bottle Jack looked to his aunt, wondering what he had said to offend the gentleman.

Deb smiled kindly at her nephew. "Why don't you take Nero for a run before we head back?" And as soon as he was out of earshot rounded on Julian full of angry embarrassment for Jack. "That was uncalled for, sir! Jack is a sensitive, caring boy. He wasn't pouring scorn on Harry's malady. Anyone with eyes could see poor Harry's affliction affects him deeply. Why you should see it differently—"

"Your nephew has no right to speak on matters he knows nothing about: nor should they concern you!"

"Is that so?" she enunciated, shaking out her silk petticoats and snatching up her bonnet. "I know not the first thing about you, who are your family, your connections, indeed what you do with your time, apart from getting yourself involved in duels with the odds stacked against you, and yet I am expected to allow you to concern yourself in my affairs? Indeed, you expect me to give you a full and open account of my history, without the same courtesy being offered me in return—"

"If you loved me…"

"Loved you?" Deb stared at him. "*Loved* you?" she repeated in a whisper, the color draining from her cheeks. "How dare you presume…"

He smiled sheepishly. "Ah. I have over-stepped the mark." He bowed. "Forgive me for such over-bearing presumption."

"God, I wish I'd never set eyes on you!" she said savagely, the straw bonnet crushed in her hand. "Life was so much the simpler before I bandaged you up. I wish you'd never come back to Bath. Damn you! Don't think I've spent my days pining. I haven't. No! I won't allow you to hold me," she said, trying to push him off. "You presume that I have fallen in love with you just because…Oh! I can't believe you had the effrontery to— to…"

He caught her to him and held her until she stopped struggling and fell against his chest. "I want you, Deborah," he murmured, lifting her chin so that he could gently kiss her mouth. "I've never wanted any female more than I want you. I want you as my wife in every sense. Do you understand me? *Do you?*"

She nodded, staring up into his handsome face with its fine nose, head of blue-black curls turning to gray at the temples, and at the deep green of his lovely eyes. He was the handsomest man she had ever set eyes on, so like the boy in her dream that it made her shiver, and she was in his arms and he wanted her. *Her.* And as his wife. She knew she loved him. She'd known that from the moment she'd set eyes on him in the Avon forest. It was love at first sight for her. Until she'd come across her injured duelist in the forest she wasn't at all sure she believed it possible to fall in love with someone within a blink of an eye. Otto and Rosa had. Rosa had told her that when she and Otto had first met each knew instantly that they wanted to be with the other and no one else for the rest of their lives. But she had always presumed her brother and his wife to be a special case. She never dreamed it would happen to her.

So if she loved him and he wanted her to be his wife, why did she hesitate at the thought of giving herself to him body and soul? It was true that she knew not the first thing about him. He looked and spoke and had the air of a gentleman of means and position, yet he had avoided telling her anything more than his name. But did his wealth and social standing really matter to her? It certainly hadn't mattered to Otto and he and Rosa had been blissfully happy. Why then did this feeling that he was withholding something fundamental to their future happiness niggle at her so? But surely, if she loved him and he loved her they could overcome any obstacles put in their path...?

She made a movement and he let her go and stepped back, awaiting her response. For want of something to do, because he felt awkward and clumsy standing in the middle of a blanket, his embraces rejected, Julian set to packing away the picnic things.

She knelt to help him, saying over the basket, "You are under no obligation to me because I saved your life in the forest."

"I am eternally grateful for your assistance but that episode has nothing to do with us being husband and wife."

Deb looked him in the face. "You want me even though I ran away from home, that I almost eloped with a musician myself, that I play a viola, *and* can handle a pistol as good as the next man?"

He smiled. "I am determined, Miss Cavendish."

She sat forward on her knees. "And if I accept? Perhaps it is I who am entering into a bad bargain?"

He gave a bark of laughter. "That depends on whether you want the man or his consequence."

At this she gave a tinkle of laughter and relaxed. "Oh, give me the man!"

He grinned self-consciously and together they folded the blanket.

Deb glanced at him. "You are determined to have me."

"Quite determined."

"And if Gerald objects?"

He took the folded blanket from her and dropped it across the basket, saying lightly, "If you marry the man and not his consequence then Gerry's opposition should hardly weigh with you, should it?"

Deborah blinked. "It doesn't."

"I've given Jack's situation some thought," he stated, changing the subject, an eye on the boy who stood at the edge of the clearing playing at fetch with Nero. "Naturally he must live with us when he is not in school. And Evelyn should tutor him, if he can be induced to return to England. Then again, Jack may prefer to spend part of the year with Har—Come along before we are soaked to the skin!" he said, grabbing at her hand as large drops of rain began to fall. "Jack! The bat and ball, if you please!"

They ran back to the carriage, Thomas with the forethought to put up the top and secure the windows. It did not stop them receiving a soaking, or Nero putting muddy paws over his young master's buckskin breeches. To Deb it seemed as if they had just settled themselves comfortably when the carriage swept through a set of iron gates and on up a gravel drive, and came to stand in front of a Queen Anne house: Martin Ellicott's residence.

Before Deb could ask the question Julian apologized. "I must confess to a slight deception. Our picnic was not half a mile from here. I had Thomas drive about the countryside in circles."

"I thought you would have discovered that, Aunt Deb!" Jack grinned, a knowing exchange with his lordship.

"Traitor," Deb said lovingly. "As for you," she said to Julian, who was peering out at the constant rain, "I'm not at all certain I should allow Jack to spend time with such a corruptive influence."

"Aunt Deb!"

"I shouldn't take your aunt's words too seriously; her actions speak volumes," Julian commented as he opened the carriage door. "The rain is easing," he added and stepped down and offered Deb his hand. "Jack, be sure and change out of those wet clothes when you get home." He handed the boy a sealed packet from his frockcoat pocket. "Give this to Joseph. He'll know what to do."

Deb stood in the rain, not knowing what to do next. A footman came dashing out of the house and took delivery of two portmanteaux from the driver. She recognized them as belonging to her. She was speechless. Julian was issuing last minute instructions to Jack and had solicited his utmost secrecy, which the boy readily gave. With a last pat for Nero, he gave the word and Thomas sprung the horses. The carriage left without her.

Deb pointed to the portmanteaux as the footman disappeared with them into the house. "Those are my bags!"

Julian looked up from studying the face of his gold pocket watch. He slipped it back into his flowered waistcoat pocket. "Yes. How convenient they were packed and awaiting me in your hallway. And we are getting wet," he said and unceremoniously pulled her toward the house. "No doubt they contain everything you'll need."

"Everything I need? For what?" she demanded, oblivious to the rain and the droop of her bonnet. "But they are packed for my trip to—"

"You can't go on your honeymoon without luggage. Now come along!"

Deb ignored the butler's bow of welcome. "*Honeymoon?*"

"You'll be pleased Brigitte was in total agreement and wished me luck."

Deb looked about her wildly. "Agreement to what?"

"We have already kept the vicar waiting twenty minutes."

"Vicar?" Deb almost screeched.

She brought herself up short. Julian held wide the drawing room door. Deep in the room there was hushed conversation and the tinkle of glasses. Somebody laughed. Deb kept her feet firmly planted in the hallway. She looked enquiringly at the doorway, then at Julian but said nothing.

He smiled in understanding. "No one who bites," he assured her. "The vicar, his good wife, her sister to stand as matron of honor, and Frew, of course. Sadly, no Martin, who always spends this time of year with my parents. I have a special license in my pocket and the vicar is willing to forgo a church service as a favor to my deep-seated need for absolute privacy. Shall we...?"

Deb shivered and pulled the damp shawl closer about her shoulders. She felt ill. "I—I—What about Gerry and Mary and your family and—"

Julian laughed. "My father had begun to despair of ever becoming a grandparent, and as I have your brother's blessing to our marriage that's all that matters really, isn't it?"

"How did you get Gerry to—

"Let's not spoil the moment by talking about your groveling brother." He smiled reassuringly and kissed her hand. "Shall we go in? The ceremony must be performed before three of the clock; that is the law. The vicar—"

"But our clothes," Deb argued, "are wet and—and—Oh! A hundred other objections I'm sure I could think of if I wasn't in a state of utter nervous collapse! You can't be serious!" When he did not answer, just stood there expectantly, fingers about the door handle, her shoulders slumped. "Must it be now?" she asked in a tiny voice.

"If it will make you feel better able to struggle through the ceremony, I am just as nervous."

Deb wrung her gloved hands. "I'm not dressed! We're wet through! My hair..."

"The sooner we set off on our honeymoon the sooner we can get on with our lives."

Slowly, Deb stripped off her soaked gloves, removed her drenched bonnet and dropped these and the wet shawl onto a chair in the hallway. She did not bother to take a step back to glance at her reflection in the looking glass. She knew her hair was untidy, that her lips needed color; her boots were muddy, and her bodice damp, as were her pale-blue silk petticoats, which had acquired a large grass stain about the knees.

Such petty details, and the vicar kept waiting...

$\mathcal{S}$even

$\mathcal{D}$eb woke to the muted sounds of dawn; of waterfowl in the tangle of tall reeds shrouded in mist at the river's edge, and beyond that the breeze rustling the tops of the beech trees in the awakening forest. It was still dark enough for the light of a full moon to shine through the open curtains and across the heavy coverlet on the four-poster bed. She lay amongst the tumble of feather-filled pillows listening sleepily to the distant noises outside her window, reveling in the warmth under the covers and feeling supremely happy. Married three days and yet she felt so comfortable and unself-conscious in her new role as wife that it was almost as if she had been married to Julian for years and years.

The marriage ceremony seemed a lifetime away. The vicar and the attendants looked as nervous as she herself had been. Julian held her hand so tightly it was as if he feared she would flee. And in their nervousness neither bride or groom looked left or right, nor did they glance at each other until their vows had been exchanged. It was only with the ink dry in the Parish Register and the couple toasted with a glass of Martin Ellicott's finest champagne that tension eased enough for there to be light conversation.

Deb had been too overwhelmed by the progress of events from picnic to wedding service to finding herself married that she had been oblivious to the finer details of that wet afternoon. She could not recall the inconsequential chatter over champagne and cake, only that there was an atmosphere of uncomfortable self-restraint. The vicar, his good wife and the attendants never once initiated conversation nor looked at their ease, and barely sipped the bubbles in their crystal glasses. Yet, when her husband spoke, they became animated and hung on his every word, answering him in monosyllables. It reminded Deb of a king surrounded by his courtiers who, acutely aware of their lowly station in life, knew they were not worthy of engaging their liege lord in proper conversation. If Julian was aware of this he did not show it. In fact, he went out of his way to put everyone at their ease, even her, for when the vicar announced it was time to leave the young couple to themselves, Deb knew she had blushed rosily. Julian had winked at her with a kind smile and quickly ushered everyone from the room to farewell them on the portico.

She wished Rosa and Otto had been there on her wedding day to share in her happiness, and Rosa had been right about the marriage bed. Deb had followed her advice, given long ago and not understood at the time. Love must be on equal terms, she had said: honesty, mutual respect, pleasure, all must be given and received in equal measure and from the first night alone together as man and wife. And so on her wedding night, in this very bed, Deb had followed Rosa's advice.

Naturally, she had been a little afraid of the unknown and apprehensive that she would be clumsy and awkward. But she was no shrinking violet. And who had worried about her maidenly virtue when she had nursed Otto? She had done everything for Otto: fed him, administered his medicines and washed and clothed him. She knew what a naked man looked like. That is a sick man; a dying man. A healthy, well-muscled athletic man with whom she was in love was an entirely different proposition.

Alone together in the bedchamber that first night, she forgot her own embarrassment at being naked as soon as she saw her husband. She had stared at Julian, fascinated by his virility, and was momentarily taken aback when he appeared shy by her open look of admiration. It made her wonder if he had ever been so candidly scrutinized in all his glory before. His shy smile made her appreciate that for all his experience, at that moment, naked and alone with her, he was feeling just as nervous as she. It made her forget about her own inexperience and realize that if she was true to herself making love for the first time with her husband would be the beginning of a wonderfully joyous union. And so she had joined him in the big four-poster bed unafraid and on equal terms.

She turned her head on the pillow, smiling at the remembrance of that first time, wanting the touch and warmth of his body, only to discover she was alone. She immediately sat up, brushing the tangle of long hair from her face, and frowned at the light coming from under the door that led into the next room. She threw an embroidered silk dressing gown over her nakedness, buttoning it up carelessly, and in bare feet silently went through to the warmth and light of the small dressing room.

Julian sat at the gilt writing desk by the window adjacent to the blazing fire in the grate of the marble fireplace. He was dressed in an elaborately embroidered silk banyan that gaped at the throat, and wore a pair of silk breeches without stockings. He held back the mop of black curls from his forehead with one hand while his quill moved quickly across a sheet of parchment, totally absorbed in his writing. When the page was filled with his elegant sloping script it was put to one side to be dried with a wash of sand and another sheet of parchment was selected to continue the correspondence.

Standing to one side of the cluttered desk was his valet, Frew, sleepy eyed yet immaculately dressed for such an early morning, his features perfectly blank as he waited patiently to offer assistance with affixing the wax seals to the parchments. A small stack of answered correspondence had been placed on a silver salver by the valet's left hand and only one letter remained unanswered.

Deb watched from the doorway, unnoticed, waiting for her husband to finish this letter before going forward. Yet he took his time and when he had come to the end of the second page his eyes wandered to the flames amongst the burning logs in the grate. One of their number suddenly popped, cracked, and fell amongst the ash, sending a snow of gray-white flakes up into the chimney. Onto this fallen burning log Julian tossed the remaining pages of an opened letter and watched it curl in on itself, the look on his face so intense that in the flickering light he appeared a stranger. It occurred to her then, as it had on numerous occasions over the previous couple of weeks, that she had learnt very little about her husband since the day she had stumbled upon him bleeding from a sword wound in the Avon forest.

The thought stayed with her as Julian turned away from the fireplace and ordered Frew to fetch a pot of coffee and some rolls to sustain him while he wrote a reply to this last letter, a letter that was to be sent at once by separate dispatch to his Grace in Paris. When the valet saw Deb and hesitated, causing his master to coldly enquire without looking up why he stood as a statue in the middle of the carpet, she announced herself. It brought Julian's head round with a snap. Such was his scowl of preoccupation that Deb faltered in surprise to receive such a cold reception. Yet in the next moment he was out of his chair with a warm smile, pulling the banyan tighter about his shoulders and dismissing the valet with a sharp word that brought the servant to a sense of his social lapse.

Deb glanced at the cluttered surface of the writing desk with its scatter of parchments, silver Standish holding quills and ink, melted sealing wax and a heavy gold seal on a length of gold chain, all bathed in the glow from the guttering candles of a six stemmed candelabra.

"You've been awake for some time," she commented with a shy smile and took the hand he held out to her.

"Letters that can't wait," he answered as he softly kissed the palm of her right hand. "I have one more to write... to Martin."

"Who is staying with your parents?" she asked in a tone she hoped sounded disinterested.

"Yes."

"You and he are close," she stated, and moved to the fireplace to spread cold hands to its warmth. "Closer than what is usual for godparent and godchild. I've never met my godparents. They used to send a gift on my birthday, until I fled to Paris to be with Otto. I guess I fell from favor."

Julian followed her, scooping up his gold seal and slipping it into a pocket of his banyan before placing himself between Deb and the writing desk. "Frew is brewing Turkish coffee—"

"Turkish coffee?"

"Yes. I acquired a taste for the filthy stuff when Martin and I lived in Constantinople."

"Constantinople? How fascinating," she said, wondering what had taken him to such an exotic city. The Grand Tour perhaps? "Did you and Martin live there for awhile?"

"We were there three years," he answered, remaining fixed in front of the desk. "Long enough to enjoy the wondrous architecture of the Infidel, the unique smells and explore the burying fields that are surprisingly far larger than the city itself. You're shivering, my dear. A hot chocolate would warm you."

Deb shook her head, fingers playing with a long strand of autumn-colored hair, determined to pursue a line of thought he continually avoided. "Strange, you and M'sieur Ellicott lived in such a far away city. I dare say you shared many an interesting adventure, and yet in all my visits here he never once mentioned his godson."

He smiled and shrugged self-consciously. "Martin is a very discreet and loyal creature. Accompanying a wayward youth on the Grand Tour was not his idea of restful retirement, yet he never complained. And I dare say the antics of his godson was not what Martin would've thought an appropriate topic for French conversation with a young lady." He lifted an eyebrow. "You have a measure of my godfather's upright character. You never once mentioned your penchant for playing a viola in the forest."

"Ah! But I was at pains to ensure he didn't know for fear he would ask me to play, which would've necessitated being impolite and refusing him," she answered in a rallying tone. "I am competent and I enjoy playing for my own pleasure, but I have a morbid fear of public performance."

Julian grinned. "That makes two of us. I told you once how I hate being the center of attention. I too dislike being on display. You would never know it to see me in society." He took her in his arms and kissed the top of her head. "Now that, my darling wife," he whispered at her ear, "is to be kept between you and I and no other."

"Do you go into society very often?" she persisted, snuggling into his warm embrace by the fireside.

"When required—"

"—by your family?" she asked too quickly and wished she had held her tongue for he let her go and moved to the sofa.

At that awkward moment Frew came through the servant door carrying a tray holding the coffee things. The valet placed this on the table and quietly departed.

Deb watched Julian arrange the coffee things, items that were richly patterned and lacquered and Oriental in design; a souvenir from his stay in Constantinople he told her. The pear-shaped coffee pot of fine porcelain patterned with gold rested on an elaborate silver stand that had at its base a candle warmer to keep the pot's contents at drinking temperature. There were two fine porcelain dishes one of which Julian poured out into, a liquid so thick and black it was the consistency of treacle. He stirred a precise amount of sugar into the coffee with a long handled silver spoon and this he set aside on a lacquered spoon rest before picking up the dish and sipping the Turkish brew to test for the correct proportion of bitterness to sweetness.

"The wine of Islam," he commented, savoring the taste. He held out the dish. "Would you like to try it?"

Deb did not immediately answer. She had been watching him intently, how his long fingers curled about the curved handle of the coffee pot, the way he sprinkled sugar into the little dish and stirred it gently before bringing it up to his lovely mouth to take the smallest of sips. Such fastidious movements were in marked contrast to his want of dress and the black curls that fell unbrushed about his shoulders. She found herself wondering for the hundredth time how she had come to be married to such a man; a man who reminded her of a boy she had once dreamed about. It was a foolish and absurd thought and she wished it would leave her alone, and yet it continued to haunt her.

When he repeated his offer she took the dish, feeling the heat in her face for being distracted by absurd thoughts. Gingerly, she sipped at the dark liquid and such was the bitterness on her tongue that she screwed up her mouth and quickly thrust the dish back at him. He laughed at her expression of disgust and drank up, chiding her under the chin for her bravery. She in turn playfully grabbed at his hand. Then suddenly they both felt awkward in each other's company and fell silent.

Deb returned to the fireplace to warm her hands while over the rim of the porcelain dish Julian watched her. His green-eyed gaze travelled from her bare toes up to the swell of her luscious breasts under the silk dressing gown, and he knew that if he did not immediately return to the writing desk to complete his correspondence he would give in to the intense ache in his loins and make love to her there and then.

Since deciding to claim his wife he had presumed that the consummation of their marriage would bring him a sense of closure and release: The marriage in name only would finally be legally binding and, God willing, his wife would soon be pregnant and provide the Duke with a grandson; tangible evidence of the continuance of his line. As soon as she was pregnant he had intended to return to Paris, to his life there, and to the unfinished business of dealing with an overly ambitious Farmer-General who had plotted to entrap him into marriage with his very beautiful but scheming daughter.

What he had not counted on was returning to England to discover that the girl to whom he was married had blossomed into a beautiful desirable woman. There was no denying he was instantly attracted to her. He'd wanted her from the moment she'd straddled his lap in the forest. And so he had eagerly anticipated the consummation of his marriage. But their first night together as man and wife, when they rode to Heaven and back as one on three separate occasions, had turned out very differently from what he had imagined. Far from providing closure and release, he found himself intoxicated; the ache of wanting her growing more acute rather than abating. He felt as an alcoholic must who tastes wine for the first time and is instantly addicted.

She surprised and delighted him with her candid enjoyment of his arousal, and the way in which her warm fragrant body responded to his lovemaking without reserve. No woman had ever been so honest with him before. The efforts of the most skilled courtesan now seemed tawdry by comparison to his inexperienced wife's honesty. In making love with Deb he discovered that honesty mattered a great deal, and that her physical honesty was the most potent aphrodisiac of all.

He forced himself to look away from her and returned to the writing desk. Putting aside the empty coffee dish, he needlessly shuffled through a few pages of correspondence. "This letter cannot wait," he apologized. "It must reach its destination with all speed or two Parisian lawyers will be on our doorstep."

Deb took a step toward him. "Parisian lawyers, *here?*"

"Not if my letter reaches them first," he said, keeping his gaze on the page. "But I won't be able to put them off indefinitely. I have unfinished business in Paris."

Deb would have crossed to him but he looked up then, sensing her nearness, and steered her away from the desk. She frowned, wondering what he did not wish her to see; yet mention of Paris was uppermost in her mind. "Paris? You are going to Paris?"

"Yes. To clear up a tiresome legal matter that need not concern you."

"To do with your duel in the forest?" When he nodded she said, "I will come with you."

"No. I won't have you subjected to such an absurd ordeal."

She put a hand on his broad chest and stared up into his frowning countenance. "Ordeal? Will Paris be an ordeal for you, Julian?"

He smiled reassuringly but could not bring himself to reply with a lie. The warmth radiating from her, the pleasing scent in her hair, the touch of her hand on his stubbled cheek, all combined to melt what little resolve he had secured by going to the desk. He brushed aside the tumble of heavy, dark red curls that fell forward over her shoulder to caress the round fullness of her breast. "Paris is the last place I wish to go," he murmured, delighting in the delicious sensation of his thumb lightly rubbing her nipple through the silk. "I want you to myself a little longer... Three days is not enough time..." He bent and kissed her gently. "Go back to bed. I'll be there shortly. Today we set off on a proper bridal trip."

Her arms went up about his neck as she sought another kiss. "Where are you taking me?"

He kissed her again, this time passionately, causing instant arousal; one hand cupping her breast, the other catching up the folds of the dressing gown to feel the roundness of her bare bottom beneath. "Where they won't find us."

"Will you be writing many letters whilst we are on our bridal trip?" she teased as she slid the banyan off his wide shoulders and down his muscular arms.

He kissed the base of her throat. "This letter is the last for a month, that I promise you."

She smiled under her lashes, enjoying the feel of his swollen hardness straining against the silk of his breeches as he rubbed against her belly, knowing that the writing of this last letter would be put off until they had made love. "Are letters to be my solace while you're in Paris without me?"

"Every night separated from you will be wretchedly cold and lonely."

"I'm glad to hear it, for I'm not above protecting what is now mine alone. Must I remind my husband that I am a deadly shot?"

He chuckled as he carried her effortlessly through to the bedchamber and fell with her amongst the tumble of bedclothes. "You deserve a good thrashing for such uncharitable thoughts, madam wife!"

She stared up through the gray morning light, into his lovely emerald green eyes and wondered not for the first time if it was all a wonderful dream from which she would awaken at any moment to find Nurse smiling down at her, holding a little silver tray with a porcelain mug of sweetened hot chocolate upon it. But this wasn't a dream. This man was her husband and he was muscle and bone and she was his wife and they now shared a bed. Those facts were indisputable.

"Make love to me, Julian," she whispered, seeking his mouth, fingers at the buttons of his breeches.

He shuddered at her touch and groaned for release from the confines of tight silk, reveling in her teasing caress as she undid the silver buttons of his breeches with a deliberate slowness. His whole body tensed with pure pleasure as he stooped to kiss her breasts. That her need of him was no less strong than his desire for her, that she gave herself to him honestly and without reserve, her enjoyment equal to his own, aroused in him a passion beyond anything he had ever experienced.

"Sweet Jesus, Deb," he uttered thickly as his kisses travelled from the round firmness of her breasts, over the flat plane of her belly and down to the pleasurable, ready wetness between her warm luscious thighs, "you've utterly ruined me."

⁓◦—◦⁓

Frew had been polishing the same pairs of shoes for a fortnight. He had little else to occupy his time. Once a day he rode into

Bath, to kick his heels at one of the taverns, to take a stroll to the Pump room to see if there were any new faces in town, and then he visited the Barr Hotel in Trim Street to collect his master's re-directed mail. After a bite of lunch and another stroll he then returned to Martin Ellicott's Queen Anne House. If he had collected any letters and cards of invitation these he placed with the rest accumulating in a pile on the sideboard in the book room. That was the extent of his day.

He had returned to Bath from the Lakes District with the news the Marquis of Alston and his bride were only a day's ride behind him. That had been fourteen days ago. Frew had expected the old gentleman to question him about his seven-week stay at the Elizabethan manor house by the shores of Lake Windermere. Martin Ellicott did not once enquire about his godson's honeymoon, thus denying Frew the opportunity to confide in him the goings on during his stay. One episode in particular still made him grin from ear to ear...

The Marquis and his bride had taken a basket nuncheon down to the lake, where they spent the afternoon swimming and fishing. They came back up to the house, dripping wet and in such animated conversation about the merits of the pistol over the sword as a preferred dueling weapon that the housekeeper and Frew were left to stare at one another open-mouthed as they were passed on the stair. Water had pooled at the doorway and the carpet made wet on the stair. And as if this wasn't enough to make Frew's jaw swing, Deb was wearing a shirt that belonged to his master. This blatant disrespect for his master's wardrobe scandalized the valet more than anything and he was in such a state of shock to think she had dared to don male attire that the subsequent noises above his head, of unrestrained laughter, of running about and of the slamming of doors went entirely unheard. The loud, almost deafening report of a pistol did not.

Frew had burst into the paneled bedchamber unannounced. What he saw horrified him. He thought he would faint. He wanted to lean up against something to steady his legs but his feet would not move. His hands were shaking so much that he drove them deep into his coat pockets, and clenched hard his fists. His eyes would not blink.

The Marchioness was standing in the middle of the room, side-on to the window, her bare feet slightly apart, the weight of her long wet curls clinging to the wet shirt, making the whole transparent. Her right arm was outstretched, pointing toward the open doorway that led into the dressing room and beyond that to the closet. In her hand was a smoking pistol. Frew recognized the pistol by its silver handle inlaid with pearl. It belonged to his master.

"Damn!" she said with a frown. "I didn't do that at all well," and dropped her pistol arm.

She's found him out! Had he finally told her the truth? Or had one of the servants... But no, none of the household servants knew the Marquis's true identity, that's why they'd come north. To them, as to his bride, he was simply Julian Hesham Esq. But she must have found out somehow and she'd taken her revenge for being duped. And now, she's shot him! screamed in Frew's brain. But he could not work his mouth to say it out loud.

Then the mundane intruded into his disordered thoughts and he felt uncannily calm. By the large carved mantle of the fireplace a pile of discarded clothes lay sodden on the hearth; they would need laundering. He glanced quickly about the room, carefully avoiding the tumble of bed linen occupying the massive four-poster bed. Nothing was amiss with the heavy Elizabethan furniture. No signs of a scuffle. In the next breath he was suffering from an acute attack of embarrassment, far worse than any feelings of faintness or panic.

The Marquis bounded barefoot into the bedchamber from the dressing room, clad only in his breeches, damp hair pulled off his face and left to fall about his bare shoulders. Laughingly, he grabbed his wife's hand and dragged her after him, through the dressing room into the closet. Without realizing it, Frew followed them.

"Not at all well?" the Marquis declared. "You're much too harsh on yourself, darling! I told you it would pull to the right and you compensated for that splendidly. Look! Not a mark on the canvas and only the slightest of shaves to the frame. No one would be the wiser save for the dent in the paneling."

There was a small hole in the closet wall; it had split the heavy walnut paneling. The gilt wood picture frame had fared less well, the bullet shearing off a long sliver of wood before impacting the wall. The painting of the Elizabethan manor house's topiary garden was unharmed. The damage to the wall was forgotten in Frew's admiration for the Marchioness's accuracy of eye with a pistol. She'd be deadly in a duel.

But Deb continued to frown. "I meant to miss the canvas and I certainly didn't intend to hit the frame." Then she smiled saucily, saying from under her lashes as she inspected the pistol, "Perhaps if I was to have a second try...?"

"No you don't, vixen!" The Marquis grinned and took the pistol from her. "A dent in the paneling can be patched up. A second shot would require an explanation to the Dunnes I don't care to give." He then swept his wife off to the bed.

Frew stood in the doorway until it was almost too late for him to depart with his self-respect in tact. Finally, he closed the door behind him, and slowly went downstairs shaking his head, a spreading smirk still in evidence when the cook handed him a mug of ale.

And now he was back in Bath, sent on ahead with the luggage to ready the Queen Anne House for the couple's arrival. The valet waited and so did the pile of correspondence, one letter in particular. It was from the Duke and had come by liveried courier three days earlier. Martin Ellicott had sent a response without knowing the letter's contents. Also awaiting the Marquis were two lawyers who had landed on the doorstep and also sent by the Duke.

Frew met them as he crossed from the stables, having just returned from Bath with the day's mail. He presumed them to be travelers who had lost their way on the Bath road, but the taller and elder of the two men dismounted and divested himself of his traveling cloak, revealing a richly embroidered frockcoat with a froth of fine white lace at his throat. He dumped the traveling cloak on Frew and stripped off his riding gloves to show hands that had never done a day's manual labor and which were covered in rings studded with precious stones. He then turned to his companion and remarked in French about the quaintness of the English architecture. His companion, who had the look of a lawyer's flunkey with his ill-fitting brown bagwig and nondescript suit of worsted wool, was preoccupied with the unpacking of the saddlebags. He replied that the English fascination for quaintness was exceeded only by their generous helpings of bland food. He prayed a good drop of wine was to be had within doors, unlike their lodgings in Marlborough, where the food had been unpalatable and the wine insipid, to which the elder man snorted his pessimism.

"M'sieur Muraire, he is here to see M. le Marquis de Alston," the soberly dressed Frenchman announced, juggling an armful of documentation tied up with ribbon. "You will tell him at once: We have arrived."

Frew pushed the heavy cloaks onto Fibber, who had appeared at the front door, and acknowledged the two Frenchmen with a curt bow. He began to explain that his lordship was not in residence but was cut off by the lawyer, who said with a haughty sniff,

"Me he will see!" and accompanied this command with a wave of his heavily scented, lace bordered handkerchief. "It is most necessary." After which pronouncement the two men minced past the butler to be greeted by Martin Ellicott who spoke to them in their own tongue and showed them into the book room, where they remained for the entire day, filling every space with mountains of documents, paper, quills and ink, and demanding that their nuncheon be brought to them on trays. They could not possibly interrupt their work by taking food in the dining room. Martin Ellicott took this all in his stride as he did everything else, and Frew could only marvel at the old man's calm, putting it down to his absolute and unquestioning loyalty to the Duke of Roxton.

Martin Ellicott's butler was clearing away the remnants of dinner from the parlor late one night when he heard carriage wheels on the crushed stone drive. Such was his haste to be the first in the tiled entrance vestibule that he collided with his master who had come downstairs in his embroidered night robe and matching night cap with tassel, taper in hand.

The old man gave the taper to his butler and unbolted the front door, sending Fibber out into the night air to greet a dusty and mud-spattered coach, the horses worn and thirsty from the speed of travel rather than the extent of their journey. The carriage door was thrown open and out jumped the Marquis of Alston dressed in a many caped greatcoat and boots. He put up a gloved hand to Martin in greeting, who waited under the lighted portico, then turned to assist his wife to firm ground.

Martin bowed to both of them, eyes keen and bright, yet features schooled to show polite interest. "I am very pleased to finally have you both here safe and well, if a little overdue...?"

"Are we overdue?" Julian asked rhetorically, gripping the old man's hand and smiling broadly. "I hope Frew hasn't been under your feet this past fortnight?" he asked, a glance at his sleepy-eyed valet who had just stumbled out into the night air half-dressed to see what all the commotion was about.

"Not at all," came the bland reply as the old man bowed over Deb's outstretched hand. "Welcome back to Moranhall, my dear. You must be tired and hungry after your journey."

Deborah smiled shyly, feeling a little awkward at this first meeting with the old man since her marriage to his godson, but she rallied herself enough to say, "Thank you, sir. Tired, yes, but not the least hungry. I should be grateful for a warm bath; we have been on the road all day."

"Fussy appetite," Julian said cheerfully.

"Fussy? *Fussy!*" Deb said with a gasp and laughed. "Just because I didn't feel like sitting down to a banquet when we stopped for dinner after bumping about for miles and miles on end."

Julian grinned. "You did look quite green when the beef was put before me."

Deb giggled and gripped Julian's arm affectionately. "Did I? How awful for you."

The Marquis linked arms with his wife and godfather and walked them into the house. "After the green episode," he explained to Martin, "we travelled the rest of the day at a more sedate pace."

"So that's why we are here in the moonlight," Deb added, "for which I apologize." She glanced at the bowing valet, who had stepped out of the way to allow the three persons to enter the house, "Poor Frew. Has he been twiddling his thumbs in our absence? We sent him on ahead with most of the luggage, expecting to be only a day or two behind him." She looked up at her husband with a shy smile, "But the day stretched into a fortnight..."

"He has been kept busy, my la—"

"Come to think on it, I am quite ravenous," Julian interrupted, cutting the old man off as he thrust his traveling cloak and gloves on his sleepy valet. "You must eat something," he said in an under voice to Deb, but with a quick look at Martin who had turned to give Fibber directions for the disposal of the bags and trunks and to see that a bath was drawn for the Marchioness. "You've not eaten all day," he added, looking down at her with concern.

"I did. A piece of bread at the Duckpond Inn," she whispered back with a smile. She stripped off her gloves and put a hand to her disheveled hair. "I really do want a bath, so you go ahead and I shall say good night to M'sieur Ellicott."

He kissed her hand and left her to Martin, while Fibber followed him to the dining room, Martin taking the Marchioness up to the suite of rooms she had occupied the first night of her marriage, and with apologies for not being able to provide her with a female attendant; but as Deb pointed out, she had not had the benefit of her maid for over two months now, save for a girl from the local village coming each day to help her with her hair and her dress, that she was quite used to doing most things for herself.

When Martin entered the dining room he found his godson staring out of the window into the shadows of a moonlit night, a deep scowl of preoccupation on his handsome face and the food on the table of no interest. Fibber came and went with covered dishes and wine glasses and a bottle of burgundy, and still Julian remained at the window, oblivious to the activity at his back and the fact his godfather stood watching him intently.

Martin closed over the door. "You haven't told her, have you, Julian?"

The Marquis took a few moments to answer him. He did not turn around. "No."

"Do you think she has any idea?" When his godson merely shrugged the old man sat down with a sigh and poured wine into two crystal glasses. "My boy, was there not a single moment in the time you were away to confide the truth of your consequence?"

"Have you been to the estate in Cumbria?" Julian asked the windowpane, as if Martin had not spoken. "The house is an Elizabethan monolith that needs modernizing; but the Dunnes, they're the present tenants, have made a reasonable job of maintaining the rooms and grounds. In fact, the topiary garden is coming along splendidly, given it was planted by James the Second's gardener. I've given the Dunne's permission to restore the south wing. And I want a jetty built. Harry and Jack will enjoy the fishing."

"Prolonging the revelation has only made it that much more difficult for you. Especially," Martin added with a kind smile, "when your wife is so very much in love with you."

At that, Julian turned and stared at the old man, face white and throat tinder dry. He felt ill. "Christ, Martin, I didn't need you to tell me that!" and returned to the night sky, dropping his forehead on the silken arm that rested against the window frame. "It wasn't supposed to turn out this way. I never anticipated I would— she would... I imagined how it would be hundreds of times, but it—*she* is unlike any female—Oh, God..." He swallowed hard and said impatiently, "It's impossible for me to explain!"

Martin came over to stand beside him, a frown between his white brows. "The time away did not go at all—well?" he asked gently, handing over a wine glass.

To Martin Ellicott's amazement Julian gave a ghost of a laugh. "Are you enquiring if I enjoyed the shooting, the fishing and the wilds of the Cumbrian landscape, or if I was able to perform my conjugal duty with mutual and satisfactory regularity? To which I must answer yes to both. If she's not with child by now, the Duke had best look to Harry to supply an heir!" The startled expression of embarrassment on his godfather's face that accompanied this blunt speech made him immediately recant. "*Excusez-moi, mon parrain.* That was uncalled for," he murmured in French. "You, more than any other, understand my morbid morality. Why I forced myself to-to—*wait*. Why I am so eager that she now give me a son and soon."

"Yes, *mon filleul,*" the old man muttered, face still flushed with heat from his godson's frank confession.

The Marquis nodded self-consciously and for want of something to cover an awkward embarrassment at voicing what his godfather had always privately known about him, he pretended to notice for the first time the neat stack of correspondence on the sideboard and asked, "Any letters needing my immediate attention?" and picked up the top packet and broke the seal. "When did this arrive from his Grace?"

"Three days ago."

Julian scanned the elegantly sloping handwriting then folded the page and laid it aside to flick through several other letters. "I've been summoned to Paris," he said conversationally and held up a letter drenched in scent and sniffed at it tentatively before tossing it aside with a frown.

"The Duke is not—pleased—you chose to ignore his earlier summons," Martin told him. "You were to be in Paris six weeks ago."

"Put bluntly, he's as mad as hell fire with me," said Julian, continuing a casual search through the cards and letters, picking up an invitation here, a letter there, aware his godfather watched him with a critical eye.

"Two Parisian lawyers, sent by his Grace, arrived this morning," Martin stated. "They spent the day in the book room consulting their papers and tomorrow morning will brief you on matters in Paris. I should warn you that the Lieutenant of Police for Paris has issued a warrant for your arrest. M'sieur Lefebvre has brought a charge of breach of promise against you on behalf of his daughter."

When Julian shrugged and looked unconcerned, it put up the old man's hackles. It angered him that his godson could be so nonchalant about so serious a charge. He expected the Marquis to at least be concerned how M'sieur Lefebvre's publicly declared accusation was affecting his parents, particularly his mother. The Duchess might show the world a beautiful face of disinterest that her eldest son was being vilified and lampooned by French news-sheets as the embodiment of the worst sort of English nobleman, but in private she looked so worried about the affect this charge was having on the ageing Duke's deteriorating health that it broke Martin's heart. It made the old man forget decades of trained restraint and say curtly,

"Will you alert the Marchioness as to why two French lawyers have invaded the book room, or shall I?"

"My wife is not your concern," came the flat reply from behind the pages of a closely scripted letter.

"I beg to remind his lordship of the considerable part I played in watching over your wife these past few years," Martin Ellicott replied in a steady voice. "My letters to the Duke concerning her welfare have placed me in a most awkward position. My loyalty is and always will be to the House of Roxton but I cannot but feel a responsibility for her well-being and—and *happiness*."

Julian tossed the letter aside and met the old man's gaze with an unblinking stare. "That you were Father's most trusted and devoted servant for over thirty years gives you a certain latitude, but it does not give you leave to lecture the son on his duty as a husband. I repeat: My wife is not your concern."

The two men stared at one another; the old man was the first to look away. He inclined his gray head with extreme politeness.

"Duty to one's name and rank is indeed a heavy burden, Julian, but it should never be endured for its own sake; or to the arrogant exclusion of everything and everybody else. The Duke your father learnt this lesson when he fell in love with your mother. Good night, M'sieur." He bowed and left the room, and as he closed over the door he heard Julian swear loud and long in vernacular French, fist coming down hard upon the table, rattling the china and the silver domed dishes and toppling the wine glasses.

Early next morning, Fibber directed Deb to the terrace where Martin sat with his morning coffee perusing a London newssheet. When he saw Deb hovering by the table in shy expectation of being noticed he quickly folded the paper and stood up. He thought she looked far lovelier than his remembrances of her from her weekly visits to his house. She was dressed very simply in a day gown of yellow cream silk and wore matching mules. A single ribbon pulled the weight of her deep red curls across the back of her slender white neck and over one shoulder. But it was not only her choice of gown that complimented her natural beauty; there was a radiance about her person, of good health and happiness that served to further depress the old man. He noted her one piece of jewelry, a long single strand of exquisite milky pearls. He knew them well. They were the Alston pearls: Passed down through the generations and presented by the heir to the Roxton dukedom to his bride on their wedding day.

"Did you sleep well, my child?" Martin asked, managing a bright smile. He took the hand she held out to him, offering her the seat opposite with the warmth of the sun on her back, and sent Fibber away to fetch her breakfast.

"Very well. So well in fact that I am much more the thing this morning," she said with a smile. "I may even be able to eat something."

"Good. I am glad to hear it. There are fresh fruits of the season and newly baked croissants."

"Do you know, I don't recall, in all the times I rode out here for French conversation, that we ever spoke in English," she said with a laugh. "And here we are! Not one word of the French tongue! You have no accent at all. I had assumed you to be French all along."

"My mother was a Frenchwoman. And in my other life, before I retired here to Bath, my master and I conversed mostly in French. His mother too was French, as is his wife. But no," said Martin with a warm smile, "my English is not accented, although the same could not be said of Julian's mother who has not spoken two words of English in my presence these twenty six years."

Deb took the mug of chocolate offered her. "Julian's mother is a Frenchwoman?"

Martin cursed himself for not guarding his tongue better. "Yes."

"Will she approve of me, do you think?"

The old man saw the apprehension in her brown eyes and smiled kindly. "Very much, child."

Deborah was not so certain, yet there was a twinkle in her eye. "Perhaps upon first introduction I should not mention that I play a viola or that I am a better marksman than I am an embroiderer?"

"Not at all, my dear. I think it is you who will be pleasantly surprised by her—Julian's mother. She is, to say the least, a most fascinating lady."

"And his father?"

Martin put down his coffee dish. "Ah. Now Monseigneur, he is an acquired taste."

"M'sieur Ellicott," Deb said with a heightened color, "you may find this strange and almost unbelievable, but I have been married to your godson for almost ten weeks now and still I know so little about his family. Oh, he has spoken of them in a general sense but I know no specifics and while we were in Cumbria I did not feel the necessity to question him; indeed my happiness made me not want to ask for fear of discovering some awful impediment to our marriage. It was as if by the very act of asking I would somehow shatter my hopes for the future." She gave a tinkle of laughter. "Oh dear, you are looking at me as if I am the silly goose I feel I am!" She took a croissant from the plate Fibber placed in the middle of the table and gently teased apart the layers of flaky pastry, yet the thought of eating it made her inexplicably nauseous. She had suffered the same unpleasant sensation at the Duckpond Inn, and before that in the last days of her stay in Cumbria. She pushed the plate a little away from her. "Forgive me if I have made you uncomfortable by my confidences. I am being one of those missish females I so despise and I can't account for it."

The old man lightly touched her hand but could not bring himself to look into her eyes. "My dear, if at anytime you feel you need—support... What I am trying to say is," he stumbled on, "that we have known each other for a number of years now, and I have come to regard you as one would a granddaughter. You must know that I care for you and that your happiness is important to me. What I am trying to say is that I—I am here if ever you should need me."

Deb stared at his thin white hand and then at his clear blue eyes and frowned. Her heart thudded against her chest. "Thank you. Your support means a great deal to me, M'sieur," she said gratefully, and then voiced in a whisper her inner most dread, "Am I truly married to Julian?"

The old man's smile was reassuring. "Very much so. And before you ask it, yes, Julian truly is my godson; an honor bestowed upon me by his parents. Those two facts are not in dispute." He squeezed her hand before sitting back in his chair. "And as you are married to my godson I would like you to call me Martin."

"I should like that very much. Thank you." She nervously toyed with the curls that fell into her lap. "It would be naive of me to think Julian hadn't discussed me with you, so perhaps you offer your support because you are worried lest his parents object to his choice of bride. After all, I did defy my brother to live in Paris and did not come home again until forced to by him. Well bred young ladies do not behave that way." Her face flooded with color. "Nor do they elope."

"My dear girl, Julian's parents cannot but love you as I have come to love you. I do indeed know a little about that episode in Paris, and it does you credit that you felt compelled to defy Sir Gerald to be at the bedside of your very ill brother. You, a young girl, nursed him and took care of his wife and young son when other family members, more obligated than you, failed him. You are to be commended not condemned, and I am sure this must surely be the view of Julian's family."

Martin refilled his coffee dish wondering how best to explain his inner most and most pressing concern without being disloyal to his godson.

"His father can be overwhelming. Indeed, Julian was over-whelmed by him when a youth, so much so that he found it almost impossible to live under the long shadow cast by his father's consequence. I would not be exaggerating if I told you my godson's boyhood was stormy and somewhat notorious." He glanced up at Deb. "In the coming months you will, I have no doubt, hear many conflicting reports. Some may be true, others are the fabrication of those who seek to damage Julian in retribution for what they believe are past wrongs. I make no excuses for his behavior, nor do I judge him. All I ask is that you remember that he is shaped by what he is destined to become. I have every faith in you being able to come to terms with these unalterable facts. If you cannot..." He stopped himself and forced a smile and changed the topic completely before Deb could utter a word. "I have not been to Crewehall, but I am told its situation on the foreshores of Lake Windermere is something to behold..."

Deb was still digesting his advice that his inane question about her honeymoon destination did not immediately register. She wanted to probe the old man further about Julian's background but they were distracted by a horse and rider, galloping across the lawns between the terrace and the river and heading for the stables. It was her husband.

The Marquis reappeared on the terrace, in a lather of perspiration and dust. His thick black curls were damp, as were his white shirt and buff breeches. He looked as if he had ridden himself and his horse to breaking point, and as if he hadn't slept at all the night before. Deborah and the old man slowly rose to their feet. They waited for him to speak. He wiped the hair out of his tired eyes and focused on the broken but uneaten croissant on Deb's plate.

"You need to eat, and more than that," he stated and turned to Martin, saying in French, "I've put a stack of correspondence on the table in the hall. Would you see it is taken into Bath today?"

"Certainly," Martin answered in kind and without a blink.

"Has M'sieur Muraire risen?"

"Yes, M'sieur."

"I won't keep him waiting. I need only bathe and change."

"I shall have Fibber inform M'sieur Muraire that you will see him in—say—an hour's time?" the old man asked politely as if nothing was amiss.

Deborah glanced from Martin to Julian, unable to fathom the formality in the tone of their French tongue nor the fact that both men were at pains to avoid stating the obvious. It was too much for her.

"Good God, Julian, you're exhausted!" she blurted out in English. "You've been up all night. You need sleep."

The Marquis bowed to her but did not make eye contact. "Thank you for your concern, my dear," he answered. "Now you both must excuse me," and he went into the house, Deb watching him go, biting her bottom lip, and she hadn't done that in months.

*E*ight

"*D*oes Monseigneur understand that if we are unable to persuade Mlle Lefebvre to change her outrageous claim then it will
be necessary for him to be interrogated by M'sieur Sartine, the
Lieutenant of Police for Paris?" M'sieur Muraire, the celebrated
French lawyer, explained patiently. "I tell you, her father he is
determined to have you up before a judge. If we cannot convince
Sartine that the girl she is a liar then our efforts they are wasted. I
am sorry for it, Monseigneur, but Sartine he will have no choice
but to charge you with breach of promise."

"That is very bad for you, Monseigneur, very bad indeed,"
Auguste Pothier, the lawyer's flunkey, breathed with something
akin to relish.

"Pothier! You great fool! Be quiet!" snapped the lawyer and
glared so hard at the flunkey that Pothier bowed deeply to the
straight wide back of their noble client and retreated behind a sheaf
of dog-eared pages, muttering to himself about the correctness
of his pronouncement.

M'sieur Muraire cleared his throat loudly. "I apologize if
Pothier's great stupidity alarmed you, Monseigneur."

"Lefebvre's threat hardly strikes dread in my heart," drawled
the Marquis, refilling his glass with claret. "Once I state my case
to Sartine this preposterous charge will be dropped."

M'sieur Muraire eyed his client warily. "There is a way perhaps
that might be considered worth pursuing with the girl's father.
M'sieur Lefebvre he is a very proud and very rich man. This

breach of promise nonsense it can be overcome if Monseigneur was to—to—" The lawyer fortified his nerves with a luxuriant sniff of his scented handkerchief. Pothier stared at his master with breath held. "If Monseigneur was to agree to *marry* Mlle Lefebvre."

The proposition hung in a heavy silence with both Frenchmen staring at one another with breath held.

"Marry? Marry a *putain?*" Julian growled in angry incredulity. "Have you taken leave of your senses? That is precisely why that whore has accused me of seducing her, you imbecile! Christ, I'd rather take my chances with a hanging judge!"

"Of course! Of course!" muttered Muraire. "An imbecile! Pothier you are an imbecile for suggesting such a thing!" he admonished the flunkey with a vigorous wave of his handkerchief. "Why do I listen to you? It is preposterous to suggest Monseigneur he would ever contemplate marriage with a bourgeoisie whore! That is her object is it not? Did I not tell you so? What we must do is get to the girl to interrogate her," he continued in a level voice, taking a tottering turn about the book room in his steepled shoes. "But her home it is an impenetrable fortress! Her father he lets no one in and no one out without his express command. The place it is crawling with thugs who pretend to be servants."

"With all due respect to Monseigneur, the girl she has given an intimate description of his—er—*equipage* to the Lieutenant of Police," Auguste Pothier said with a nervous snort, addressing himself exclusively to his esteemed colleague, not daring to look in direction of the nobleman. "I realize that this is not proof in itself that Monseigneur offered the girl marriage so that she would allow him to share her couch, but is a damning piece of evidence nonetheless."

"Do not be an ass, Pothier!" M'sieur Muraire threw at the flunkey contemptuously, another luxuriant sniff at his heavily scented handkerchief. "Again you are acting the idiot! Why do I put up with you? So this silly wench, this Mlle Lefebvre, is able to describe to Sartine M'sieur's sizeable *telum*. But what does that prove, eh? It proves, Pothier, that she is a calculating little *putain*. And that is all it proves. *Infin.*" He turned on a high heel of his damask covered shoes with their enormous buckles and came away from the window where the Marquis stood staring out at the knot of trees at the far end of the drive. "A young lady who claims to have permitted her lover to take full liberty of her person only after he had promised her marriage, and then goes on to describe her lover's sizeable genitals with glaring clarity to the Lieutenant of the Police, she is no seduced innocent but a seasoned whore who willingly opened her legs to a nobleman in the hopes of entrapping him into marriage."

"*Touché!*" Auguste Pothier declared, all admiration for his colleague's emotive reasoning, but the appreciative light died in his little eyes when their noble client spoke from the window without turning around.

"I don't give a damn one way or the other," Julian said with bored indifference. "What I want is this distasteful episode dealt with."

"Of course. Of course," Pothier the flunkey murmured nervously and addressed himself to his esteemed colleague. "There is the rumor, unsubstantiated you understand, that Monseigneur has impregnated Mlle Lefebvre. Leaving aside her claim of breach of promise, penetration can lead to impregnation. A pregnant Mlle Lefebvre would surely win the sympathy of a judge." He burst out with another of his annoying nervous snorts. "*Infin.* That too then is a problem worth considering, is it not, M'sieur Muraire?"

The lawyer exchanged a meaningful look with his noble client before the Marquis turned again to the view. Muraire bent and whispered in Auguste Pothier's large florid ear a piece of intimate information the Marquis had shared with him but which had so far been denied the flunkey. It sent Pothier into a spasm of embarrassed choking.

"Poor Auguste! His rudimentary skills at being pleasured by a whore do not run to the imaginative." M'sieur Muraire sniggered with a shake of his powdered head. "Perhaps if Monseigneur would be so kind as to write him out an introduction to Mme Celeste's cathouse in Saint-Germaine, one of her sweet-mouthed sapphists would be only too willing to broaden his education?"

No sooner had the lawyer said this than he instantly regretted such free and easy speech, for it was immediately apparent by the rigidity in the tall nobleman's wide back that such unguarded remarks had crossed the deep social divide that separated them.

But before the lawyer could rectify his social solecism he caught sight of a vision of loveliness framed in the doorway. That Auguste Pothier saw her too and had stopped his choking fit convinced Muraire that he was not witness to an ethereal apparition.

Deb hesitated on the threshold in embarrassment and uncertainty, oblivious to the sight she presented to these strangers. Without the services of a maid and not in expectation of receiving visitors, she had dressed for comfort. Without the requisite wide hoops the layers of yellow cream silk fell naturally about the curves of her tall voluptuous figure and in such a revealing way that she invited open admiration: Her dark red hair cascaded in unrestrained waves to her thighs, her face was delicately tinged with color and the string of lustrous pearls about her neck drew the eye down to a deep and inviting décolletage. She appeared to the two French lawyers a statue of a Greek Goddess come to life.

Both Frenchmen instantly doubled over. Pothier upsetting the pile of documents spread out on the table as he made Deb a hastily executed bow, and Muraire bowing until the lace at his wrists swept the carpet. They were all appreciative smiles of such beauty, but their appraisal was not at all respectful of her rightful position, for they assumed she was the latest and almost certainly the freshest in the English nobleman's long line of beautiful mistresses.

The unnatural quiet caused Julian to turn into the room again, and he saw at once the reason for the Frenchmen's distraction. They stared at his wife in mouth-gaping silence, their silly, lascivious grins widening as they dared to visually strip her bare. Ill at ease and embarrassed at being so openly and carnally admired, Deb's usual self-assurance deserted her and Julian was witness to the red stain of embarrassment that spread across her white breasts and throat; evidence she was aware these Frenchmen thought her a whore.

For Deb, it was the look on her husband's ashen face that completely unnerved her. For although he had bathed and shaved after his exhausting morning ride and was dressed immaculately in clean linen shirt, buff breeches and oyster silk waistcoat, his green eyes were dull and hollow, circled by the deep shadows of a sleepless night. His mouth was set in a hard line; gone was the friendly smile and there was something altogether cold and aloof about him. To Deb he could very well have been a handsome stranger.

Julian's anger at these Frenchmen who dared to openly appraise his beautiful young bride was so intense that it inflamed a jealous and covetous anger that was new to him and not at all welcome. Yet it never occurred to him to correct the Frenchmen's presumption, and his pride would not allow him to offer up an explanation he did not think they deserved. His one thought was to remove Deb as quickly as possible from an embarrassing situation. He strode forward, pushing both men aside. But before he could act, Deb came further into the room, speaking French in her clear strong voice, long fingers plucking at the string of heavy pearls that fell between her breasts; the only sign of her nervous embarrassment.

"Monseigneur," she said, taking her lead from the way the Frenchmen addressed her husband, "I thought perhaps you would care to introduce me to our guests before we are called to nuncheon?"

She may be embarrassed but Julian was quick to see the spark of defiance in her brown eyes and knew at once she must have been standing in the doorway for a considerable time. He addressed her in English.

"I am sorry, my dear. This tiresome legal matter is taking longer than anticipated."

"Oh? Perhaps I may be of some assistance?"

He frowned. "It need not bother you in the slightest."

"Need it not?" Deborah replied swiftly, trying to keep the tremble out of her voice. She shot the Marquis an angry look as she went over to the window and out of earshot, saying in English, "Need it not bother me that my husband and his lawyers see fit to discuss the finer points of his—of your—Discussing you as if you're a prize bull put out to stud!" She gave a half-hearted laugh of unconcern but inside she was falling apart. "To think that the most intimate of personal details are the stuff of a written deposition taken from a French whore. Is that what you call a tiresome legal matter that should not concern your wife? Perhaps they would care to take my statement, or do they wish to measure for themselves *Monseigneur's offending implement?*"

"Madame has no right to speak on matters she knows nothing about!"

Deb gave a practiced sigh and lowered her gaze in a gesture

of mock humility, her interest seemingly on the long strand of pearls. "That is very true, sir. After all, I am only your ignorant little bride, and as such am unable to make the necessary comparisons. No doubt the whores of Saint-Germaine would be only too willing to give a glowing report of your-your—*telum*."

"Enough," Julian growled as he took a stride toward her.

Deb stepped back, a hand about her burning throat and made herself look him full in the face. She could feel the hot tears behind her eyes but she willed herself not to cry. If she started crying she would soon be sobbing. And she didn't want to cry, she wanted to make sense of what she had overheard. She wanted Julian to tell her, to reassure her, that she was mistaken, that these Frenchmen were talking about someone else, anyone else but her husband. But he did not reassure her, nor did he speak. He just glared at her in mute anger. She gave a little laugh that broke in the middle and said archly,

"Oh? I had no idea it was perfectly acceptable to discuss such intimate details with flunkeys but not with your wife, who has enjoyed you in all your glory." Just as Julian reached her, face livid with acute embarrassment, she turned to the two Frenchmen and said lightly in their own tongue as she put out a hand, "Will you not introduce me to these charming gentlemen?"

The Marquis turned to the two bright-eyed lawyers, thankful they were ignorant of the English language and said in an arctic voice that wiped the appreciative and lewd grins from their swarthy faces, "M'sieurs Muraire and Pothier, I give you my wife: Mme la Marquise de Alston."

Muraire was so overwhelmed he wondered if he had heard right and he staggered back and dropped his perfumed handkerchief, quickly readjusting his features into a look of respect as he executed a bow fit for a royal audience at Versailles. Pothier was just as shocked, and to think he had dared to openly appraise the girl's magnificent breasts in front of her noble husband! He bowed until he fell to his knees to pick up the dropped documents littering the carpet for want of something to cover his state of agitated embarrassment. Both men respectfully averted their gaze.

"Mme la Marquise de Alston?" Muraire repeated in shocked

surprise as he bent over the long white hand extended to him. "Indeed! Of course! How delightful! How enchanting!"

"Delightful! Enchanting!" Auguste Pothier mimicked, his bulbous nose amongst an armful of creased parchments.

The lawyer looked expectantly at his noble client as if he was entitled to further explanation but Julian ignored him. He was staring fixedly at Deb who had snatched back her hand and turned to glare at him as if he was an apparition, her shock far outstripping anything the two Frenchmen felt at their social *faux pas*. The mixture of disgust and angry incredulity on her white face did not surprise him. He had been dreading the coming of this moment for months, had thought about the best way of approaching her with the truth and had managed to convince himself that perhaps after two and a half months of marriage it wouldn't now matter to her that Julian Hesham and the Marquis of Alston were one and the same gentleman. But it did, he could see that it mattered to her a very great deal. His own acute discomfort and bitter disappointment made him sound supercilious.

"I see that you are not best pleased to discover you are Marchioness of Alston."

Deb was so paralyzed with disbelief that she could not move or speak for several moments. She was numb from her toes to her ears.

"This is a cruel jest!" she finally blurted out, looking at him in frantic expectation that he was merely play acting for the benefit of the Frenchmen, or that she had misheard his pronouncement that she was the Marchioness of Alston, wife of the heir to the Roxton dukedom.

But he did not look down at her and wink away her worst fears. In fact he was not looking at her at all but took snuff by the window with all the nonchalance of a gentleman attending a card party. He nodded to the two French lawyers as he pocketed his gold snuffbox and came to stand beside her, saying near her ear as he took hold of her upper arm, "I suggest we continue our *tête-à-tête* without an audience," and began to propel her towards the door.

She tried to shake him off as she fought to keep a grip on her dignity as the full force of her predicament hit her in a wave of denial and angry disbelief. No. Her husband could not possibly be the Marquis of Alston. Her husband was Julian Hesham. It was utterly absurd to think she had eloped with a conscienceless libertine. But the sordid details she had overheard in this very room merely confirmed the rumors about the Marquis's disreputable reputation. Why had she put her faith in such intangibles as instinct and intuition? Why had he eloped with her? It set her brain reeling, and with the hideous new knowledge that he had married her for any number of reasons known to himself but that love was certainly not one of them. Ruminating on this she realized another startling piece of information, one that made her feel sick to her stomach: Not once, at any stage in their time together, be it at the height of passion or in the quietest of moments, had he ever declared his love for her.

Her married life collapsed in on itself and turned to dust.

She tried to remain upright, to not let the two Frenchmen, who watched from under hooded eyes, and this nobleman she now did not know in the least and who jostled her to the door, know that she was ill and empty and panic-stricken. Her bones felt as brittle as burnt paper and her heart ached as if it had been stomped under foot. And then the enormity of her situation became all too much. Her knees buckled and the carpet rushed up to meet her.

<hr />

When Deb opened her eyes and tried to sit up a wave of nausea forced her to lay still a little longer amongst the cushions. She was on the sofa by the fireplace, the lawyers were gone from the book room and Martin Ellicott was peering down at her with concern. She turned her head away, a sob catching in her aching throat, and there staring into the fire with his hands in his breeches pockets was the tall brooding figure of the Marquis of Alston: her husband.

The Marquis of Alston was *her husband*. Part of her still did not believe that the gentleman she had married, with whom she had shared the most intimate of moments, was the notorious heir to the Roxton dukedom. How could she have been so stupidly naive and trusting? How could she have followed her heart? Had her wits been sleeping? Why had her head not cautioned her heart?

What madness had possessed her to marry him out of hand? Was it the same impetuousness that had seen her run off to care for Otto? But Otto was her brother and their love for one another was unquestioning. She had thought her love for this man and his love for her was of the same unquestioning kind. Love must truly be blind. Not only blind, she thought, but completely witless!

She despised herself for fainting dead away. She had no idea what had come over her to react in such an absurdly weak-willed way. She had not been herself lately and although she had her suspicions she had not voiced them because she wanted to be absolutely certain before giving her husband the wonderful news. Now, her news was not so wonderful: it terrified her. And she would not faint again. She must be strong. She needed to make sense of this shocking situation in which she now found herself. Not since she had boarded the ship for the Channel crossing to France to be with Otto had she felt so alone in the world.

"I've never fainted before in my life," she said aloud in disbelief as she slowly righted herself and put her feet to the carpet.

"Not surprising," Julian said dully, addressing the flames. "You haven't eaten a proper meal in three days."

Deb stared at his wide back, illness giving way to a heaviness of heart and mind. She addressed herself to Martin. "I would be grateful for a glass of water."

The old man brought her the water with a stricken look. "I meant what I said to you this morning, my lady," he murmured in a rush. "Had I realized the shock would... I—I am so very sorry."

The Marquis looked over his shoulder. "Martin, leave us."

"No!" Deb stood up and swayed. In one stride Julian had her by the upper arm but she shrugged him off, not wanting the touch of him, and steadied herself with a hand to the back of the sofa. "I need someone here other than you to help me make sense of this—this *nightmare* in which I find myself. Please, M'sieur Ellicott, tell me: Is this man in truth the Marquis of Alston?"

"Yes, my lady."

"And are we truly man and wife?"

"Yes, my lady."

Deb took a few moments to collect herself, breathing deeply as she fought off panic. It did not help that Martin's short answers were followed by a heavy silence. Neither man spoke and she knew they were watching her and waiting. She let out a small hysterical sob but stifled the urge to burst into tears, a shaking hand to her trembling mouth.

"How ironic! It wouldn't have mattered in the least had my husband been the bastard son of some illustrious nobleman," she confessed. "Yet finding myself married to the heir to the premier dukedom in the kingdom fills me with sickening dread. London must be overflowing with bird-witted heiresses willing to marry you despite your sordid reputation. Why me?"

"Dozens," Julian answered bitterly. "But none so bird-witted as to dare insult my lineage!"

"What was I to think when you never once spoke of your family, in fact you were at pains not to divulge their identity," Deb argued. "Yet M'sieur Ellicott is your godfather, a man who had been valet to an old aristocrat, whom I now realize is the Duke of Roxton. How many noblemen of your acquaintance have made godfathers of their valets to their legitimate children?"

"My lady, that great honor was bestowed upon me because—"

"Martin! You need not justify yourself!" Julian cut in angrily.

"Yet, her ladyship has a point," the old man answered calmly, adding with a smile at his godson, "Your wife was left to draw her own conclusions about your parentage, and still she married you."

Julian threw up a hand, a dull red glow of embarrassment to his lean cheeks. "And that is supposed to appease me; that my wife thought me of bastard blood: the debased product of a lustful mount?"

"Your pride is insufferable!" Deb exclaimed angrily. "It's a wonder it permitted you to lower yourself to take to wife a female who puts more store in a man's character than she does his impeccable pedigree. A noble title does not make a gentleman; nor does it give a nobleman the right to look down his aristocratic nose at those who shouldn't be blamed for the sins of their fathers!"

"My bride was chosen for me when I was *sixteen* years old," Julian stated without preamble, taking out his snuffbox, her blink of incomprehension making him add coldly, "The last thing I wanted to do on this earth was go through a wedding ceremony in the middle of the night with a skinny chit still in the nursery. But my father, in his infinite wisdom, considered it the wisest course for a wayward heir about to venture off on the Grand Tour, and who would reach his majority on foreign shores. Who knows what might have happened in those years in exile? I may have returned home with a wholly unsuitable bride."

Deb blinked at him, a crease between her brows. "In the middle of the night? Sixteen?" She swallowed, mind turning over his words, and then her eyes opened wide with dawning realization and she swiftly looked across at Martin. Julian smiled crookedly.

"You were quite a drab brown thing when you were twelve years old," he drawled. "Luckily for me you blossomed into a rose of rare sensual beauty. It makes our marriage that much more palatable."

"But—how? No. *No.* That was a dream. A vivid opium in-duced dream. Nurse had given me a dose before bedtime. I don't remember what for. She said it would help me sleep. And when next day I told her about my dream she told me to forget all about it," Deb argued, fingers clenched in the folds of cream silk. "She said it was the laudanum. I was on a swing and Otto was playing his viola and we were in the forest and the very next moment I was standing before a-a fat bishop and there were these two old men and a sad boy with green eyes. Indeed everyone seemed sad and it made me sad. It was all too fantastical to be real. It had to be a dream. It made perfect sense to me that it was a dream." She shook her head, trying to shake off the memory. But one look up at the Marquis, at his emerald green eyes, and she knew he was telling her the truth.

She put a cold hand to her constricted throat and slowly sank onto the edge of a wingback chair. "I was half-asleep... It was midnight. I—I don't remember the half of what was said to me. To be married off in the middle of the night in such a barbaric way... It's positively *feudal.*" She turned to Martin. "You were there," she stated in wonderment. "You and the—Duke? Yes, the Duke *his* father and Gerry and the bishop. Otto wasn't there at all was he? That part was a dream..." She shut her eyes to blink away tears. "Gerry never said a word. He must've ordered Nurse to give me the opium to guarantee my complicity. Much easier to marry me off drugged! And then to tell me it was all a

142

dream? My God, what a despicable *coward*. How-how could he do this to me?" she asked herself in a tiny voice. Disbelief gave way to anger and her fingers dug in again and crushed the silk of her petticoats as large tears fell into her lap and stained the fabric. "How *dare* he marry me off in such a deceitful, underhanded way. I was a mere child, his *sister*. Not a farm animal to be blindly taken to market and auctioned off to the highest bidder!"

"My dear girl, you know as well as I that in our circle females aren't entitled to decide for themselves," Julian interrupted matter-of-factly. "It matters not if you be twelve or twenty." He gave a lop-sided grin. "Yet, my insufferable pride aside, given the choice, you married me anyway. You certainly didn't think twice about eloping with a stranger you found bleeding from a sword wound in the forest. What's the difference? Best make the most of it."

Deb gaped at such sublime arrogance. "You deceived me into thinking I had a choice because you allowed me to fall in love with a false being: a gentleman of fine feelings and elevated thought who loved me for myself; all the things you are not! All you truly cared about was getting me into your bed!"

The Marquis took snuff, a sidelong glance at his godfather who had politely retreated to the far corner of the room. "Of course I needed to get you into bed, you foolish girl. You are my wife. I couldn't have you seduced into a bigamous union with the likes of Robert Thesiger. You belong to me, body and soul, and to no one else."

"So you think?" she threw at him, up on her feet again. "I may be female but I have a mind and a will. I won't be party to a cold-blooded marriage contracted for your dynastic self-preservation! And I won't be paraded about society as your wife, an attachment to your consequence. That is a hollow, shallow existence. You may legally own me for the present but you will never have me."

The Marquis shut his snuffbox with a snap, his smile hovering between lewdness and embarrassment. He glanced her over and put up his brows. "But I have had you, my dear. Two, often three times a day."

"How dare you degrade our most intimate—"

"Oh, I'm not complaining. Far from it. I was delightfully surprised to discover our physical appetites are well matched.

143

Although… such carnal enthusiasm is not what one expects from a virgin—"

She slapped his face, a hard stinging blow that made him reel back in shock.

"You *disgust* me. Did the stallion hope to put the mare in foal? Was that the purpose of-of *mounting* me three times a day for ten weeks? What a tiresome business for you! Oh? Does my base language *offend* you? Ha! Or perhaps it is the bald truth that makes you wince? I just thank God I discovered the truth before the *hideous* prospect of conceiving your child befell me. I will *never* have your children!"

He caught her wrist and yanked her up against his chest, forcing her arm into the small of her back and holding her fast so that she could not move. "For better or worse, my love, you are my wife," he whispered viciously in her face. "Mounting you, as you so indelicately put it, is my right. And, by God, when I want to mount you, you will part those lovely long legs as wide as I please, and accommodate me. Do you understand?"

Deb stared up into his face contorted with rage and shivered with loathing. "I can readily believe a-a *monster* capable of cold-blooded deceit capable of forcing himself on his wife. I will never again come willingly to your bed. If you hope to get me with child you will have to *rape* me."

Julian pushed her away with a huff of furious embarrassment, the sting still smarting in his reddened, close-shaven cheek. He turned to the window. "Take comfort in the fact that the sooner you give me a son the sooner our relations are at an end. You can then go your own road for all I care."

Such a prospect froze Deb to her marrow and she sat down on the sofa with head bowed, tears of anger, frustration and disbelief now sliding freely down her hot cheeks. She mustered what reserves of dignity was left to her and took a deep breath. She had to make him see reason for both their sakes.

"If you have no thought for me then spare a thought for a child of such a hateful union," she said quietly. "Surely you would not want your son to grow up to one day discover that his father is a libertine who begets bastards by French whores and then abandons them to their fate? You would not want your son to go through life knowing his is one of privilege while his bastard brothers and sisters are forever marked as social outcasts, unable to marry well, unable to enter this society to which your son belongs, facing God knows what adversities all because of their noble father's uncontrolled lust? What if one day a half brother or sister confronted your heir with the truth about his libertine father's whoring ways? What would your son think of you, the father he was taught to look up to, to emulate one day, how you treated with contempt and disrespect the marriage bed shared with his long-suffering mother? Whatever your feelings for me, could you in good conscience be such a monster to your son and heir?"

The audible intake of breath came from the old man and he crossed the room in a few quick steps and put a hand on Deb's shoulder, his eyes wide in warning, a finger to his lips, and a worried, nervous glance at his godson. But Deb would not be silenced.

"Never mind that as your wife I am supposed to hold my head high and ignore your whores and your ill-gotten off-spring because as Marchioness of Alston they are but dirt beneath my feet." She put up her chin. "You are grossly mistaken if you think I will meekly submit to a cold-blooded marriage of the sort entered into by your parents—"

"*Enough.* I've heard *enough*," Julian growled, suddenly coming to life and turning on Deb with a face flushed with absolute fury. "Ten. *Ten* weeks in my company and you've learned nothing— *nothing*—about *me?*" he spat out incredulously and took a few moments to master his emotions, bright green eyes fixed on Deb's flushed face. "You have insulted my esteemed parents more than is humanly possible to forgive," he continued with icy formality. "Know this madam: You are my wife for better or worse and as my wife you are also the Marchioness of Alston. You will learn restraint and the manners befitting your elevation. You have a month to have your belongings in order before I send for you to join me in Paris. And you will come to Paris when I bid, even if I have to return to carry you across the Channel myself. Is that understood?"

Deb bravely looked him in the eyes, determined to be as in control of her emotions, but she could not keep the deep note of sadness from her voice. "And you, my lord, have so cruelly used me and abused my trust and love that I will do everything in my power to see us forever parted."

Because my heart is irreparably torn asunder, she wanted to add but felt too emotionally drained and listless of mind to continue. Her life, the life she had so looked forward to sharing with Julian Hesham, was now so turned inside out that her head ached to think about it. Through a haze of disbelief and unbelievable sadness she watched this stranger, this nobleman to whom she was irrevocably wedded, turn away from her without another word and speak in rapid French to the old man. He then strode from the room and slammed the door so hard it reverberated on its hinges.

"My lady, I have been charged with the care of you until—"

"Please, Martin. I cannot think any more today."

The old man was regarding her with such sadness and pity in his troubled eyes that Deb wanted to burst into fresh tears and run from the room. Instead she walked quietly to the door, only stopping when he called her back. She looked over her shoulder hoping her features did not betray her disordered emotions.

"My lady, these revelations today have been a great shock," Martin said quietly. "I wish matters had been handled differently. I make no apologies for my godson, only that he has the unrestrained temper of youth. More I am not at liberty to say. I just trust that in time, when you know the truth behind the rumors about the Marquis of Alston, and finally meet his illustrious parents, perhaps then you will gain a deeper understanding of the man to whom you are wedded and... find it in your heart to forgive."

"I have no heart, Martin," she answered softly. "Your godson just tore it from me."

Nine

Paris, France *1770*

*S*ir Gerald and Lady Mary Cavendish were hosting a select soiree for relatives and friends newly arrived in Paris for the celebration of the Dauphin's marriage to the young Austrian princess, Marie-Antoinette. The royal wedding was taking place in the French capital and to mark such an auspicious and historic event all of Paris was rejoicing. Balls, routs, open-air concerts, plays, operas, fireworks and a hundred free entertainments had been organized for Parisian society high and low. The whole city was in a festive mood. Cards of invitation crossed back and forth society's gilded salons. Every invitation was accepted, to show off a painted face and the latest towering powdered hairstyle if only for half an hour in a crowded salon before being whisked away in a sedan chair into the heady perfumed atmosphere of the next soiree.

Yet, despite the typically French surroundings of gold-leaf furniture, polished parquetry flooring and white and blue paneled walls, the Cavendish soiree was quite markedly an English affair. The guests were either from the English Embassy or young Englishmen staying briefly in Paris at the start of the Grand Tour; people with whom Sir Gerald, who did not have an ear for languages and thus knew no French, could have a decent conversation. Unlike twittering, effeminate painted French nobles, the guests at Sir Gerald's little gathering knew his worth as a favored relative of the Duke and Duchess of Roxton; Englishmen with whom he could feel a natural superiority.

He congratulated himself on how well the evening was progressing as he looked out across the large square courtyard with its avenue of chestnut trees, gravel walks, fountains and shrubbery illuminated by flickering flambeaux; and at the southern end the imposing black and gold iron gates which kept out the world as it traveled up and down the Rue Saint-Honoré. His wife had been the perfect hostess and the guests were suitably impressed by his noble connections and surroundings. After all, not every relative of the Duke and Duchess was given use of one of the large apartments within the compound of the Hôtel Roxton: a collection of four-storey seventeenth century buildings with mansard roofs, awe inspiring in size and aspect even by Parisian standards.

But as Sir Gerald drank the Duke's excellent claret and surveyed the aristocratic landscape with his usual pompous self-consequence his thoughts were niggled by the specter of his recalcitrant sister and her lunatic demands.

Every morning he awoke with the expectation that Deborah had come to her senses and accepted her arranged marriage. But every day he was disappointed. He had hardly believed his eyes when reading her letter damning him for marrying her off to the Marquis of Alston. He had expected, at the very least, gratitude, and for his troubles he had received words dripping with reproach and ungratefulness. And when she had demanded he contact his lawyers to discover an impediment to her marriage so that it could be annulled forthwith his bowels had opened of their own accord.

He did not understand her. One day she would be a duchess. And not just any duchess, but the Duchess of Roxton, wife of the most powerful and wealthy noble in England. What better incentive did she need to remain married to Lord Alston than that? The nobleman's nefarious lifestyle, the fact he was being sued for breach of promise by a Farmer-General and was being daily lampooned in Parisian newssheets, was of small consequence; a mere trifle that his sister, if she had her wits about her would, like any good and obedient wife, dismiss as beneath her notice.

Fortunately, he had avoided any unpleasant face-to-face confrontation with Deborah because of her refusal to come to Paris to join her husband. This also had the added advantage that her esteemed parents-in-law were still none the wiser about her lunatic whim to seek an annulment, and in so doing, discover that he had given in to her demands to contact his lawyers. After all, he had to hedge his bets as it were.

Let Deborah believe he was obliging her for as long as it took for him to sufficiently ingratiate himself with the Duke so that when the thunderstorm of his sister's annulment plans poured a cold torrent on any Parisian nuptial announcement he could cut his connection with her without fear of being socially ostracized by the distinguished family into which she had been married.

And then the moment came. A footman whispered in his ear that he had a visitor awaiting him in the adjoining small reception room. The visitor was his sister. A frisson of unease tingled his spine and his bald head under its snug powdered wig began to sweat as he excused himself to his guests.

Deb was looking out on the same view as her brother, admiring the avenue of chestnut trees. Disheveled by travel, tendrils of her red hair had escaped from under the small peaked velvet trimmed bonnet and fell about her face. Despite a warm evening, she wore a silk-lined woolen cloak over her traveling gown. She was tired and need of a good night's sleep in a decent bed after a three day journey from the French coast, but she was determined to speak with her brother before reluctantly presenting herself at the main entrance to the Hôtel Roxton.

When her brother came into the room and closed over the door, she barely had time to turn from the window before he was across the parquetry and had taken possession of her gloved hands. He guided her to sit with him on a hard-backed red velvet settee, his face flushed from too much wine and wearing an embarrassed smile that put Deb on her guard.

"What a delightful surprise, my dear! Yet I cannot help but wonder if it was quite the right thing to make such an arduous journey when at last report you were still in your sick bed being attended by Dr. Medlow. A most distressing episode. I had hoped you would heed my wise counsel and remain in Bath. Such a long journey can only have taxed your reserves of strength."

"Medlow assures me that I am now in no danger whatsoever," she interrupted, her brother's pompous speeches never failing to grate. "In fact, Gerry, I'm so much better that I'm plumper beyond even Medlow's expectations."

Sir Gerald screwed up his mouth at this, unconvinced. "Yet, I don't understand, despite Medlow's assurances, why you felt you had to come, when I quite specifically stated in my last letter that you remain in Bath to receive Bishop Ramsay."

Deb let out an involuntary laugh. "Gerry, Ramsay can't help me out of my predicament. Nor should I think he would want to. After all, he was the one who performed the original marriage ceremony."

Sir Gerald shook his powdered head sadly. "This is a most distressing business. Naturally I blame myself—"

"Oh, it is only right and proper you blame yourself! That you can sit there enquiring after my health when I know you don't give a button for me... But I didn't come all this way to go over old ground. My letter to you was blunt enough, and if it wasn't for the despicable situation I now find myself in I would gladly be anywhere than here with you!"

"Deborah? How can you abuse me when I have only your best interests at heart?" he answered, casting her a wounded look. "Naturally, your offensive and unladylike letter did not please me, and the accusations and plain language directed toward your eldest brother were such that I did seriously wonder at your mental state." He sniffed and stretched his neck in its tightly bound silk cravat. "Yet when it was made known to me that you were ill and had taken to your bed, I was more forgiving and of the belief that you wrote that letter under the duress of illness, because you have never been ill a day in your life, so for you to take to your bed meant—"

"Did you do as I requested and write to your lawyers?" Deb asked bluntly, the only sign of her frustration showing itself in her tightly clenched gloved hands.

"Of course. My lawyers thought it prudent to brief Bishop Ramsay on this most distressing business, to garner his support, if possible, for an annulment. The bishop was willing, despite his age and infirmities, to undertake the journey to Bath. I thought perhaps you would appreciate the comforting words of a man of God."

"You have a very odd sense of comfort!"

"I fail to see why you must treat this very serious and quite shocking matter with levity!" Sir Gerald lectured through a tight mouth. "I admit that I had hopes that a match between our family and the Roxtons would be a great success and set you, my only sister, up for great things in life. Yet, I should have known that it would come to this. You and Otto both have been a sad disappointment, but I have strived to do my utmost for you as your guardian and as a Cavendish, and what is my reward? Otto's total disobedience and stupidity and your ungratefulness! Deborah, I have bowed to your wishes for an annulment, because I want what is best for you. Do you think it is an easy thing to hold one's head up high when Otto saw fit to contract a marriage with a gypsy and now my only sister's marriage to a future duke is to be annulled on the grounds of her husband's lunacy?"

Deborah listened to her brother's impassioned speech with suspicion. She had been wary of his eagerness to help her since his letter of reply to her request for a dissolution of her marriage. She had expected a downright refusal and was prepared to seek assistance from lawyers recommended to her by Lady Cleveland. After all Sir Gerald did not exert himself for others unless there was something to be gained for him. Yet when he had jumped at the chance to engage the family lawyers in a case of litigation that was sure to create a major public scandal of the sort Sir Gerald deplored, she had been so surprised that she was certain he was up to something underhanded. Reason enough for her to travel to Paris; but it wasn't the reason she had done so.

She caught on the word lunacy and raised her arched brows. "You think Lord Alston mad, Gerry? Is this a new thought, or did you know him to be of unstable mind when you married me to him?"

"My lawyers inform me that there are only two possible avenues for a marriage to be annulled," Sir Gerald said, ignoring his sister's sarcastic question but feeling acute discomfort under her cool gaze. He was not a perceptive man but there was something different about his sister that he could not put his finger on. He had expected her circumstances to have turned her into a weeping pot, instead she might have been fashioned from stone, such was her frosty manner. She unnerved him and more than usual. "One is non-consummation of the marriage," he muttered, clearing his throat and avoiding her widening smile. "In the event the husband is— the husband is—er—incapable of the—um—the um—*act* the bride's guardian has every right to seek an annulment on her behalf."

"Incapable of the act? Ha! As any Parisian whore will tell you, Alston is more than capable of satisfying a female between the sheets."

"Deborah! Indeed! For you to talk of such matters is—is…"

She shrugged indifferently, Sir Gerald oblivious to the film of tears across her soft brown eyes that belied her cold tone. "Do stop this pretense of offended sensibilities, Gerry. I am a married lady and as such have learnt a thing or two about the marriage bed. What is the second circumstance for annulment?"

Sir Gerald wiped a sweaty hand across his glistening brow at such blunt speech and stumbled on. "That is complicated and more difficult to prove. An act passed in '42 makes provision for the annulment of a marriage on the grounds that the husband was of unsound mind at the time vows were taken. If this can be proved then the marriage is void."

"And was Lord Alston mad the night we were wed?"

Sir Gerald wandered to the window. Suddenly the majestic view of illuminated chestnut trees and fountains lost its appeal. "You may not recall the night you were married, but I can, vividly. I was most uncomfortable with the way the marriage was conducted. There had been a long understanding between our families, since almost from your cradle, that you and Alston would wed, but I could hardly credit it when His Grace demanded a most hurried affair. And when one saw the boy's unstable condition, I was most reluctant to proceed."

"Not enough for you to call the whole thing off!" Deb scoffed. She joined her brother by the full-length windows. "And I do remember aspects of that night, *vividly*, despite being drugged. Oh, you can look the stunned trout, Gerry, but you can't deny that you had Nurse give me a dose of laudanum to keep me biddable. No wonder I thought I was dreaming! I could barely put two thoughts together. As I recall Alston was extremely distressed and that there was an ancient gentleman with white hair who looked very sad."

"The Duke." Sir Gerald nodded and swallowed. "Yes, a very sad business indeed. If the rumors be true it was also a very shocking business."

Deb regarded her brother's look of contrition with the suspicion it deserved. "Gerry, why are you so eager to have my marriage annulled when it will surely mean disfavor with the Roxtons?"

"Isn't it enough that I want to see my sister parted from a man who is of unsound mind?"

"No. I don't believe you. But tell me why you believe Lord Alston of unsound mind the night we were wed."

"You had best sit down, my dear, for it is a most appalling business."

Deb bit her lip and stared out at the deserted courtyard, the flambeaux flickering in the breeze of a balmy evening. "No. I will stand. Tell me."

"On his sixteenth birthday, Alston attacked his mother."

"When you say attacked, what do you mean?"

Sir Gerald threw up a hand and blustered. Where were his sister's feminine sensibilities? If he had been telling Mary she would have been satisfied with the word, no details necessary. Why did his sister always have to be so annoyingly quick witted?

"Well, Gerry? Please don't feel you need to go all big brotherish on me now and shield me from any unpleasantness. That ended the night you married me off."

He let out a sigh of defeat.

"Attacked as in he dragged the Duchess out into the middle of Hanover Square in full view of the world and denounced her as a whore and a slut and a witch."

Deb decided she did need to sit down after all and sank onto a nearby spindle legged chair, a hand hard about the ornately curved arm. She took a deep breath and nodded for her brother to continue.

"That in itself is shocking enough but the Duchess at the time was heavy with child. She and the unborn babe came close to death. Alston's insane actions brought on his brother's premature birth. It is the opinion of learned medical men that Lord Henri suffers to this day with the falling sickness because his mother went into an early labor."

Deb looked up at Sir Gerald, a sickening tightness in her chest, realizing he lacked the imagination to invent such a tale. "Does Harry suffer badly with the falling sickness?"

"Yes. A physician is his shadow."

"Poor little fellow."

She recalled what Jack had said that day in the forest and Alston's anger, incomprehensible at the time, at Jack's confidences about his best friend Harry. No wonder the Marquis had been uncomfortable at the mention of his brother's affliction. She took a few moments to collect herself then asked, "How did you come by such information? Surely Mary didn't—"

"Good God, no!"

"If not Mary, then who?"

"Does it matter where I heard—"

"It matters a great deal! A very great deal, especially if I hope to convince a judge as to Alston's state of mind at the time of our marriage."

"I am certain you will take the tale as fact when I tell you it was confided in me by someone who was witness to the whole sordid episode and who cares deeply for your welfare. In fact, he has asked for your hand in marriage."

"Hand in marriage? But I am already married."

"Can you have forgotten in what deep regard Robert Thesiger holds you?"

"Robert Thesiger?" Deb was not only surprised but again her suspicions were aroused. "You put store in the word of Robert Thesiger, a gentleman you have long held in aversion because of his shoddy parentage, at the expense of your illustrious connections by marriage? Gerry, for shame on you! When have you not condescended to birth over all other considerations?"

"I should wash my hands of you! Stay married to a lunatic!" Sir Gerald growled in frustration, all semblance of understanding and patience evaporating. "I've done everything in my power to assist you, and you repay my loyalty and duty with sarcasm and ungratefulness. And there is Robert Thesiger, a gentleman of wealth and polished address who still wishes to have you as his wife, would elope with you now, before the annulment came through, if you let him."

Deborah stood up slowly and stared at her brother through narrowed brown eyes. "Let me understand you: You are in favor of Robert Thesiger eloping with me *before* my marriage is annulled?"

Sir Gerald's quickly averted gaze was evidence enough for

Deb that there was an ulterior motive lurking somewhere in the recesses of his mind. Under her silent penetrating stare he finally blurted out in annoyance, "If you had any common decency left you would do the noble thing!"

"The *noble* thing? I beg your pardon? What are you driveling on about?"

"You must see that any judge in his right mind would grant you the annulment you seek given the evil Alston perpetrated against his own mother. But do you truly want such scandalous and shameful revelations to be aired in a court of law for all the world to hear? Do you sincerely wish to break the health of the old Duke, see the Duchess heartbroken, her youngest son wise to his brother's mad folly? Can you truly be so cold hearted and calculating?"

"Am I to understand that you want me to run off with Robert Thesiger in preference to going through the proper legal channels and seeking an annulment to a marriage that was forced, yes *forced*, upon me?" When hope sparked in her brother's eyes, Deb looked away, sickened. "How much better that would look for you, that a sister's scandalous actions cause her own downfall, than the truth cause yours." She looked at him hard. "And that is what you consider is the noble thing? For me? Your sister?"

Sir Gerald took a step toward her, hopeful. "Then you will consider Thesiger's offer?"

"Get away from me, you sniveling coward!"

He struck her, an instinctive swipe across the left cheek with the back of his hand. She was so stunned that she dropped back onto the spindle-legged chair, a hand to her smarting flesh. He immediately repented and fell to his knees to clutch at her hands but she pushed him off.

"You made me strike you! You did!" he blubbered in a gasping voice. "You shouldn't have called me a-a coward! Don't you see that if you go ahead with this annulment, if you air the Roxtons' dirty laundry in public, I will be utterly, *utterly* ruined. I will be struck off the register at White's. I will never again be able to set foot in this house. Alston will turn his back on—If not for me, then for my wife! Think of Mary!"

"You're pathetic, Gerry! Get up before Mary comes in and sees you for what you truly are! Mary? Mary! How lovely to see you again!"

Mention of his wife sent Sir Gerald diving in the pocket of his frockcoat to find a kerchief to wipe dry his florid face. He dropped his snuffbox close by his silken knee, as if he was down on the floor to retrieve it, scooped it up and scrambled to his feet, all the while keeping his back to his wife. But Lady Mary had eyes only for her sister-in-law who, despite being travel-weary looked, in glowing good health, so much so that she appeared radiant.

Instead of returning Deb's warm embrace she sank down into a respectful curtsey, acutely aware that Deb was now Marchioness of Alston and as such outranked her.

Deb frowned and pulled her up.

"I was so certain you would be pleased to see me, Mary," Deb said with a nervous smile, the mantle of hard indifference she had cultivated since discovering she was married to the Marquis of Alston slipping ever so slightly. Mary's cool reception hurt her more than she cared to acknowledge. God help her to keep herself in check when she was reunited with Jack! "Forgive me for disturbing your little gathering," she apologized. "Perhaps you will come and see me tomorrow when I am well rested from my journey. I do believe I need to eat something soon or I shall be ill again, and that would never do. Dr. Medlow insists I take nourishment every few hours for the sake of the baby. Excuse me. Mr. Ffolkes is expecting me."

Without waiting a response to her momentous news, Deb left her mouth-gaping brother and his equally speechless wife and had herself and her portmanteaux shown upstairs to the spacious apartment occupied by the Honorable Evelyn Gaius Ffolkes, musician and composer, nephew of the Duke of Roxton and closest friend and cousin of the Marquis of Alston.

The composer sat at his gilded clavichord with a viola balanced on his silken knees, and a parchment spread across the ivory keys. He was busily making notations, the music running on in his head faster than he could scrawl it down; the fine white lace ruffles at his wrist trailing across the parchment as he wrote. At his back, through the open double doors of his grace and favor apartment, a rowdy dinner continued unabated in the dining room.

There was laughter and belching and the three musicians at his table continued to eat and drink as if they had no idea where they would find their next meal. Between mouthfuls of roasted pheasant, pate stuffed fowl, seasonal vegetables swimming in creamy sauces and all washed down with the best wines the Duke's cellar had to offer, they shouted out for their host and fellow musician to join them.

It was the very early hours of the morning and a cursory glance at the ornate mantle clock told Evelyn what his drooping eyelids already knew: The sun would soon be up and he and his musicians had worked through the night. He picked up his wine glass and returned to his seat at the dining table.

"May the Marquis of Alston's amorous adventures continue to provide entertainment for the Parisian masses and choke our salons with inconsequential babble!" declared Georgio, a barrel-chested baritone in a threadbare frockcoat that had once belonged to the valet of the Duke d'Orleans. When his two fellow musicians glanced knowingly at Evelyn and then looked down at their dirty plates, the baritone gave a grunt of annoyance. "What? It is better I toast Evelyn's noble cousin behind his back and not to his face? This scandal involving the Marquis, it continues to rage through Parisian salons faster than a fire through Saint-Germain, and you think I should not speak of it? I for one would like to know the truth of it from the mouth of the horse's cousin!"

"To be honest, I've not picked up a newssheet in three years," Evelyn confessed, reaching for an uncorked bottle of champagne.

"Then what do you make of this!" Georgio continued and slapped down one of a number of crumpled pamphlets scattered amongst the dinner things. "These are being distributed every-where. Funded by the Farmer-General Lefebvre, so it is said, though he denies all knowledge of their very existence."

Evelyn picked up the dog-eared and wine stained piece of parchment and gave it a casual glance. He didn't bother reading the text. The cartoon was enough. The drawing depicted a noble-man, naked from the waist down with an enormous erection, his arms about the hips of an aristocratic female, her hair festooned with ribbons and bows piled outrageously high upon her head and her many layered petticoats up around her waist. He was smiling lewdly down at her while she stared up at him in abject terror. The caption under the cartoon read: *An English nobleman's Grand Tour: pillaging foreign works of art and the maidenhead of virtuous middle class French virgins.*

Evelyn screwed up his mouth and put the pamphlet aside as if it was something unclean. He realized well enough that the cartoon depicted the Marquis of Alston and Mlle Lefebvre and he was shaken by the extent to which the Parisians were vilifying his cousin. "Casimir," he said quietly to a consumptive musician with a bad complexion, "be good enough to collect up all this waste of paper and ink and put it to the flames."

"I have heard there is a trial brief with M. le Marquis's name upon it," offered Casimir as he put paper to flame.

Georgio turned a blood shot gaze on a man of middling years and faded good looks who wore a mouche at the corner of his painted lips. "Sasha! There! If Casimir he has heard of a trial brief then this rumor is no longer rumor it is a situation most serious for M. le Marquis!"

"I'd hardly call his name on a factum serious, Georgio," Sasha drawled. "Three-quarters of what is set in ink is inflammatory and the other quarter? It isn't to be believed. This trial brief, it is a piece of high drama, it too is wasted paper, it is fit for the stage not a court of law."

"And you would know this, Sasha, aye?" Georgio scoffed, sticking out his fat bottom lip and looking about at his friends to support him. No one offered it.

Before Sasha could answer, Casimir spoke.

"And so he should. Sasha he gave up the law to follow his passion: music. Is that not so, Sasha? His father and grandfather before him they were barristers and members of the prestigious *Ordre des Avocats*. Sasha—"

"Enough, Casimir," Sasha ordered although he smiled approvingly at such praise and ignored Georgio's gaping mouth. "I, too, was a great lawyer but…" He shrugged. "Music! Ah now that is much the purer form of entertainment, yes?"

"So pray tell us oh-great-lawyer-that-was, what is your learned legal opinion of this imbroglio in which M. le Marquis finds himself?" ordered Georgio.

When Evelyn shrugged a powdered shoulder, as if to say it was Sasha's decision whether he took up the challenge or not, the musician sat back in his chair, an arm over the padded back and took the floor.

"The lawyers engaged by either side, and who have penned these factums, naturally have their own barrows to push," Sasha began. "M'sieur Lefebvre's lawyers they have painted M. le Marquis de Alston as typical of his kind, whose wealth, charm and polished manners are a veneer to hide a sinister nature, one of arrogance, of insufferable pride and of power through intimidation. M. le Marquis he symbolizes what is most repellent with the aristocracy of this country; never mind that he is an Englishman. His noble sire the Duke of Roxton's mamma was the daughter of the Comte de Salvan, and M. le Marquis's divinely beautiful maman is French to the ends of her delicious fingertips. Does she not speak our tongue more elegantly, more fluidly and with more prettiness than any French Duchesse? Is she not the only non-royal Duchesse whom Louis permits to sit on a tabouret in his presence, as if she were royal herself! Is that not truly a mark of her Frenchness?

"So, M. le Marquis he is French when it suits and English when it suits the purposes of Lefebvre's lawyers to point out he is a heretic who has taken advantage of a good Catholic convent bred female of the French bourgeoisie. Mlle Lefebvre she is the innocent victim of an unscrupulous nobleman, whose very arrogance of nobility he used shamelessly to take advantage of the girl's innocence and trust. It is said he offered her marriage to get her into his bed and once he had tasted enough of her delights he abandoned her, she with child, to her fate. Viola! It is done!"

He motioned for Casimir to pass the crystal port decanter and poured himself out a drop before continuing.

"M. le Marquis's lawyers, headed by that most gifted and idiosyncratic of barristers, M'sieur Linguet, who likes nothing more than to bask in the glow of a dozen chandeliers, has painted his client as the innocent victim of a bourgeoisie plot. It is asserted that M'sieur Lefebvre he schemed to have M. le Marquis as his son-in-law. At every opportunity he made certain his pretty coquette of a daughter, who was well-aware of her father's ambitions on her behalf, danced in M. le Marquis's orbit. She was seen where he was seen. Dressed in the most ravishing of creations, her young breasts pushed up in her corsets and her lips painted invitingly. She rode about in carriages painted to compliment her gowns. She paraded in the park whenever M. le Marquis was there. She dropped her pretty painted fan at his feet at the Opera and made certain that she danced with him at every masked ball. It did not take many weeks before M. le Marquis was bewitched by this nymph of seduction! And it took even less time before she permitted him her couch. *Infin!* He is ensnared! Or so Lefebvre wished in his heart of hearts to believe."

He paused, sipped from his crystal glass, a satisfied look at the rapt faces of his friends.

"To sum up: What he Lefebvre failed to understand is the nobility's great arrogance for marrying within the confines of its own class. Being ignorant of the entrapment, then discovering the little Mlle's flattering attentions and masterful coquettery were not for his person but wholly for his title, her objective: marriage all along, M. le Marquis turned his broad back, leaving the little mlle to a fate of her and her father's making.

"This is the essence of Linguet's case. And unlike the inflammatory and highly emotive accusations in Lefebvre's brief, the arguments put forward by Linguet are seductive and believable by their very restraint. Thus, who are we to believe?" He smiled crookedly and threw up a lace covered wrist. "You, my dear friends, must decide for yourselves."

There was a moment of awed silence and then enthusiastic applause from Casimir, who was up on his steepled shoes and clapping wildly. Even Evelyn raised his glass in praise of his friend's eloquence. Sasha inclined his powdered head in acknowledgement and for one moment wondered if he had made the right decision all those years ago to give up the practice of law for his love of music. It was left to the barrel-chested baritone to disabuse him. Georgio plunged the conversation back into the scandalmonger's gutter by saying with a punctuated belch,

"That's all well and good, Sasha, but Eve, tell us: Is there truth to the rumor that your well-endowed cousin has never penetrated a female, whore or no whore, for fear of fathering bastards?"

This outrageous question went unanswered for the outer door opened with a squeak and a bleary-eyed footman appeared in the doorway, then did an about face and scurried away, leaving the door ajar. The three musicians looked at one another, seeing this as sign for them to depart yet reluctant to do so for their meager lodgings on the Left Bank. They hoped Evelyn's generosity would extend to allowing them to catch a few hours' sleep on the sofas and chairs in his study, a regular occurrence when they rehearsed for an upcoming performance.

But Evelyn wasn't paying attention. He was thoroughly bored with the incessant and mindless speculations regarding his cousin's amorous adventures, real or imagined, and he sipped from his champagne glass, blue-eyed gaze wandering to the row of undraped French windows with their view of the hôtel's large rectangular courtyard of manicured lawn, cobblestoned walks and trickling fountains. His thoughts were not on his cousin but on his cousin's beautiful young wife and how she must be dealing with the strain of an arranged marriage to a nobleman accused of breach of promise. At least Deborah had the good sense to remain in far away Bath.

She had not only defied her husband by remaining on the other side of the Channel, she had openly flaunted her total disregard for the Duke of Roxton's authority by turning away at her door the Duke's secretary and a six man escort sent to bring her to Paris. He smiled to himself at such audacity. No one ever challenged his uncle's authority, ever.

Evelyn yearned to see Deborah's smiling oval face again, with those candid brown eyes and wild mane of dark red hair. But why were her eyes so bright? Had she been crying? And surely he hadn't seen her in that particular velvet traveling cloak with its collar and cuffs trimmed in fox fur. And why was his valet, Philippe, hopping about on the balls of his feet babbling something about instant dismissal if his master was disturbed for any reason except the hôtel burning to the ground.

Philippe? Why was his valet intruding in one of his daydreams?

Evelyn must be more tired than he imagined. Drinking champagne on an empty stomach didn't help...

He put aside the glass and rubbed his eyes. Good God! She was still there. Deborah was standing in his apartment, in his very dining room and smiling at him while his valet continued to spew inanities at her. He glanced swiftly at his three dinner guests and they had risen as one and were bowing to the unexpected visitor.

Evelyn shot up off the padded chair, offsetting his wig and sprinkling powder down his high forehead. "Deborah?" he whispered with mouth-gaping awe, as if speaking to an apparition, and took a tentative step forward. "*Deborah.*"

"It's wonderful to see you again, Eve," she replied in English, a nod at the three bedraggled men who shuffled their feet and smiled sheepishly, not least because she had scooped up off the turned arm of a silk covered chair one of the Lefebvre pamphlets accidentally dropped by the consumptive musician on his way to the fireplace. "Eve... I need—I need *your* help."

The composer smiled sympathetically and kissed her forehead, gently removing the crushed pamphlet from her fist as he did so. He tossed the offending paper onto the crackling fire behind him. "Yes, *ma cherie*, I rather think that you do."

Ten

Evelyn was sitting at the breakfast table by the long windows with their view of the rectangular courtyard when Deb appeared from his bedchamber dressed in a pretty day gown of muslin, her hair in a single plait down her back. She was feeling very much better for a good night's sleep. He had insisted that she take his bed; he slept as best he could on the daybed in his dressing room. They had not exchanged more than half a dozen sentences the night before, leaving what was most important to be said for the morning.

Deb knew Evelyn's gaze never wavered from her profile as she sipped *café au lait*, but she pretended an interest in the cobblestone walk lined with chestnut trees and the team of gardeners working in the flowerbeds. She picked up a warm bread roll, relieved that she no longer felt nauseous at the prospect of eating with her maid one step behind holding a basin. And that had been on the good days when she was well enough to take a little fresh air in the back garden of her house in Bath. Then one day, after four months of morning sickness, and as Dr. Medlow had continually assured her on his frequent visits, the nausea had disappeared as instantly as it had begun.

She had so much to say and discuss with Evelyn that she did not know where to begin. That she had not seen the composer for three years made conversation all the more awkward. Particularly when he must know by now about her arranged marriage to his cousin. She wondered how much he knew and what he knew. Her marriage and the consequences of its consummation had consumed her every waking moment since that hateful day at Martin Ellicott's Queen Anne house, and were still so painfully raw she avoided talk of it altogether and asked after her nephew, whom she had missed dreadfully and who had been living with the Roxtons since their eldest son had orchestrated the mock elopement.

"Have you seen much of Jack?" she asked lightly then added in a rush, meeting Evelyn's unwavering gaze, "Is he well? Is he happy? Do they make him welcome? Does he ever ask after his aunt?"

"Yes, *ma cherie*. He is well and he is happy and yes, he is made very welcome by the Duke and Duchess. And Henri-Antoine likes him, which says a great deal about Jack, for my haughty young cousin doesn't like many people," Evelyn replied with a smile, reading the apprehension in her brown eyes. "And yes, he has asked after you on many occasions; particularly the question of your arrival. But of course he is a boy who wants to appear a man, so he does not reveal to anyone that he misses you terribly. The Duchess she sees this and does her best to make him comfortable."

"Her Grace is very good," Deb murmured with downcast eyes.

"Yes, my aunt is, as always, very good."

"My house—My house was very empty without Jack," Deb admitted quietly. "But an aunt with morning sickness is no company for a nine-year old boy... You say he has played for you? Tell me honestly your opinion of his playing. Does he live up to his aunt's high praise?"

Evelyn put up his brows at her open pronouncement of her condition but ignored it for the time being, saying evenly, "When he plays he reminds me of Otto."

Deb heard the note of sadness and put out her hand across the table. "Did I not tell you in my letters? There is the same natural grace in his style and he feels the music as I never can and—"

"Deb, dearest. He has his father's ability to be sure but not his passion," Evelyn told her seriously. "Jack enjoys playing for its own sake but he is first and foremost like other boys his age. And that is no bad thing."

Deb bit her lip. "I see. I've pushed him too hard."

"Not at all, *ma cherie*. I think you miss Otto; I do, very much. And when Jack plays it is as if Otto is with us again. Jack is his father's son and he has talent but you must permit him to decide if composing and playing music will be his way of life. One may have a love of music and the love of playing a musical instrument without making it their sole purpose for existence as Otto did. Look at me. I pretend to be a composer—"

"—but you are!"

Evelyn laughed. "I compose music but I am not the composer or even the great musician that Otto was. He lived for his music. He sacrificed his comforts and his wants, his good name and even his family, yes, even Rosa and Jack, came second to Otto's compositions. I, on the other hand, could never sacrifice my all for music." He held Deb's hand across the cluttered breakfast table. "To put it bluntly, *ma cherie*, I indulge my musical eccentricities because I have the wealth and family support to do so. My musical composition is seen by family and friends alike as a passing interest, to be indulged, not taken seriously." He shrugged and sat back. "So be it. Music is at least an escape from the mundanity of one's social position. Being related to a ducal house is a tiresome business: every move watched by a thousand pairs of eyes; most of us with little to do but parade about in fine silks from one social function to the next, with your social equals for the entertainment of your inferiors. And if you are unlucky enough to be an eldest son life is spent in limbo waiting to inherit title, estate and the seat in the House of Lords. I have escaped such an existence by immersing myself in music. Alston spent several years wandering Italy, Greece and the Ottoman Empire and thus he too managed for a time to avoid social suffocation. However, he can no longer do so, nor delay the inevitable. His father, the grand old Duke of Roxton, is ill. It is whispered he is dying from a complaint of the lung."

"Dying?" Deb repeated softly. "How dreadful..." She stood up, a hand to her aching lower back, and stared out of the window, down at the velvet green lawns where a huddle of lackeys were creating a commotion struggling to erect a striped marquee. "Do the physicians know how much time is left to him?"

"We have widely differing opinions from numerous physicians. The more morose say it is only a matter of months; those who wish to remain in their noble client's pay tell him confidently he has many more years of earthly pleasure; then there are those who see the sorrow in my aunt's lovely eyes and lie, predicting M. le Duc will live to see three score years and ten."

"Then I see why Lord Alston felt some urgency in getting me with child," Deb said bitterly.

Evelyn went to her, took hold of her hands and met her sad gaze squarely. "I do not excuse my cousin's conduct any more than you do, *ma cherie*. But perhaps I understand it a little better knowing the Duke, and the arrogant shadow he casts over his family and retainers. Tell me honestly: Do you love your husband?"

"I cannot answer that," she said in a stricken voice, her brown eyes meeting his steady blue-eyed gaze, "because I do not know to whom I am married."

Evelyn was more attuned to her confused feelings than she realized for his response startled her. "You may not know the Marquis of Alston, indeed your feelings for him must be quite repellent after such a deception, but what of the man you willingly eloped with and married, the man you know as Julian Hesham? What are your feelings for him?"

Deb stared at Evelyn through a blindness of tears, overcome with such sadness as her mind's eye flooded with memories of her honeymoon with the man she loved and had known only as Julian Hesham. The hard emotional shell she had cultivated and shown her brother cracked down its center and fell away.

"You are right," she answered quietly. "I do not know the Marquis of Alston at all, except to say he is detestable and arrogant and everything hateful and despised that is written in that disgusting pamphlet." She took the lace handkerchief he offered her and smiled a watery smile as she dabbed dry her eyes. "Eve, it's as if I married two men. One is very caring and easy-going and enjoys the simple pleasures of life. I care about that one deeply; I love him. The other one is this insufferably arrogant creature who was banished by his father for his unspeakable actions and who it is whispered is depraved beyond redemption. That one I hate."

"I sometimes wonder if he knows which one he is himself," Evelyn said on a sigh and at Deb's sudden intake of breath was quick to reassure her. "But no, I don't think him beyond saving. And rumor has become mingled with historical fact. My mother spoke once of a most shocking incident that occurred soon after the Duke and Duchess were married. A mad young nobleman, the Duke's natural son, attacked and tried to abduct the Duchess. She was with child, with Alston in fact, and came close to having her throat cut." Evelyn pressed Deb's hands and smiled ruefully. "When my cousin was seen to repeat, in a different way, the folly of this mad half-brother, there were those who were quick to magnify a hideous error of judgment of a wayward youth. History repeating itself, you might say."

"Then my brother did not lie... For Julian to attack his own mother... Eve, why?"

Evelyn took a deep breath. "You can blame my cousin's reckless and most shocking outburst on Robert Thesiger who knew very well the sad story of the mad young nobleman and used it to advantage—"

"Robert Thesiger?"

"Yes." Evelyn's smile was tight. "Robert was at Eton with Alston and I and he made a point of informing my cousin of their connection by blood; that the Duke was also his father, something of which Alston was unaware and which truly shocked him. He had no idea about his father's nefarious past, nor that such a debauched existence had produced rotten fruit. Suffice for me to say Robert used his connection by blood to sinister effect."

Deb's mind was awhirl with new knowledge. "But what could Robert Thesiger possibly say to make Julian condemn his own mother as a whore and a witch?"

Eve looked down at the lace ruffles covering his long hands. "It is not my place to say and what I have said is too much, *ma cherie*. You must ask Alston for the truth. Let me just add that Robert's motives have always been transparent. He is eaten up with bitter envy; envy that but for the Grace of God he would be heir to the Roxton Dukedom, not Alston. His mother, who had expectations of marrying the Duke and was rebuffed, taught her son from a young age to loathe the Duchess." He touched Deb's cheek. "What is important is that Alston can be forgiven his one act of youthful folly."

"I can readily forgive the disordered emotional *drunken* outbursts of a naïve and misguided sixteen year old boy," Deb said with a wry smile, "but the impetuous naivety of youth cannot explain away the actions of a grown man, one who is not only accused of breach of promise, but who went to great lengths to deceive his own wife about his identity and intentions!"

Evelyn grabbed Deb hard by the shoulders and looked into her eyes. "If there is one sure thing I know about my cousin it is that he would never offer Lisette Lefebvre, or any other female for that matter, marriage merely to get her into his bed! Believe me, Deborah, I know. *I know.* You are not to believe the inflammatory writings in a filthy pamphlet. They are putrid nothings, written to inflame a starving populace by uninformed hacks that don't know the real circumstances or motives behind the accusations against my cousin. Do you understand me?"

"I understand what you are saying, Eve," Deb answered levelly. "But how am I to believe you when Lefebvre's lawyers have instituted proceedings against my husband?" She pulled free and stepped back. "Eve, Lefebvre and my husband fought a duel. A man does not follow another over water and into a foreign land to cross swords, not unless he believes his daughter was grossly wronged and as a father he has the right to defend her honor."

Evelyn threw up a lace-ruffled wrist. "Of course Lefebvre believes his daughter was grossly wronged but—but there are always two sides to any imbroglio!"

"Oh? Don't tell me the girl ensnared Alston with her charms and he was powerless to resist her, because that is a very lame excuse and not one I am willing to entertain!"

"Alston is a stiff-necked bloody fool!" he blurted out savagely. "I warned him how it would be when he returned from exile. But no, he follows his own path and won't live by society's dictates! That's what has landed him at the center of this absurd scandal." He put an arm about Deb's shoulders, seeing her hurt and confusion and said in a much calmer tone, "Forgive me, *ma cherie.* Alston and I are the best of friends but we do not see eye to eye on this matter." He led her through to the blue and white gilded salon, saying with a smile, "You and I, we must help him be more Julian Hesham and less the Marquis of Alston, yes?"

Deb wished in her heart of hearts for nothing truer. But Evelyn's confidences were far from reassuring. After all, he had made no excuses for the Marquis's deceiving her into consummating their marriage, nor had he adequately explained the sordid business with Lisette Lefebvre. It was all very well for Evelyn to assure her his cousin had not seduced the girl with the promise of marriage, but where was the proof? And until she had the same assurances from her husband she could not believe Evelyn out of hand.

"Seeing you, knowing your mind, has decided me, *ma cherie*," Evelyn announced as he tucked his viola under his square chin. He handed Deb a sheaf of musical notations and then began to play a pretty piece he had composed. "Follow the notations. Give me your opinion of this piece of froth I've written for Dominique. It is a betrothal gift I will play for her at tomorrow afternoon's concert in the Tuileries gardens. Jack has consented to be part of my small string ensemble. Having the boy will add a certain tender piquancy to the occasion, don't you think?"

Deb indulged his whim and reclined on the striped silk chaise longue by the clavichord with the sheets of musical composition while Evelyn pranced about the room in his high-heeled shoes, seemingly lost in his playing, but acting the clown for her benefit, anything to take her mind off her present troubles. She couldn't help a giggle at such antics.

"It is a pretty piece," she admitted with a laugh as the composer pirouetted in front of her, the silk skirts of his waistcoat flaring out around him. "But how can you expect me to concentrate on your music when you talk of betrothal pieces, a girl called Dominique, and Jack performing with you at the Tuileries all in the same breath? Is he truly playing in your ensemble?"

Evelyn finished playing his composition with a flourish. "Yes, *ma cherie*. And his aunt must be there to applaud his efforts, and mine in persuading the boy to perform before an audience. His talent must not remain in a cupboard, and so I told him."

Deb's brown eyes lit up and she clapped her hands. "I knew you would see my Jack's talent!" She cocked her head to one side, adding quizzically, "And Dominique?"

Evelyn put aside the viola and came back to the chaise longue.

"Ah, Dominique... I will tell you a secret, *ma cherie*. I am about to incur the wrath of the Duke and my parents. My mother will naturally take to her bed, declaring never to rise again from the shame I inflict on her and my illustrious ancestors. But I beg you to wish me happy. I am about to elope!"

"Elope? Elope with this Dominique? But, Eve, you've never once mentioned this girl in any of your letters. Who is she? Why must you elope? Why won't your parents approve of her?" Deb's arched brows contracted sharply when Evelyn smiled ruefully. "Of course I wish you happy but... Are you truly happy, Eve?"

He flicked out the embroidered skirts of his Italian waistcoat and sat on the striped silk footstool beside the chaise longue. "Ha! You were ever the perceptive one. Yes, I am *determined* to be happy."

"But you do not love her?" Deb said gently and felt his fingers convulse in hers, which said more than his words of explanation thus far.

"It is not a *grande passion*. But perhaps it is for the best," he confessed with a smile of resignation. "I have a distracted and obsessed musician's disposition and she, for all her youth, has a firm grasp on reality: Unable to catch the prize, she magnanimously settled for a dilution in the noble blood and a connection by marriage."

Deb touched his close-shaven cheek with the back of her hand. "Oh, Eve, but if she is marrying you merely because of your noble connections, why elope with her?"

He kissed her hand. "*Ma cherie*, I assure you, the sooner I am married the sooner this hideous entanglement we all find ourselves in will be resolved and we can return to a semblance of normality. Although, I fear the Duke will send me into exile, if only to keep Alston's fingers from choking the life out of me. Poor Maman, she will not recover from the shame of having Dominique for a daughter-in-law."

"You've not told me more than her name."

"Trust me. Soon all will reveal itself. For now she is simply Dominique. I was her pianoforte teacher."

"Teacher? When did the son of a viscount, nephew of a duke, ever need to descend to earning a living from his talent?"

Evelyn's blue eyes were alight with mischief and he grinned. "Didn't Otto ever tell you that passing one's self off as a musical genius who must needs earn his keep as a teacher makes for easy entrée into the best houses, and the best houses have the prettiest daughters!"

170

Deb playfully pinched his cleft chin. "You are execrable. What will my husband think—"

"If you cared anything for my opinion, Madam wife, you'd have thought twice about sleeping in my cousin's bed!"

~⟩——⟨~

An hour earlier Joseph had been kicking his heels at the Roxton stables, waiting for the Marquis of Alston's return from Versailles. He did not have to loiter long when a mud-spattered carriage and four turned into the courtyard, sending an army of lackeys into a frenzy of activity, and came to a halt close to where Joseph was propped on a low, ivy covered stone wall, smoking a Turkish cheroot.

The first noble to alight from the carriage was Alston. He lingered on the portable steps two liveried footmen had rushed to place on the cobbles under the carriage door and spoke to its occupants. From the noise and laughter, Joseph reckoned there were at least half a dozen aristocrats deep within the velvet-upholstered interior. A pretty painted female, her powdered hair swept up in a confection of dyed plumes, satin ribbons and strings of pearls managed to stick her head and arm out of the curtained window and demanded Alston kiss her fingertips. He did so with a flourish and she disappeared inside with a giggle to be replaced by another female with an equally complicated and absurd headdress. The Marquis was required to kiss her plump wrist, just above the string of pearls. He obediently complied and then descended the steps, three bewigged noblemen emerging from the dark interior to follow him onto the cobbles. That the carriage door remained wide told Joseph that the Marquis's friends were not staying.

"Perhaps another time, Bertrand. Give my regards to Mme D'Aprano, and thank her for the invitation."

"You can't refuse Madame's invitation so brutally, Julian! It is most unfair of you. You must come to Chaillot for a few days. It is expected, no?" asked the young Vicomte de Chaillot, looking to his two companions for support. "Henriette and Marguerite,

171

they are expecting you. Their disappointment, it will be unbearable." He indicated the carriage window. "You saw just now how they miss you already."

"Alas, Sebastian, your dear sisters must be denied my company upon this occasion."

The Vicomte frowned. "This absurd trial, it is bothering you more than it should, my friend."

"Sebastian he is right in this," the Vicomte's younger brother, Bertrand agreed. "This stinking fishmonger does not bear a moment of your thoughts. He is absurd. This business, it is absurd. Ugh! I do not know why you do not turn your back on it all. Then it is done with. Touché!"

"That you do not turn your back, that is what feeds the rumors. But what of that, I say? It is not the truth that is important. It is that this tax-collector had the effrontery—"

"*Excusez-moi*, Frederic," interrupted the Marquis with an embarrassed half-smile, turning to the third nobleman, one Chevalier du Charmond, "I beg to differ. The truth it is very important to me."

"M. le Duc your father he will arrange everything, I am certain of it," the Vicomte put in hurriedly, hoping to avoid offending his English friend. "This middle-class *putain* who opened her legs to you and her ridiculous father they will be paid off. Then all will return to normality."

"Yes! Yes. Sebastian, he is in the right," Bertrand nodded, offering the others snuff. "All Farmers-General, they are open to bribery. Is that not how they gathered up their great wealth in the first place? Is it not criminal that they should be so wealthy?"

"M'sieur, as I am innocent of the charge I do not see the need to resort to bribery," Julian said flatly, ignoring the commotion in the carriage. "And were I to do so, what would that say about my innocence?"

The three noblemen pondered this as if the idea was new to them, the Chevalier adding good-naturedly after he had snorted a goodly quantity of snuff up one fine nostril, "But... Alston! That is being too stiff-necked about a trifle of a thing. This bribery of which you speak, it is a commonplace thing. It is done at the highest levels. It is expedient, no?"

There were calls from within the carriage for the noblemen

to hurry along or they would be late for the recital. Henriette had to change her gown and Marguerite her hair needed more powder. Why were their brothers so unthinking? Bertrand? Sebastian? *Frederic?* The three noblemen exchanged comments and gestures of hopelessness and forgiveness about the excessive needs of sisters, bowed to their friend with a flourish and piled back inside the carriage to be off.

Julian waved them away with a smile. The Vicomte de Chaillot calling out from the window that he and his brothers would next see their friend when they came to collect him for the Opera. But when he set off across the courtyard Joseph saw that the nobleman's face was devoid of laughter. He pulled at his cravat as if eager to be rid of it and walked as fast as he could in red high-heeled court shoes that were meant for mincing about not striding at pace.

He had not gone far when he was bluntly commanded to wait up. The shock of being so rudely addressed caused him to turn about with a thunderous expression that scattered the stable hands to all corners of the stable yard.

Joseph stood his ground and waited for the Marquis to come to him. Now was not the time to show nervousness. He had genuine concerns about Deb to raise with his lordship, and it was for her that he must remain resolute. Yet, when Alston came over to him, a liveried flunky in pursuit, Joseph quickly stubbed out the cheroot under the toe of his boot and was momentarily lost for words under the lofty, angry, yet nonplussed gaze of a pair of emerald green eyes.

"Joseph? Why are you in Paris? I thought you had returned to England?"

"I've been to Bath and back, my lord," Joseph answered levelly and in English, a glance at the steward who had come part-way across the cobbles in anticipation of Joseph receiving a whipping for his insolence. "I went to see Miss Deb for myself."

Alston flinched and, sensing the steward at his back, turned on the astonished lackey, who couldn't believe his master was conversing socially with this inferior oaf, and growled at him to go away. He turned to Joseph with a scowl. "Favored family retainer you may be," he enunciated in English, "but you will

173

address my wife as is her due. Is that understood?"

"Aye," Joseph answered demurely. "Beggin' your lordship's pardon, but it's her health and happiness which concerns me, not her elevation."

Julian took a step forward. "Damn your impertinence—"

"'cause I care about her, my lord!" Joseph argued, taking a nervous step away. "She's never been ill a day in her life and when I'm told she's taken to her bed and is so weak she can't eat, that worries me. That ain't like her. So I decides I have to see her for myself. I don't care to take the word of a saw-bones and leave it at that! Beggin' your lordship's pardon, but... neither should you."

"I cannot leave Paris at this time," Alston muttered, a heightened color in his cheeks. "The trial..."

"Well I can and I did!"

"And is my wife as ill as Medlow makes out?"

Joseph heard the note of sneering disbelief. "It ain't like her to feign illness, my lord. And Medlow ain't the sort of man who exaggerates. And he ain't one of them quacks who panders to a man's imaginary ills."

"So satisfy my curiosity: What illness does her ladyship suffer that has made it impossible for her to join me?"

"Medlow wouldn't say. Said it was against his hypocritic oath."

"Hippocratic oath," Alston corrected. "Very convenient. Now you will excuse me. I need to get out of these Court clothes." He turned his broad back and strode toward the imposing archway that proclaimed the entrance to the inner courtyard and the main building of the hôtel where only soft-footed household livered servants were permitted.

"I do know what's kept her bed ridden, my lord!" Joseph announced, scrambling across the cobbles to keep up with the big man's strides, never mind he was in heels. When the Marquis did not stop, he added, "And I know where she is!"

That stopped Julian in his tracks. He turned from the stairwell. "So tell me: What has kept her ladyship bed ridden?"

Joseph swallowed under the mutinous gaze. "I don't think it's my place to tell you, my lord."

"For the love of God! Out with it or leave me in peace!"

"I know Deb would prefer to tell you herself."

Julian looked out across the inner courtyard and then down at his large feet before meeting the old retainer's gaze openly. "Joseph, believe me when I tell you that had it been in my power to do so, I would gladly have gone to Bath to fetch her ladyship myself. But I cannot leave France. Lefebvre's lawyers have seen to that."

Joseph nodded. "I thought that was how it was, so when she was well enough to travel I went and fetched her for you."

Julian grabbed his elbow. "She's here? Here in Paris? Tell me. Where?"

Joseph pointed to the clouds. The words were hardly out of his mouth before the Marquis turned on a heel and took the stairs two at a time.

"Upstairs. M'sieur Ffolkes' apartment."

The Marquis entered his cousin's apartment on a soft scratch and made his way toward the melodic sound of the viola, ignoring the goggle-eyed valet who hopped about on the balls of his feet screeching in a whisper that there was no female in his master's apartment and if there was she was a lady, despite owning a pistol which she kept in a holster sewn into her boot. He Philippe had seen it while tidying the bedchamber, where the lady had most definitely *not* slept and not had a bath. So would his lordship kindly leave before the young lady splattered their brains across the paneled wall.

The valet then retreated, a quick glance into the salon in time to see his master kiss the beautiful young lady's fingers and say something that made her laugh. She playfully pinched his chin in response. Philippe glanced swiftly up at the dark look on the impassive handsome face of the Marquis and ran back through the rooms of the apartment and down the servant stairs as fast as his fat little legs would take him. He wasn't going to be the one to wipe the blood off the walls!

The Marquis stopped in mid stride just inside the door. Reclining on a chaise longue with her stockinged toes to the warmth of the fire was his bride. She was more beautiful than his remembrance of her; with liquid brown eyes full of laughter, luminescent skin, and a thick braid of hair that he knew shone wine red in the sun;

hair he had once caressed and brushed and liked best when it cascaded freely to her thighs. She also glowed with vitality.

In fact, she was such the epitome of bountiful good health that his happiness at seeing her turned to anger, at being duped by the physician Medlow's written assurances that his wife was too ill to travel; that he had worried himself needlessly about her welfare; that he had spent every night wanting her, needing the touch and the warmth of her, and seeking solace in excessive exercise to take away the constant ache of not having her, and all the while she was feigning illness to bide her time so that her lawyers could find her an escape from their marriage.

Annulment be damned!

He had been without her for twelve long weeks. They had been apart longer than they had shared a marriage bed and it felt like a lifetime.

And so his words to her were cold and mean, fuelled by jealousy and thoroughly unwarranted and served to startle apart the couple by the fire. Evelyn scrambled to his high heels and Deborah sat up, tucking her stockinged feet under the froth of her pretty muslin petticoats, and in so doing scattered the sheets of musical composition across the Turkey rug.

The Marquis ignored his cousin, a smoldering eye on his furiously blushing bride. "Well, Lady Bountiful, how gratifying to find you in good health. I can now look forward to an immediate resumption of my conjugal rights." He glanced at his cousin. "Of course I need hardly remind you that your paramount wifely duty is to remain chaste until you've given me a son. I want no by-blows, however closely related." And with that blunt speech he turned on a heel and was across the room before Deborah's retort made him return to the chaise longue. "What—did—you—say?" he said in a voice that was barely above a whisper, hoping his hearing had not deceived him.

The Marquis had been in the room a full thirty seconds before it registered with Deb that the nobleman in Court dress was her husband. His face was powdered and patched, his shoes had stacked red heels with enormous diamond encrusted shoe buckles and his black unruly curls were plastered to his scalp with pomade and wax. It was only his deep mellow voice that alerted her to the fact that somewhere beneath all that grease paint and gold thread was Julian Hesham, the man she had fallen in love with. But as he appeared first and foremost the epitome of a French courtier, it was easy for Deborah to appear just as cold and unsentimental as he.

Her chin had tilted up in defiance with his first sneering words, and she clasped her hands behind her back, effectively bunching up the yards of light muslin so that her petticoats were taut across her stomach, exposing the growing roundness of her belly and leaving him no doubt she was heavily pregnant.

"I assure you, my lord, I pray daily to be delivered of a son," she repeated as he came back to stand before her, adding with an icy calm she did not in the least feel, "Because *nothing* will induce me to share your bed again!"

For what seemed an eternity of minutes the Marquis stared at her and such was the change in his expression, the softness that came over his handsome features, that for one heart-stopping moment he was again Julian Hesham. His gaze finally met hers as he gingerly put out a hand but Deb released the bunched up yards of muslin and quickly stepped back out of his reach.

"So that's why you could not come to Paris; why you were ill?" he asked in a voice filled with wonderment, and when she nodded without looking at him added gently, "When—when did you know?"

"On our return from Cumbria."

"Back then? How far along is the babe?"

She bit her lip and focused on his intricately tied lace cravat with its single large diamond headed pin. "Five and a half months."

"*Five and a half months?*" he repeated in the same tone of disbelief. He smiled broadly. "Then you conceived almost from our first night together...?"

Deb hesitated, confused. This nobleman certainly appeared the arrogant Marquis of Alston, but the deep, gentle tenor of his voice was pure Julian Hesham. She wondered which man she should answer. But when she looked up and saw that grin, when she caught movement out of the corner of her eye and realized Evelyn, who had stooped to pick up the sheets of musical notation from the Turkey rug, was sharing in his cousin's delight, she blanched white with embarrassment that the Marquis was openly discussing intimate details that were the private preserve of husband and wife.

"Impregnating a bride on first mount must be a feat worth bragging about to your male compatriots. Eve certainly shares in your conceit. What a shame your lordship wasted two tiresome months in Cumbria. Had I realized my condition earlier, you could've returned to France and your whoring—"

"I beg your pardon?"

Julian looked so shocked and affronted that Deb almost burst into incredulous tears that he could stand there pretending moral outrage. Instead she turned away and fell into Evelyn's embrace, burying her face in his silk waistcoat on a shattering sob.

"Deborah, *ma cherie*," he murmured soothingly on a heavy sigh and looked imploring to his cousin. "Julian, you must understand—her condition…"

"I understand all too well, Cousin," Julian enunciated bitterly, a significant look at the composer's hand that stroked his wife's back. He turned on a heel, saying at the door before he strode from the room, "When you've done *comforting* my pregnant bride, be so good as to send her to the library. The Duke will be home on the hour."

Evelyn called him back but Julian strode on not looking left or right until he reached the stairwell that led up to his spacious apartment on the second floor. Here he stopped and hesitated to ascend the stairs. It was as if all the emotional fight suddenly drained from him. He slumped back against the wall and slowly slid down the paneling to the bottom step where he covered his face with his hands.

Eleven

$\mathcal{S}$ir Gerald Cavendish stumbled upon the Marquis ten minutes later and made a bumbling speech full of verbose compliments and inane observations about the weather because he was nervous at having a private word with his noble brother-in-law. But what made his delivery even more blundering was the fact he had not expected to find his lordship slumped on the floor with his head bowed, particularly when he was dressed in gold thread and diamonds.

He just didn't understand it and wondered if the Marquis was drunk, or having an attack of some kind, because the nobleman's face was flushed and his eyes were red and glassy, as if he'd been sobbing like a girl. It certainly wasn't the sort of behavior Sir Gerald deemed usual for the son of a Duke.

With a heavy sigh of resignation Julian invited his wife's brother into his sitting room where Frew kept a good fire burning. The valet momentarily emerged from the closet off the bedchamber but as his master appeared distracted and was not alone he retreated, leaving the connecting door ajar and affording Sir Gerald a glimpse within his lordship's inner sanctum. He saw the valet quietly going about his duties; with him were two lackeys, one carried a pail of steaming scented water that was poured into an enormous hipbath central to the room, the other draped a richly embroidered banyan of red silk over an ornately carved arm of a gilded chair.

That these preparations for the nobleman's bath continued unabated made Sir Gerald realize how ill judged was the timing of his visit. He felt most unwelcome and this feeling deepened into acute discomfort knowing the Marquis was newly returned from Versailles and obviously wished to change out of full Court dress. When Julian silently stood his ground by the fireplace and did not offer Sir Gerald to sit on any of the chairs in the room, but merely took snuff from a gold and enamel snuffbox, Sir Gerald coughed to clear the nervousness from his throat.

"I must tell you how grateful I am to your esteemed parents and to you, my lord, for permitting my nephew the honor of spending time in the company of Lord Henri-Antoine." Sir Gerald ended this rehearsed speech with a smile but the Marquis remained unmoved. It was as if he stared straight through him, with emerald-green eyes so piercingly clear that they were unnerving. Sir Gerald's palms began to sweat. "No one was more surprised than I to learn Jack had such an esteemed school friend. He has always been an impetuous youth, somewhat wayward at times, and often given to speaking his mind—"

"A circumstance of residing with his aunt perhaps?"

"Yes. Yes. Not the most ideal of circumstances for my nephew."

"Yet, the only option open to him?"

"Um—er—Well, I am confident that time spent in the elevated company of your brother, who is a most worthy young nobleman, will be most beneficial to my nephew's uneven temperament."

"Are you? I'm hoping Jack will teach Harry a thing or two."

"Oh, no, no, my lord," Sir Gerald assured him with a shake of his powdered wig. "I am hopeful Jack's unpleasant over-exuberance will be subdued while under this exulted roof. And in Lord Henri-Antoine's superior companionship his manners can't help but improve. My nephew has had a rather provincial upbringing," he apologized, showing his distaste. "I cannot bring myself to say more for fear of offending your lordship. If you knew the circumstances your lordship could only agree with me."

"I do not agree with you."

Sir Gerald blinked. "I beg your lordship's pardon?"

"I am delighted Jack has befriended my brother. His influence has considerably improved Harry's somber outlook on life. In fact, their divergent personalities compliment one another very well."

"Do—do they indeed?" Sir Gerald stuttered with incomprehension.

"Your nephew is a fine young man."

"He is? Well, yes, I suppose he must be. Yes, I'm sure he is!"

"A credit to his aunt, who has had the rearing of him since he was—five? Yes, five years old. But I'm sure you aren't keeping me from my bath for the express purpose of discussing the merits of your esteemed nephew."

"I—I—No! No, indeed, my lord! No. I besought this interview to make it known to you that Lady Mary—Lady Mary and myself—we—you—have our unconditional support regarding this—um—unpleasant and most tiresome business. To think it has gone as far as the publication of slanderous pamphlets shows what opportunistic little swine are these French tax collectors. That they dare think they can bring down a member of the nobility defies the imagination," Sir Gerald blustered on, a glance up at the Marquis whose face remained infuriatingly inscrutable. "This tax-collector deserves to be locked up! His daughter put in the stocks for her wanton and outrageous behavior. Of course, those of us who know you—"

"But you do not know me."

"—would never seriously entertain the notion of the Marquis of Alston dangling after a mere tax collector's daughter," Sir Gerald concluded with a snort of bombastic self-consequence. "And as I told my sister, as the Marchioness of Alston she is obliged to ignore such inconsequential chatter, whether there be truth in it or not."

"Told your sister?" Julian repeated and so quietly Sir Gerald wondered if he had spoken at all and continued on as if he had not, oblivious to the cold hard light that dulled the normally friendly and expressive green eyes.

"Before Lady Mary and I embarked on the voyage to Paris, I made a point of calling on Deborah in Bath."

"And how did you find my wife upon that visit?"

Sir Gerald blinked again. "Find her, my lord?"

The Marquis came a little closer. "Her health. Her person. How did she appear to you?"

"To tell you a truth, my lord, she was not keen to see me. She sent down some lame excuse with her maid about being too ill," Sir Gerald said confidentially. "But as I know she has not been ill a day in her life I thought the maid's pronouncement that my sister was too weak and too ill to see anyone save her quack doctor a bit rich to swallow and my persistence finally paid off. But of course Deborah will play her tricks on her brother and when I was shown up to her boudoir I found her lying upon the chaise under a coverlet with a basin at the ready!" He forced a laugh but when the Marquis did not join in he quickly banished the smile and added gravely, "Upon reflection, I must own that Deborah did look quite green and she listened to my advice without one word of dissent, which is most unlike her."

"Advice?"

"I made it clear to her that it was absurd to make more of a situation than was merited," Sir Gerald stated confidently. "That when a nobleman seeks the favors of a French whore it should be of no consequence, in truth a mere nothingness, to a nobleman's wife. I stressed to Deborah that it was beneath her dignity to even acknowledge the existence of such females. I told her it was time she stopped her pretense of outrage by remaining in Bath, and that feigning illness was merely delaying the inevitable. I let it be known that she could not expect a grain of sympathy or support from me and that it was her duty to be here in Paris at your side." He smiled with satisfaction. "And I am most happy to report that Deborah took my advice for she arrived in Paris only last night."

"You miserable worm," Julian muttered, surveying his wife's pompous prig of a brother with such an ugly pull to his mouth that he was the image of his ancient parent. "You have the bare-faced audacity to tell me you took it upon yourself to lecture Deborah on her duty as my wife and that you spoke to her about a piece of trumped-up filth you know not the first thing about?"

"My lord? It was not my intention to offend you," Sir Gerald apologized, completely misreading the direction of the Marquis's anger. "Indeed, if you only knew to what lengths I have gone on your behalf to support you in this matter."

"Your sister is no longer your concern. She is mine. Do you understand? Stay away from her!" With that Julian turned and strode through to the dressing room. The inviting sweet smell of the heated water caused him to breathe in deeply as he removed the diamond headed pin from the folds of his lace cravat, then tug restlessly at the intricate knot. "Frew? Frew!"

The valet came scurrying from one of the inner rooms carrying a pair of new high-heeled shoes just sent from the shoemaker. His master's black mood did not surprise him. It was Frew's considered opinion that the Marquis's frequent black moods and restless nights could be blamed on the strained relations with his bride and that the sooner the couple resolved their differences and once again shared the marriage bed the sooner life could return to placid normality. But Frew kept his thoughts to himself and showed his master a perfectly neutral expression.

Julian fixed his scowl on the high heels and pulled a face.

"For the ball this evening, my lord," the valet explained.

"Send those ridiculous affectations back where they came from!" Julian ordered and kicked off the high heels he was wearing. He tugged again at the tightly bound cravat as if it was choking him. "Get me a shoe fit for an *Englishman's* foot, not some effeminate steepled creation only a midget should wear!"

"An Englishman's shoe," repeated Frew. "Very good, my lord."

"In fact, toss out any shoe with a heel higher than the width of my thumb."

"No higher than your thumb. Very wise, my lord."

The Marquis strode over to the cluttered dressing table and sat down in his stockinged feet. "And, Frew, I won't be wearing powder this evening."

"No powder, my lord?" said the valet in accents of horrified outrage at the thought of such a social solecism. "But the ball..."

"What of it? I've had enough of this wretched grease and powder itching my scalp! No more powder! *Ever.*"

"No more powder—*ever?*"

Julian looked up sharply. "For God's sake, Charles, are you a parrot?"

"No, my lord. Not a parrot," Frew murmured, turned to scurry away and came face to face with Sir Gerald standing as a statue by the hipbath. If the valet was reeling from his master's orders to banish the powder cone from the dressing room, he was goggle-eyed to discover a trespasser in this inner sanctum. But not as goggle-eyed as the time he had walked in on the Marquis sharing his bath with his bride. Since accompanying his master on his bridal trip to Cumbria, Frew determined that nothing or no one could ever again ruffle his valet's feathers. So he took Sir Gerald's presence in his stride, bowed to him and departed, leaving the round faced gentleman to face the Marquis's wrath alone.

Anger made Julian speechless. He was incredulous that Sir Gerald had the stupidity to continue the discussion and worse, the social ineptitude to follow him into the inner sanctum of his dressing room. Sir Gerald took the silence as permission to speak; such was his overwhelming panic and selfish concern.

"My lord, I must tell you that no amount of cajolery on my part has persuaded Deborah to change her mind from a course of action that will be the ruin of her family name!" Sir Gerald declared on a nervous snort, feeling inexplicably hot under the Marquis's steady gaze. "It will shock you to learn that she had the effrontery to ask for my assistance in seeking an annulment to your marriage!" When this dramatic pronouncement was met with icy silence he added, "When she expressed this wish I was as revolted into silence as you are now."

"Liar," Julian muttered, taking a step forward. "You put the idea of annulment into her head."

"No, my lord! It was my lawyers! My lawyers advised that there was no other way out of an arranged marriage," Sir Gerald said in a thin voice, backing across the deep rug as Julian continued to come at him. "I had no idea, no idea whatsoever, of the existence of the Act of '42 until told by my lawyers. You must believe me, my lord!" He stumbled over the side of a wingchair and scrambled to pick himself up, adjusted his lopsided wig and immediately tripped over the carpet as he was backed against the door. "Deborah will attempt to use the Act to persuade a judge to grant her an annulment. That is why I came to warn you; to assure you of my undivided support. I warned Deborah that there is not a judge in the kingdom who would go up against your family to grant her an annulment."

"You despicable piece of filth," Julian seethed in white-lipped fury and gripped Sir Gerald by the narrow lapels of his velvet frockcoat. "God knows what unnecessary distress you've caused

her with your pompous self-important lecturing and interference!"
He let him go with a shove and opened the door that led onto the
passageway, saying flatly, "Tomorrow you will return, not to
London, but to your estate, and stay there."

Sir Gerald's eyes widened in disbelief as he stepped out into the
servant passageway, little realizing he had been relegated to lackey
status. There came a distant rumble like thunder from somewhere
further along the warren of narrow corridors. Far off a bell began
tolling. Sir Gerald recognized that distant rumble; it wasn't thunder
but the scampering of a hundred soft-footed servants belonging to
the Duke's household. The tolling bell signaled that the Duke's
carriage and entourage had turned in through the black and gold
gates of the Hôtel Roxton.

Sir Gerald blinked, distraction with the household goings-on
evaporating as he realized the enormity of the Marquis's order.
"Tomorrow, my lord? To my estate? I am to be *banished*?"

"I never want to see your lily-livered face again. Frew? Frew!"
Julian called out as he slammed the door on Sir Gerald and so
hard that a small watercolor of Constantinople in a large ornate
gold frame jumped off the wall and crashed to the parquetry.

A blank-faced footman in livery escorted Deborah to a large
anteroom and politely requested she remain until summonsed to
enter the library. She felt wretched and shivered with nerves.
Although she had rehearsed what she intended to say to the
Duke and Duchess over and over while confined to her bed in
Bath, she dreaded forgetting her carefully crafted speech now she
was to come face to face with her husband's parents. She kept
telling herself that she held the trump card; that whatever they
said or threatened her with, news of her pregnancy was surely so
momentous that they had to listen to her demands and ultimately
agree to her request for a formal separation from their son. His
behavior in Evelyn's apartment merely confirmed that he cared
nothing for her personally, only for what she could give him. So
be it, but his dearest wish would come at a price.

As she paced the polished floorboards she caught sight of her reflection in an ornate gilded looking-glass over an empty fireplace and noted with a frown that her hair, despite time spent arranging it herself, appeared to be in an imminent state of unraveling down her back. She hastily rearranged a number of pearl-headed pins before turning her attention to the sit of the square neckline of a new velvet bodice trimmed with tiny bows that was already too tight across her breasts. She really should have remained in the sacque back muslin gown she'd changed into in Evelyn's apartment, but perhaps it wouldn't do to be too comfortable in the presence of the Duke and Duchess; after all she needed to keep her wits about her.

Such was her nervous preoccupation with looking presentable that when the library doors opened and a footman appeared to quietly usher her within, it was the servant's reflection at her shoulder that caused Deb to jump away from the looking glass. She went at his bidding, her slippered feet taking a moment to respond, hands clasped tightly in front of her.

The long book lined room with its heavy velvet drapes and gilded furniture, blazed with light despite it being the middle of the day. Every sconce held lighted candles and as the footman took her deeper into the room Deb peered nervously about at the three walls covered from parquetry flooring to painted ceiling with bookshelves crammed with leather bound volumes. She passed by a wide heavy mahogany desk and glanced at its surface where several opened picture books displayed maps and colored sketches of exotic lands. In the large ornate fireplace central to the room an inviting fire blazed. On the mantelshelf were propped gilt edged cards of invitation and pride of place over this carved mahogany mantel was a family portrait of the Duke and Duchess with their two sons and four faithful hounds. It was a recent portrait for Lord Henri appeared close to his nine years of age, yet the Duchess was painted as a young woman, closer in age to her eldest son and that could not be. Deb supposed the artist to be a flatterer for the Duchess was surely closer in age to the Duke?

Two wing chairs, a deep cushioned sofa and a large tapestry-covered ottoman were arranged on an Aubusson carpet near the warmth of the fireplace. On the ottoman was an ancient backgammon board with its ivory pieces still in play, a small leather bound volume with a silk riband between two pages to hold a place and several opened letters tucked in under a corner of the backgammon board. Nervousness gave way to curiosity as Deb took in this quaint domestic scene at odds with the surrounding masculine magnificence of the library, and it was only with the swish of stiff silk petticoats from the sofa that she realized that the footman and she were not alone in the library.

In fact the servant had formally announced her and departed before Deb came to her senses and dropped into a respectful curtsey to the two persons who had risen as one from the sofa. She felt a hand on her elbow as she straightened and a perfumed kiss lightly brushed one cheek and then the other while words of welcome were uttered in French by a pleasing feminine voice. Deb caught the flash and sparkle of diamonds and emeralds about a slender white throat before space was put between her and the exquisitely embroidered silk-hooped petticoats of Antonia, Duchess of Roxton.

A masculine drawling voice offered her the wingchair opposite the sofa and when she declined to sit the Duke and Duchess remained standing. There was a moment of awkward silence that brought color and heat up into Deb's throat and her gaze remained firmly lowered to the carpet. It was only when she reluctantly sat where requested that her illustrious hosts did likewise.

"Under the—er—circumstances, I won't insult your intelligence with inane words of welcome into the family fold," drawled the Duke and took snuff. "You have come to us in your own good time so perhaps you would do the Duchess and I the courtesy of knowing how we may be of service?"

Deb's gaze flashed up angrily at the Duke's face. He was regarding her with a thin smile of sympathetic insolence and yet his dark eyes held a spark of mischief, as if he was enjoying her discomfort. He looked just as Deb pictured him from her sleepy, late night remembering: a shock of snowy white hair, coal black eyes, and a long face etched with the deep lines of dissipation. It was impossible to guess his age, only that he was ancient. She had expected him to be taller, but perhaps that was because she had been only twelve years old, and all grown men were tall to a child. But he was frailer and it was as if breathing was an effort for him now. She looked away, lest she appear bad mannered and more importantly, lost her train of thought.

"I sincerely hope you may be of service to me, M. le Duc," she answered with a slight clearing of the throat, then continued forthrightly. "I am in this predicament through no fault of my own. My marriage to your son was for your political and dynastic preservation, and although such cold hearted reasons for marriage are commonplace amongst the nobility, it is not the sort of marriage I had envisioned for myself."

The Duchess leaned forward, hands clasped in the lap of her billowing petticoats. *"Ma belle-fille,* what kind of marriage did you have in mind?" she asked gently.

Deborah did not raise her gaze above the Duchess's slender bare arms where, encircled about both wrists, were half a dozen sparkling diamond and gold bracelets. "Mme la Duchesse, it is very difficult to explain to someone who cannot possibly under-stand that I find the idea and practice of arranged marriages abhorrent. Forgive me if my blunt speech offends you for that is not my intention, but I had hoped to marry for reasons that would appear foolhardy and incomprehensible to you."

"You hoped to marry for love, *ma petite.*"

It was not a question and the sadness in the soft pleasant voice made Deb swallow and hard clench her hands in her lap. *I must remain strong,* she told herself, *emotion must not get the better of me.*

Yet her conviction could not stop her curiosity and she stole a glance at the face that owned such a sweet, sad voice. Her shock was evident in the way she could not help staring openly until the Duchess smiled at her kindly. Only then did Deb blink and quickly avert her gaze. This noblewoman could not possibly be the Marquis of Alston's mother! She was far too young. Yet, Julian had those same emerald-green eyes. Deb had thought the Duchess beautiful, the family portrait over the fireplace was testament to that, but in the flesh the word beautiful seemed a rather inadequate and inane description for this elfin creature. The Duchess of Roxton was so breathtakingly beautiful she was dazzling. And even more startling, if that was possible, she had to be closer in age to her son than she ever would be to the Duke.

She must have been a child bride, reasoned Deb, and was revolted by the thought of her as a beautiful young girl forced into an arranged marriage with a lecherous rake; resigning herself to a life of titled privilege as wife and devoted mother and suffering in silence her husband's excesses and infidelities. No doubt the Duke expected the same of her. How wrong he was!

"I trust you are recovered from the illness that kept you bedridden and a—er—prisoner in your own home for an astonishing twelve weeks?" enquired the Duke with that hint of insolent disbelief Deb found annoying. It served to shatter her mental musings and further inflame her anger.

"Illness or not, M. le Duc, I was a prisoner in my own home until such time as I agreed to come to Paris," Deb replied in a steady voice. "The only visitors I was permitted were my brother and M'sieur Ellicott. The latter, no doubt, sent to confirm that I was indeed as ill as reported."

The Duke inclined his white head, saying with a smirk, "Sir Gerald's visit was a regrettable oversight. As for Martin, I—er—presumed you would not object to his company. He is very fond of you."

"And I of him," Deb answered quietly and met the Duke's look squarely. "But that does not explain why my house was being spied upon by your thuggish servants, M. le Duc. It was not as if I was about to run off. Not that I could, had I wanted to. Those buffoons would have found me soon enough."

The Duke put up his white brows in mild surprise. "I gave you credit for more brain, Madam. It was my son who requested that your house be watched for your own protection. There are those who could seek to do you a harm now that you are intimately connected with my family."

"Lord Alston's concern is gratifying but I doubt a worse fate exists than being intimately connected by marriage with your family!" Deb retorted in English before she could help herself.

"Flippant sarcasm does not become you!" the Duke rasped in such an icy voice that Deb involuntarily swallowed and dropped her gaze to her clenched hands.

"The physician Medlow he assured us you are restored to full health, *ma petite*?" gently enquired the Duchess.

Deb nodded. "Yes, Mme la Duchesse, I am well." She glanced at the Duke. "I trust Medlow's assurances were in response to your enquiry, M. le Duc, and not the other way round?"

"If you are concerned Medlow broke his Hippocratic oath, you may rest easy," the Duke answered with a ghost of a laugh. "That is one physician who is—er—incorruptible. However, I regret to inform you that Sir Gerald's lawyers are not."

Deb breathed in quickly but instantly regained her composure. "My brother is not to blame, M. le Duc. He contacted his lawyers at my request, and most reluctantly too."

"Your honesty is to be commended. Perhaps you would care to inform the Duchess why you had Sir Gerald approach his lawyers?"

Deb frowned and bit back a retort. So he was going to humiliate her in front of his wife. Not if she could help it!

"As you are well aware of my reasons for doing so, your Grace, I am surprised you did not tell the Duchess yourself," she enunciated calmly in English, eyes bravely focused on the Duke. "Then again, you did not consult your wife on your son's marriage, did you? Was that because you consider females little better than children and thus incapable of rational thought and understanding, or because you do not wish to upset her with the news her son's marriage is to be dissolved using the Act of '42 that grants annulment on the grounds of lunacy?"

The Duke's dark eyes sparked with anger and his thin lips parted in reply but something made him pause, and in that small hesitant moment Deb's gaze dropped from his lined face to his silken knee where two hands rested, fingers entwined.

The Duke and Duchess were holding hands!

That the Duchess had merely to move her fingers in his to silence the Duke amazed Deb, but what shocked her more was the fact the Duchess must understand the English tongue for her to give such an instant response to a speech she knew would anger the Duke.

"Forgive me, Mme la Duchesse," Deb apologized quickly, reverting to French. "Had I known you understood the English tongue I would not have been so blunt."

The Duchess's green eyes twinkled.

"I understand that you did not wish to upset me, yes? That is very considerate of you, *ma belle-fille*. But me I am not one of these females who wishes to be treated as a child. You understand?" When Deb nodded and looked suitably chastened, she added, "And I must tell you, *ma petite*, that my son Julian he has a quick stubborn temper like his Maman and a little of Monseigneur's great arrogance—yet that is not such a bad thing for a man in his position—but one thing he is not is a lunatic."

"Your son is not a lunatic, Mme la Duchesse," Deb agreed, bravely keeping her gaze on the Duchess's beautiful face. "But as I understand it, for a marriage to be annulled it need only be proved that one of the parties was of unbalanced mind *at the time the marriage took place*. The night we were forcibly married off he was very drunk. I believe he had drunk himself into a stupor in order to forget his quite shocking behavior towards you, Mme la Duchesse." She glanced at the Duke. His eyes were all for his wife and he had raised her hand to his lips. Deb swallowed. "I do not know why he did what he did, but he did and that's all that matters. Such action goes a long way to proving his mind was unhinged at that time. According to my brother's lawyers that one act of lunacy is all that is required to have my marriage declared null and void."

When the Duchess looked down and away, green eyes bright with tears, it was the Duke's turn to squeeze his wife's fingers and Deb stumbled on, eager to bring this painful interview to a close; willing herself not to be overcome with emotion, to let the tears run down her cheeks.

"I am so very sorry to speak of events which are still painfully raw for you both, but surely you cannot blame me for wanting to end a marriage based on deceit and false promises? I was robbed of the choice to marry for love and companionship. Yet," she said on a deep sigh of resignation, "matters have conspired against my wish for an annulment and I have requested Sir Gerald's lawyers to halt the annulment proceedings... for the time being."

There was a long silence before the Duke spoke.

"That begs the question, Madam: Has Sir Gerald's lawyers been instructed to pursue such proceedings at a later date?" he responded with his peculiar insolent drawl. "A time perhaps when you can again inflict cruelty on Mme la Duchesse—"

The Duchess interrupted her husband.

"*Ma belle-fille*," Antonia said earnestly, "tell me honestly that you do not love my son and I will see to it that he Julian never bothers you again."

Deb gave a laugh that broke in the middle, a shaking hand to her trembling mouth. "Mme la Duchesse, I'm afraid your assurances cannot help me now. I am five and a half months with child."

There was an audible intake of breath from the Duchess and she spoke in rapid French to the Duke something Deb did not catch. The Duke's silence brought Deb's eyes up to his face and she was startled by the smile of tenderness he bestowed upon the Duchess and one he must keep exclusively for her because it transformed his harsh aquiline features into someone quite human and approachable. The Marquis had that same smile. His father was made of flesh and blood after all.

This intimate scene was all too much for Deb and she was up on her feet to pace the space between the sofa and the wingchair, her thoughts tumbling forth into speech as tears spilled onto her cheeks, hoping the sooner she managed to say all that was on her mind, and they agreed to her wishes, she could flee their presence for the solitude of the rooms assigned her. That they were over-joyed by her news only made her feel more wretched because in every other circumstance she too would have shared their joy at her pregnancy.

"I will keep up the pretense of an amicable marriage until the birth. But after the child is born I want a formal separation and ultimately a divorce."

"And if I do not agree?" asked the Duke.

"If you do not give me your word that I may go my own road once the child is born then I will have no alternative but to force your hand, M. le Duc."

"What—er—method of spiteful coercion do you intend to employ, Madam?"

Deb continued her pacing, not looking at the couple on the sofa.

"It would be an easy thing for doubt to be cast on the child's paternity given that our marriage is yet to be publicly announced nor are the circumstances surrounding your son's deception in legalizing our union universally known."

The Duke's upper lip curled in distaste. "You would do that to your own child? Put his future in jeopardy, make his life an uncertainty, all to exact revenge?"

"*Revenge?* I do not seek revenge M. le Duc," Deb said simply. "I desire to have my freedom returned to me. With all due respect, it was you who forced your son and I into this intolerable union and thus it is you who must concede to my wishes if your grandson is to be born in unexceptional circumstances."

"If I sanction a formal separation you relinquish all rights to the child."

Deb stood with her back to the fire and faced them. "Yes, M. le Duc," she answered with resignation. "That would be for the best."

The Duchess looked anxiously from the Duke to Deb. "*Quoi?* A child needs its maman, *n'est-ce pas?*"

"A child needs loving parents, Mme la Duchesse," Deb argued sadly. "If I continue in this loveless marriage I will become a hateful, resentful wife and as such I cannot be the kind of mother my child deserves. Besides," she shrugged, gaze dropping to the carpet where the shadows of little leaping flames from the crackling fire played upon the woven oriental patterns, "once our marriage is at an end I am very sure Lord Alston will do everything in his power to keep our son from me."

The Duchess stood and the Duke did likewise. Antonia came across to Deb and took hold of her hands. "If you think that he Julian would do such a dreadful thing to the mother of his child you are greatly mistaken in my son's character, *ma petite.*"

"I thought I knew your son very well," Deb replied, a sob in her throat and tearful gaze on the small hand that held hers. "But, yes, you are quite right, Mme la Duchesse, I find that I do not know Lord Alston at all."

A polite cough had all three occupants of the library turning to the double doors. The butler had quietly trod the length of the room and had been waiting to be noticed. At the Duke's nod he announced that nuncheon was ready and that family and guests had assembled in the dining room anteroom. Deb was all for making her excuses to decline nuncheon when the butler departed, leaving wide the door.

In strolled a tall, thin boy with coal-black curls tied back with a large white ribbon and dressed in a waistcoat and breeches of exquisite embroidered richness. His skin was so pale it was translucent and his black eyes were ringed with dark shadows. There was no mistaking his parent. He was the image of the Duke and had the beginnings of his father's strong nose. At his heels pranced four whippets with diamond collars that upon seeing their master scampered up to the Duke to receive his adoration.

And lastly into the room bounded Jack, copper curls falling into his eyes, clothes slightly crumpled and with his shoes scuffed, which is what Deb expected of a rough and tumble boy almost ten years of age. Not at all like Lord Henri-Antoine who was precise to a pin and carried himself with a languid upright insolence, the antithesis of Jack's easy gait and friendly open look.

At sight of her nephew all Deb's pent up emotion spilled forth and she rushed forward to enfold Jack in a tight embrace. Through her tears she told him how much she had missed him and that if it had been in her power to come to Paris earlier to be with him, she would have done so. Did Jack forgive his aunt's neglect?

Jack suffered Deb's tears and hugs with good grace for he had genuinely missed her very much but was embarrassed at such overtly female carryings-on in front of his best friend. But Lord Henri-Antoine did not seem to care. After being introduced to Deb as his brother's wife he bowed politely, showed mild interest in the fact that this tall female was also Jack's aunt and then promptly returned to the problem uppermost in his mind.

"Bailey says I'm to have an afternoon nap," Lord Henri grumbled, tucking his hand in that of his ancient parent's. "I don't want to, Papa. He had the impertinence to tell me that he will bar me from attending my own brother's marriage ball tonight if I don't. It's most unfair!"

"But nonetheless a necessary evil," the Duke answered and brought the whippets to heel with a snap of his long fingers. He kissed his son's thin hand. "If you want to stay awake for the ball you will take Bailey's advice and have a nap. Versailles made you overly tired."

"I think it's the most tremendous news that you and Alston are married!" Jack was saying eagerly to Deb. "He lets me call him

Alston, Aunt Deb. He says that it's only proper I should, now that he's my uncle. Alston says I'm to live with you both and that Harry can stay with us whenever he wishes. Can he, Aunt Deb?" He looked at the Duke and Duchess, as if for confirmation and felt heartened when the Duchess smiled. It made him add in a rush, forgetting his French, because his aunt looked as if she was about to burst into tears again, "Harry and I had the most wonderful time at Versailles. There's a great hall of mirrors and everything, I mean *everything*, is covered in gold and marble and there are fountains that spring up everywhere along *l'Majesty's* walk, and we saw the King! He's always surrounded by hundreds of gentlemen in truly outrageous skirts and very tall-heeled shoes! And he has a great hooked nose just like on the coins and—"

"Oh Jack, I am very pleased King Louis did not disappoint you and I cannot tell you how happy it makes me to see you so well and enjoying yourself, but perhaps it would be best to tell me the rest after nuncheon?" Deb said with a watery smile, aware that Lord Henri-Antoine was very pale and had slumped against the Duke's arm. "You must be hungry after your trip to Versailles?"

"But Harry and I aren't the least bit hungry. Alston's set up a row of archery boards on the courtyard lawn. There's to be a tournament for our friends and us this afternoon before the ball. Did he tell you about it? Did he show you the marquees? Are there circus performers with a bear like he promised? I know there's to be ribbons and cake and—" Jack stopped at his aunt's knowing look and, suitably chastened, apologized and bowed to the Duke and Duchess. "Come on, Harry. We'd best eat something. If we don't eat, Bailey will—"

Lord Henri-Antoine scowled. "A curse on Bailey! What does he have to say to anything?"

The Duchess looked up from the dogs, at Jack and then at her son who was paler than usual, his skin almost gray in hue and his eyes dull and sunken. He was completely worn out. "He has a great deal of say, if it is your health which is of concern, *mon chou*," the Duchess said quietly. When Lord Henri-Antoine shot Jack an angry look she added, "Jack you must not blame. He is only concerned like us all for your well-being."

"But, Maman, Bailey would have me forever in doors if he

had his way! You can't imagine what it's like to be always resting and being forced to eat pap when I don't want to in the least!" he sulked. "Why should I miss out when other boys—*Jack*—doesn't have to *nap* in the middle of the day? He isn't cosseted and clucked over. It's insulting to be saddled with a jailer physician who won't even let me pee in private!" At this outburst the Duchess couldn't help an indulgent giggle but the Duke raised his white brows in displeasure, which was enough to make Lord Henri-Antoine drop his head in penance. "Forgive me, Papa, but it makes me madder than anything."

"Yes, it must," the Duke sympathized.

"Alston! Tell Papa what a kill-joy Bailey was at Versailles," Lord Henri-Antoine called out to his brother. "Tell Papa how Bailey followed me *everywhere* like a beggar! It was most embarrassing." He went up to his elder brother and slipped his hand in his. "You'll keep an eye on me this afternoon, won't you?" he pleaded, looking up at him expectantly. "I need not have a nap or I might miss the start of the tournament. I don't *want* Bailey behind me. Not this afternoon and tonight with Henriette and Paul and Rene here. *Please*, Alston, *tell* Papa!"

The Marquis had strolled into the library with his hands in the pockets of his embroidered waistcoat, dressed in tight buff breeches, white shirt with a plain linen stock and polished jockey boots. His black curls were freshly washed and simply dressed, and he'd shaved. He was as far removed from the pomaded and powdered courtier that the breath caught in Deb's throat and her heart gave the oddest flutter.

Julian pulled Lord Henri-Antoine into an affectionate embrace, an arm about his brother's thin shoulders, and came up to his parents. He acknowledged Deb with a slight bow but that was the extent of his attention. After kissing his mother's hand and nodding to his father he ruffled Jack's hair, before saying,

"Come, Harry, you can't expect me to spend my afternoon in Bailey's shoes, following you about like a beggar." He winked at Jack. "I have better things to do with my time than watch over a couple of scapegrace boys—"

"But, Alston," Lord Henri-Antoine whined, "You promised..."

"He's roasting you, Harry!" Jack said with a grin. "Of course

Alston will keep an eye on us. The tournament was his idea after all. And if you want, I'll pick up all your spent arrows so you need not get tired."

Lord Henri-Antoine rolled his eyes, leaning against his brother's tall frame. "Don't be an ass, Jack," he drawled in very much the manner of his father. "We keep dozens of lackeys to do such menial tasks—"

"Thank you, Jack, for your kind offer," interrupted the Duchess with a smile, a reproachful glance at her younger son as she slipped her arm over the Duke's velvet sleeve. "With a house full of guests and tonight the ball, I am sure not one servant can I spare to run after my son's whims. Is that not so, *mon chou*?"

"Yes, maman," Lord Henri-Antoine agreed reluctantly, and when the Marquis gave him a friendly nudge he apologized to Jack, who good naturedly said there was nothing in it, and the two boys fell in behind the Duke and Duchess as they went into nuncheon.

Deb turned to follow the little procession, watching the Duke who, she noticed for the first time, leaned on a Malacca cane whenever he was upright, and who now used his wife's arm for support as they left the library.

"The cane is a recent addition," Julian commented, coming up to her, watching his father. He offered her his crooked arm. "Only eight months ago he was astride his horse every morning. Now... His breathing is labored taking the main stairs."

"His Grace seems little altered since that night nine years ago," Deb mused, walking with Julian through to the dining room. She looked up at him pensively. "Is he very ill?"

"Yes."

"I am truly sorry. The Duchess your mother is—is—"

"—much younger than he," Julian interrupted, finishing the sentence for her. "There in lies the greater tragedy." And added in a whisper at her ear, before stepping back to allow Deb to be introduced to family and friends who were all gathered in the ante-room, "Today is his birthday. Your news is by far the most precious gift..."

$\mathcal{T}$welve

$\mathcal{C}$rystal, silver and gold winked in the blaze of light of two chandeliers that were suspended over the long mahogany dining table. Deb was sure that there was enough silver cutlery laid out at each place to confuse even the most fastidious of diners. Elaborate arrangements of fruits of the season were displayed in worked bowls of finest porcelain, and crystal vases were filled to overflowing with large heavily scented roses. A roaring fire in the marble grate of the fireplace, over which hung a portrait of the Duchess by the fashionable painter Fragonard, kept the company warm, as did the many and varied courses served at table by the army of soft-footed and attentive liveried footmen under the direction of a blank-faced butler.

Only immediate family and Martin Ellicott were in attendance. Sir Gerald had excused himself with a head cold, but everyone knew his French was so poor he could not sit through a dinner without his wife as interpreter, and Lady Mary was visiting friends at a nearby hôtel. Julian's godfather arrived a few minutes late, and in time to hear Lord Vallentine declare loudly that he had yet to meet a musician whose delicate sensibilities permitted more than the ingestion of a thin broth. He conveniently ignored his son Evelyn's plate, which was piled with capon, a wedge of pigeon pie and enough vegetables to fill a small garden plot. But the Duchess did not ignore this fact and she defended her nephew at the expense of his parent; their usual playful banter easing the formality of sitting through a nuncheon with an illustrious host who rarely joined in the conversation, except to make an acute observation designed to turn the topic to one he considered more worthy of discussion and which usually left family and friends alike floundering until the Duchess steered the conversation in the right direction.

The laughter had barely died away from one of the Duchess's sallies at Lord Vallentine when his wife, a fascinating gray-haired lady, blue eyes very large and resembling her elder brother the Duke, was heard to complain loudly about the rigid formalities observed at the Court at Versailles.

"It is quite unbelievable to me," Estée Vallentine said with a sniff of annoyance, "why an old lady is made to stand for hours and hours in the presence of the King until her bones seize up, and dearest Antonia, who is young enough to be my daughter, is permitted to sit on her tabouret. I tell you, I do not see the fairness in it."

"Fairness has nothin' to do with it," Lord Vallentine stuck in, gnawing on the bone of a fowl soaked in garlic. "You ain't a duchess and only duchesses get to sit in the presence of Louis. I told you how it would be but you insisted we go. Never more bored of a place in all my days!"

"You did not enjoy the spectacle of the Court then, my lord?" Martin Ellicott enquired politely.

"Spectacle?" Lord Vallentine snorted. "A gentleman'd need glass bottle spectacles to get a glimpse of His French Majesty! Forced to stand around kickin' me heels for most of the day with a room full of prosin' struttin' birds of a feather; powdered, patched and beribboned, all to be able to bow and scrape to Louis' back whenever he passes-by, surrounded by an entourage of perfumed fools! Not my idea of entertainment, I can tell you, Ellicott."

"We did not ask you to come with us," the Duchess said loftily. "It was you who would not be left behind by Monseigneur. What was it you said...? Ah, yes! *To rattle around alone in this haunted mausoleum.*"

Lord Vallentine grinned and looked about at the other diners for confirmation of his own cleverness. "Did I say that? Well, I'll own to it!"

The Duchess opened her green eyes very wide. "But, Lucian,

I do not like at all for you to call our home such a thing, especially when it was the childhood home of Monseigneur and of your wife, too. If this hôtel *is* haunted by ghosts I should think they are of the living-dead variety only." There was a hint of a smile about her lovely mouth as she exchanged a glance with the Duke and Martin Ellicott, the Marquis's godfather hiding his mirth behind his napkin.

Estée Vallentine glared across the table through the roses at her husband. "Lucian! Me you owe an apology!"

"Eh? An apology?" blustered Lord Vallentine. "But I didn't mean anythin' by it. She's teasin' again, you can see that, can't you? And I'll tell you all somethin' for nought: This place is full of ghosts." He shot the Duchess a dark look, catching her smile, and blinked. "Eh? Now, now, Mme la Duchesse, who are you callin' the livin'-dead?"

Deb laughed along with the rest of the family, feeling very much at ease for the first time in a long while. She took an instant liking to Evelyn's father Lord Vallentine. He reminded her of a stick insect with his long, loose-limbed frame and square cut jaw; his saffron yellow silk frockcoat she presumed to be all the rage amongst the dandy set of the aging nobility. And the Duchess she liked very much. Her youth and beauty were truly startling, but watching her now as she held court at the dining table Deb was surprised and delighted to discover that her beauty was matched in kind by a loving personality. There was an aura about her tiny person, of vitality and joy and an eternal optimism that infected all those about her. Deb had never met a couple so dissimilar. The Duke certainly lived up to his reputation of being a phlegmatic and arrogant nobleman. Yet when he spoke with the Duchess or either of his two sons he became a wholly different being.

It was obvious the Duke and Duchess were devoted to one another and whatever the Duke's previous life as an unconscionable rake, Deb was certain he had mended his wicked ways upon marriage. She wondered how such cruel lies about the Roxtons' private life had continued to circulate and was of the opinion that the Duke's reputation as a debauchee must have been very bad indeed. But she could not now imagine him being anything but a kind and loving husband and father and thinking back on the baseless remarks she had hurled at her husband about his parents she felt shame and wretchedness.

Suddenly the delicious food on her plate became unpalatable and she lost the thread of the chatter going on about her. But in her abstraction of self-castigation she became aware of another quite separate conversation between devoted servant and master. Martin Ellicott and the Duke chose to converse in English at a table overflowing with French repartee. It was the first time Deb had heard the Duke speak his country's native tongue and if his tone in French was haughty, in English he sounded positively chilly.

"May I enquire if you gained your objective with his French Majesty, your Grace?" asked Martin Ellicott.

The Duke looked away from the Duchess. "The private audience went well. Louis, like I, is most concerned Antonia should not suffer any undue—er—distress."

"Then one can presume the trial...?" Martin began, letting the sentence hang because he found the topic of his godson's upcoming trial a difficult one to broach with his father.

The Duke spooned oysters onto his plate from a silver dish lying on a bed of ice and held by a blank-faced footman wearing white gloves. "It is most lamentable, but I fear not only has the trial judge fallen victim to an undisclosed—er—contagion, which has delayed proceedings now for some months, but that the entire fraternity of judges has succumbed to the same illness. An early recess was called; cases are postponed for several more months." He speared an oyster with a small silver fork. "The precise nature of the illness remains a mystery..."

Martin Ellicott grinned and waved away the gloved footman. "I'm sure it will, your Grace." He sipped his wine thoughtfully, a sidelong glance down the crowded table at the Marquis who was heaping garlic drenched quail onto Jack Cavendish's plate. "Yet, I believe your son was looking forward to his day in court. He will be disappointed."

"Yes," came the flat reply.

"After all, he is blessed with that rare quality amongst his kind: a strong moral code, if you will."

"Yes. He is his mother's son."

Martin patted his mouth with a corner of a linen napkin to hide a knowing smile. "Yes, your Grace, he is. That must please you?"

The Duke put up his white brows in mock hauteur. "Are you daring to suggest I would not want my son and heir to follow in my—er—rakish footsteps?"

"Pardon, your Grace, but even did you desire it, which I know you do not, he would not do so. It is not in his nature."

"Ah, my declining prestige…" The Duke finished his oysters, pushing aside the plate to take up his wine glass. "Defending his honor in a French court of law against an upstart merchant prince and his cunning bitch of a daughter serves no worthwhile purpose," he said acidly. "If my son has a taste for speeches let him satisfy it in the Lords where his—er—*values* can be put to good purpose; he'll be Duke soon enough." He signaled to his butler to refill the Duchess's wine glass, and raised his own to her with a smile. "Yet, my dear Martin, this infirm old satyr is determined, God willing, to remain for as long as possible upon this earth; for her sake, you understand."

"Yes, your Grace, I understand perhaps better than any other."

Deb followed the Duke's gaze down the length of the table to the Duchess and was witness to the look and the private smile they exchanged, and for one moment it was as if the ducal couple were dining alone together at the long table and not amongst their chattering, happy family. The Duchess returned the Duke's toast with one of her own, and with the spell broken the couple's attention came back to the dinner table. It was then that Deb sensed that she too was being watched.

From under her lashes she looked across the cluttered surface of the mahogany table between two bowls overflowing with white roses and found Julian's green-eyed gaze upon her. It was obvious he had been regarding her for sometime while she had had an ear to the conversation between his father and godfather, for he quickly looked away, pretending to adjust the silver knife and fork on his empty plate, but not before Deb glimpsed the abject sorrow reflected in his lovely eyes.

It was too much for her and she shot to her feet, none of the silent liveried footmen lining one wall able to catch her chair in time before the ornately carved back clattered to the parquetry floor.

Instantly, Julian was on his feet. The rest of the gentlemen, with a lady out of her chair, politely rose but at a more leisurely pace. The Duke, however, remained seated, regarding his son and daughter-in-law over the rim of his glass with an expression that remained unfathomable. All conversation and laughter came to a halt.

"I—The heat—This gown—I-I should rest before the ball," Deb heard herself babble in the deafening silence. She dropped a curtsey, first to the Duchess and then to the Duke. "Please, excuse me…"

Without waiting to be excused, she ran from the room with a shaking hand to her mouth.

Evelyn threw down his napkin to follow her but two sharp words from his cousin and he remained where he was.

Julian cast a smoldering eye over the table as the gentlemen sank back slowly onto their chairs, Evelyn included. "Deborah has had enough of this family's good intentions for one morning. Harry? Jack? If you've finished eating we will inspect those archery boards before the guests arrive."

And with a bow to his parents, Julian left the room with the two boys in tow; Lord Vallentine heard to comment loudly,

"What's that? *With child?* Alston's bride? Well, stamp me! The chit's only been here five minutes!"

Lady Mary found Deb seated at a cluttered boudoir table, a cotton dressing gown over her flimsy chemise and frothy under petticoats. She was staring, not at her reflection, but out the window, chin cupped in her hand and a mass of dark red hair tumbling freely down her back. Draped over a spindle-legged chair by the ornate Oriental dressing screen was Deb's ball gown of heavy silk embroidered with gold thread and pearls, and a matching pair of silk covered shoes with diamond buckles. Deb's maid Brigitte, who held a silver-backed hairbrush, lifted her shoulders at Lady Mary's look of enquiry, as if to say she had done all she could to hurry her mistress along to finish her toilette in time for the ball. She then stepped back with a curtsey to allow Lady Mary to draw up a chair. Such was Deb's distraction with the view that it was only when she rose half off the padded stool to take a better look at what was going on beneath her window, and then turned to comment to Brigitte that she saw her sister-in-law.

"Mary! What a pleasant surprise. But how formal you look with your hair so tall and powdered and feathered and—Is that truly a sailing ship atop a small straw hat?"

"It's all the rage. Do you truly like it?" Lady Mary asked anxiously, a tentative hand to her steepled coiffure. She failed to notice the quick look that passed between Deb and Brigitte, Deb biting her lower lip to stop a smile. "Of course I told *Maurice* my hairdresser that I did not want my hair so outrageously tall that I would have a crick in the neck before the first dance; which is what happened to the little Countess Lowenbrue and she had to sit out an entire ball with a bag of ice at her shoulder!"

"Is that so?" commented Deb, returning to stare out the window. "I am in two minds: Wear my hair down my back in the manner of a medieval princess, or let Brigitte work her magic. If I had my way I would simply braid it and be done, but Brigitte says I must wear it up and so I shall. Oh, well done, Jack!" she announced and this time did get to her stockinged feet. "Come look, Mary. Jack and Harry are having the most wonderful time with their archery bows."

Lady Mary came to the window with its view of the courtyard.

Gaily colored tents festooned with ribbons and flags were erected at the far end of the rolling green lawn and under their shade lounged the crème de la crème of Parisian aristocracy, their every whim attended to by an army of liveried servants who came and went with heavy silver trays laden with food and drink. At some distance from these marquees a row of large bullseyes had been nailed to the chestnut trees lining the cobblestone walk, and it was at these bullseyes Deb drew Mary's attention. A cluster of children watched over by their nurses and tutors, dressed in rich fabrics and diamond buckled shoes that mimicked those worn by their fashionable parents, were each possessed of a bow and a quiver full of arrows. They stood a designated distance from the bullseyes, ranked according to age, and fired off their colored arrows at the targets. When their supply of arrows was exhausted liveried servants ran about gathering up the spent arrows and returning them to the quivers of their rightful owners.

Lord Henri-Antoine and Jack stood shoulder to shoulder amongst this excited group of laughing, happy children and fired off their arrows in turn. Standing off to one side was the Marquis of Alston, shirtsleeves rolled to the elbow, and Martin Ellicott, who looked to be keeping score with quill and blotter; both offering collective encouragement to the children in their efforts to strike the bullseyes. As Deb and Mary continued to watch, the Duchess came up in a whirl of silk embroidered petticoats and stood between them, holding Martin Ellicott's arm and barely reaching her elder son's shoulder. When her younger son waved she blew him a kiss. At that Lady Mary turned away from the window with a frown and sat down heavily with her back to the view.

"I've never understood why that old servant is treated better than any relative!" Mary commented pettishly. "Gerald says it's because Ellicott knows too many of the Duke's secrets and so can't be easily fobbed off. And if he wasn't as ancient as his master we would all be left to wonder at the true nature of his relationship with Cousin Duchess."

Deb swiveled about on the padded stool, mouth agape. "Mary! How appalling to hear you, of all people, repeat such horrid and quite malicious gossip, particularly about a woman who I suspect hasn't a malicious bone in her body."

"When you've been a member of this family for as long as I have you—"

"While I am a member of this family, I never want to hear any of the untruths spread about the Duke and Duchess and Martin Ellicott or, for that matter, my husband."

"So you intend to remain Marchioness of Alston?" Lady Mary enquired archly.

Deb glanced at her own reflection, a protective hand to her round belly. "I—The baby..."

"The baby will at least be a consolation."

"How's that, Mary?"

"You'll have something to love and someone who loves you. All the ugliness of your marriage will disappear and, if you are truly blessed, you'll have a son and then, well…" Mary looked down at her plump white hands. "You won't have to submit to any more unpleasantness."

"Unpleasantness?" Deb gave an involuntary laugh. "Mary, you goose! This baby wasn't conceived in unpleasantness. Far from it. That first night… It was the beginning of quite the most wonderful experience of my life," she said wistfully and inexplicably burst into tears. "Damn! What is wrong with me these days?"

Lady Mary offered Deb her handkerchief. "Females in your delicate condition often cry for any reason. I did and at the oddest of moments."

"Well I can't bear it! First I'm bedridden with nausea and now I'm a weeping pot. How Medlow can tell me pregnancy is a perfectly normal condition… And how you can honestly sit there and say a child can make up for a loveless marriage is beyond me." She wiped her eyes and disappeared behind the ornate dressing screen, calling for Brigitte and saying through gritted teeth, the wet handkerchief twisted in her hands, "How dare he do this to me so soon!"

"Don't you want this child?"

"Want?" Deb called out bewildered, as if the question had never occurred to her. "Of course I want this baby. I wanted a brood. But now… Brigitte? Good. Let's see if I can fit into that wretchedly heavy gown. And then perhaps I can go for a walk for I need some fresh air before I enter a ballroom full of strangers."

"I know you've only just arrived, and I'd hope to spend some time with you," Lady Mary called out, watching the maid come and go from behind the screen, first with the heavy silk gown and then return for the shoes, "but Gerald and I are returning to England tomorrow morning. Gerald says I've been away from Theodora long enough, which I quite agree, and there are pressing estate matters which require Gerald's immediate attention." She stood close on the other side of the screen. "And what with the baby you will have enough to do without worrying about a nine-year-old boy. Gerald insists Jack return to England with u—"

"No!"

"Gerald said you'd take the news badly, but you must be reasonable, dearest," Lady Mary continued patiently and in a voice that was beginning to grate on Deb's nerves. "Jack can't impose on the Duke and Duchess forever."

Deb came out from behind the screen and stood in front of the full-length looking glass, side-on at first to see if her expanding waistline was at all noticeable under so many layers of petticoats and a heavy silk over-gown, and then face on to inspect the sit of the bodice across her swelling breasts. The square cut neckline was indecently low but there was nothing she could do about that now. In the reflection she caught her sister-in-law's frown of disapproval.

"Jack belongs with me," she stated, and carefully spread out her voluminous petticoats to sit again on the boudoir stool, to allow Brigitte to work her magic with pearl-headed pins and threaded silk ribbons on her untamed mass of long dark red hair.

"You're in no condition to look after him, dearest," Mary argued. "Indeed in your present condition I'm very sure you'll be expected to spend your days resting quietly—"

"Really, Mary, you make out I'm an invalid. I assure you I am healthier now than I've ever been. It's just that I find myself unexpectedly bursting into tears.

"—because you are carrying Alston's heir, after all," Lady Mary continued in that same patronizing tone, "So you can't afford to do anything silly that might jeopardize the baby, such as running after a particularly boisterous nine-year-old boy who gets himself into all sorts of scrapes. Did you know that not only does he take viola lessons from Cousin Evelyn, which is against Gerald's express wishes, worse, these lessons are conducted amongst Evelyn's pack of drunkard, good-for-nothing musician friends? Sad company for a child of nine, and after one considers what a horrid mess Otto made of his life consorting with such musical riff-raff, is it any wonder Gerald is concerned that Jack may go the way of his father?"

"For pity's sake, Mary, Jack is only a child!" Deb retorted, an impatient glance up at Brigitte to see if her maid had finished dressing her hair.

"He is also Gerald's heir and Gerald will not have his heir playing a viola with musical vagabonds nor one who imposes himself on Cousin Alston. He really has become a nuisance, pestering Alston with all sorts of nonsensical requests, not to mention leading

Henri-Antoine astray with games of hide-and-seek and late night mischief. I wouldn't be at all surprised if Jack was the cause of that poor boy's next fit of falling sickness."

"Indeed, Mary," Deb replied in a deceptively mild voice. Her large brown eyes narrowed. "Then pray tell me why Julian gives so much of his time to those boys? And why do Jack and Harry seek him out so readily, if not encouraged to do so?" Absently, she handed Brigitte the last of the pearl headed pins, her long hair now expertly upswept with tortoiseshell combs, pins and interwoven with a number of silk ribands threaded with pearls. "How do you account for Julian's involvement in the archery tournament below my window? You think he was pestered into it against his will? For the best part of two hours he has been with those children, applauding their efforts, offering encouragement to the little ones, and most particularly to his brother and Jack—"

"Oh, that's only because he has his mother's mild temperament," Mary said dismissively. "Cousin Duchess is exceedingly patient and caring and sees the good in everyone, qualities that aren't particularly praise-worthy in a duchess surrounded by fawning sycophants."

"Possessing a kind nature does not exclude a sense of discrimination nor does it assume the person is simple-minded."

Lady Mary's blue eyes widened and she gave Deb's acute observation a contemptuous smile. "That may be true, Deborah, but the fact remains: Alston has also inherited a bucket-full of his father's most unsavory traits which far outweighs the noble characteristics gained from his mother. His outlandish behavior caused Cousin Duchess to go into an early labor and Henri-Antoine to be born with the falling sickness; no coincidence that. His early birth and Alston's banishment certainly ruined both their lives thereafter."

"And you would now be Marchioness of Alston save for Julian's one bout of youthful imprudence?" Deb enquired, taking a leap of faith with her intuition, and not surprised when her sister-in-law blanched. "Poor Mary," she added with genuine sympathy. "I knew your heart had been broken all those years ago, but not by a sixteen-year-old boy. You were very much in love with him when you were fourteen, weren't you? Not that he knew it. How could he at his age? That's why you, an heiress and daughter of an earl, rejected all suitors season after season in the hopes that when Julian returned from his travels he would finally offer for you. I suppose his rejection was easier to accept if you convinced yourself his character was beyond saving. Was it when you discovered Julian was already married that you accepted Gerry's offer? Yet like the rest of your suitors, Gerry will never measure up to Cousin Alston, will he, Mary?"

Lady Mary opened her mouth to refute Deb's assertions, face bright pink with embarrassment, but as Deb had spoken the truth, she could not bring herself to speak. A soft rap on the paneling rescued her from total ignominy and she was most grateful for the interruption, even if the pleasant drawling voice at her back subjected her to playful ridicule.

"What a fetching coiffure, Mary. It reminds me of a church-steeple. But I'm not entirely convinced about the boat motif, perhaps a church steeple after a receding flood...?"

It was the Marquis and Deb practically jumped off the stool, sending the last curl to be pinned up under Brigitte's deft fingers tumbling forward over her bare shoulder. "You enjoy sneaking up on me, don't you?" Deb said with asperity to his looking-glass reflection.

Julian grinned. "Naturally. Men are merely large boys after all." He retreated to stand by the ornate dressing screen.

"I was just telling Deb that Sir Gerald and I are returning to England in the morning," Lady Mary announced in a clipped voice, smoothing a hand over her shell-pink damask petticoats. "Jack is to accompany us."

Julian glanced at Deb with a raised eyebrow before looking directly at Lady Mary. He sat with a deliberate slowness on the lattice-backed chair by the dressing screen, flicking out the stiff skirts of his black velvet frockcoat with gold lacings and crossing his long stockinged legs at the ankles so as not to overly crease a pair of thigh-tight black satin breeches. His black hair was dressed but unpowdered and his only jewelry was the familiar heavy gold signet ring on the pinkie of his left hand. He took out his gold snuffbox and tapped the lid.

"You have been singularly misinformed, Madam. Jack remains here with Lady Alston. It is for her ladyship to decide when her nephew will return to England. But I certainly won't release him into the care of your husband: ever."

Lady Mary noted the Marquis's use of his wife's title and she knew when to submit to an implacable higher authority. She curtsied. "Naturally I will inform Sir Gerald of your lordship's wishes."

The Marquis swept a lace-ruffled wrist carelessly into the air. "Inform whomever you like, Mary," adding with a wink at Deb, "but Gerry certainly knows my wishes. You are returning to England tomorrow, are you not?"

Lady Mary gaped at him but as the Marquis continued to regard her with an air of insolent amusement she shut her mouth tight, shot a suspicious look at Deb, who was hiding a smile behind an unfurled fan of carved ivory she had quickly grabbed up from amongst the clutter in front of her, and with a mutinous expression stomped out of the bedchamber; the little sailing ship atop her towering headdress bobbing from side to side as if caught in a gale force wind.

Thirteen

"I thought you might like to take a walk in the courtyard gardens before we get caught up in all the nonsense of this wretched ball," Julian suggested in that conversational tone he had used the day he'd walked into Deb's sitting room in Milsom Street.

"Yes, I'd like that," Deb replied with a shy smile, adding in a tone she hoped sounded off-hand, "Will it be nonsense?"

Julian remained silent at the window, taking snuff with an eye to the activity down on the velvet-green lawns. In front of the marquees, the children were all sitting in a row, adults standing behind their chairs, all rapt attention as a troupe of circus performers in brightly colored outfits, funny hats and exaggerated shoes went through their routines; one juggler in particular causing gasps and giggles as he tossed three colored balls high up in the air while he swallowed fire from a lighted baton. Finally, he looked over his shoulder at her reflection in the looking glass and held her gaze. "Not if you are there beside me."

The afternoon sun was still bright and warm but the air was crisp and a light breeze stirred the tops of the avenue of chestnut trees. The couple strolled down one length of the cobblestone walk, neither saying a word, Deb with her hand comfortably in the crook of her husband's velvet sleeve.

Where the avenue ended and the sweep of lawn began a game of bowls was in progress, watched on by several spectators lounging on chairs and drinking champagne and hovered over by attentive footmen. The Marquis stopped a little way off from this group so as not to disturb the game, but close enough to hear the banter between the players. He grinned. Deb understood why for the repartee between Lord Vallentine and the Duchess of Roxton was constant and unflagging and very entertaining.

"Me? I do not believe it!" stated the Duchess. "Lucian, you do not have the eyes to see the ball, so how is it that you think you can hit it?"

"Now you listen to me, Mme la Duchesse. I ain't finished with you yet. I know gamesmanship when I hear it," grumbled Lord Vallentine, standing at the end of the bowling green with knees bent, ball in hand, sizing up his shot with a practice swing before making his drive. "Be on the ready to lose ten pounds! There! What a shot! See, Estée? What did I tell you, aye?"

From her chair beside Martin Ellicott, Estée Vallentine sighed her exasperation. "You will never win against Antonia, Lucian."

Vallentine straightened his thin frame and with a dark look at his wife stomped off down the green. "Loyalty! Ha!"

Antonia went after him, passed him, and blew him a kiss as she skipped on ahead, the many layers of her embroidered silk petticoats swishing about her. At the end of the green, where Lord Vallentine's bowling ball had come to rest, she clapped her hands and called to his lordship to see for himself her triumph. After many minutes sizing up the state of play, his lordship finally conceded defeat and with a flourish, bowed to the Duchess before turning on a heel and stomping back up to where his wife sat.

"Estée! I need ten pounds," grumbled Lord Vallentine, and fell into the chair on her other side. He accepted a tumbler of wine from a footman and pointed it at the Duchess as she came to join them. "I still say if it hadn't been for a dip in the grass I'd have beaten you, minx!"

The Duchess, who had spied Julian and Deb standing a little way off on the cobblestone walk, waved and smiled at them before turning on Lord Vallentine with a twinkle in her green eyes. "No, Lucian," she told him bluntly, "that is a great piece of nonsense. Martin! Tell him: He Lucian is a very bad bowler and me I am a very good bowler."

"You are indeed a very good bowler, Mme la Duchesse,"

Martin Ellicott agreed demurely and received such a thunderous look from Lord Vallentine, who had sprung half out of his chair, that he was forced to put up his shoulders in a gesture of total capitulation.

"You will support me, won't you, Estée?" Vallentine growled at his wife.

"But it would be a lie, Lucian," she answered matter-of-factly. "I do not know why it is you never listen to me. Antonia has always been and will always be by far the better bowler."

"Then why did you allow me to waste ten pounds if you knew I couldn't win, damme?" he complained. "I could've saved m'self a pain in the back and just handed over the ten, blast it!"

"Yes, you could," agreed his wife.

This sent the whole company sitting about the bowling green into whoops of laughter. Even Julian and Deb could not help having a laugh at Lucian Vallentine's expense but quickly turned away to hide their smiles when his lordship realized his loss had provided entertainment for an extended audience and turned a hostile eye in their direction. So Julian led Deb away from the lawn, and away from the striped marquees beyond the bowling green that were now overflowing with guests, with the smaller children being scooped up by their nurses to be taken home.

From this activity Julian realized there was not much time left to him before he and Deb would be called to join the guests for supper indoors and the formalities of a long evening would begin. But he wanted Deb to himself a little longer, and so, just as they passed a group of gardeners busy tilling flowerbeds and Deb turned to admire one of the many Greek and Roman statues dotting the walk, Julian pulled her sideways into a shady grotto of tall trees.

"Deb! I'm not a monster," he burst out, letting go of her arm. "You've every right to think me a-a bestial *fiend* given the lurid gossip about my past. And when I think of what I said to you in Martin's bookroom..." He ran a hand through his thick hair. "God, I've made such a damned muddle of this speech already and I've barely begun!"

Deb blinked at him as he paced in front of her, the feeling of lightheartedness that lingered after watching the antics of the bowlers evaporating. Yet she remained remarkably calm despite the quickening thud of her heart as she sank onto a low marble bench and placed her closed fan in the lap of her billowing petticoats. "If you're referring to that incident which occurred when you were sixteen years old, I know a little of that sad story…"

"Sad story? Ha! My actions were reprehensible. So much so that it is still gossiped about in drawing rooms to this day. Let me recount it for you, then you tell me if a judge will agree with you, that I was mad on the night we were wed."

Deb gave a start, opened her mouth to tell him it was unnecessary for him to recount such painful details but then just as quickly she realized that she did want to hear what he had to say, very much, so pressed her lips together and waited.

"I burst into my parents' Hanover Square residence demanding to see my mother," he said matter-of-factly. "My father was still at the House. Several of their friends had arrived for a dinner party. I'd come down from Oxford with Robert and Evelyn to celebrate my sixteenth birthday. Yes, Robert Thesiger. He, Evelyn and I drank all the way to London. It was on the journey that Robert asked me how I felt about sharing my mother with another brat. I had no idea what he meant. Evelyn did. I could see it written all over his face. Robert had already confided in him, and to the last salacious drop by the look on his face.

"So Robert told me. He gave a Convent Garden performance. At first I refused to believe it: that my mother was pregnant with her lover's child; that my father, for the sake of the family name and because his arrogance would not allow for any other outcome, was telling the world he was its sire. But Robert and Evelyn convinced me to open my eyes. A beautiful young duchess, sweet-natured and full of life married to a white-haired old noble who showed as much emotion as an iceberg. Why wouldn't such a vital creature look elsewhere for love and affection? It made perfect sense. I swallowed the bait whole, as it were."

"Oh, Julian, how could you when five minutes in your parents' company is enough to convince a blind man they are so very much in love!"

The Marquis swallowed. "Well, I wasn't blind, I was a sixteen year old prig eaten up with his own self-consequence! I did not try to understand my parents' marriage. At that age, a boy wishes his parents to conform to the society to which they belong so he is acceptable to his friends. At Eton I was taunted mercilessly because my parents have an unconventional marriage by any standards. Theirs wasn't an arranged marriage, a bloodless union for the transfer of property and wealth. My parents thumbed their noses at convention and eloped."

Deb looked abashed, remembering the hurtful and totally unsubstantiated remarks about the Duke and Duchess she had hurled at her husband. "I admit to being astonished by your parents. I do not know of another exulted couple that have married for anything but dynastic self-preservation, certainly none who married for love. The last Cavendish to do so was Otto and he was banished from the family. My parents, Gerry, indeed most people I know have had their marriage arranged for them. But I have interrupted you..."

Julian stopped his pacing and stood before her, clenching and unclenching his hands. That he took a few moments before he spoke, that he cleared his dry throat and swallowed and looked at first anywhere but at her, but then found the courage to meet her steady gaze, color deepening in his cheeks, was indication enough that he still found it difficult to speak of that night without emotion getting the better of him.

"My mother was in her boudoir. The physician was with her. The scene that presented itself to me in my drunken state was such that I... God, I didn't even see that they were not alone, that my mother's ladies-in-waiting were in attendance! I let myself believe, after what Robert and Evelyn had told me, that the physician was my mother's lover. I went into a rage. I overpowered the physician and dragged my mother, who was dressed only in her chemise and nightgown, out of the house and into the cold night..."

He sat down on the bench beside Deb, elbows on his silken knees and stared at the hedgerow, as if seeing the events as he retold them. "I remember there was a great deal of noise. People scurrying about with tapers. And there was shouting. There was lots of shouting. A gathering had formed at one end of the Square. They were held back from coming closer by our servants. The only person who wasn't shouting was my mother. She hardly made a sound. She was crying but she never once shouted at me." He turned his head into his shoulder and looked at Deb, a glaze to his eyes. "I called her a whore. I said she was a witch. I called her a *putain* and other foul names that I won't sully your ears with. You get the idea. I denounced her to the world as an adulteress. I proclaimed to the mob that the child she was carrying was not my father's but the ill begotten progeny of a bastard whoreson. And then it all went very quiet. No shouting. No one talking. No one moved. There was only the sound of my mother whimpering in pain. She had gone into early labor. It was then that I saw the-the blood on her chemise and I came my senses…

"And my father… He came home to a nightmare, a nightmare of my making. I may have been insensible with a rage fuelled by claret, but it was my father who was sent to the brink of madness. He punished me the only way he saw fit, and for that I do not blame him." He smiled sadly. "One brief moment of madness should not consign a man's entire life to Bedlam … Should it?"

Deb took the hand he held out to her and rose up to be enveloped in his embrace. Instinctively, she rested her head against his chest and was comforted by the strong beat of his heart. Her voice was barely audible. "No. No, it should not."

They stood in the grotto, silent in each other's arms, listening to the sounds of celebration and beyond the high brick walls that surrounded the Hôtel Roxton, the continuous rumble of carriage wheels and hooves on the cobbles of the Rue Saint-Honoré. And when she finally looked up at him wondering how best to respond to his heartfelt confession to assure him she understood, that she did not condemn him for his youthful folly, he bent and kissed her gently.

"Do you believe in fate?" he asked, nuzzling her neck, enjoying the scent of her perfume. "I never did, despite my mother's belief that she and my father were fated to be together. But that day on Martin's terrace, when you splashed wine on your petticoats, I knew our marriage was destined." He took her silence for complicity and kissed her again, this kiss more urgent, more needful and he pressed her against him. "Since we parted on that most hideous of days, I've spent every day wishing you were at my side," he confessed. "I'm lonely without you. I need you to make me laugh, to make me forget my cares and responsibilities, to just be there for me *Julian*."

Deb so wanted to believe him, and she wanted *Julian* to kiss her again more than anything, but the specter of Mlle Lefebvre and the upcoming trial made her hesitate and to doubt his sincerity. She thought of the lewd pamphlet she had seen in Evelyn's apartment, and of the stranger dressed as a French courtier just returned from Versailles, and she reasoned that there had to be a grain of truth to the scandal or why else would the Farmer-General insist on a very public trial? But even a grain of truth was one grain too many for her. She did not want to share her days, least of all her nights, with such a creature as the Marquis of Alston.

She looked up into his eyes. "And while Julian spends his days with his wife, forgetting his cares and responsibilities, with whom does the Marquis of Alston spend his nights?"

"I beg your pardon?"

He looked as if he had no idea to what she was alluding that she was almost convinced. But not enough that it did not stop her from pulling out of his arms and brushing down her silk petticoats with an agitated hand.

"I forgive you your youthful folly. You were only a boy, and misguided by others. I understand that your parents have a marriage that is not in the common way, and I applaud them for that. But I cannot forgive the Marquis of Alston for deceiving me into his bed, just as I cannot forgive the Marquis of Alston for deceiving Mlle Lefebvre in the same way!"

He baulked. "You dare to make such a comparison? You are my wife. She is nothing but a tawdry French harlot who would do anything to catch herself a titled husband."

"Which gave you permission to seduce her with impunity?"

Julian did not blink. "I have maintained all along that I did not seduce her. I will say again: I did not seduce Mlle Lefebvre. My word should be good enough for you to believe me, for *my wife* to believe me."

His arrogant self-assurance made her blurt out, "You are vastly mistaken if you believe I am the sort of wife who will meekly sit in a big house by a lake waiting for the occasional visit from

217

her philandering husband so he can impregnate her. I will not be used as a-a—*vessel* to beget your children!"

"For pity's sake, Deb! Stop this self-torture at once!" he demanded and sighed as if she was making a scene about a trifle of a thing. It was the handkerchief that he held out to her that was the last straw. "Take it and dry your face. We are expected at the ball any moment. Take it!"

"I saw the pamphlet distributed by M'sieur Lefebvre. Have you? It boasts a cartoon of the Marquis of Alston with the biggest organ not housed in a church. Imagine!" she said on a note that was half hysterical laugh, half sob. "You and your French cronies must find such notoriety vastly entertaining, my lord."

Julian's face fired red and he scowled. "Don't be absurd, Deborah."

"Oh? Don't tell me you're *embarrassed* to be so compared? Most men would be flattered."

"Now you are being unreasonable and hysterical."

She was being slightly hysterical but she could not help herself. She blamed her pregnancy on this new-found desire for self-castigation, and plunged deeper into recrimination.

"I dare say you must feel some sort of male pride knowing your wife derives just as much satisfaction from your body as any whore of your acquaintance?"

Julian's jaw locked hard and he turned his head away, as if she had slapped his face. Deb interpreted this action as the mute obstinacy of a noble husband's right to keep his sexual life to himself. So be it. She had had enough of the Marquis of Alston. She picked up her petticoats and turned to depart, when he grabbed her elbow and spun her back to face him.

"If it's a confession you want, if nothing else will convince you, then you shall have a full and frank declaration of your husband's whole sordid sexual history. But, by God, you will say not one word until I'm done!"

"Beggin' your lordship's pardon," Joseph muttered with a cough into his hand and a bow. He came further into the grotto with a sheepish half-smile. "Wouldn't have interrupted you for the world but... Lord Henri-Antoine is missing."

"Missing?" Deb and Julian said in unison.

"No one's seen him since the circus folk left half an hour ago. Jack says his little lordship wanted to see a bear and when the circus folk didn't bring one with them he went off in a bit of a huff to—"

"—to sulk? Yes, that sounds like Harry," Julian agreed, concern for his brother masking any embarrassment at the old retainer's interruption.

"The house and grounds are being searched," Joseph continued, a sidelong glance at Deb, "and the guests have all been herded into supper none the wiser. Her Grace remains on the lawn but says she can't do so for much longer without raising the Duke's suspicions. She sent me to find you."

"I will go to her at once," Julian answered, and with a quick nod to Deb disappeared through the trees.

A handful of liveried servants were combing the avenues of chestnut trees when Deb and Joseph followed the Marquis out of the grotto. Jack was darting in and out amongst these servants, and when he saw the Marquis, his aunt and Joseph he waved a hand high above his head and ran to them as fast as his long thin legs would carry him.

"Alston!" Jack called out as he finally ran up to them, out of breath and dry in the mouth. "You've got to come *now*! Harry *needs* you!"

"Thank God," murmured Deb as her nephew fell into her arms. She cuddled him to her saying with a smile, "That's good news, Jack. I knew Harry wouldn't be far away."

Julian squatted beside the boy, realizing he was crying into his aunt's petticoats. "Where is Harry, Jack?" he asked gently, and when the boy flung an arm out in direction of the lawn added, "In one of the tents with his mother?"

"He's by the walled gate," said Jack with a sniff, turning his head out of his aunt's silk petticoats and dashing a sleeve across his eyes. "He'd followed the circus, wanting to know about the bear. I'm sorry I'm not being a man about it but he gave me a fright, y'see. He was on the ground. He'd had one of his attacks. But he's all right now, I think..."

"Shall we go and see how he is?" Julian suggested with a smile, though he felt anything but calm. He held his hand out to

Jack. "Don't worry about Harry. Bailey always knows what to do."

Jack looked up at his aunt and then at Joseph before moving out of Deb's embrace altogether to speak to the Marquis in a confidential tone. "There's a gentleman... He came in the gate just as Harry fell down. He said he'd keep an eye on him while I fetched Bailey. But I remembered what you said about strangers outside the gates, and so I wouldn't leave Harry until Bailey was fetched."

"What gentleman, Jack?" asked Deb.

The boy looked up at his aunt as if she should know the answer. "You know the one. He was always calling at our house in Bath and Saunders was always sending him away with some lame excuse. Well," he glanced at Joseph, "we thought it was lame, didn't we, Joe?"

When Deb looked none the wiser, the boy added, "You must remember him, Aunt Deb. He has a dueling scar on his cheek."

"*Parbleu. Non,*" Julian muttered in French and in two strides was off running up the avenue of chestnut trees towards the lawn.

He did not have far to go. At the entrance to the furthest marquee the Duchess stood in silent vigil, a lady-in-waiting pacing at her back, while, striding across the cobbled courtyard from the direction of the tradesmen's entrance gate, and carrying Lord Henri-Antoine to his chest, was Robert Thesiger. At his side, Dr. Bailey and five liveried footmen tried to keep step. The Marquis was at his mother's side by the time Robert Thesiger entered the tent and placed the limp little figure on the divan.

The attack had passed and had not been as severe as the previous one some months before. That was Bailey's opinion as he felt the boy's pulse, and it received a collective sigh of relief from those surrounding the divan. The physician's diagnosis was born out by the patient himself who managed a weak smile when the Duchess sat on an edge of the divan and put a cool hand to her son's bloodless cheek.

"They promised me a bear," Lord Henri-Antoine complained weakly. He turned his head and blinked at Robert Thesiger. "He says there'll be a bear at the Tuileries tomorrow."

"I do not doubt it, *mon chou*. There are many wondrous sights throughout the capital to honor the Dauphin's marriage. But we cannot see all of them," the Duchess said with a smile and kissed Henri-Antoine's forehead, her heartbeat slowing knowing her young son was out of danger. She stepped back to allow the physician to apply lavender drops to her son's temples. "Now you must rest and I will thank this gentleman on your behalf for bringing you back to me, yes?" And in a move Julian found admirable, she turned and bravely looked up into the blue eyes of the son whose mother the Duke had discarded in order to marry her. "Thank you, M'sieur, for restoring to me my son."

Robert Thesiger met her gaze, face devoid of emotion, and rudely turned his back and left the tent without comment or according her the low formal bow her status demanded.

"You're damn impudent showing yourself here!" Julian snarled at his back.

Robert Thesiger looked up from brushing down the creased sleeves of his sapphire blue embroidered silk frockcoat and, over the Marquis's shoulder, saw Deborah coming across the lawn with her groom in tow. "Show some proper gratitude. After all, I did restore the little pup to his bitch—Steady!" he added with a nervous laugh as he jumped away from the Marquis who took a stride toward him, fists clenched. "You wouldn't dare bruise your own flesh in the house of our father, now would you, Juju?"

Julian mentally winced at the use of a long discarded boyhood name but said in a perfectly controlled voice, "Can't bruise what is already rotten to the core—Steady!" he mimicked and grinned as he ducked a wild swing then caught Robert Thesiger's closed fist in his hand and held it in a vice like grip. "Mustn't be impolite in the house of our father, Bob."

Robert Thesiger tried to pull his hand free and his inability to break Julian's iron grip melted his cool façade and he swore under his breath before saying through gritted teeth, "And if it is rotten, whose fault is that? Not my mother's, to be sure!"

The Marquis gave a bark of harsh laughter as he opened his hand and let go of Robert Thesiger with a contemptuous little push. "Are you still using that pathetic twaddle to gain entree to society's salons? For shame! Isn't it about time you freshened your calling card?"

Robert Thesiger seethed at his inability to match the Marquis in strength and agility, nursing bruised knuckles as he waited for Deb and Joseph to come within earshot. "And what pathetic twaddle did you use to get Mlle Lefebvre's petticoats up over her knees? The same line of seduction the Duke used on my mother: the false promise of marriage?"

"Lord, no! That technique is as stale as last week's bread," Julian said with disdain. "Oh? Did *you* offer *her* that inducement? Dear me, I presumed you better practiced at the art of seduction than that."

"You sneer, but my pursuit of Mlle Lefebvre was wholly honorable," Robert Thesiger replied stiffly, a glance at Deb who was now at her husband's elbow.

Julian was genuinely surprised. "And she refused you? Why?"

"You know perfectly why she refused me!" Robert Thesiger said savagely. "You dangled a dukedom on the end of your *telum* and she obliged because she thought you meant marriage!"

"If she told you so then she is not only a whore but a liar."

"If Mlle Lefebvre is either it is your doing!"

Julian threw up a hand. "Robert, show some wit. Whether I was the girl's lover or not is quite inconsequential to the fact she rejected your suit. So if you're done, leave via the tradesmen's entrance from whence you came."

Robert Thesiger could hardly contain his anger and frustration at the Marquis's cavalier dismissal of his predicament and it made him say recklessly, knowing he had an audience in the Marchioness, "This is not over! I will have my revenge, for the wrongs done my mother and for your cold-blooded seduction of the woman I hoped to marry! Even if it takes five, ten, twenty years—"

"Yes. Yes. I've heard all your melodramatic nonsense before," Julian said with a languid wave of one hand. But the light in his green eyes was hard. "Or perhaps you've forgotten how you came by that scar; that you would not now be alive if it wasn't for your sordid claim to the dregs of my father's blood."

Robert Thesiger pretended offence. "Is it my fault I am your father's son?"

To everyone's surprise and bemusement the Marquis gave a bark of unrestrained laughter as if told a good joke. "Now *that* is a winning performance and a much better calling card!" And almost in the same breath the laughter died. "You are a thorn in my side, to be sure, Robert, but I shall live. Your bitter, petty attempts to disrupt my life are merely that, and are not worthy of my thought or time. But harm any member of my family, and I won't show you the same courtesy I did in Athens."

He then dismissed Robert Thesiger with a contemptuous wave as he turned his back to enter the tent to see how his brother was fairing. That he had no idea he had an audience was evident by his startled expression when he came face to face with Deb. But she wasn't looking at him. She was looking at Robert Thesiger and Joseph had a hand on her upper arm, as if to restrain her.

"Beggin' your ladyship's pardon, but his lordship wouldn't want you to—"

"Damn you, I must know!" Deb muttered under her breath and pushed his hand off as she stepped past the Marquis to extend her hand to her husband's mortal enemy.

"Mr. Thesiger? Oh, how remiss of me! *Lord* Thesiger," she said with a smile, as if it was only yesterday they had parted in the Assembly rooms in Bath, and was relieved when he bowed over her hand. "So much has happened these past few months," she said conversationally. "To both of us…"

"Just so, my lady," Robert Thesiger replied, a triumphant glance at the mute Marquis who, unable to hide his bitter disapproval of his wife's actions, walked away and disappeared inside the tent. He smiled crookedly and tugged at the white ruffles covering his hands, a sweeping look at the mansard roofed palace that dominated the skyline. "I have acquired a title and wealth while you, my lady, have sacrificed your independence of spirit to live in a gilded cage."

Deb continued to smile, ignored the slight and said with practiced calm, "Once we had a discussion at the Assembly rooms about business in Paris keeping you away—"

"Business with blue eyes? Yes, intriguing that you should remember."

"Because you were adamant the adorable Dominique was more beautiful than I."

"Ha! You remembered her name. So you were piqued after all!"

"Is there a point to this?" Joseph muttered in Deb's ear.

"May I know if the blue-eyed Dominique is Mlle Lefebvre?" Deb enquired calmly, ignoring her groom, but with the blood drumming in her ears as she anticipated Robert Thesiger's reply

Robert Thesiger was bemused as to where the conversation was leading, but happy to oblige. He inclined his powdered head. "Just so."

"Dominique Lefebvre." Deb whispered the name as if it was reverential and in that same breath a thick fog of uncertainty that had enveloped her for months suddenly dissolved and everything was given clarity and meaning. Now she knew what she must do to secure her future. Decided, she flicked open her fan and held out her hand in farewell to Robert Thesiger, barely giving him a second glance, although, when he bowed over her hand she was not so distracted that she did not hear his invitation.

"At the Tuileries tomorrow," he said in an under voice. "Mlle Lefebvre arrives at noon. If you desire the truth, be there..."

Deb made no reply and watched him saunter off across the cobbled drive towards the tradesmen's entrance gate before turning away to find her husband waiting for her by the tent. She was so caught up in her mental strategies on how best to escape the Hôtel for the Tuileries tomorrow without alerting Brigitte, the Duke's army of servants or her husband, that she was oblivious to the Marquis's stiff-necked silence and Joseph's jaw swinging look as she was escorted indoors to be presented to the hundreds of guests waiting to be introduced to the Marquis of Alston's English bride.

Fourteen

$\mathscr{I}$t was four in the morning when the last of the guests straggled out of the Hôtel de Roxton and were helped into their carriages by liveried footmen who did their best to keep yawning to a minimum. Half an hour later, Julian padded through in his bare feet to his wife's apartment via the secret door concealed behind an enormous floor to ceiling tapestry. Deb had been put to bed well before midnight and he wished he could have followed her, such was his aversion for large public gatherings where he and his family were the main attraction.

He really would have to tell his wife about the door, if Brigitte hadn't already. But he suspected he was right about the very discreet Brigitte: a gem amongst paste. And how did Deb think he had arrived in her boudoir via her bedchamber earlier that day, by conjury?

He found Deb curled up amongst the pillows, an arm caught in the tumble of her long dark red hair that enveloped her like a blanket. He set aside his taper, to pull the coverlet up over her, and to draw the curtains about the bed to keep in the warmth, when she woke and blinked in the muted candlelight.

"I'm not asleep," she said drowsily.

"No, you're not," he replied gently, and sat down on the edge of the bed.

Deb propped herself up on an elbow and frowned under heavy lids. He was still dressed. He had removed his velvet frockcoat and matching gold thread waistcoat and thrown a silk banyan loosely over his opened neck shirt and breeches. "You're not dressed for bed."

He laughed at her blunt disappointment.

"I didn't come here to be a nuisance. I just wanted to see how you fared after such an exhausting evening... And I couldn't sleep," he confessed. "Our conversation today was interrupted by Joseph."

Deb was suddenly wide-awake. "Would you like to tell me now?"

He glanced at her fleetingly, and pretended an interest in a pulled thread on the embroidered coverlet. "I've been meaning to tell you something about myself that you should've known from the very beginning..."

"May I ask you one question before you tell me?" she asked, filling his silence. And when he nodded, said frankly, "Do you know Mlle Lefebvre's actual Christian name, Julian?" When he gave a start she grabbed at his hand and smiled. "Please. It is important."

He shrugged. "I have no idea."

"And the color of her eyes?"

"That's two questions."

Her smile brightened. "I promise it will be the last time I mention Mlle Lefebvre."

Again he shrugged his ignorance. "Why does her Christian name and the color of her eyes interest you?"

She bit her lip to hide a grin. "Oh, they don't interest me at all. But no more. I promised. Tomorrow. First I must speak with Eve. Now what is it you want to tell me?"

He shook his head at her mischievous twinkle and swiftly kissed her hand. "Tomorrow then." And stopped, not knowing how to go on with his confession. Finally he took a deep breath and said softly, "Perhaps it would be for the best if I begin at the beginning... The night of our hasty midnight marriage I made a vow."

"A vow?" Deb clutched at the word, intrigued and she scrambled to sit up amongst the feather pillows.

The action was simple enough but the arousing sight of her full breasts brushing against the silk of her nightgown in the soft light of the flickering taper was all consuming. Finally he tore his gaze away, determined to complete his confession once and for all time.

"This vow was in the form of a promise to the children that

would one day eventuate from our marriage. I have always wanted a large family..." He looked into Deb's eyes, the frown between his black brows a little deeper than before. "Very few noblemen take responsibility for the corollary of their immoral behavior. After all, it is arrogantly assumed that any children that result from such a base union are the female's responsibility. But it was this appalling consequence, that there was a very real possibility that somewhere out there I had bastard brothers and sisters who struggled through life, forgotten and in poverty, while I was given every advantage in life, all my wants and needs, *my whims*, attended to without question, that had a profound affect on me.

"You can then well imagine my feelings when I discovered Robert was my natural brother. To come face to face with a boy who was my father's son, who blamed my mother for his base birth, yet was proud of his ignoble connection with my father... The shock... The idea that one day a son of mine could be approached and his innocence of the world, the image he held of his loving parents and all that he held dear, could be shattered and corrupted by the existence of a bastard half-brother, so appalled me that I vowed there and then that such a hideous prospect would never befall my children."

Deb blanched. "What I said to you that horrid day in Martin's house—"

"—echoed the truth of my youth. But you could not have known that..." He smiled crookedly. "And yet I was delightfully surprised to discover how attune are our views on the subject of infidelity and the upbringing of children."

The heightened color in his face was indication enough that he had made this speech with difficulty and a good deal of embarrassment, but he had yet to tell her the exact nature of his vow, although she had a fair idea by now what it was. Still, she wanted to hear him say it. But his next words caused her to blush rosily.

He pressed her hand. "In Constantinople, I had a lover—"

"I'd really rather not know."

"—ten years my senior," he continued in a measured tone. "She was from a minor branch of the Russian royal family and wife of the Russian Ambassador. She taught me many valuable lessons about life and love in at least four languages. More importantly, she offered me the reassurance I needed that I'd no reason to be apologetic or feel ashamed of my convictions."

Deb kept her gaze lowered to where their intertwined fingers rested on the coverlet. "You talk of a vow to ensure your own children are never plagued by bastards fathered out of wedlock, and in the next breath you are fondly reminiscing about this older woman who was clearly your mistress."

"Darling, listen to me. She and I—we—we were never lovers in the *strict* sense of the word. In fact, I have never—that is, I have *experience* in certain particulars of lovemaking but I—I—*Damn it!*" he growled in frustration, a hot flush burning his stubbled cheeks. He pushed a hand through his thick black curls. "Why can't I just come out and say it?"

Deb drew herself up off the pillows to kneel before him, her nightgown so outrageously askew that Julian's appreciative gaze fell on luscious thigh and rounded buttock and his mouth went dry. He completely lost his train of thought as he felt himself stir.

"God, Deborah, don't do this to me, not now, not at this moment. Not when I'm trying to tell you—"

She put her arms about his neck. "I think I know what it is you want to tell me…" and leaned forward to brush her lips over his dry mouth. "Abstinence is nothing of which to be ashamed."

He kissed her mouth, wanting to fulfill the promise in her brief alluring kiss, then pulled back saying candidly, "A bride expects her husband to be a consummate lover, to initiate her into love making… Not an over-eager virgin armed with raw instinct and expert lessons in foreplay!" He frowned, cheeks burning hotter than ever. "I'm a fraud, Deborah."

"Fraud?"

"The vow I made was far more important than any momentary tawdry satisfaction to be gained from a casual liaison, yet I never corrected the assumptions Society made about me, in particular about my love life. That's nobody's business but my own." He smiled shyly. "And then I met my wife and I was determined she would not be influenced by slander and gossip that swirled about the Marquis of Alston, but get to know me, Julian Hesham, as I truly am, in every sense."

"And what are you, Julian?" she asked softly.

His smile was bashful. "I'm afraid your noble husband is rather straight-laced and conventional."

"Oh? You aren't one of these noblemen who is a sad rake and a profligate, with a string of discarded mistresses left in your wake?" She feigned disappointment, adding with an encouraging smile at his surprise, "That is as well because this wife intends to keep to herself that she has a husband who is a wondrously inventive lover."

"Am I?" he said with a self-conscious grin, her simple sincerity vanquishing any discomfort he felt at being so brutally honest. "Do you have any notion how very necessary you are to my health and happiness?"

"Tell me."

He kissed her, first gently and then savagely, a kiss full of urgency and need as her lips parted to receive him.

"No. Let me show you..."

Julian went to sleep smiling with his wife in his arms. It was the most contented sleep the couple had had for many months. They would've been greatly surprised to know that not only did they enjoy an unbroken slumber but so did the Marquis's valet and her ladyship's maid. Julian was not smiling when Brigitte woke him five hours later with the news he was to present himself in the south wing at once. She was asked to repeat the command; he had not been in that part of the Hôtel since a boy. The south wing was his parents' private domain, off limits to family and guests alike and was serviced by a half dozen of the Duke's most discreet and trusted servants.

There could be only one explanation for his summons by the Duchess and so he quickly returned to his apartment, telling Brigitte to let her mistress sleep for as long as possible. He bathed quickly in tepid water and dressed in haste. Frew was lost for words when his master refused to be shaved and went off with the beginnings of a beard and in his shirt-sleeves, only throwing on a dark-blue damask frockcoat as he went up the wide main staircase two steps at a time. Before he had reached the top step, where two sentries stood guard at the entrance to the private rooms the Duke and Duchess had shared for over a quarter of a century, the news had whipped through the myriad of servant passages like a blast of cold November air: The Duke of Roxton was on his deathbed.

⚬⚬⚬

The Duchess was seated at a black lacquered breakfast table, dressed in marked contrast to the rich Oriental magnificence of her surroundings in a simple low-cut gown of printed Indian muslin, white skin devoid of cosmetics and jewelry and her thick honey curls braided into plaits and caught up in a silver net at the nape of her slim neck. She was reading a letter while a soft-footed footman cleared the table of the remnants of breakfast. A curl of steam rose from the coffee pot and two clean porcelain coffee dishes had been placed on the table.

Julian took all this in with one hurried glance as he strode across the wide room buttoning his frockcoat without announcing himself. "Maman!?"

Antonia looked up, startled. "Oh! I did not expect you so soon."

"I came at once." He glanced at the footman. "Where's Father? What's happened?"

She slowly folded the letter but did not return it to the pile of correspondence and invitations stacked on a silver salver at her elbow. Instead she propped it against the porcelain milk jug and stared at it as if able to read the scrawled sloping handwriting on the reverse before turning away to look up at her son.

"Monseigneur is in his library."

"In his library?" he repeated in a whisper and let his wide shoulders drop, the tightness in his limbs easing knowing his father was no better or worse than the day before. Anxiety was replaced with annoyance. "Maman, do you have any idea what your summons has done to your household?" he demanded. "If Father is well and he did not request to see me then I will return

230

to my apartment to shave. I should not linger here."

The Duchess waved away the footman and put her hands in her lap and studied her eldest son. She was well aware that her ambiguous summons would produce immediate results, and that she had been deceitful in its execution. She knew Julian would come at once because he suspected something had happened to his father. But she needed to talk to him and on a subject that had remained unspoken between them. But how to do this with a son who chose to remain aloof because it was easier than dealing with the past? She sighed and decided the best approach was to appear stronger than she was.

She put out a hand to pick up the silver coffee urn off its pedestal but Julian was quick to do this for her. He poured out only into one dish.

"You will please sit, Julian," she commanded. "I do not care in the least if you have a full beard upon your face, or if you do not drink my coffee but me I mean to speak with you."

The Marquis remained standing. "There is little we can have to say to one another within these four walls that could not be said elsewhere."

The Duchess sat up straight and raised her arched brows. "Is that so? Perhaps you would prefer to talk with your maman in the middle of the open field surrounded by animals of the barn, *hein*? That I could easily have arranged, but me I do not want to get my silk slippers muddied."

Julian's jaw set hard. "I would gladly have you sacrifice one pair of slippers, Maman, than flame speculative gossip by having me summonsed here to your private apartments."

"An open field would do you more harm, *mon fils*."

When he threw up a hand but did not contradict her she knew he understood. She watched as he went to the window to stare out at the rose garden with its rows of fragrant white blooms planted for her by the Duke and carefully tended by a team of gardeners. After what seemed a silence of minutes she said, "I have never questioned your father's judgment. But when he sent you away I thought my heart it would break. And then later, much later, when he finally told me he had married you off in such a cold-hearted way I was so very angry with him. I have never been angry with him before or since. You understand, Julian, yes?"

"He did what he considered necessary."

"But... An arranged marriage it was not what I wanted for my son."

That brought him back to the table and for want of something to fill the awkward silence between them he poured out a dish of coffee and stirred in a spoon full of sugar. His eyes locked on hers.

"But what choice did my father have? Allow me to make an imprudent match on the Continent just to spite him or secure his dynastic future by arranging my marriage with a Cavendish heiress in the hopes that one day in the future there would be children of the match before his death? It is no worse than the situation he finds himself in: old enough to be a grandfather to his own children and married to a woman almost half his age who will outlive him by thirty years. I know which I prefer." When his mother looked away swiftly, emerald-green eyes awash with tears, he wished he could have cut out his tongue than have wounded her by such unthinking truths. He drew up a chair. "Lord, Maman, I didn't mean—I just wanted to reassure you—"

The Duchess cleared her throat. "I am perfectly well aware your father... He and I we will not grow old together," she interrupted in thickly accented English; the first time he had heard her speak his native tongue in many years. "I realize this concerns you; that one day soon your father he will—that he will no longer be with us—and I will have to live—live without him..."

"There really is no need—"

"Yes. There is a very great need!" she said in a rush. "This opportunity I may never have again. You think it is easy for me to talk of Monseigneur leaving me? That we will soon be parted on this earth? It is a thing that is the most horrid imaginable and I never dwell on it. It is only that I must tell you how it is so you will stop worrying about me. And you do worry, don't you, Julian? That is the truth of the matter." She stared at the opposite wall with its patterned wallpaper of lotus flowers and cranes. "I do not know why it is so, but it is easier to explain these things to you in the English tongue, it makes it less real to me. So you will please excuse my pronunciation; I am out of practice."

She was trying desperately to be strong, but it only served to make her appear even younger, more fragile and more vulnerable. And her green eyes were so full of sorrow that Julian could not look at her.

"We understand one another, Julian. Yes?" she asked. When he nodded his bowed head, she rallied herself. "I count each day with your father as a blessing and I do not care what those fools, those idiot physicians say! I intend that your father live a great many years yet."

"Of course he will, Maman, a great many years," Julian assured her gently; privately he did not hold to such a conviction.

"You think because your father he is in frail health he does not *see*? Never forget, Julian: Monseigneur is as omniscient as ever. He knows you frown on the consequences his dissipated past has brought to his family, that you conduct your life very differently from what his was like when he first became Duke."

"But I have never judged him, Maman!"

Antonia covered her son's fingers with her small hand and smiled. "That is very true, *mon fils*," she said, unconsciously reverting to her native French tongue. "But he sees that you view your future as Duke with trepidation and reluctance."

"Of course I am reluctant! To inherit my birthright he must be dead. You think that is a prospect I relish? That in order for me to strut the world stage as Duke, my father, a man I love and respect, must be cold in his grave? Lord, Maman, you above all others must see that I dread the coming of the day when I am saluted as His Grace the Most Noble Duke of Roxton."

"Yes, I see it, Julian," the Duchess replied sadly, tears glistening on her cheeks, "but I ask that you not *show* it. He wants to leave this world knowing you embrace his exulted position with all the enthusiasm and energy in which he inherited the title from his grandfather. What he needs now, at this the end of his long life, is the reassurance that your future it is secure… and to be at peace. Deborah's pregnancy has given him reassurance but only you can give him peace."

Julian sat back in his chair, momentarily uncomfortable, and rubbed the tips of his long fingers across his stubbled cheek. "If he is concerned the annulment will go forward…"

Antonia dried her eyes on a scrap of lace she called a handkerchief and shook her head and smiled. "I am not talking about that great piece of nonsense at all! A one-eyed idiot can see that you and Deborah are very much in love. That pleases us both more than I can tell you."

In spite of himself, Julian felt his face flood with heat. "Strange," he muttered, "Deb knew instantly the same about you and Father..."

"Because she has a pure heart and thus sees the truth," the Duchess stated. She sat forward in the lattice-backed chair, as if fearing to be overheard. "Listen to me, Julian. What I have to tell you your father and I have never told a living soul, and you must promise it will go no further, *mon fils, hein?*" Julian's nod of assent made her continue. "I tell you this without your father knowing I do so. It bruises my heart to go behind his back in this way because me I have never done so before, but... It is important for your future and the future of your sons that the past is finally laid to rest. You see, Julian," she said in a halting voice, gaze lowered to where her hand rested on her son's embroidered upturned cuff, "The Comtesse Duras-Valfons has always maintained that her son is Monseigneur's son also; that her child was conceived at Fontainebleau when Monseigneur was hunting with the King. The parish records bear this out, for the boy was indeed born nine months after the King's Hunt, around the time of your own birth..." Her green eyes flickered to Julian's immobile face and then lowered again with a small sigh. "Your father and I we were married two months after this Hunt and you were born just seven months later. Before your time, we said. But that was a convenient lie. You were a small baby and that made it easier to convince others, but you had not quickened early."

Julian frowned. He wanted to stand to stretch his legs for the conversation had taken an intimate turn that he was not convinced he needed to hear. It made him shift restlessly on his chair. "What is the point of this, Maman? Given the Duke's past, I am not at all shocked to learn he bedded his mistress then turned around and married you out of hand. What's important to me is that he reformed his wicked ways for you."

Antonia squeezed his arm. "Listen to me, Julian," she demanded imperiously. "Do you not understand that if Mme Duras-Valfons and I conceived around the same time that your father he was not bedding that woman at all! I may have fallen in love with a great rake but your father he knew very well what was expected of him before I would give myself to him."

Julian cocked an eyebrow at her. "And you think I don't know who rules this noble roost?"

The Duchess waved her hands at him. "Please do not interrupt again or I may not be able to tell you all of it before Monseigneur he returns. Particularly when this is the most difficult part to explain." She sighed again. "I tell you the rest bluntly. Your father he did reform his ways for me. From the moment he became my guardian around the time of my eighteenth birthday—while I was living here in this house—which was many months before we were married, he rejected all other females, and this while I was still engaged to another. It is true I tell you, Julian!"

"I believe you, Maman," he reassured her, hiding his astonishment and spreading smile at her scowl.

"The day Monseigneur relinquished his guardianship of me I was to go to London to stay with my grandmother. Your father he went off to Fontainebleau and your Aunt Estée she went with Vallentine to visit her Tante Victoire in St. Germain, and so the Hôtel it was shut up. But I did not go to England straight away and Monseigneur he did not go to Fontainebleau. He returned at nightfall... to be with me. Martin he is the only one who knows this. We spent a week here alone in this apartment. That is when you were conceived." Her gaze flickered to her son's face. "You understand now, Julian, yes, why your father he will not speak of this time. Why it must remain between us?"

Julian could sit still no longer and he wandered to the windows and back again and looked down at his mother, at the heightened color in her porcelain cheeks and the hesitation in her large emerald green eyes. He thrust his hands in his frockcoat pockets. "Because if the world discovered that the dissolute Duke of Roxton had taken advantage of a young innocent girl in his care, under his very roof, it would forever blacken his honor?"

Antonia hung her head and then bravely looked up at her son.

"*Mon fils*, you know as well as I that Society it is indulgent of the degenerate ways of a great rake but a nobleman of advancing years who seduces a-a virgin who is under his care and protection… If this girl she is of the same social standing and betrothed in marriage to another, then this nobleman he has broken the unwritten code of his peers."

"And his peers will no longer consider him a gentleman," Julian continued when she could not. "They will turn their noble backs on him. He is condemned forever as an abhorrent monster."

"It wasn't like that, Julian. *He* isn't like that! Monseigneur and I we were in love and we did not think through the consequences of our actions. All that mattered was having those few days alone together before we were to be forever parted. The future—living without each other—it was inconceivable." When Julian gave a grunt she added in a rush, "You are not to think of your father in that way, *mon fils*. If you must think badly of one of us then it is I you should condemn. He would not have crossed the great divide that separates guardian from ward had I not enticed him to it!"

Julian shook his head solemnly and took a turn about the room but when he came back to her it was with a grin on his face. "Maman! As if I could think worse of you or Papa knowing what you have just told me. So I was conceived out of wedlock. What of that? Who am I to judge when I myself deceived my own wife into thinking me a common man so that she could get to know me as Julian, not the Marquis of Alston. I gave no thought to the consequences of my actions. Who thinks beyond the immediate when the heart rules the head?" He pulled her out of the chair and hugged her to him, a great shudder of relief coursing through his body. "*Merci, ma mere.* Your secret it is safe with me. And it has lifted a great burden from my shoulders."

Antonia stepped back and looked up at him. "Because that man he is not your brother, yes?"

Julian bowed over her hand and kissed it. "Yes."

Their moment of intimacy was abruptly ended when the breakfast room door opened and the Duchess's lady-in-waiting came into the room, bobbed a curtsey and whispered near Antonia's ear before departing, leaving the door wide.

"Mme le Duchesse, please excuse the intrusion. I wouldn't have disturbed you for the world but Alston is not in his apartments and his valet—*Julian?*" Martin said with considerable surprise, suddenly spying his godson by the undraped window as he bowed low over the Duchess's outstretched hand.

"What is it, Martin?" asked the Duchess with alarm; her first thought with the Duke.

The old man looked from mother to son. Julian came away from the window to stand by his mother. Both were ashen-faced. "Not the Duke," he assured them, though he still looked very worried. "It's Henri-Antoine. He's disappeared. Bailey thinks he's gone to the Tuileries with Master Cavendish." He smiled crookedly at the Marquis, eyes widening imperceptibly at the day-old growth on his godson's face. "It seems he's determined to see that wretched bear."

Julian put an arm about his mother's shoulders. "Don't worry, Maman. I know exactly where to find them." He rubbed a hand over his stubbled chin and grinned at his godfather. He had seen the flash of disapproval cross the old man's face. "I suppose a shave will have to wait until my return from the Tuileries."

Antonia touched Martin's arm. "Thank you for not telling Monseigneur. He has enough to worry him what with that oaf Sartine daring to bother him."

Julian's head snapped round at his mother. "The lieutenant of police is here annoying Father? Why?"

"That it is unimportant," the Duchess said dismissively, propelling him towards the door. "Your brother he is what is important. So please you will now go fetch him home so that I may scold him severely and before Mon—Monseigneur!" she declared with a bright smile as she went forward to greet the Duke, who stood in the doorway, leaning lightly on his cane, and surveying his wife through his quizzing glass. "You have sent those horrid policemen away, Renard, yes?" she asked eagerly.

"What's this, Antonia?" the Duke drawled, twirling his quizzing glass on its black silk riband. He was frowning but there was a decided twinkle of mischief in his black eyes. "Twenty-six years of marriage, twenty-six years of—er—uninterrupted privacy in our own chambers, and yet in one morning I am gone less than an hour and return to find my wife entertaining our son and his godfather without me?"

Antonia went up on tip-toe and kissed him. Her smile was

impish. "But, in those twenty-six years, you have never left me to breakfast alone and so me I was lonely."

The Duke returned her kiss and playfully chided her under the chin. "Dear me, I see I must never leave you alone again."

"Sir, if Sartine was here, why wasn't I told of it?" Julian asked with annoyance, interrupting his parents' playful banter.

"Because, my son, he came to see me," the Duke replied simply. "There has been an interesting—er—development in the Lefebvre case."

"Such as?"

The Duke regarded his son with an inscrutable gaze. "Correct my grand presumption, but I believe you know well enough already."

Julian's eyebrows lifted with surprise. "Exceedingly interesting. So he's finally done the honorable thing and confessed?"

"The words *honorable* and—er—*confess* do not readily spring to mind."

Julian's lip curled. Martin Ellicott was nonplussed. The Duke took out his snuffbox and tapped the lid. Antonia looked at all three and said bluntly,

"Me I do not understand at all! What is this development of which you speak, Renard?"

"I'm only too willing to allow Julian to tell you, my love. I find the whole Lefebvre imbroglio fatiguing in the extreme."

The Marquis opened his mouth to speak when unannounced into the breakfast room rushed the Duke's sister. Estée Vallentine crossed the room in a whirl of voluminous hooped petticoats and a mass of disordered gray hair festooned with curling ribbons, as if she had left off in the middle of having her hair dressed and powdered. She clutched a crumpled letter to her heaving bosom and spying her brother she waved this at the Duke. Roxton rolled his eyes to the ornate ceiling and sat down as his sister launched herself, sobbing, into the Duchess's arms.

"Antonia! He's eloped! My son! My *darling* boy. *Evelyn.* He's run off with a filthy *bourgeois!*"

Fifteen

*D*eb would have preferred to make the short trip to the Tuileries on foot. It was a lovely day. But Brigitte, Joseph and two of the Duke's burly footmen had other ideas and they arrived at the formal gardens by carriage. So much for slipping quietly away without anyone knowing her whereabouts! Yet she realized it was better to have her entourage with her than leave them behind to alert her husband and his father that she had absconded. The carriage was met at the terraced steps leading down to a broad central avenue by Evelyn Ffolkes, who had with him Jack, an odd assortment of musicians, and a small band of servants carrying musical instruments and chairs.

While the musicians and their retinue of hangers-on went off to ready themselves for their performance by one of the large fountains, Deb took the opportunity to stroll with Joseph and Brigitte amongst the crowded stalls that lined the walks. The two beefy footmen who had accompanied the carriage fell in behind the Marchioness and her party, keeping a discreet distance, yet ever watchful of the crowds. The noise of carriages and barrows plying along the streets was not so deafening within the expanse of the Tuileries where promenaded groups of pleasure seekers out to enjoy a spring day of entertainment. News reporters huddled under the trees, old men played at chess in the shade, some enjoyed skittles, and groups of men and women partook of *cafe au lait* from one the many gaily colored stalls. Stilt walkers, puppeteers, mime artists and even the quack doctors provided endless amusement for the passers-by.

There was such a carnival atmosphere within these walled gardens, with everyone intent on enjoying the festivities staged by the Parisian city officials to celebrate the Dauphin's marriage to the Austrian Princess Marie Antoinette, that Deb almost forgot her dual purpose for coming to the gardens. To hear Jack play in Evelyn's string ensemble was paramount, but she also hoped Mlle Lefebvre would show as promised by Robert Thesiger.

As Evelyn had helped her alight from the carriage, she received the distinct impression that he had no wish to be private with her, conveniently avoiding her eye. She hoped Mlle Lefebvre would be more forthcoming.

A chance glance over her shoulder and she saw the Duke's henchmen not far from her back jostling with a boisterous group of street performers. Their presence gave her an odd sense of comfort, so did the small pearl handled pistol she carried in the pouch sewn onto her boot; a gift from Otto on her arrival in Paris, who warned her to carry the weapon whenever she went onto the streets of Paris.

Just as she was beginning to wonder how she was supposed to recognize Mlle Lefebvre or find Robert Thesiger in such a festive crowd, the gentleman himself materialized before her. He had broken away from a group of powdered and patched young men and came strolling towards her, a decided twinkle in his blue eyes, and bowed low over her out-stretched hand.

"Will the bride take a stroll with an old friend?" he asked smoothly, a glance over her shoulder at the stony faces of Joseph and her lady-in-waiting, and at the two brutes in Roxton livery who hovered further afield of the Marchioness's little party. Boldly, he offered Deb his silken arm and his smile widened when Joseph gave a start. "Yesterday, I failed to wish you happy on your marriage. Are you happy, my lady?"

Deb met his blue-eyed gaze openly. "Yes. Very happy."

He smiled as if he did not believe her and they walked in silence amongst the fashionable Parisians who were enjoying the sideshows and entertainments. A few powdered heads turned to admire this handsome couple being shadowed by two sour faced servants and a couple of ape-sized brutes in distinctive silver and red livery. Did anyone know to whom the livery belonged? A *Duke* you say? Which one?

Three stilt walkers and their entourage of tumblers and small band of musicians were making slow progress up the broad avenue towards them, scattering the promenading Parisians either side of the walk, teasing some and surrounding others with their antics. Deb and Robert Thesiger took refuge by a refreshment tent serving *café au lait*, to wait until this band of merry performers passed by. The commotion gave Thesiger the opportunity to face Deb, saying with concern in his blue eyes and a frown on his brow,

"I cannot help wondering: Had I confided in you from the very beginning Mlle Lefebvre's sorry predicament, would you now be Alston's wife in more than name only?"

"Tell me, sir: Did you pursue me in Bath to exact revenge on my husband because of Mlle Lefebvre's ruin?"

"My dear, you are quite beautiful and I very much wanted to bed you, for its own sake as well as to cuckold your husband," he said with a grin, puckering up the scar indenting his left cheek. "Unfortunately, this absurd tenacity of yours to engage your feelings before tumbling into bed proved my undoing. It necessitated I rethink how best to secure my future." His blue eyes scanned the sea of faces moving along the avenue, and then he looked at her again saying with a sad shake of his powdered head, "It pains me to involve you in this matter between the Roxtons and myself. But father and son must be brought to account for their actions."

"I fail to see how my involvement in the matter will make an ounce of difference to father or son."

"Don't you? Strange you should be so naïve," he pondered. "Tell me: Is it right that the Duke's legitimate son has all his needs, wants and desires, indeed the world, placed at his feet, all because his father rutted his mother with the blessing of church and state, while I, the Duke's natural son, is not recognized as of the same flesh?"

"And that's my husband's fault? You conveniently neglect the part played by your mother. The Comtesse raised you in resentment and bitterness all because of her unreasonable and spiteful jealousy of a girl whom the Duke fell in love with and who never did her a harm." Deb's smile was sad. "No, you are not to blame for the actions of your parents but your mother is just as blameworthy as the Duke."

For the first time in her company Robert Thesiger's calm veneer fell away.

"Rutted five minutes and you're persuaded by that family's arrogant line of argument? You simpleton! My mother was enticed into playing the whore with the same false promise that led to Mlle Lefebvre's seduction: the promise of marriage!"

"I have not the least interest in your opinions, of me or of the noble family into which I am married!" Deb retorted, a glance around to find the most convenient path back to Evelyn and her nephew who were at the large fountain. But all exits were blocked by the contingent of circus performers and their appreciative audience. She came as close to Robert Thesiger as her damask striped hooped petticoats would allow. "Be reasonable, sir. Surely it has occurred to you that perhaps Mlle Lefebvre pursued my husband for his rank and fortune. That when he rejected her advances she turned her attentions to another who could offer her a pale imitation of the same, a gentleman who has a close association with the Roxton family?"

Robert Thesiger stared at her as if she was raving. "Good God, Madam! Why the devil would she name Alston if he wasn't her seducer?"

Deb shrugged a bare shoulder. "Because rejection cut her to the quick. Because she did not want to reveal the identity of her real lover for fear of the consequences from her father, who had encouraged her to pursue the Marquis of Alston. They are but two reasons I can think of. You must admit, to the vast majority of females it is one thing to be seduced by a future Duke, quite another to allow a mere commoner between the sheets."

Robert Thesiger opened his mouth to refute this, had second thoughts, and said with a crooked smile, "Is that what persuaded you? That you will soon be Duchess of Roxton?"

"Why do you persist with this futile quest for retribution from the Duke of Roxton, a nobleman whose pride and arrogance will never permit him to acknowledge you as his son?" Deb asked calmly, ignoring Joseph's loud clearing of his throat. "Why do you assume my husband is cast from the same die? Is it because you cling to the absurd notion that to fill the Duke's shoes his son and heir must also be an arrogant and depraved debauchee as the Duke once was? Can't you see that my husband has always been the man his father became upon his marriage to the Duchess?"

"Madam, your husband doesn't deserve the rank thrust upon him by luck of birth. Who can respect a nobleman who'd prefer to live in the obscurity of his estate surrounded by his peasants, his pigs and his sheep rather than take up his rightful place at the helm of society? At Eton he never put himself forward, and yet his peers, those idiotic fawning brats who now make up Society, thrust him center stage as they do now, all because one day he'll be Duke of Roxton!"

"You ridicule him only because you do not understand him," Deb answered with exasperated patience. "Would you care to go through life never knowing who are your true friends; if you are chosen on merit, fawned over and praised, not because of who you are but because of what you will one day become? Just because he doesn't strut about society like an over-blown peacock full of his own consequence, lording it over all who are cast under his shadow, but has a natural deference for his social position and the huge responsibilities that will one day be his, you judge him as weak?"

Thesiger shoved his enamel snuffbox in a frockcoat pocket, Deb's line of argument dismissed as credulous sincerity. "Had the Duke done the honorable thing by my mother I'd be heir to a dukedom!" he seethed. "And I tell you this, Madam: I'm no social cripple. I'd know how to use such an exalted position to best possible advantage!"

Yes, for your own self-serving ends and with no regard for others, Deb thought sadly. Her husband and this man were so dissimilar in every way that it was pointless to continue the discussion. Robert Thesiger was so twisted up with jealousy and resentment that her arguments were incomprehensible and unheard. Nothing she could say would make an ounce of difference to his distorted view of life. It was time she ended this circular discussion before she missed Jack's performance altogether. And she was reasonably confident Mlle Lefebvre would show herself at this concert. If only she knew what the girl looked like. Another glance about her and she was relieved to see the walks were now clearing of spectators and the tumblers and stilt walkers had moved on up the avenue. She signaled to Brigitte and Joseph she was ready to leave and in a gesture of goodwill put out her gloved hand in farewell to Robert Thesiger.

"Good day, my lord. I hope that in time Baron Thesiger's inheritance brings you some comfort and joy. Now, if you will excuse me, I must return to my nephew where, I hope, Mlle Lefebvre may be found amongst the audience for Mr. Ffolkes performance?"

"I wouldn't know, Madam," he said softly, taking a step closer, blue eyes scanning the view over her head. "She has refused to see me these past three months or more."

"But—Did you not say she would be here today at noon?" Deb asked with a confused frown, a look out over the sea of faces. "And I am very sure she will be because—"

"I don't care one way or the other," Robert Thesiger purred, and before Deb could step away, his hand shot out to hard-grip her wrist. He pulled her against him and in one deft maneuver had her back hard up against his torso, her arm twisted tightly into the small of her back. Thus bound together he shuffled them along the walk toward the closest group of circus performers, her capture accomplished before Brigitte and Joseph knew what was happening.

"It's time to end this charade." he hissed in her ear, staring fixedly at Brigitte and Joseph who stood as stone in the middle of the avenue, gaze riveted on his face. He glanced at the two burly servants in livery and they too remained fixed, as if awaiting his next move. He caught up Deb's free hand and with his hand covering hers pressed her open palm hard against the front of her damask bodice. "Made quick work of impregnating you, didn't he, your diffident Adonis." At Deb's gasp of surprise, he sniggered. "Did you hope to keep such momentous news a secret from me, the child's uncle? For shame!"

"It's none of your business!"

"It is very much my business. Have you any idea what the birth of a male grandchild will mean for the Roxtons?"

Deb tried in vain to struggle free, but she was pinned against his torso, his hand that pressed against hers now uncomfortably tight on her abdomen. "Let me go before you find yourself swinging from the end of a rope!"

"A grandchild would give the Roxton Dukedom a future—"

"It already has a future in my husband! That is indeprivable."

Thesiger was incredulous. "Roxton want a son to succeed him who prefers to rusticate on his estates than strut the world stage? Ha!"

"You won't force the Duke's hand by taking my child hostage!"

"Don't take me for a fool, Madam," he growled, forcing her deep within a group of acrobats who closed ranks about them, dancing and twirling and tumbling, and making an unholy racket. "It's not a hostage I want. It's *revenge*."

A tumbler back-flipped, came face to face with Deb and winked with a tobacco stained, almost toothless grin, and then she knew with an increasingly rapid heart beat that these performers were in Thesiger's pay for the specific purpose of aiding her abduction. The appreciative crowd of onlookers, oblivious to the crime being committed under their very noses, applauded the tumblers' antics, as they swept Thesiger and his captive along the avenue in a processional that was heading towards the river.

"Look straight ahead," Thesiger commanded when Deb tried to catch a glimpse of Joseph and Brigitte.

The closeness of the performers surrounding her, Thesiger's arm about her waist and the fact she had only picked at her breakfast contributed to the feeling of nausea rising within her and which was fast beginning to overwhelm her.

And that's when it came to her to pretend to faint.

Surely Thesiger would be forced to stop and revive her if he hoped to get her to the riverbank? So without another thought she let her knees buckle, and as her legs collapsed under her she expected Robert Thesiger to catch her in his arms and right her. Actuality was far more frightening.

As she crumpled into the dust of the graveled walk Robert Thesiger's hold on her slackened and he stepped away. Unable to right herself in time, she fell towards the ground expecting to be trampled by the performers who continued to tumble and make merry while their band of players crashed cymbals together and played their tin pipes a little louder than before, her cry for help unheard and unheeded. She wondered if this wasn't how Thesiger had planned for her to lose the baby all along; no blame attached to him. Just as blame hadn't been apportioned to him all those years ago when he had whispered such horrid, foul lies in Julian's ear about the Duchess and her unborn child.

Yet just as her feet became entangled in the yards of silk of her crumpling petticoats she stuck out a hand and grabbed for the nearest billowing shirt of a sinewy acrobat. His split second reflexes reacted to pull Deb to him before she was trampled underfoot by his companions and he picked her up in his strong arms and carried her the short distance along an avenue that led to the river.

Her stockinged feet in mid air, Deb felt a hard object knock against the ankle of her old kid boot. It was Otto's pistol. How foolish of her not to remember before now that she had worn her boots specifically because she could carry Otto's pistol on her person! She was so relieved knowing she had her pistol and grateful to the swarthy faced acrobat for saving her that she made no attempt to struggle or cry out. She merely awaited her opportunity to reach down and remove the pistol from its holster. Her chance came soon enough.

The procession halted at the end of the avenue at the edge of the gardens. Beyond was the Seine where a boat awaited them. Over-confident of their success, one of the kidnappers performed a victory tumble and back flipped, over balanced and fell on his buttocks into a hedge. His fellows laughed and did nothing to help him up, the acrobat holding fast to Deb finally setting her on her feet now they were away from the main avenue. Her moment had arrived. As she was put to firm ground she carefully lifted her boot and slipped the pistol from its holster and hid it amongst the folds of her crushed and disordered petticoats, her captors none the wiser as they continued to laugh at the expense of their fellow's embarrassing fall in the shrubbery.

One of the tumblers exclaimed that before they departed for the river they should have a little fun with their hostage. His suggestion was laughed away as the emotive talk of a drunkard, not to be taken seriously. Yet, when the observation was made that none of them had ever been so close to a titled lady before and that this was a once in a lifetime opportunity to discover if a noblewoman's porcelain skin was indeed as soft as the fine silks she wore, more than one of their number turned lascivious eyes on Deb. The tumbler who had fallen into the hedge offered to have first feel of the girl and he grabbed a handful of Deb's petticoats and began to tug up the yards of an exquisite fabric he had never before touched, much to the delight and appreciative hoots of his fellows. They urged him on, to lift the gossamer layers to the girl's thighs where garters held up her fine white silk stockings.

A cheer went up followed by the explosive discharge of a pistol.

The report from Deb's pistol was deafening. It instantly silenced the tumblers and musicians surrounding her, and then one of their number let out a blood-curdling scream. The drunken tumbler who had dared to lift Deb's petticoats had been shot. The ball had pierced the leather of his jackboot. He fell to the ground, writhing in agony, clutching his ankle with both hands while his fellows stared at Deb in horrified silence. The silk of her gown smoldered, the bullet exploding from the cocked pistol searing the top layers of her many layered petticoats, but she was unharmed and had great presence of mind to keep the smoking pistol leveled at her abductors.

Shock gave way to anger tinged with wariness at such outrageous behavior from a female, a lady at that! More than one of the performers wanted to abandon the girl and flee. After all, they had already committed a hanging offence by abducting her. That she had the courage to fire upon them was enough to put paid to their plans. Tumblers and musicians scattered, most running back into the gardens, their escape route to the river blocked by the two burly liveried footmen who had accompanied Deb to the Tuileries. Even the man she had shot managed to hobble away supported by two of his fellows, heaping curses upon her head between his continued whimpers of agony.

The Duke's servants did not give chase. They had their orders. The safety of the Marchioness was paramount; everything and everyone else was of no consequence. To this end one of the footmen mutely removed the pistol from Deb's hand, scooped her up, despite her objections that she was quite capable of walking, and carried her to the steps where he sat her gently down. His twin made Deb a formal bow of recognition and then boldly offered her the contents of his hip flask to calm her nerves. Deb was about to tell him she was perfectly calm when she realized that her whole body was trembling and that perhaps a drop of brandy would help settle her and so she gratefully drank of the fiery liquid.

She felt remarkably calm, helped by the gulp of brandy, given she had just foiled an attempt to kidnap her. Unharmed, she did not let herself dwell on possibilities. Yet, despite foiling the kidnapping and the protection of a footman the size of a Russian bear, she did not feel her baby would be completely safe until she had returned to Julian and the safety of the Hôtel Roxton. Her fear was justified when she chanced to glance up the stairs and there on the top step was Robert Thesiger. She gave a start and the footman protecting her went forward, ready to meet any challenge Thesiger cared to throw at him, the pistol leveled and cocked.

Thesiger came lightly down the stairs, passed the footman standing over Deb as if he did not exist, not a glance in Deb's direction. She watched him follow the line of the ancient stone wall and wondered what held his attention. He did not look left or right but out across the gardens at the fleeing hordes as he stripped off his frockcoat, tossed it and his ruffles aside and unsheathed his sword. And then she saw the reason for his preoccupation. Coming along the gravel path was her husband.

It was while striding the avenues in search of his brother, over a head taller than those around him, that Julian had caught sight of Deb in company with Robert Thesiger. It brought him up short. He had left her safely tucked up in bed and that's where he supposed she had remained, sleeping peacefully. And then he remembered something about Jack being involved in a musical performance and he should've realized Deb would do all in her power to ensure she did not miss her nephew's first public appearance. That she was strolling the Tuileries gardens in conversation with his nemesis not only angered him but also brought with it an unwanted sense of trepidation for her safety. He was in no doubts that it was Thesiger who had sought out his wife, and he wondered what mischief the man meant.

He stood in the middle of the crowded avenue as stone, watching them, for how long, he had no idea. He stared at Robert

Thesiger, willing him to look up, and when the man finally did their eyes met and Thesiger's face broke into a grin. It was only then that Julian found his legs and he strode towards them, anger and fear extinguishing all thought of finding his younger brother. His green eyes did not leave his wife and when Thesiger grabbed Deb to him, her back up against his chest and his arm about her waist, she struggling in vain to break free of him, Julian felt a gut-wrenching sense of helplessness for the first time in his life.

Frantically he tried to push his way through the immoveable crowd that seemed to swell in number by the minute. Swarthy faces, toothless and unshaven, began to replace those of the gentleman and women come to the gardens for a leisurely stroll. Tumblers, stilt walkers and a band of rowdy musicians clogged the avenue and when he tried to break through their ranks he was rudely and unceremoniously shoved backwards and told that this section of the gardens was now closed to the public.

His second attempt saw him knocked off his feet, the promise of gold extinguishing all deference to rank, for although the acrobats who wrestled Julian to the ground took in the fineness of his clothes, the whiteness of his soft hands and the ornate hilt of his sword and rightly concluded that here was a gentleman if not a nobleman, they had their orders. Besides what could one nobleman do against a gang of muscular circus performers?

What they failed to assess was that the nobleman's fine lace ruffles and exquisite coat of superfine disguised a well-exercised physique whose strength was fuelled by a furious anxiety in his need to rescue his wife and unborn child from danger. He refused to stay down and had knocked out cold two tumblers and was all for taking on the third when Joseph materialized beside him. The groom's nose was bloody and he had the beginnings of a black eye but his grin was enough to convince Julian that the man was enjoying the fray hugely and obviously looked worse then he felt.

He jumped in to assist the Marquis, who was beating off a particularly hard-set gypsy, and shouted out for his lordship to go after the Marchioness. He, Joseph, would take care of this ugly customer. Julian nodded his understanding and took off running down the avenue. He was almost upon the procession of performers and musicians when he saw the two footmen in Roxton livery leave the path and set off across the flowerbeds. He slowed, wondering what they were up to and whom he should follow, the liveried footmen or the procession, and then to his surprise Robert Thesiger appeared from the back of the procession and disappeared between two stalls, alone.

And then not a minute later there came the deafening noise of a pistol being discharged. The explosion rang out across the expanse of gardens and for one shocked moment an eerie silence descended on the Tuileries. The sound of pistol fire brought out everyone's worst fears and panic overwhelmed even the most phlegmatic of temperaments. Pandemonium ensued. Fearing shots meant a pistol-wielding madman was on the loose, visitors to every quarter of the terraced gardens panicked and instantly sought escape.

People ran in all directions. Wild-eyed parents scooped up crying children, agitated shopkeepers and their customers dived under chairs and into the back of stalls seeking refuge from the unknown assailant and the stampeding hordes. Puppeteers, mime artists and street performers, animal handlers with their screeching monkeys and barking little dogs, all leapt out of the way or were pushed aside as hundreds of people trampled over carefully tended flower beds, dived into ornamental ponds to hide with the fish or raced with frenzied determination for the nearest exit.

Shouts went up for the militia.

At the sound of pistol fire Julian's heart missed a beat and the blood rushed up into his ears. He had a nauseous presentiment that the pistol fire was connected to Deb's abduction and it fuelled a furious determination to get to her as quickly as possible. He elbowed his way through the fleeing hordes, withstanding the mindless jostling and knocks from the onslaught of a frenzied mob. Size and height saved him from being trampled but it also meant he stood out in a crowd seeking help to escape from a phantom madman. More than once he was appealed to, but he ignored all requests for assistance and ran on.

And then Julian saw her, his beautiful, courageous wife, watched over by the two liveried servants he had instructed to be her shadow whenever she ventured outside the protective high walls surrounding the Hôtel Roxton. She was sitting calmly on the steps that led up to the river, clothes and hair disheveled, but very much alive. The noise and madness surrounding him ceased to be important, the shouting and the screams barely registered. It mattered little that somewhere in the Tuileries there might be a madman with a pistol. Deb was unharmed and no one and nothing else mattered. He breathed deeply, as if, for the first time since he saw her together with Robert Thesiger, a great stone weight had been lifted off his chest.

He strode towards her, a hand held up above his head to let her know he had seen her. When she waved back, he smiled for the first time since entering the Tuileries. Yet she did not look happy and when she averted her face with tears in her eyes his happiness evaporated and in its place was a heaviness of heart that made each step closer to her as if he was wading through thick mud. He felt empty and hollow thinking that some harm must have come to her or the baby, for what else would make Deb look so stricken? He then chanced to follow her tearful gaze and there standing at the end of the avenue, sword drawn and waiting him was Robert Thesiger.

$\mathcal{S}$ixteen

$\mathcal{S}$o it had come to this: A duel in the Tuileries in the broad light of day, with the formalities ignored and his pregnant wife watching on. The ludicrous reality brought a crooked smile to Julian's mouth as he watched Robert Thesiger make an elaborate display of flexing his rapier. The man's intentions couldn't be cruder, nor his methods more dishonorable. Julian was in no doubt that Thesiger meant a duel to the death. So be it.

Julian stripped off his frockcoat and tore the ruffles from his shirtsleeves, rolling the ragged edges up out of the way to his elbows. He then scraped back the curls that had fallen into his eyes during the fight with the acrobats and retied the ribbon at the nape of his neck. Preparations concluded (he would not allow himself even one brief glance at his wife) he approached Thesiger with sword drawn. They briefly saluted one another in the formal manner, and then steel hissed against steel.

The duel commenced.

From the moment the swords crossed, Thesiger went in for the attack, his frenzied swordplay instantly putting Julian on the back foot. Time and again Thesiger lunged, employing every trick of the fencing master's art, forcing his opponent back across the gravel at a furious pace in the hopes of wrong-footing him. He saw an opening in Julian's defence and delivered a lightening thrust. At the last moment, it was expertly deflected. But the tip of Thesiger's rapier caught inside Julian's rolled sleeve, flexed the steel shaft of the sword bow-like and then it sprung forward and upwards. The sleeve of Julian's shirt ripped, the needlepoint tip of Thesiger's blade glanced up along his bared upper arm and split the taught flesh of hardened muscle. Blood instantly flowed from the stinging wound and trickled down Julian's arm and the blades disengaged.

But Thesiger wasn't about to give Julian any respite. He snarled "on guard" and the fight went on. Far from giving Thesiger any advantage, the wound made little difference to Julian's ability with the sword, the stinging and the trickle of blood ignored as he met Thesiger's every thrust and parry with a strong-wristed foil of his own.

Repeatedly the blades clashed with a sing of steel on steel, neither achieving supremacy. Each man was able to counter every move of the other but Thesiger was beginning to tire, evidence in the sweat that soaked his shirt and beaded his forehead. At one point he leapt back and wiped the sweat from his brow and Julian gave him the moment, lowering his blade to wipe the sticky blood from his forearm onto his damp shirt. Thesiger's blade came up again and the fight resumed, a little less frenzied than before.

They came in close, blades sliding off one another, Thesiger scrambling backwards and fending off a powerful lunge. He fell hard up against the stair wall where just above his powdered sweating head Deb was seated on the step, watched over by a bear-sized footman wielding a pistol. He pushed his shoulders off the wall and righted himself, Julian awaiting his pleasure. It was Thesiger who called "on guard". With a smile and a sideways glance up at the Marchioness he taunted the husband hoping to whip him into such a white-hot rage of unguarded passion that he would let down his guard. Panting air into his deprived lungs Thesiger said with a sneer as their swords disengaged,

"Your wife—Your cousin—When she was in Paris last— They were lovers—He had her first."

"Liar!" Julian growled savagely, white-lipped fury and not the cool-headedness of time honored tactics drummed into him by his fencing master causing his lunge to go awry and giving Thesiger the tactical advantage he was seeking.

It was Thesiger who now forced Julian against the wall, flexing the nobleman's wrist sideways and twisting his grip so that the rapier came down at an angle, enabling Thesiger to get under his guard. He made a final thrust for the nobleman's heart but Julian's reflexes were the quicker and his sword came up to thwart the thrust. He managed to push himself off the wall and using his superior strength and stronger wrist forced Thesiger back again, Thesiger's sword wide of its mark, the point stabbing at air between Julian's arm and torso.

Unable to halt the momentum of his final lunge, Thesiger stumbled forward and, as Julian leaped out of the way, he fell hard against the wall and then onto his knees in the gravel. He scrambled to pick himself up and put out a hand for his rapier that had spun out of his grip. But the Marquis was there, looming large over him and he grabbed Thesiger by the collar of his wet shirt and hauled him to his feet. Righting him he then scooped up his sword and this he tossed to him, stepping back and calling "on guard".

But Thesiger knew he was spent and that if he put up his sword Julian would surely kill him in the short encounter to follow. He marveled at the nobleman's reserves of strength and wondered how best to extricate himself from a no win situation. Wiping the sweat from his eyes, he glanced first at the Marchioness sitting as a marble statue, oval face bleached white and an unblinking gaze on her husband. He then regarded the large figure of the Marquis of Alston, standing tall, damp black curls falling into his eyes, green eyes ablaze and so resembling those belonging to his mother the Duchess that it brought a sneer full of hatred to Thesiger's lips, the scar puckered and pulsating with heat. He made a half-hearted effort to raise his sword and then did the unexpected. Tossing his sword at Julian's feet, he rushed towards the stairs leading up to the river.

In two steps he was standing over Deb.

Deb had watched the duel as if it was something of a blurred bad dream. When Thesiger's blade flashed up and split the muscle in her husband's arm she muffled a cry behind shaking hands, wanting to put a stop to the encounter there and then. Yet she sat calmly on the step as if she was attending an Assembly ball and she watching a couple dancing a minuet, as if it was the most natural thing in the world for her husband to be fighting a duel with this fiend who had sought to destroy her.

When the Marquis finally had the better of his opponent her sigh of relief was audible and the tension eased in her back and shoulders, although Thesiger's last desperate lunge at her husband's heart had her eyes tightly closed for the briefest of moments only for her to open them wide to discover Julian standing over Thesiger who was now prostrate on the ground.

Thus when the man leapt up on the step beside her she was startled into wondering what he was about, for the duel looked for all the world as if it would end in Thesiger's death. Behind her she heard the cock of a pistol and was about to order the footman to hold his fire when the Marquis shouted out for the servant to lower his weapon. Yet before the footman had a chance to obey the command Thesiger made a grab for the pistol.

There was a brief, close struggle between the two men.

The pistol discharged.

The shot rang out across the eerily deserted Tuileries.

The footman and Robert Thesiger stood very still and then fell apart. For a brief moment it was unclear which man had been shot. Then the footman took a step back, the pistol still in his hand and blood splattered across the front of his liveried uniform. Thesiger turned slowly and came face to face with Deb, who had risen to her feet, and his blue eyes were wide and blank. He had both hands to his belly and blood was flowing from between his splayed fingers. He took a step, pitched forward and fell off the stairs.

In three strides Julian was at his side and went down on a knee to cradle the dying man's head. Thesiger's eyes flickered open and recognizing the blurred frowning face high above him he grimaced, showing blood-covered teeth.

"Couldn't give you the—the satisfaction..." he said with great effort, expelled a last breath and was dead.

Julian fetched the dead man's frockcoat and laid it across his upper body before reaching into his own breech's pocket for his handkerchief to bind up his own wound. Deb came down the steps and took the handkerchief from him and did the deed, her long fingers shaking as she deftly tied a tight knot in the material to staunch the bleeding. He thanked her and there followed a moment's awkward silence in which neither was able to form the words to express their feelings. All they could do was stare at one another until Deb fell into her husband's arms to be enveloped in a warm and protective embrace, relief bringing tears and fear of what might have been.

"Sweet Jesus, Deb," Julian finally whispered in her hair, voice low and unsteady, holding her more tightly against him, "what hell have I put you through?"

"We're alive and we have each other. That's all that has ever mattered."

He smiled and cradled her, face buried in her mussed hair, shudders of relief coursing through his exhausted body. After what seemed an age he kissed the top of her head and looked up at the sound of approaching voices.

Coming along the deserted avenue was his cousin Evelyn Ffolkes and a rag tag bunch of disheveled musicians, two militia on horseback not far behind them, no doubt come to disperse the small crowd gathered to ghoulishly view the dead duelist. Out from behind this gawping group appeared a blue-eyed beauty dressed in a confection of white and lavender petticoats who, having spied the Marquis of Alston, immediately rushed up to him as if her life depended on his protection. Julian stepped forward, not to greet her, but to shield his wife from the prying eyes of the morbid mob. The blue-eyed beauty took his advancement as an invitation to throw herself against his broad chest in a fit of mild hysterics.

"Dominique! Desist with these theatrics at once!" Evelyn Ffolkes called out, and tottered up to his startled cousin in his high heels to prize the beauty from his chest only for the girl to turn and throw her arms about his neck. He bore her suffocating embrace for ten seconds and then demanded in a voice one used with a spoiled child that she release him at once or be responsible for the ruin of a perfectly good Brussels lace cravat and his favorite silk Chinoiserie waistcoat. He had endured enough this afternoon to fill three lifetimes and he wasn't about to add the ruination of his clothes to the list!

"You missed the performance, such as it was, and are extremely fortunate to find me in one piece," he grumbled, still so overcome with angry annoyance that his first open-air musical performance had turned into a musical fiasco when it was interrupted by gunfire and then a riot, that he was completely oblivious to the situation at hand and that not twenty feet away lay the covered bloodied body of Robert Thesiger. "If it hadn't been for my quick thinking in overturning our chairs to form a Roman barricade of sorts, I doubt we would've survived our ordeal with the stampeding cattle!"

"Cattle?" The girl's blue eyes opened very wide as she looked about her. "But, Evelyn, there are no cows here, surely?"

"Cattle! Cows! *Canaille!* They are all one and the same! Philistines!" Evelyn argued, setting his wig to rights and shrugging his shoulders in a bad-tempered way.

It was then that out of the corner of his eye he caught sight of the state of the carnage: Two militia were inspecting the lifeless body sprawled out in the gravel, lifting a corner of Thesiger's embroidered frockcoat as if needing to verify for certain that the man was indeed dead. More militia on horseback was dispersing a group of onlookers to this macabre scene.

The composer looked swiftly up at his cousin, took in his tousled hair and soiled shirt, saw the makeshift bloodied bandage about his upper arm and drew an audible breath. "What happened here, Alston?"

"I thought that obvious," Julian stated coldly. "Thesiger attempted to kidnap my wife and child and now he is dead."

"*Mon Dieu!*" cried the composer and crossed himself, a shaking hand to his mouth. "Is Deborah—Is she—safe?"

Deb stepped out from behind her husband then, gown brushed down but irreparably creased, and with her long dark red hair littered with pins and tumbling loosely about her shoulders. She glanced curiously at the blue-eyed beauty clinging possessively to the composer's silken arm and knew her identity at once. "I am safe, Eve. I used Otto's pistol. I'm afraid that's what started the riot."

Julian viewed his wife anew, eyebrows raised. He was not pleased but was all admiration for her quick-thinking courage. "Did you indeed. Shoot my pheasants by all means, Madam wife, but no more carrying pistols on your person. Do you hear?" When Deb nodded meekly, but couldn't hide the twinkle in her eye or the dimple in her cheek, Julian put his arm about her shoulders to whisper near her ear, "I shall deal with you in my own way later, vixen."

"*O là là!* So this one, she is Madame la Marquise d'Alston?" the beauty blurted out with something akin to awe. "Evelyn," she said accusingly, "you omitted to tell me how very beautiful she is!"

"It is Dominique, yes? But you prefer to be called Lisette?" Deb asked calmly and stuck out her hand when the girl dropped a respectful curtsey.

"*Oui*, Mme la Marquise," Lisette Lefebvre answered diffidently, a shy glance up at the Marquis who was staring fixedly at his cousin.

"Well, Cousin, this is your last opportunity to explain yourself," Julian stated coldly. "If not for my sake, then you owe it to Deborah to tell her the truth."

The musician swallowed and looked from his noble cousin's expression of implacability to Deborah who was smiling kindly upon him. But before he could offer a word of explanation, Lisette Lefebvre took a deep breath and decided it was time to be brave.

"M. le Marquis, Evelyn you cannot blame for the—the *predicament* in which you find yourself with the Lieutenant of Police! The blame it rests entirely with me. I had no idea that one little lie, told so long ago, would fester into an even bigger more horrible lie." She glanced at the composer and confessed with guilty downcast eyes, "I was most offended, M. le Marquis, when you ignored me at the Opera, and at the Duc d'Orleans ball when you would not stand up with me, which was most cruel of you so I told a-a lie—"

"Ah! Dominique!" Evelyn burst out in despair. "I told you over and over but you refused to listen! Alston loathes being the center of attention."

"But, Evelyn, that is inconceivable to me. Why would the son of a duke not want to be the focus of everyone's adoration? It is most natural and expected that a nobleman—"

"Dominique, for God's sake, get on with it before my mother

has the Duke send out the militia for me and then we will never be able to marry," pleaded the composer, a shaking hand to his throbbing temple.

The girl flushed scarlet and continued, a fearful glance up at the handsome nobleman whom she had failed to ensnare with her sweet voice and great beauty. "When M. le Marquis you would not dance with me my friend Beatrice she laughed that I should be so cruelly ignored. I was angry at Beatrice for making fun of me so I told her a lie in the strictest confidence, knowing she would tell the other girls: That M. le Marquis you were only feigning to ignore me and that in truth we were lovers."

A groan escaped from the composer and he hung his head.

"Evelyn! If you look at me in that horrid way again I will cry and not be able to go on. I admit I did not see the harm in adding myself to the string of beauties M. le Marquis has seduced! What was one more name when it is rumored—"

"*Rumor?* A rumor has no more substance to it than a meringue, you little fool! Rumor is mere speculative nonsense! It is not fact," Evelyn argued angrily, adding with no regard for the presence of his stony-faced cousin, "If you want fact, my love, then let me disappoint you and all those scheming, doe-eyed creatures who have ever thrown their heaving bosoms at my cousin's noble chest, by telling you that M. le Marquis is the greatest stiff-necked moralist I have ever met. He would no more get between a whore's legs as willingly step on a dog turd!"

Lisette Lefebvre sniffed back tears and said pettishly, "Evelyn, you are merely jealous because these females they did not thrown themselves at your chest too! But as I have told you before today M. le Marquis he is to be a duke one day. Besides, what I said to Beatrice was not so very far from the truth because you and I we were lovers by the time of the Duc d'Orleans' ball and as M. le Marquis's cousin you—"

"And that makes it acceptable to—"

"Allow Mlle Lefebvre to get on with her story," Julian interrupted coldly.

"Thank you, M. le Marquis," Lisette answered in a small voice, the quarrelling lovers coming to a sense of their surroundings. "When I was telling this little lie to Beatrice we were sitting in the Duc D'Orleans' beautiful gardens, with Chinese lanterns in all the trees and floating candles on all the ponds, but it was too dark for us to notice that our conversation it was overheard by M'sieur Thesiger who was in the shadows. Me he must have followed out into the gardens. When Beatrice returned inside M'sieur Thesiger revealed himself to me and wanted to know if what I said was indeed the truth." Lisette shuddered and appealed to the Marquis with big blue eyes swimming with tears. "You know Robert Thesiger, do you not, M. le Marquis? He wanted to marry me. Many, many times did he ask and me I said no, no and no! I could not marry a man who boasted of being a bastard son of a Duke! That is a thing most abhorrent to my family. And so I thought if I confirmed the truth of my lie to M'sieur Thesiger he would hate me and leave me in peace."

She glanced at Deb and hung her head, feeling the heat of shame in her cheeks. "Robert Thesiger did indeed believe me and he did indeed hate me after that. He told my Papa and it broke my Papa's heart. I did not think such a little lie would turn into one big scandal. After all, what could Papa do against a nobleman? I never dreamed Papa he would lock me away and have his lawyers question me. That horrid Lieutenant of Police he had me sign a paper condemning you, M. le Marquis. I did not want to sign it but Papa he would not let me out of my rooms until I had done so. And how could Evelyn elope with me if I remained locked away? Please, M. le Marquis, I beg of you, if you cannot forgive me please forgive Evelyn. Evelyn he loves you like a brother but he could not tell you the truth until our elopement it was all arranged and my Papa he was not to find out the truth before we were on our way to Italy. None of this is Evelyn's fault. It is mine entirely!"

She burst into tears and clung to the composer who took her in a comforting embrace and whispered soothing words in her ear until she took a great shuddering breath and was quiet. A heavy silence followed this confession, broken only when Julian addressed cousin.

"I gave you ample time and opportunity to make a clean breast of it and still you hesitated to do the honorable thing and tell the Duke and your mother the truth," he said bitterly. "And, by

God, when you finally drummed up the courage to set matters to rights you left it damnably close! What would it have taken, the loss of my child, Deborah's death perhaps, before you claimed responsibility for the consequences of your despicable actions?"

"Julian! I'd never have let you enter that courtroom, my word on it!"

"Your word became worthless the instant you bought into Mlle Lefebvre's lie. If you've a shred of decency left, find a priest and marry her without delay!"

Evelyn glanced pleadingly at Deborah. "I did not mean for this business to drag out as long as it has. It's just that I didn't want Thesiger to know about us until I could safely get Dominique away without him—"

"—challenging you to a duel?" Julian interrupted contemptuously. "Heaven forbid you should risk your precious life for the woman you love!"

Evelyn lowered his gaze, unable to refute his cousin's inference because it was true. He was only too glad it was his cousin and not himself who had fought a duel with Robert. "Dominique and I are eloping to the Italian States," he said quietly. "Who knows when we will see each other again; if the Duke will ever allow me back into the family fold... Julian, you and I, we were once the best of friends, as close as brothers. I need—no I *beg*—your forgiveness."

The Marquis met his cousin's impassioned gaze, features implacable as ever, but it was Deborah's hand in his and the faint scent of perfume in her tumble of hair that softened his features. It made him say on a more conciliatory note,

"Not yet. When you return from your bridal trip—perhaps. That's the best I can offer you." And with that he turned on a heel and walked away to greet two happy laughing boys coming along the avenue. Beside them Joseph, black-eyed and bloodied but looking none the worse for fighting a bunch of sinister acrobats with his bare hands, and Brigitte, hair mussed and gown crumpled; both servants looking relieved and pleased to see Deborah and Julian unharmed.

Deborah put out her hands to Evelyn and kissed his cheeks.

"I wish you happy, Eve. I truly do. If you ever return to England, please come and see us. I'm sure, given time, Julian will forgive..."

Evelyn embraced her. "*Ma cherie*, he may forgive but, like his father before him, he will be a most obdurate Duke. But I shall come, if only to visit your brood and to see how Jack progresses with his viola. I expect great things of that boy."

Lisette Lefebvre bobbed another curtsey, and then with Evelyn's hand in hers, they walked off up the avenue, neither one looking back. It was only when they'd disappeared from view behind a row of abandoned stalls that Deb turned her back on them to discover the body of Robert Thesiger being loaded onto a cart by a couple of men under direction of the militia. She averted her eyes and walked over to where Julian had carefully herded Harry and Jack to the other side of the steps, out of the line of sight of such a macabre scene.

Jack and Lord Henri-Antoine were regaling the Marquis with a vivid account of their adventures, considering it a great lark that people had panicked and begun running everywhere at the sound of a single shot. And they had enjoyed themselves immensely helping to build a barricade of chairs with the musicians from behind which they had front row seats, particularly to the futile attempts of the animal handlers to regain control of their stampeding, squealing and rearing charges. Lord Henri-Antoine magnanimously conceded that it was a pity the concert had been interrupted at the precise moment of Jack's solo performance but both boys exclaimed that never in their wildest imaginings had they dreamed a dull garden concert would turn out to be the best day's entertainment they had ever seen. What did Alston think?

The boys were so bright eyed and keen for the Marquis to enter into the spirit of their adventures that Julian hadn't the heart to deflate their exuberance with recriminations about his brother's truancy. And he was so relieved that both boys were unharmed and unaffected by the day's traumatic events that he merely ruffled their hair with a grin and sent them off with Joseph to await him at the carriage. He then returned to Deb, whom he found sitting on the bottom step of the stairs, with her face in her hands.

He immediately went down on one knee beside her. "Darling, what is it? Tell me!"

"'tis nothing," she replied with a watery smile as she lifted her face. "Just a thought. I'm sure my condition is making me exceedingly missish."

He frowned. "Thought? You are well? You aren't hurt?"

"No. That is... I don't think so," she said quietly, looking with concern at his unshaven face. "But what if later—What if... Julian, what if I lose this baby?"

"Nonsense!" he said with a bravado he didn't completely feel.

"But... What if these exertions today bring on the child too early? Then, Thesiger, he-he gained his objective..."

Julian sat on the step beside her, pulled her into his embrace, and kissed her.

"If, for argument's sake, the baby did not make it to term," he said patiently, entering into the discussion not out of any fear of believing that such a consequence was likely to occur but to humor her, "then it would be a tragic loss to both of us. No one can deny that but... Thesiger can never win because you and I we will always have each other." When she turned her head into his shoulder he lifted her chin to look into her eyes. "Deborah, our being together is not about this child. I admit that before I knew you I was intent on consummating my marriage to provide my father with an heir. But then I met you and from that moment I wanted our marriage to be first and foremost about us. Since you stumbled upon me in the forest all I've ever cared about is being with you. I want this child as much as you do, but if it is not to be then we shall both come through the tragedy and try for another. Darling, I hope we have six children, God willing. But more than anything, I want to spend the rest of my life with you and no other."

Deb smiled through her tears. "Then won't you please tell me here, in the light of day, what you told me last night while we were making love; what I've been waiting to hear you say since I fell in love with you in the forest?"

He laughed, understanding immediately her request, and went down on one knee beside the stone steps. He took hold of her hands. "My dear Lady Alston—Deb—My *only* love," he said as he leaned in to gently kiss one hand and then the other, "I love you. I pledge my love to you and no other. I love you so very much that I intend to go on saying those three little words for the rest of our lives."

$\mathcal{E}$pilogue

Treat: the Roxton ducal seat
Hampshire, England

$\mathcal{T}$he Duchess threw down her hand of cards and smiled mischievously at his lordship. "That is our rubber and, I think, the game, Vallentine. Monseigneur and I, we have beaten you for a third time!"

"When don't you, minx," Lord Vallentine grumbled good-naturedly and slowly rose from the walnut card table to stretch the aching joints in his bony knees. "Damme! I can't take much more of this waiting! They should've been here by now."

"You've been saying the same thing for three days, Lucian. It is most annoying of you," Estée Vallentine complained. "Is it not, Roxton?"

The Duke, who sat in his favorite wingchair by the fireplace, looked over at his sister. "Four days, my dear. And yes, annoying in the extreme."

"Two, three or four days! What of it?" Lord Vallentine demanded, beginning to pace this particular drawing room with its view of the ornamental gardens. He took out his gold pocket watch and stared at the pearl face without noting the time. "Six days and still no word. A man could die from waiting!"

"I do not see at all why it is you who is so put out," argued the Duchess, sweeping up to his lordship in a froth of lace and muslin petticoats to tap a finger on the gold case of his pocket watch. "And this, you look at it to tell you that they will be here in what? An hour, perhaps two?' she teased. "Or does this watch count days as well as hours?"

There was laughter at his lordship's back that caused him to snap shut the pocket watch and shove it in a deep pocket of his saffron yellow frockcoat. "You can all laugh but I'll be laughing the loudest when I win the wager! Heed my words!"

Antonia's emerald green eyes widened with mock surprise. "But, Vallentine, I have wagered against you and so it is not possible that you will win. When have I been wrong in this? Renard?"

Lord Vallentine turned on a high heel to wag an accusatory finger at the Duke before he could comment. "I don't need you to tell me m'losses, your Grace! Nor do I see what the two of you find to laugh at! It's a nerve-wracking business. Tell 'em, Estée!"

"As you did not give birth to our son I do not see at all why you think you are suddenly an expert," Estée Vallentine lectured. "Furthermore, Lucian, you are making a big fool of yourself. After all, it is not you who is about to become a grandfather."

"Thank you for your wifely support, my dear," Vallentine muttered with annoyance and eased himself into the wingchair opposite his host. When the Duchess handed him a glass of claret he eyed her with loving hostility. "Never will be able to get it into my head you're a grandmother, minx." He raised his glass. "Your health!"

Antonia perched herself on the rounded arm of the Duke's chair. "So, Vallentine, you will please stop this nonsense and concede that Julian and Deborah they are to have a daughter."

"And why would I do that?" his lordship asked belligerently. "D'you know for certain the outcome?" When Antonia raised her arched brows he sat up with a start. "Hey! What's this? You know! Those two rascals, they sent you a letter!"

The Duchess appeared to be offended. "Monseigneur and I we have not had word from Henri and Jack since before Michaelmas. Nor do I expect word until the boys they return here in person: today, tomorrow or the next day!"

"So why are you so confident you'll win the wager?" his lordship asked silkily. "The odds at Whites are fifteen to one it'll be a girl; three to one for a boy. Those are mighty strong odds, your Grace.

Besides which, you have the family history of boys against you."

Antonia shrugged a bare shoulder. "What of that? I told Deborah that please you will give me a little granddaughter and she said she would do her best and so the bébe she will be a girl, I know it."

Vallentine stared open-mouthed at this explanation and then fell into such whoops of laughter that he slapped his silken knee and almost spilled his wine. He dried the tears from his eyes with a scrap of lace and shook his powdered head saying, slightly out of breath, "Well, that's the best argument I've heard for stickin' to me original wager! What say you, Roxton?"

"My dear Vallentine, in these matters I leave it entirely to those who are most expert."

When the Duchess and Estée Vallentine exchanged a look of triumph his lordship mumbled something about a female conspiracy, but he had to have a final say. "You can't tell me, Roxton, that it don't mean a whit to the odds when Alston has already given you three healthy grandsons in as many years. Stands to reason this fourth child will be a boy."

"Lucian, I do wonder at your brain sometimes," his wife sighed impatiently. "Deborah she has given Alston three fine sons, so it is reasonable her fourth little one will be a girl because Antonia she would like a granddaughter."

Vallentine opened his mouth to refute this illogical argument when sounds of arrival in the anteroom closed his mouth and had him on his feet. All eyes were on the door. There were voices and then the door burst open and in strode two long-legged and travel-worn youths, shoulder to shoulder. Antonia ran up to them and was embraced by both boys before being scooped up into the arms of her son Lord Henri-Antoine. He set her down again with a laugh, crossed the room to stoop and kiss his father's cheek, then his aunt and shook hands with his uncle; Jack shaking hands all round. Henri-Antoine again turned to his mother and this time he kissed her hand and smiled into the light of expectation in her emerald-green eyes.

"All's well with the Alstons, Maman," he assured her. "I have letters and much news. Mother and child are well and the babe is thriving. Deb sends her love and looks forward to visiting you and Papa at the end of the month. The boys can't wait to visit. Jack and I had a devil of a time getting them out of the coach! We had to bribe them, didn't we, Jack?"

Jack grinned. "Frederick says that at *almost* four years of age he is man enough to own a real pistol. And the twins, well, Louis and Augustus would be satisfied with a whirly top each but—"

"—Frederick, as their elder brother and leader of the push, demands that we take all three of them fishing on the lake," added Henri-Antoine, a knowing look at his best friend. "That's our days filled."

A discussion on the exceptional talents of all three Roxton grandsons was cut off by Lord Vallentine before it had a chance to take hold, startling the butler and two footmen who came into the drawing room carrying a jug of weak ale and trays of food for the two young travelers.

"Hey! You two rascals! That's enough of your blather! Damme," his lordship demanded rudely. "You haven't told us what's important. What's had us pacing the boards this past month or more."

Henri-Antoine and Jack merely blinked at the old man. Accustomed to his eccentricities and knowing all about the wager between his lordship and the Duchess neither boy could suppress a grin.

"Uncle Vallentine?" Henri-Antoine drawled in surprise, much in the manner of his ancient parent, as if the answer was self-evident. "Maman requested a granddaughter and Lady Alston has obliged her with Juliana Antonia."

"But we are to call her Julia," Jack proudly informed them all.

Vallentine stuck out his hand to his wife. "Estée! I need ten pounds."

Inspired by real events

The inspiration for Julian and Deb's unusual marriage came from the real life marriage of Charles Lennox, 2nd Duke of Richmond and his wife Lady Sarah Cadogan in 1720. The noble couple met for the first time on their wedding day, when Sarah was thirteen and Charles nineteen. Reportedly Sarah just stared at her future husband when brought out of the nursery for the marriage ceremony, while he, gazing with all the sophistication of his 19 years at the plain 13 year old, burst out in horror "Surely they are not going to marry me to that dowdy?". After the ceremony the young husband set off on the Grand Tour, spending three years on the Continent. Upon his return to London he went to the theatre and there spotted a beautiful young woman. When he enquired who she was he discovered to his surprise and delight that she was in fact his wife! The couple went on to have a happy marriage and 12 children. You can read more about the real-life Lennox family in *The Aristocrats* by Stella Tillyard.

To be continued... ~

The Roxton Series continues in Book 3 *Autumn Duchess*

Autumn Duchess

*P*review

*H*e saw her from across the ballroom.

A striking beauty was staring straight at him.

Jonathon brought himself up short and stared back.

He couldn't help himself.

He could count on three fingers the occasions he had crossed paths with exquisite feminine beauty that it stopped the breath in his throat; twice on the Indian subcontinent, once in the East Indies, and now here, this very minute, in this ballroom, on this green wet island. So it was only natural he should give himself the leisure to drink her in. His admiring gaze wandered from her honey-blonde hair that fell in heavy ringlets over one bare shoulder, to the porcelain skin of her décolletage glowing flawless against the bottomless black of her gown. He would not have been male had his gaze not lingered on her ample breasts, barely contained in a square cut bodice. He tried to find fault with her heart-shaped face, with the small straight nose and determined chin, and with her unusually oblique eyes, but what was there to fault?

Smiling to himself, he fancied everything he saw, and everything he could not he was sure was just as alluring.

He wondered at her age. Not that it mattered. It was a game he played to pass the time at social functions such as this. Dressed all in black and wearing no jewelry about her slender throat or wrists he supposed she was a widow, and thus not in the first flush of youth.

What was a widow doing here?

His fascination increased tenfold.

For all his limited experience of the London social scene, Jonathon knew well enough that widows did not attend social gatherings of this sort, particularly not such a renowned event at the height of the Season. Perhaps her mourning was almost at an end and she was chaperoning one of the young things here tonight? Surely, she was not old enough to have a daughter of marriageable age? Jonathon pulled a face. For some unfathomable reason he did not like the idea that she may have been a child-bride.

Why was she staring at him?

She stood so still, with her hands clasped in front of her, it was as if she was a statue carved of alabaster draped in black cloth; as much a fixture of the ballroom as a blazing chandelier or the enormous, richly woven tapestry hanging behind her. And so it seemed when dancers began pairing up and passed her as if she was indeed no more than part of the furniture. Why? Perhaps she was so well known in Society that her incredible beauty was taken for granted? In a ballroom awash with beautiful young things draped in silks of soft creams, pinks, and blues, she was a real head turner.

Jonathon found it impossible not to stare.

He watched as some of the guests even went so far as to go out of their way not to look at her, passing in a wide arc, eyes fixed forward or down to the polished floorboards. The one or two young ladies who did cast a curious, furtive glance in the beauty's direction were instantly reprimanded in furious undertones by parents and guardians alike and quickly cast their gaze away, heads hung, as if in shame at having committed a grave transgression.

Why was she being deliberately avoided?

Why did no one acknowledge her?

Why did no one stop and talk to her?

Why was she being neglected?

It burned him up to see her alone and forsaken.

It was unlikely the beauty had a sordid past or lived openly as some lucky nobleman's mistress for she wouldn't have been invited amongst this august company. The Duke of Roxton was an incorruptible prude and devoted family man, a rare bird amongst his preening peers. The King couldn't praise the Duke's example highly enough; a compliment that was so much sniggered about in Society drawing rooms that even Jonathon, just six months in the capital, had heard it repeated often enough. Whatever the reason for her social ostracism, it was of supreme indifference to him. He was determined to make her acquaintance, curiosity and allure compelled him.

A burst of wild laughter close by brought him out of his reverie. Tommy would know the beauty's identity and her story. He always had the latest gossip. Collecting social minutiae about Society that families desperately tried to suppress was Tommy Cavendish's favorite pastime, second only to eating. And so with no regard for the two turbaned dowagers who were filling Lord Cavendish's insatiable appetite for scandal with the latest wicked crumbs, Jonathon caught at the stiff skirts of the nobleman's frockcoat and unceremoniously pulled him backwards to stand at his side.

"Tommy! Tommy, attend me!" he demanded without taking his gaze from the beauty. "She's in widow's drapery and she's being ignored. Why? What is she doing here?"

"Good Lord, don't tell me one of the fairer sex has finally piqued your interest? Bravo! Who, old dear?" asked his lordship, a wave of his lace handkerchief to the departing dowagers who flounced off in disgust at being so rudely interrupted by a tanned colossus of undetermined social consequence. He hurriedly plastered his quizzing glass to a watery eye and swept an eager roving stare out across the ballroom, the first minuet of the evening underway, before running his eye down to Jonathon's large feet, then up to his head of thick, shoulder-length hair. "Are you truly six feet *four* inches?"

Jonathon pulled the quizzing glass out of Lord Cavendish's chubby fingers and let it drop loose on its riband. "Have done with that silly affectation, Tommy. And that hideous black patch, if that's what it is, is also beyond enough. A wart at best."

"Brute," Lord Cavendish responded without offence as he touched the corner of his mouth with a fat pinkie to assure himself the heart-shaped mouche remained in place. "Those of us who can't be Samsons must attract Delilahs in other ways."

"Patch and paint doesn't do it for you, Tommy. Trust me.

What would Kitty say?"

Lord Cavendish shrugged and patted his portly belly, very snug in its tight-fitting Chinoiserie silk waistcoat. "*M'wife?* Told me to wear a half-moon rather than a heart, and at the temple not the mouth. But what would dearest Kitty know about patches and paint? And, I'm not the one who needs a wife——"

"Tommy, don't start."

Lord Cavendish pretended ignorance and swept a silken arm out towards the crowd gathered on the edge of the dance floor. "Start? My dear friend, the bridal campaign started in earnest months back, if you hadn't noticed. And where better to find a nice little wife than at this august gathering. Pick of the grapes, this bunch. No one with a relative below the rank of Viscount and it's not as if you have to marry money. There's a few dainty dishes with a pedigree as long as *your* arm and no funds to match. Kitty thinks——"

"No, Tommy! *No.*"

"——that there are at least five delicious puddings for you to choose from; all in their early twenties and in their second Season. Although, I wouldn't discount the Porter-Lewisham pikelet, even if she is eighteen."

"*Eighteen?*" Jonathon was revolted. His daughter was just nineteen years old. He turned his portly friend's shoulder towards the dance floor. "Attend, Tommy! The beauty over there. Who is she?"

Lord Cavendish fumbled for his quizzing glass.

"Where is this vision of loveliness, this delectable éclair that has whet your manly appetite?"

"Not over *there*. Over *here*," Jonathon said impatiently. "To my left. The tapestry. She's staring straight at me."

Lord Cavendish made another sweep of the ballroom with his magnified eye, careful not to linger on any particular pretty face for more than a few seconds, but if there was an eligible beauty amongst the press of silk petticoats and fluttering fans, he could not discover her; pretty, yes, but no female so striking as to cause his tall friend to get steamed up under his cravat, unless... No! His smile remained fixed but his brow furrowed. He glanced up at Jonathon and followed his unblinking gaze... *Oh God. No.*

273

He mentally gulped and let drop the quizzing glass, mouth at half cock, and mumbled something unintelligible. It was a few moments before he found his voice, long enough for Jonathon to witness two dour faced creatures, both dressed in dove-gray silk and with all the charisma of strong-armed jailers, approach the beauty from behind to stand two paces back on either side of her. They reminded him of a couple of gargoyles. The almost imperceptible way in which the beauty squared her snowy white shoulders told him she was aware of their presence and that they were an unwarranted intrusion. But she did not speak, nor did she look at them.

His assessment of these women was justified when a gentleman carrying two glasses of champagne staggered out of the refreshment room, skirted the dance floor ringed with onlookers, and headed straight for the beauty. He lifted both glasses in the air as he twirled this way and that to avoid spilling a precious drop of bubbly, and came face to face with one of the humorless gargoyles who stepped forward and waylaid him before he could get within ten feet of their mistress. He was quietly taken in hand by two liveried footmen, who appeared from the crowd as if from thin air, and was marched away, the champagne soaking the front of his canary-yellow frockcoat.

"Well?" he demanded of Lord Cavendish as the Countess of Strathsay curtsied low before the beauty and then rose up to speak a few words. "Who is she that such a sanctimonious stickler for breeding and rank as the Lady Strathsay curtseys until her long nose scrapes the floorboards?"

Tommy Cavendish's mouth was still forming words but then it fixed itself in a tight smile and he tapped Jonathon's arm with the edge of his quizzing glass. "Strang! You cunning steak and kidney pie. For a moment you had me believing you. You can't bamboozle me that easily."

"I'm not. I've never seen her before tonight and I want to know who she is so I don't make a fool of myself upon first introduction. Your contribution would be much appreciated but I will do without it if I must."

Lord Cavendish's usual bonhomie evaporated. He wished Kitty with him. His wife would know how to explain matters much better than he.

"Ah… Yes… Should've realised. She doesn't go out in society any more. Damn shame, if you ask me. Damn waste of a beautiful woman."

"Well?" Jonathon repeated rudely. He watched Lady Strathsay take her leave, shuffling backwards a few feet before turning and abandoning the beauty to the watchful eye of the two gargoyles. "Come on, Tommy. If she's a recluse she could up and leave this claustrophobic social get-together at any moment. So out with it before I lose patience and take the plunge and ask her to dance without the benefit of your assistance."

Lord Cavendish shook his powdered head.

"No, Strang. You do not want to go over there. It will be very bad for you if you do. Believe me, by going over there you'll certainly make a fool of yourself. You'll be boiled mutton for broth before you can be minced for steak tartar." When Jonathon gave a huff of disbelief, his lordship sighed and dropped his quizzing glass to say without artifice, "Strang. Trust me in this. Deb Roxton has favored your dearest Sarah-Jane with her patronage. The Duchess doesn't favor all her Cavendish relatives. Such noble benefaction is not to be scorned. If your daughter is to bag a baronet at the very least, you want to avoid incurring the Duke's displeasure at all costs. Believe me, you, like the rest of us red-blooded males, must admire that divine beauty from afar."

Jonathon was unimpressed. He stared out across the noble bewigged and powdered heads gathering in the vast ballroom and caught sight of the very nobleman whom they were discussing. He watched the Duke make his way through the crowd to come stand beside the beauty. She reached no higher than His Grace's shoulder and, Jonathon suspected, this in heels. The Duke inclined his head, took out his snuffbox and said a few words to which the beauty did not respond. Finally, she turned and tilted her chin up at him, gave a response, and flicked open her fan of black feathers with a quick agitated movement. After an exchange that lasted a few minutes she dared to turn her bare shoulder on the Duke to look the other way. His Grace remained at her side, watching the dancers with an enigmatic smile, and by the inclination of his head he was continuing to talk to her under his breath despite being deliberately ignored. It was Jonathon's opinion that one would have to be blind not to see the impenetrable wall of ice bricks that separated these two.

"If the man who offers for Sarah-Jane is spineless enough as to put his Grace of Roxton's good opinion of him before his love for my daughter, then I do not wish Sarah-Jane to be so favored."

Lord Cavendish threw up a lace-ruffled hand in defeat.

"You always were an unashamed romantic." He sighed. "And the family had to wonder why Emily ran off with a penniless second son of a second son who worked for the India Company. Ha!"

"The name of the beauty at Roxton's elbow, Tommy."

"What about your quest to have the Strang-Leven inheritance returned? Put the Duke offside and you can throw the ancient ancestral pile and Sarah-Jane's marriage prospects out with the bathwater!"

Jonathon gave a grunt, annoyed. He hadn't spent twenty years sweating it out on the subcontinent making a fortune for his plans to slip out of from under him now before he'd had a chance to fully persuade the Duke of his moral obligations to return what rightfully belonged to the Strang-Levens. So he wasn't about to tread lightly on the off chance he might offend the Duke and thus ruin his daughter's chances of marrying into the nobility.

"Sarah-Jane can find herself a titled husband in Edinburgh just as easily as she can scuffing her silk mules on these noble floorboards."

Lord Cavendish was shocked. "Strang! A *Scottish* lord? One might as well say Macbeth to an actor!"

"Do stop the French cook theatrics, Tommy, and tell me the beauty's name."

Lord Cavendish avoided the question. "Kitty is a remarkable woman," he said and touched his eyeglass to his nose knowingly. "Has the ear of the Duchess. But that's between you, me and the saucepan, old dear."

Jonathon cocked an eyebrow. "Well, *old dear*, the saucepan knows more than I, so out with it!"

"It should please you to know that Roxton is rather ambivalent about your long-lost inheritance, particularly the Hanover Square residence. He's bought a larger, more palatial house on the edge of Hyde Park which better suits his growing brood and, so say the cynics, puts more distance between his dukedom and the nefarious past of previous title-holders. As for Crecy Hall... It's said he's in a dilemma about the Elizabethan turreted terror; his words not mine. As you know, the house was let go to ruin and unfit for habitation, that is until four years ago, when the old Duke, breathing his last, decided to restore Crecy to its former glory."

Jonathon was surprised enough to take his gaze from the beauty to look down at Tommy Cavendish. "For God's sake, *why?*"

"Hold on to the cream in your éclair," Lord Cavendish ordered and continued *sotto voce*. "This Duke of Roxton sees himself as a morally upright nobleman and thus once the true nature of the acquisition of the Strang-Leven inheritance was made known to him by your lawyers, holding on to Hanover Square and the Elizabethan manor does not sit well with our Duke's high principles."

Jonathan was surprised. "Is that so? The clouds part yet again and the sun shines through. And? There's more to tell. Your painted lips are twitching."

Lord Cavendish rocked on his heels. "But what the Duke feels and thinks is here nor there to your cause, I'm afraid. It's the Duke's French mamma who will be your undoing because it was for her the old Duke restored Crecy, as a dower house in her widowhood. And that is where she took up residence on his death three years ago. And so it is *Antonia*, Duchess of Roxton you must not only persuade Crecy should be returned to the Strang-Levens but also whom you must *evict*."

"Roxton's *mother?*" Jonathon rolled his eyes to the ornate ceiling, muttering, "A cantankerous old widow to contend with, and French into the bargain! *Fabuleux. Un malheur n'arrive jamais seul!* The weather is ever cold in this country and now it turns frigid." He let out a sigh and squared his shoulders, giving Tommy Cavendish a nudge as he returned his gaze to the beauty, who said something to the Duke over a bare shoulder that made the nobleman clench his snuffbox and shut his mouth hard. That they were arguing couldn't be more obvious had they been shouting insults at each other from opposite sides of the ballroom. "So who is she, Tommy, that Roxton dares let off steam in public?"

Lord Cavendish made a noise in his throat that greatly resembled the sound of a startled pheasant. He coughed into his fist politely to find his voice.

"The—um—beauty who has aroused your lust is the Duke's—Lord! I can't *believe* the first female to heat your blood since your return to England is the Duke's—"

"—cousin? Sister, distant third cousin, poor relation—"

"Antonia, Duchess of Roxton. The cantankerous old widow as you so amusingly put it."

Jonathon swallowed hard.

"I'll be damned," he muttered in utter disbelief.

"And so you will be if you go near her."

Jonathon cleared his raw throat.

"She's not old enough, Tommy. Roxton must be my age if he's a day."

"We were at Eton together. He's turned thirty. His grizzled locks and the fact his mother is cursed with being absurdly youthful for her years don't help."

Jonathon frowned with distaste. "Child-bride?"

"Do you doubt it? She was snatched from the schoolroom. The fifth Duke was a notorious rake who reformed for her. They were devoted to one another until his death. Enough said." Lord Cavendish waved to a gentleman across the room who was making exaggerated head movements in direction of the refreshment room. "Time to move on, Strang. Cards, conversation and comfits await us through those archways, and I for one intend to enjoy what's on offer."

Jonathon stayed him; gaze still very much riveted to the Duchess. "Tell me you're hoodwinking me, Tommy. Tell me the truth. Tell me that such an extraordinarily beautiful woman has no blood connection to Roxton. Tell me, Tommy."

Lord Cavendish let out a heavy sigh. "I wish I could. I cannot."

"Then tell me what you do know."

"Will you have done staring openly at her," Lord Cavendish hissed, pulling at Jonathon's velvet cuff. "Roxton's glanced at us twice already, and no wonder with your eyes glued covetously to his mother. He's damned protective of her, and who can blame him? The old Duke's death signaled open season on his much younger wife. Her incredible beauty is matched only by her personal wealth, an inheritance left her by the old Duke to do with as she sees fit; the Strang-Leven inheritance amongst those riches, old dear. Roxton's hands are tied while she is alive. So you see why he keeps her in a gilded cage. Well, that's the line…"

"And the unauthorized version?" When this was met with silence, Jonathon forced himself to look away from the Duchess, down at Lord Cavendish's frowning countenance. "Oh, come on, Tommy! Tell me and then you're free to stuff yourself from the buffet tables with abandon."

His lordship sighed. "You're doggedly persistent."

He again took up his quizzing glass to pretend an interest in the dancing, for not only was the Duke regarding them under heavy brows but those who milled about on the edge of the dance floor were beginning to turn heads in their direction and whisper behind fluttering fans and perfumed lace handkerchiefs.

"The old Duke died almost three years ago. He was three score years and ten and had been ill for a number of years, so his death was not unexpected. Except, that is, by his Duchess, who still mourns his passing as if it was yesterday. She is a divinely beautiful, sweet-natured creature who is to be pitied. Rumour has it sorrow has unhinged her. Sir Titus Foley, a dandified physician who's made a name for himself in the study and treatment of female *melancholia*, has been summonsed to Treat by the Duke, and for the second time in as many years. It begs the question about the balance of Her Grace's mind, does it not? And you didn't hear this from me, old dear, for Kitty would surely have me trussed and spit-roasted."

Jonathon pulled a face of disgust.

"The poor woman has lost her husband, who was the love of her life, her home and her exalted position in society, and her son keeps her under lock and key? Is it any wonder she's suffering from *melancholia*? She has no life at all; bullied and badgered and totally misunderstood is my guess. She don't need the peculiar attentions of a supercilious quack. What she needs is someone to talk to and a sympathetic shoulder to cry on."

Lord Cavendish's burst of high-pitched incredulous laughter was heard across the ballroom.

"*T-T-Talk to*? Oh, *S-S-Strang*! You are my bowl of chicken broth; so necessary to my comfort. Your remedy? So appealingly uncomplicated that you have me almost convinced. I take it you're going to do the manly thing and offer Antonia Roxton your own broad shoulder to cry on?" He wiped his watery eye on the lace covering the back of a shaking hand. "And for your efforts she'll be eternally grateful and not only sign over the Strang-Leven inheritance to you, but vacate Crecy Hall forthwith, for you to do with as you wish?" He shook his powdered head in disbelief. "May I live to see the day!"

Jonathon grinned. "Just watch me."

Lightning Source UK Ltd.
Milton Keynes UK
UKHW010749060121
376458UK00001B/57

The Little
Book of
Dreams

For Anoushka F, my namesake,
who taught me to sleep,
perchance to dream

The Little
Book of
Dreams

Anoushka F Churchill

An Hachette UK Company
www.hachette.co.uk

First published in Great Britain in 2020 by Gaia Books,
an imprint of Octopus Publishing Group Ltd
Carmelite House
50 Victoria Embankment
London EC4Y 0DZ
www.octopusbooks.co.uk

Distributed in the US by Hachette Book Group,
1290 Avenue of the Americas, 4th and 5th Floors, New York, NY 10104

Distributed in Canada by Canadian Manda Group
664 Annette Street, Toronto, Ontario, Canada M6S 2C8

ISBN 978-1-85675-422-4

A CIP catalogue record for this book is available from the British Library.

Printed and bound in China.

10 8 6 4 2 1 3 5 7 9

Publishing Director Stephanie Jackson
Art Director Juliette Norsworthy
Senior Editor Alex Stetter
Copy Editor Clare Churly
Design and illustrations Abi Read
Senior Production Controller Allison Gonsalves

Contents

1. Such Stuff as Dreams are Made on

What are Dreams?

There is, perhaps, no subject more studied than dreams. Humanity has been attempting to understand how and why we dream for thousands of years.

Of course, all the Abrahamic religions (mostly Judaism, Christianity and Islam) have dream stories in their holy books. But the *Epic of Gilgamesh*, a poem featuring the meaning of dreams, was written two thousand years before Christ came on the scene, and Aboriginal Australian folklore – known commonly as 'Dreamtime', or 'Dreaming' – is said to stretch back as far as sixty thousand years.

For as long as human beings have been able to record their thoughts, they have recorded their dreams and struggled to understand them: *why me?, why this dream?, what does it mean? and how can I use it?*

You have picked up this book because you, too, have wondered this.

Interpreting Dreams

Have you ever dreamed something horrible and then woken up, battered and baffled, wondering: what was *that*?, where did it come from? and what does it even mean? Perhaps you've dreamed about kissing Queen Elizabeth II and wondered if that meant you secretly had a weird fetish for royalty. Or maybe you've dreamed about being stuck in a lift with a man who was simultaneously your former maths teacher and your current boss, while knowing you needed to get to Caracas before five o'clock to deliver a parcel of bees, or your mother is going to kill you. (And was your teacher/boss flirting with you?)

I'll level with you: I can't tell you what these dreams mean. Nobody can tell you for sure. We don't even really know what dreams *are*, or how they happen. We certainly don't know definitively what each individual dream might absolutely *mean*. Nobody does. The more we learn about the brain, the more we realize we just don't know.

So why read this book at all? Why bother? Well, because, over sixty thousand years, humanity has amassed a great many ideas about how dreams – so mysterious, yet somehow universal – can help us.

Over the course of this book, we'll find tools to interpret dreams for ourselves. These tools, drawn from everything from neurological hard science to spiritual beliefs, pull together the wisdom of all who came before us to give us the best possible chance of using our dreams for good.

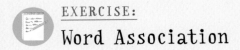

EXERCISE:
Word Association

This exercise is an incredibly useful warm-up for thinking about dreams critically, analytically and interpretatively. This is because dreams work a lot like word association.

Below you'll find a space for a word association activity. Around the word 'dreams' in the bubble, jot down anything that the word 'dreams' calls to mind: clouds, pillows, the American Dream, night terrors, nightmares or perfect fantasies, it can be anything you like. Don't worry if you can't explain it – and definitely don't overthink it.

DREAMS

Do you see how your ideas spin off from one another? Do you notice how words can mean more than one thing at once? Sigmund Freud called this phenomenon 'condensation'. It is the idea that things can have many layers of meaning and complications, some useful, some not.

Dreams are all things to all people; real/unreal, art/science, personal/universal, routine/wonder, ourselves/not ourselves, prophecy/reality. They can affect many areas of our life in a very real way, whatever they are and whatever you believe.

You see, if you were to compare the results of your exercise with someone else's, you'd probably find some similarities – as well as some serious differences. Acknowledging this is key to understanding the problem with most books about dream interpretation – but this book is a bit different.

The Language of Dreams

There are lots of books that promise to 'decode' your dreams, as if your dream language might be the same as the author's. Now, it's possible that you and I may have similar dream languages, given that there are obvious points of similarity between us. We're both interested in dreams, for a start, which might suggest we share a sensitivity. Perhaps we're both people who think it's worth considering how we interact with the world. Let's go further: we both worry that we are running out of time to do everything we want, and we both feel that there's more to us than others necessarily see. Seem about right?

The great neurologist Matthew Walker, in his book *Why We Sleep,* describes an exercise he does with each new class he teaches, where he asks a random student to tell him a dream. The student is always amazed at the accuracy of Walker's interpretation. How does he do it? The solution is simple: he gives the same interpretation every time, whatever the dream. As with lots of fortune-telling tricks, the answer lies in the fact that the feelings he describes are common to almost everyone.

Dream interpretation that relies on basic human commonalities, without digging down further into the individual psyche, is pretty silly – and unlikely to tell us anything useful. But don't throw this book away just yet. We are, after all, such stuff as dreams are made on, and an understanding of our dreams can help us understand our own 'stuff' better. It can help us to know ourselves and our deepest desires and fears.

So how is this book different to those other books about dreams? Well, instead of providing a 'dictionary' decoding the meanings of individual dream symbols, it will talk us through various approaches to understanding different dream qualities.

Dream Qualities

In this book I've chosen to focus on several dream qualities, with tips, exercises and space for you to try things out for yourself.

We're going to start with how you *feel* in your dreams: your emotions, the simplest dream quality to interpret. Then we're going to look at what you're *doing* in your dreams: the plot, the story and the journey. After that, we'll focus on the people in your dreams, which can be the hardest quality to interpret. And once we've mastered interpreting those three qualities, we'll move on to using those dreams in our real life – including prophecy, projection and lucid dreaming.

But before we begin to examine those qualities, there are two things we need to consider: are we sleeping well enough to even *have* dreams?, and do we remember them when we wake?

In the next chapter we'll look at how to sleep better.

2. Rounded with a Sleep

Better Sleep, Better Dreams

We can't talk about dreams without talking about sleep. Specifically, we can't talk about dreaming better, or more usefully, without talking about sleeping better. Without good sleep it is impossible to have good dreams. Without good sleep, actually, it's impossible to do almost anything.

You probably know for yourself that it's harder to concentrate after a disturbed night; and that a number of disturbed nights in a row can make executive functioning almost impossible. Sleep, you see, is as vital as food or water; exhaustion as pressing a concern as hunger or thirst.

We understand what food and water give to our bodies: it's a simple in-out equation. Sleep is far more nebulous. We know that sleep triggers the release of a growth hormone that mends our muscles and tissues and promotes growth. We know that sleep allows proteins in our body to synthesize better, which promotes healing and improved function. We know that sleep allows adenosine — a by-product of brain cells' activities — to clear from our mind, and that this might be part of what restores us to peak mental fitness the next day.

Scholars, after studying the problem for many years, eventually concluded that sleep was defined by four things: a period of **reduced activity** and **decreased responses to stimuli**, taken in a **typical posture** (lying down, eyes closed), that was **easily reversible**. (That last one, presumably, is there to distinguish sleep from...well, death.)

If you're thinking that you could have written that description yourself: well, yes. You're probably right. The study of sleep is hampered by the researchers' inability to see into the minds of their subjects. Once again, the best person to observe your sleep is, in many ways, yourself.

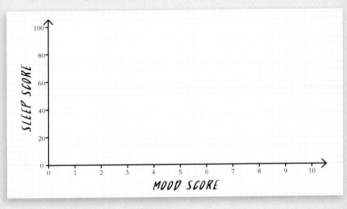

EXERCISE:
Sleep Tracking

Let's begin with a sleep-tracking exercise. We're going to draw up a simple chart, and use it to track just a few factors over a couple of weeks. And here's a stretch goal, if you feel like it: we're going to plot these values on the graph below.

Tracking Your Sleep

Each day, we'll track the time we go to bed, the time we wake up and any periods of wakefulness (just jot down the time, if you wake up!). Then we'll work out how long we slept (excluding any wakeful hours) and rate the total sleep quality out of ten. To get your sleep score, multiply the hours slept by sleep quality. For example, if you slept for seven hours, with a sleep quality of six, you'd multiply 7 × 6 for a sleep score of 42.

Tracking Your Mood

At the end of the day, we'll rate our mood during the day out of ten. Things might have been tough for external reasons, but how did we handle it? Did we feel composed? Did we feel overly stressed? Did we cry on the way to work or feel like hiding underneath the bed? (A score of ten being flawless composure; one being hiding underneath the bed.) To get your mood score, simply take that reading out of ten.

Plotting the Scores

Plot the sleep score against the mood score, and make a little x on the graph. Do this for every day you track your sleep. You'll probably start to see a pattern emerge after a few days, but keep going for at least a couple of weeks: there is a clear correlation between quality of sleep and quality of life.

Improving the Quality of Your Sleep

Maybe the sleep-tracking exercise revealed a low score in sleep quality, and a low score in resulting competency, and you're wondering how to change this. Is this just your life? Is there anything you can do?

Of course there is.

First, you need a routine. To start signalling to your brain that it's time to wind down, get into the habit of taking a bath (a muslin bag filled with lavender and oats, tied with kitchen string, and dropped in the bath will release a soothing scent), dressing in pyjamas; and reading a real book (just like this one!).

No TV. No screens. And, if you can manage it, no phones in the bedroom at all. Blue light disturbs sleep because it tricks our brains into thinking it's the middle of the day, releasing chemical signals to promote wakefulness – the opposite of what we're after.

Ideally, you'd *never* have your phone in your bedroom, and certainly never in your bed. Remember the word association exercise (see page 10)? You don't want your brain to associate 'bed' with 'work', or even 'going out' – and you certainly don't want those blue lights! Make your bedroom a safe, clean, softly lit space that's dedicated only to sleep.

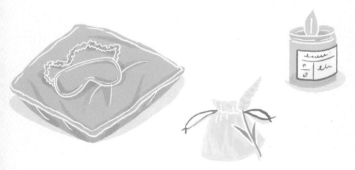

Sleep Problems

If you wake up during the night,
leave the bedroom. Go and read on the
sofa, or elsewhere — keep your bedroom for sleeping.
Similarly, never wear your day clothes on your bed.

If you often have trouble sleeping, it's worth mentioning
that alcohol doesn't help at all (passing out doesn't count as
sleeping, for neurological purposes) and coffee is a nightmare
as well (pardon the pun). Caffeine wakes you up by
temporarily blocking the flow of adenosine to the adenosine
receptors. The key word here, of course, is 'temporarily'.
When the caffeine dissipates, the brain has to process all the
built-up adenosine in a rush, instead of gradually, and thus
we get the so-called caffeine crash. This fact may, rightly,
make you somewhat wary of coffee.

And lastly, try not to worry about not sleeping too much.
I know. Much easier said than done. But think about babies,
who have no idea how to worry about sleeplessness and
sleep for something like 14 hours a day. Be like a baby.

Babies, in fact, may be the key to understanding why
sleep matters…

Sleep Stages

Sleep has four key stages: 1, 2, 3 and REM. The first two are light; the third is the deep, heavy sleep that has been said to restore the body; and the fourth is REM. We cycle through these stages in turn over the course of about 90 minutes, repeating for as long as we are asleep. So it seems obvious, then, that the more we sleep, the more REM sleep we'll get.

Unluckily, it's not as simple as that, because the cycles change through the night.

Our first sleep cycle is mainly comprised of deep sleep. This sleep stage is both the most necessary physically, and the hardest for us to wake up from, so our bodies do this part first as a kind of evolutionary priority. In the first 90-minute cycle, we get perhaps ten minutes of REM sleep. By the third sleep cycle, however, REM sleep takes priority – and after that we alternate mostly between light sleep and REM for the rest of the night.

The Importance of REM Sleep

The first four to six hours of our sleep, in some ways, is simply the time it takes for our brains to repair themselves – and it's only after that the body can begin its real dreamtime. If we skip that stage (by going to sleep too late or waking up too early), we don't dream properly.

So what does all this have to do with babies? Well, of the 14 hours that babies sleep per day, more than half is spent in REM sleep. For adults, this proportion is often less than a quarter. We learn more in infancy than at any other time, and it seems likely that this extended dream-sleep is at least part of the reason why.

We used to think our brain were inactive while we slept, but new research shows this isn't true. In fact, our brains are extremely active when we sleep. In what might be the world's cutest scientific study, researchers at the University

of Chicago in 2009 demonstrated that 'baby birds practise
new songs while they sleep'. Researchers were able to
implant tiny electrodes into the brains of zebra finch chicks.
By looking at the results of these electrodes, scientists were
able to see neurological patterns in the way birds learn. Baby
birds, it turns out, learn first by hearing themselves copy their
parents – and then by dreaming about it.

The baby birds who were allowed to dream learned the songs; the birds who weren't allowed to sleep did not. Furthermore, the neurological patterns of their dreams corresponded exactly to the neurological patterns that occurred when they first heard the parent birds sing. We think something of the kind happens in humans too: dreaming allows us to process the events of the day, and learn from it.

If dreams are what allow us to process and learn, then it's even more important that we should analyse them properly. In the next chapter, we'll learn how to make that happen.

3. Catching a Cloud

Remembering Dreams

How often do you remember your dreams? Everyone knows that dreams are hard to recall in precise detail. Like attempting to catch a cloud or holding water in your cupped hands, dreams that once seemed so tangible can slip away without your even noticing.

There are some people, in fact, who never remember dreaming. Maybe you're one of them, and you've come to this book to try and understand why. Don't worry. We'll look at the reasons we don't remember dreams, and learn some techniques to improve our recall.

Robert Stickgold, of the Harvard Medical School, has studied this problem extensively. People who don't remember their dreams tend to have similar sleep patterns to one another: sleep easy, sleep quickly, sleep deep and wake quickly to an immediate state of up-and-at-'em.

Researchers at the Lyon Neuroscience Research Center in 2013 recorded the electrical activity in the brains of a group of people, half of whom were 'high recallers' (who mostly remembered their dreams) and half 'low recallers' (who rarely did so). They found that high recallers tend to wake up for about 30 minutes per night; whereas low recallers were awake for just under half that time.

Stickgold's solution to this finding is somewhat unorthodox: he suggests drinking three large glasses of water before bed, to wake you up at frequent intervals during the second half of the night. This seems like a dedication to remembering your dreams that is at best likely to lend itself to a grouchy morning, and at worst rather risky. So what else can we do?

Well, the Lyon researchers found that high recallers were also more likely to respond easily, in their waking lives, to their name being called. In some sense, then, we can say that these people were more highly attuned to the waking world. Thus, improving our recall of the waking world can improve our recall of dreams.

Some dream theorists suggest that practising remembering real places can act as a kind of training ground for remembering dream places. Look out of the window for 60 seconds, concentrating hard on as many aspects of the scene as you can, then look away and try to recall every detail. Come back to this memory throughout the day, perhaps taking notes to compare your recollections after a minute, after an hour and after several hours. In this way, you can begin to train your brain.

You might notice, as you do this exercise, that memory can be helped and hindered. For instance, if you see something that reminds you of the scene you memorized, the memory will probably come back to you without much conscious effort. This is called the 'trigger effect', and it can be made useful to you in two ways: strengthening your brain's ability to recall things and allowing you to use a 'dream anchor'.

Strengthening Recall

To improve your recall, observe when something in your waking life triggers a memory, whether that's of your real life or a dream. Take care to notice these feelings, whether they manifest as a memory or as something like déjà vu, and note them down. You could even start making a kind of 'dream dictionary' of the feelings and ideas associated with places, objects or people. To do this, take a new notebook, and label each page alphabetically A–Z. As you start to notice the world around you, and the feelings triggered by that world, jot them down, adding to your notebook any time you have a fresh association or idea. We'll look at this idea more closely later in the book (see pages 42–7).

Creating a Dream Anchor

A dream anchor is an object that you focus on immediately when you wake, and as you meditate on the object you make a specific effort to recall the dream from which you have just awakened. It should be the first thing you focus on in the morning, and as you stare through and past the anchor you'll try your best to recall any dreams. This works by association: the more you do this, the more you'll associate the object with the successful recollection of dreams.

Some dream scholars suggest that a dream anchor can be as simple as a bedside lamp, candle or other object you have lying around – but creating one can be a fun and satisfying project that also allows you to focus your mind on your intentions. Focussing your intentions can be extremely powerful, particularly when we're dealing with questions of the subconscious mind.

Take some time to find or make a dream anchor that feels right to you. Mine, for instance, is a small bronze cube I found in a shop. You could embroider, paint, carve, draw or buy some small totem that feels right to you. As you're making it, or searching for it, focus your mind on the purpose and intention of the dream anchor: *this will help me recall my dreams, this will help me remember my dreams.* While repeating a mantra may seem like magic, it's based in the sound psychological principles of association, subconscious suggestion and determination.

After all, Robert Stickgold also suggests using a mantra before bed: *I will remember my dreams.* Repeat it out loud, while focussing on your dream anchor, as the last thing you do before you go to sleep. Try to believe it.

Dream Recall

The most useful thing you can do to improve your dream recall is to force yourself to sit and recall your dreams. You have to make dream recall a priority.

The moment you wake up, don't move, don't speak, don't turn to the person next to you and announce 'I had such a weird dream!' Instead, linger in the dream world as long as you can, with your eyes closed. Think, 'Where was I just now? What about before that? And before that?' Cling on to keywords for parts of the dream: *fire, flying, teeth, poodle, mother.* Then open your eyes, focus on your dream anchor while you try to recall every sensation, and – here's the key – immediately write the keywords in a dream journal you keep for the purpose.

EXERCISE:
Dream Journal

A dream journal is the single most efficient way to improve dream recall; and therefore the single most useful tool we have in dream analysis.

We're going to break dreams down into five categories: the **cast of characters** (who was in the dream with you); the **set** (where the dream took place); the **props** (the objects in the dream); the **action of the dream** (what happened); and the **emotions of the dream** (how you felt about it).

Take a notebook and pen, and copy the template on the next page.

To begin with, we'll consider the prompt questions. We'll scribble down keywords to jog our memory, then go back and fill in the gaps. Once we're done, we'll give the dream a title that reflects what we've written. The title will help us cement the dream in our memories, and provide an easy way for us to see if there are any recurring themes or patterns in our journal.

For now, we're going to leave the 'Awake' box empty. You'll learn how to use it later in the book (see page 44).

AWAKE:

DATE: ....

TITLE: ....

KEYWORDS: ....
....
....

CAST: ....
....
....

Who was there? Do you know them in real life? Do you know them well? What's their relationship to you, and was it the same in your dream? Did they look the same?

SET: ....
....
....

Where were you? Were you somewhere familiar or strange? What time of day was it? What time of year? Have you been to this place recently, a long time ago or never? Was it old? Was it new? What temperature were you?

PROPS: ....
....
....
....
....

What was there with you? What were you holding? What were you wearing? What material things made up this immaterial world?

ACTION: ....
....
....
....
....

What were you doing? Where were you going? What were you trying to do, or failing to do, or what did you say? Were you talking? Did you say anything that you can remember?

EMOTIONS: ....
....
....

How do you feel right now? How did you feel while dreaming? Is there a difference? Were these feelings linked to someone you saw in the dream, or where you were in the dream, or what you were doing in the dream?

4. Overnight Therapy

Emotions

Emotions are the simplest dream quality to interpret, even though they can be complex. Much expensive, sophisticated psychotherapy essentially boils down to a process of understanding what we are feeling at any given moment and in any given situation.

It can be so hard to identify exactly what we're feeling, in fact, that therapists often use a feelings chart, like the one on the following page, to help us pin it down.

FEELINGS CHART

Admiring	Disgusted	Indifferent	Regretful
Affectionate	Doubtful	Indignant	Relaxed
Alarmed	Eager	Insecure	Reluctant
Alienated	Embarrassed	Interested	Resentful
Angry	Enthusiastic	Jealous	Resentful
Annoyed	Envious	Joyful	Romantic
Anticipatory	Excited	Listless	Sad
Apprehensive	Frightened	Loved	Satisfied
Ashamed	Frustrated	Loving	Shocked
Bitter	Furious	Lustful	Shy
Blissed-out	Glad	Melancholic	Spiteful
Bored	Gleeful	Miserable	Stressed
Brave	Glum	Nervous	Sulky
Calm	Grateful	Nostalgic	Surprised
Cheerful	Grieving	Outraged	Suspicious
Confident	Guilty	Overwhelmed	Tense
Contemptful	Happy	Panicky	Terrified
Curious	Helpless	Paranoid	Thrilled
Defeated	Hungry	Pitying	Triumphant
Desiring	Hurt	Pleased	Wondering
Detached	Hysterical	Proud	Worried
Discontented	Impatient	Raging	Yearning
			Zealous

Humans have words for many gradations of feelings – and, furthermore, we can recognize them in others. We are finely calibrated to interpret facial expressions by mood.

The neurologist Matthew Walker, in his book *Why We Sleep*, explains how he showed a group of people many pictures of a face. The first picture of the face was friendly and open; the last picture was stern and threatening; and between them the pictures gradually shaded from the first face to the last, with minute differences in facial expression to convey emotion. The participants in the study were able (after a full night's sleep) to accurately assess the feelings conveyed in each image. When the experiment was repeated, and the participants were deprived of that sleep, they became unable to grade the photographs properly: they were unable to read the delicate nuances of each face.

Sleep and emotions are tied together in ways that perhaps we don't fully understand, yet understanding the emotions of our dreams can help us understand our waking lives. Dreams have even been called 'overnight therapy'.

Dreams and Emotions

We all know that there's a link between what happens when we sleep, and the way we feel. We know that a bad night's sleep makes us grouchy and irrational the next day. Many people even report carrying the emotions of their dreams into their waking lives. Our dreams and sleep, then, influence our waking emotions in many ways – but, of course, the converse is also true.

Emotions are the most thinly disguised of all the dream elements: if we feel shame in a dream, it's likely to be related to shame we feel in real life. There is a strong correlation between how we feel when we're awake and how we feel in our dreams.

This isn't to say that we'll necessarily feel the same about what we *do* in dreams as we might if we did them while we were awake – but we carry our emotions into our dreams with us. This is where almost all psychoanalytic dream assessment begins (think Sigmund Freud or Carl Jung), and it's backed up by science: studies have shown that when we note down the strongest emotion felt in our day, and the strongest emotion of our dreams, they are likely to be similar. Mark Blagrove, who led a team of researchers at Swansea University, found that events with high emotional impact were significantly more likely to be rehashed in dreams than events that meant less to us.

Let's demonstrate this for ourselves by carrying out a version of these experiments.

Emotional Diary

For this exercise, we need three things: a pen, our dream journal and the list of feelings from the chart on page 40.

Start by focussing on the 'Emotions' category in your dream journal, and that blank 'Awake' box at the top of the page (see page 36). Before you fall asleep, as part of your bedtime routine, consider the following questions, and write down your answers in the blank box, using the feelings chart to help you:

• *What was the strongest emotion I felt today?*

• *What triggered it?*

When you wake up in the morning, record your dreams in your journal and consider these questions:

• *What was the strongest emotional impression left by my dream?*

• *What triggered it?*

After a couple of weeks of this exercise, you'll probably start to see a pattern. Studies show that people suffering from stress are more likely to experience nightmares; and that people who report bad dreams are most likely to also report low levels of satisfaction with their waking life. This phenomenon is well documented scientifically – and is blindingly obvious to anyone who has ever had a nightmare. Our subconscious mind deals with the same stress levels as our conscious mind, so why shouldn't the same emotional preoccupations recur?

Happy People, Happy Dreams

Presumably exhausted by the field's obsession with the unhappy, three Australian scholars (Susan Gilchrist, John Davidson and Jane Shakespeare-Finch) attempted in 2007 to find a correlation between positive emotions and positive dreams. Happily, they succeeded: over half the participants recorded having pleasant dreams when they had had a pleasant day.

Moreover, the Australian researchers also found that there were 'significant correlations between some personality characteristics and participants' tendency to experience positive or negative emotions in dreams'. Broadly speaking, happy people have happy dreams; sad people have sad dreams.

To put it more finely, and more psychologically, if you're having repeated unhappy dreams, perhaps there's a difficult emotion in your waking life you're not processing properly. Freud believed that dreams were manifestations of repressed desires, often sexual desires, that go all the way back to childhood – but it doesn't have to be that complex. Is there something you want, but don't have?

This could be something tangible, but it could also be something like recognition or affection. Maybe you want to be acknowledged for your work, or for who you are. Maybe deep down you're lonely, stressed or unhappy in some other way.

Take a moment to look at your emotional diary (see page 44) and your dream journal (see page 35) and check in with yourself. Are there things you're not giving yourself the time or space to acknowledge? How could you best make that time? Where could you best find that space?

EXERCISE:
Free Association

An interesting way of checking in with ourselves and our deeper feelings is to play a word association game. You will need a pen and a piece of paper. Both Jung and Freud believed that this kind of work could bring out the deeper meanings behind dreams. Freud's technique is called 'free association'. Here's how we can use it:

First, decide on the strongest image you've taken from your dream. Maybe it's an object. Maybe it's a person. Maybe it's a place. This is your key symbol for the exercise. Write it down in the top-left corner of the sheet of paper.

What do you associate with that word? Don't think too much about it; don't worry if it doesn't make much sense. Jot your answers down in a kind of curve around the first word, like this:

What do you associate
with all the new words?
Write down those words
too, like this:

Keep going, until eventually
the page is full of words and
pathways.

Do any of these pathways
have a bearing on a real–life
situation? Do any of these
pathways speak to a particular
need, want or desire in your life? Do any of the final words
strike a chord with you in ways that weren't so clear in the
original dream? Does this give you any ideas of where to go
in your waking life?

This technique lets your mind wander freely, *prompted* by the
original dream but without sticking closely to the specifics.
(Jung's technique is much more interested in the dream itself,
which we'll look at in the next chapter.)

Processing Strong Emotions

While free association might sound a bit wishy-washy, it is actually legitimate hard science. Specifically, it's been posited that it's all about a chemical called noradrenaline – the neuro equivalent of adrenaline. Adrenaline in the body is linked to fear and excitement and, essentially, a kind of overdrive. Noradrenaline does the same thing for the brain. Studies have shown that REM sleep is the *only* time that the brain is not actively producing noradrenaline.

People suffering from post-traumatic stress disorder (PTSD) have too much noradrenaline in the brain, and they often have repeated nightmares. However, when they take a drug to reduce the noradrenaline, the nightmares decrease radically.

It's important to note that nightmares can be useful. Matthew Walker considers researcher Rosalind Cartwright 'as important as Freud' on the understanding of dreams. Cartwright, Walker explains, carried out a series of psychological studies into the dreams of depressed patients going through a traumatic divorce. Those patients who actively dreamed about the traumatic feelings at the time were significantly more likely to be in remission from their depression a year later. The dreams helped the patients to distinguish the memory of the event from the vivid emotions associated with what happened.

When we remember hard times from our past, we don't feel the same strong emotions we felt at the time: we remember feeling the feeling, as it were, but not the feeling itself. 'I was so sad that day,' we might say, 'It felt so lonely there.' We are capable of talking about the past without reliving it – *unless* we have a condition like PTSD, *unless* we have too much noradrenaline, *unless* we aren't getting a chance to sleep properly and process the problems at the time.

Therapies like EMDR (eye movement desensitization and reprocessing) are now being utilized to help people who suffer in this way: by having the patient recount the trauma, while the therapist induces eye movements similar to those seen in REM sleep, we mimic the processing and 'filing' effects of dreaming.

Dreams make our past into stories. Dreams, according to some researchers, are what make our past into our past.

5.

Dream Journeys

Our Dream Inheritance

'The dream acts as a piece of fiction that can be explored by the dreamer,' explains a 2019 study into the benefits of talking about our dreams, and that's what we'll look at now.

Some dream analysts, like Carl Jung, believe that all dreams are based on a series of deep stories called 'archetypes', common to all people and all cultures. Archetypes, in Jungian theory, are ideas and images that derive from the 'collective unconscious': things that crop up time and again in religion, myths and – yes – our dreams.

Jung believed that these stories were part of what it means to be human: that we are each born with an innate understanding of figures like 'The Mother' or 'The Trickster' and significant events such as 'The Apocalypse' or 'The Flood'. Jung believed that our dreams could be best understood as a new manifestation of those ancient patterns.

If you believe Jung, we inherit stories in the same way we inherit our body shape or senses.

Storytelling

Telling stories is how we make sense of the world, and it's how we make sense of our dreams too. Our waking mind constructs a narrative around the lingering images when we wake, which means that the dream is a collaboration between our conscious and subconscious. Sudden plot jumps, in dreams, are often the linking places between one dream and the next; it's just that we weave them together into a coherent narrative once we're awake.

Did the dream really
happen exactly as we narrate it?
Maybe not – how would we know?

But what's 'really' in this context? What's 'happen'? And does it matter?

The fact that a dream, once told, is a collaboration between our waking and sleeping selves – all parts of our consciousness – makes it *more* useful, not less. How is our conscious mind framing things dredged up by our subconscious? Could there be another interpretation? What other stories could we have told about this journey, or this action, and why did our subconscious present us with this interpretation? What does this say about us?

Falling or Flying?

One of the most universal dreams is the falling dream.
No, wait: the flying dream. No, wait: the falling dream.

These two dreams are sometimes referred to as two sides
of the same coin, which makes them a perfect case study.
Both are often triggered initially by similar physiological
factors, specifically the drop in heart rate and blood pressure
as we fall asleep. Both involve rushing through the air, not
touching the ground. The action of the dreams is similar,
yet the emotions underlying the dreams are very different.
We mostly wake up from flying dreams feeling elated, and
from falling dreams afraid. Our brain's interpretation of the
same electrical impulses tells us a lot about how we're feeling,
which gives us the tools to do something about it.

control

flight path

freedom

flying high

flying colours

FLYING

lucid

flight risk

travel

flying the flag

speed

come fly with me

When we look at the words on the opposite page, we can see that falling isn't always negative. Sometimes letting go of control is a good thing – too much control can hinder us. Do we need to hold on? Can we let ourselves fall? What will happen if we do? It's said that you'll die if you hit the ground in a falling dream, which definitely isn't true, but sometimes when we fall, we fly…

Dream Actions

We've learned already how to sleep, recall our dreams and track our emotions from sleep into our waking lives and back again. Emotions are easy to translate (although, of course, not always easy to solve!) and that's why we started there.

Our actions can be harder to understand: the plots of our dreams (like the cast of characters, like the objects and places that surround our sleeping selves) are symbols. All dream analysts treat these symbols as a language we can decode individually, by asking ourselves why these actions, objects and people have surfaced for us now. What do they mean when taken in conjunction with our life now, our past and what we hope for in the future?

You'll notice that this book has lots of questions, and not many answers. That's because the most important part of dream analysis, like all therapy, is what *you* think and how *you* feel. No book can give you the answers: all this one can do is help you find them for yourself.

On the following page there is a questionnaire you can use to interrogate your dream actions – and learn more about yourself in the process.

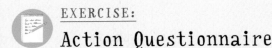

EXERCISE:
Action Questionnaire

This exercise will help you answer the questions posed in the 'Action' category of your dream journal (see page 37) in greater depth, and in a more complex fashion. You might want to jot some of your answers down on paper first, to help you work out what's important.

Emotion

• *Do you view your behaviour in your dream with shame, or with compassion?*

• *Is your 'dream self' behaving in ways your waking self approves of?*

• *Do you wish you could behave like that, or do you feel regret?*

Who's in Charge?

• *Agency is the capacity to effect a change: to choose to do something and do it. Do you have agency in the dream?*

• *Does your 'dream self' want to be doing this?*

• *Are you doing it, or is it being done to you?*

• *Are you passive or active, subject or object, followed or following?*

Get Real!

- *Is this something that's possible in real life?*

- *Is the dream mimicking your recent real life, or is it further away?*

- *Have you ever done this activity?*

- *Do you want to do this activity? Why?*

- *Is this something you are afraid of?*

- *Would you be afraid of it in real life?*

- *Is this a fantasy?*

On the Move

- *What's the dream journey here?*

- *Where have you gone?*

- *Where have you come from? Why?*

- *What do both those places mean to you?*

- *Have you ever been there in real life?*

- *When did you go there in real life?*

- *Why were you travelling in the dream?*

- *How were you travelling in the dream?*

- *How did you feel about the journey?*

6.
Cast
and Crew

Who's Who in Dreams?

Gestalt theory is a kind of therapy that emphasizes a holistic approach to the self (that is to say, looking at the whole person). So it's no surprise that it's from Gestalt that we take this maxim: *we are everyone in our dreams*. Nobody else is in our minds; nobody else can dream for us. Each person in our dreams is our projection of that person: they are a composite of our ideas about that person, our ideas about their role in our lives and our ideas about their relationship to us. They are a representation of what we think of that person (or what that person represents), crafted by our subconscious from many sources.

Think of it like a puppet show, with your subconscious as writer, director, producer and star.

Sometimes the people-puppets in our dreams represent themselves – or, at least, our ideas of them. Often this is the case when we dream of people we recently saw, or had cause to think of in our waking lives: the dream is simply reproducing real life. They seem, in the dream, pretty realistic simulacra of our friends, colleagues, family, whoever. They don't act in ways that seem too surprising; and even after we wake we aren't too shocked by their dream presence or dream actions.

This seems fairly straightforward, and it can be – but beware! They are still just puppets, and they are still just us. They are still comprised of our ideas about what they are, who they are and who they are to us. We have to keep this in mind for two reasons. First, and most obviously, because people are more than our ideas about them. They can think and speak and feel for themselves – and believing our opinion of them to be the *only* opinion that counts is the fastest way to ruin a relationship. Second, by ignoring the things the characters in our dreams *represent*, we're ignoring important symbols: important messages from our subconscious.

The Five Elements of the Self

We've agreed that we are everyone in our dreams. Let's take this one step further: what if the characters in our dreams each represented different fragments of ourselves?

This kind of thinking is mostly drawn from Jungian dream analysis. Unlike Freud, Jung didn't believe dreams were about repressed sexual traumas: he believed that dreams were the key to understanding our subconscious wants, desires, stories and personal development. Jung wrote that there are five elements of self: anima, animus, shadow, persona and self.

Anima is the feminine; animus the masculine. Shadow is the darker parts of our personality: the enemy, the frightening parts of ourselves we don't want to acknowledge. Persona is our mask: who we are to the outside world. And the self? Self is who we truly are.

These five archetypes are sometimes said to be the ones who drive the people in our dreams: the puppeteers, if you like, behind those other characters. They might look like other people, they might look like strangers, but they are shaped and crafted by the elements of the self.

The difficulty, of course, is in knowing which is which. How do you know who each character represents?

How do you know what part of your subconscious is making itself known?

The answer lies, as usual, both in keeping a dream journal and in applying some Jungian analysis.

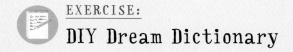

EXERCISE:
DIY Dream Dictionary

Remember those keywords we've been writing in our
dream journal (see page 35)? We're going to analyse them
now. You'll probably need a piece of paper, a pencil and a
dictionary and thesaurus or access to the internet.

Take your first keyword. Write down anything immediately
associated with it. For example, 'fire' might take you to 'hot',
'roaring', 'comforting', 'bright' or 'dangerous'. So far so good?
This time we're not going to spiral out as we did with the
free association (see page 48), but instead keep checking back
in with the symbol. This is direct association.

Consider drawing the keyword: does that bring up any other associations for you?

Look up the word in a dictionary or a thesaurus, or search it online. Do you feel a resonance with any definitions, synonyms or common links?

Do the same for each keyword you wrote down, remembering all the time to bring it back to the keyword itself. What we're doing here is making a kind of dictionary of what each symbol means for you.

After a while you will start to see patterns: things that reoccur a lot for you. You might see patterns in a single dream, or you might see them over the course of time. This process is as unique as we are, and it allows us valuable insight into what our mind dwells on when freed from regular life.

Understanding Archetypes

Part of what we were looking for in the exercise on the previous page was those archetypes we touched on briefly before (see page 53). Often, they manifest as people – or as types of people.

If you've ever studied any kind of storytelling, you'll already be familiar with lots of these character types. They exist in fairy tales, myths and legends, and they feature heavily in religious stories. You might have come across them as part of spiritualism, say the Tarot deck, or you could have encountered them in the workplace: what is the Myers-Briggs Type Indicator questionnaire, after all, except a method for sorting people into characters?

Of course, people are more than one thing – especially in dreams. We're all familiar with the way in which someone can be two people at once in a dream – your mum and your doctor, or your sister and the window cleaner. This process is called 'condensation', and it means that our brain merges symbols together when dealing with a complex issue.

For example, your mum being one with your doctor might mean you're hoping that an upcoming hospital trip will take care of you (as a mother might). That's obvious, right? But it could mean that you're starting to look at your relationship with your mother the way a doctor might (clinical, detached); or that your relationship with your mother *is* sort of clinical, or detached, and that's worrying you. It might mean any number of things. This is why there's no point in most dream dictionaries. What you need is a way to explain how these archetypes relate to *you*.

It's worth noting that some of these archetypes might seem old-fashioned — but they're worth considering anyway. It's also worth saying that the so-called 'masculine' and 'feminine' energies are present in all of us. However, we live in a gendered society where different kinds of people are praised for prioritizing certain traits, which means, of course, that our dreams may be gendered too.

On the following pages are some archetypes drawn from a wide range of sources. Which ones have appeared in your dreams lately? Which ones are relevant to you? Who in your life can you match to these archetypes? Who would represent each one for you? Have a look at the list, consider and jot down any additional notes in your dream journal (see page 35).

The Fool

(aka The Innocent,
The Jester, The
Beggar, The
Child, The
Protagonist)

In traditional Tarot
archetypes, The
Fool often represents
you: a person about to
go on a journey. It may hint
at an optimistic desire for new
beginnings, or a need for new
beginnings. When this figure
shows up in your dreams, it
might be you, it might
be a child or it
might even be an
animal. Often
The Fool is
accompanied by
a little dog.

The Orphan

(aka The Martyr, The Child, The Outcast)

The Orphan is the central figure in so many stories, and has a lot to do with The Fool. Whereas The Fool tends to be a happy figure in dreams, The Orphan tends to be a bit of a pessimist: a loner, worried that they have been rejected, worried that nobody wants them. While everyone feels like this sometimes, to dream repeatedly of being orphaned suggests a fear of being outcast — and a fear of being alone.

The Warrior

(aka The Hero, The Protector, The Crusader, The Rescuer)

This archetype is often represented by somebody tough but kind; somebody capable of using great strength. If this kind of character shows up in your dreams, consider whether you are asking for protection or whether you want to protect someone else.

The Lover

The important thing to remember when dreaming of lovers is that love is love. Dreaming about sex doesn't always mean sex, just as death doesn't always mean death. Dreaming of lovers can hint at a need to compromise, a need to be more yielding, a need to be kinder. Dreaming of sex, for Jung, might indicate a conflict with that person that needs to be solved; or it might indicate a wish to become closer or more similar to a sexual partner. (An aside: everyone has weird sex dreams – try not to worry about it. It almost definitely doesn't mean what you think.)

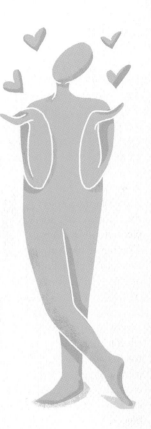

Death

Just like sex doesn't always mean sex, death almost never means death. Sometimes, of course, we're rehashing the elements of our daily lives – we can dream about death after a bereavement, but that's not what we're looking at here. (See page 50 for more on the trauma-processing element of dreaming.) The figure of Death can appear in lots of guises – a traditional skeleton, a psychopomp (a mythical figure who escorts souls to the afterlife), a friend who has passed on – and often it indicates a need for change. Change is always a kind of death (and death the biggest change of all).

The Mother

(aka The Goddess, The Divine Feminine, The Caregiver)

Strongly connected to the anima part of our psyches, according to Jung (see page 66), The Mother tends to be related to caregiving more than actual motherhood. Dreaming of our mother might actually mean we're dreaming of needing to give or receive care; of a love without judgement. If we believe Jung, dreams about this figure aren't so much about our own mothers (who aren't all perfect goddesses!) as our instinctive understanding of the maternal.

The Father

(aka The King, The Priest, The Masculine)

The counterpart to The Mother, The Father represents the animus part of our Jungian psyche (see page 66). Often historically related to issues of control and authority, this figure might show up as a boss, a headteacher or other power figure. (Yes, this labelling isn't ideal – but so much of our subconscious is shaped by a flawed society.)

The Hermit

(aka The Scholar, The Student, The Hierophant, The Institution)

Often represented by priests, doctors, academics, schools, and hospitals, this archetype indicates your relationship with institutions and authority. It can also indicate a desire for spiritual or religious guidance; a desire to know where we're going; a desire to learn and to understand. It shows a desire to pull away from ordinary life into the life of the mind. Why might this be manifesting in your life? Are you overwhelmed by demands? Do you feel unrecognized for what you've done, and swamped by what you've still to do?

The Stranger

The Stranger might represent
parts of yourself you haven't yet
unlocked – or parts of yourself
you're uneasy about recognizing.
It's a common myth that we can't
invent faces: that everyone in our
dreams is drawn from someone
we once saw in real life, even if
we don't recognise them. In 2015
an internet hoax convinced
thousands of people that
thousands of others had seen
the same face in their dreams.
It claimed that thousands had
reported meeting the same man
in their dreams, as if the man
could travel into the minds of
many strangers. It was widely
reported, and many people
believed it before it was
debunked. But why did this
story appeal to so many of us?
Why did it ring so true?

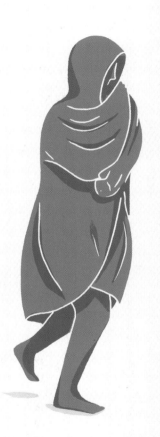

Seeking 'Real' Meaning in Our Dreams

We want to believe that the dreams we have are signifiers of something tangible and real. For example, if we see a stranger in our dreams (see page 81), we want to believe it means something more than a random face generated by rogue electrical impulses. And who knows? That might be the case. In the next chapter, we'll look briefly at how that could be…

7. Shamans, Soothsayers and Lucid Dreamers

What is Lucid Dreaming?

Lucid dreams are those dreams where you know you're dreaming – and stay dreaming. Often the realization that you're dreaming can wake you (especially in nightmares, thank goodness), but it's possible to train your brain to stay awake and manipulate the dream into something great.

Once they know they're dreaming, lucid dreamers can take control of the dream. At its best, lucid dreaming is essentially like having superpowers. Everything you've ever wanted to do in real life, you can make happen in your dreams. Flying. Falling in love with a famous person. Seeing places you've always wanted to visit and doing things you've always

wanted to do. All of these are possible. It's like homegrown virtual reality, with none of the expensive equipment.

The Greek philosopher Aristotle wrote about self-awareness in dreams, which is at the heart of lucid dreaming. Knowing yourself, your brain and your dreams well enough to understand what's a dream and what's reality is immensely helpful for encouraging lucid dreaming (one reason it's so good to keep a dream journal, as we've been doing throughout this book). Knowing that you're dreaming gives your imagination the chance to manipulate and exert conscious control over a dream in an environment that feels almost fully real.

Lucid Dreaming as Therapy

Some researchers have suggested that lucid dreaming could be a valuable tool for therapy. Imagine being able to confront someone from your past who has hurt you in a safe and secure way; imagine the closure you could gain from that kind of experience. Imagine being able to probe your phobias in order to more deeply understand why you've been afraid – without ever having to, say, get on a real plane or touch a real spider. Lucid dreaming has even been used to help people suffering PTSD, although research is still in the early stages.

Studies with an MRI machine have started to be able to predict the dreams of certain volunteers, based solely on the ways their brains light up as they sleep, as Matthew Walker reported in *Why We Sleep*. While we can't yet apply this universally, imagine the possibilities! Imagine if we could induce certain dreams for certain people in a therapeutic sense.

We began this book by articulating just how much we don't know about dreams, and that's definitely true. But what that gives us is the possibility of an extraordinary future – one that can draw on the traditions of the past. Until then, however, we'll have to try to do it ourselves. On the next page, you'll find some tips for lucid dreaming, whether you want to use it for therapeutic reasons or just for fun...

Tips and Tricks for Lucid Dreaming

If you've followed the tips for better sleep and dream recall (see pages 20 and 31), you're already ahead of the game. Studies have shown that the better your dream recollection, the more likely you are to experience lucid dreams – so keep up with that dream journal.

Set Your Intention

It can be helpful to set an intention: a mantra of not just *I will remember my dreams*, but *I will notice when I am dreaming*.

Be Mindful

Mindfulness is the real key to lucid dreaming. In your waking life, ask yourself a question like 'Is this real?' or 'Is this a dream?' to build that question into the pattern of your day-to-day mind. That way, you'll dream the same question, and hopefully, over time, become aware of the differences between sleeping and waking.

Look at Your Hands

Another common trick is to look at your hands. It's hard for your brain, apparently, to accurately dream your own hands, so it can be a really significant 'tell'. If you build in looking at your hands to your daily life, you're likely to dream the same thing – and you're likely to notice a difference.

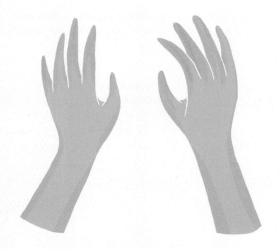

Focus on a Subject

If you want to dream about a particular subject, spend some time thinking about that subject before bed: look at pictures, read books, build up a full mental picture as if you've just seen the person or place yourself.

Make Time for Dreaming

You're mostly likely (at least in my experience) to lucid dream as you're falling asleep, or just as you're waking up, so try to build some extra time for bed into your routine. You know that swirly dark pattern you see just before you're falling asleep? That's your hint to try and imagine something you'd like to dream. It probably won't work straight away, but keep at it.

Shared Dreaming

The next stage of lucid dreaming is often thought to be something called shared dreaming, or dream telepathy. Shared dreaming is, of course, being able to meet with other dreamers. Shamans, or dream walkers, profess to be able to go into the dreams of others. Some even claim to be able to influence those dreams. Is it possible? Many cultures believe so. Certain Australian Aboriginal tribes, for example, have deep and profound beliefs in the ways the spirit can leave the body and commune with others.

These stories and ideas are ancient, deeply felt and truly important, so it seems ludicrously arrogant that we should rule it out completely. After all, how could we confirm or deny the reports of what people dreamed? How could we be sure that they were truly experiencing the same dream and not just similar dreams based on similar environments? How can we, with the technology currently available

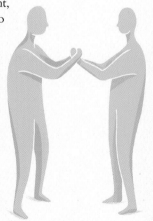

to us, even begin to parse the vast complexities of the human brain? Many people report things from and about their dreams we just can't support with science, but that doesn't mean they're not true.

Often things that once seemed strange or primitive are now revealed to be scientifically sound. In the same way that chewing the bark of a willow tree was once thought to cure headaches, then reviled as a myth, then hailed as the wonder drug aspirin, might the same not be true of what we understand about dreams?

The Native American Iroquois, for instance, believe that dreams (particularly nightmares) must be banished by the whole tribe together, in a series of rituals, to stop harm coming upon them. People must come together to explore the elements of the dream to, in a sense, banish it. While this practice might once have been mocked, studies have now shown there is therapeutic benefit to discussing nightmares. There is a clear path from acting out the things that frighten us to absolute, scientific harm-reduction.

What else might we not know? What else might we have dismissed? How else might our dreams be useful to us in ways that currently we just can't prove?

Prophetic Dreams

Dream telepathy is, of course, linked to prophecy and prediction – and dreams have been part of prediction and prophecy for millennia. The *Epic of Gilgamesh*, written in the 7th century BCE, was prompted by a prophetic dream. The Ancient Egyptians wrote dream dictionaries (dreaming of warm beer, for instance, promised harm) and the Ancient Greeks created a complex dream-analysis system whereby dreams were classified as 'false' or 'true', with true dreams further subdivided into 'symbolic', 'vision' or 'oracle' dreams, as categories of prediction.

Many ancient holy books are full of dreams that change the course of history. But not just history: these dreams change the course of the lives of the individuals concerned. The dream changes the dreamer: it changes the dreamer's mind about what they should do, where they should go and who they should be. The dream has no power alone, but must be acted upon — on waking — by the dreamer.

Perhaps, then, this is one thing we can take away from the history of prophecy: dreams have the power to change our lives, if we let them. The lessons we learn from our dreams can shape us: the lessons we learn about ourselves, and the lessons we learn about the ways we view the world, and our place in it.

Just look at what we've learned about from this little book alone. How to sleep better. How to look properly at the world around us. How to keep a journal, and record things that are important to us. How to notice how we feel, and wonder why we feel it, and how to identify those feelings. How to understand ourselves (our wants, our desires, our needs). And once we know ourselves, we will know how to act. We will know how to change our lives to accommodate those needs and desires. We will know how to go through the world, secure in our understanding of people and place and self.

Self-knowledge is self-care, and self-care is radical: caring for the self allows us to be in the best possible place to care for the world around us. And what more could anyone want, from a dream, than that?

Acknowledgements

Thank you to Chad, the first therapist to teach me about sleep hygiene. Thank you to my doctor, Emma, for first introducing me to many of the ideas in this book. Thank you to the many analysts, therapists, experts and dreamers who I consulted in the process of writing. Thank you to the neuroscientists making such extraordinary strides in our understanding of the human mind. And a particular thank you to the scholars who make their writing accessible to the non-scientist!

Thank you to my editors for all their patience while I worked on this book, and for letting me write about something I am so passionate about.

Thank you to Hannah, Lottie and Libby for a lifelong commitment to talking about our dreams in depth. Thank you to my namesake, Anoushka F, the strangest dreamer of them all and queen of sleep. This book is in honour of your dedication to ten hours a night.

Above all, thank you to Therese, chief cheerleader of gentle days and herbal baths. I could not have written this without you.